Nicholas Rhea is the pen-name of Peter N. formerly an inspector with the North Yorkshire police, and the creator of the *Constable* series of books from which the Yorkshire TV series *Heartbeat* has been derived. Peter N. Walker is also author of *Portrait of the North York Moors, Murders & Mysteries from the North York Moors* and *Folk Tales from the North York Moors*. He is married with a family and lives in North Yorkshire.

BOOKS BY PETER N. WALKER

CRIME FICTION
The *Carnaby* series pub. Hale:
Carnaby and the Hijackers (1967)*
Carnaby and the Gaolbreakers (1968)
Carnaby and the Assassins (1968)
Carnaby and the Conspirators (1969)
Carnaby and the Saboteurs (1970)
Carnaby and the Eliminators (1971)
Carnaby and the Demonstrators (1972)
Carnaby and the Infiltrators (1974)**
Carnaby and the Kidnappers (1976)
Carnaby and the Counterfeiters (1980)
Carnaby and the Campaigners (1984)
Fatal Accident (1970)
Panda One on Duty (1971)
Special Duty (1971)
Identification Parade (1972)
Panda One Investigates (1973)
Major Incident (1974)
The Dovingsby Death (1975)
Missing from Home (1977)
The MacIntyre Plot (1977)
Witchcraft for Panda One (1978)
Target Criminal (1978)
The Carlton Plot (1980)
Siege for Panda One (1981)
Teenage Cop (1982)
Robber in a Mole Trap (1984)
False Alibi (pub. Constable 1991)
Grave Secrets (pub. Constable 1992)
  *reprinted Chivers (Black Dagger) 1993
** " " " " 1994

WRITTEN AS CHRISTOPHER CORAM
pub. Hale:
A Call to Danger (1968)
A Call to Die (1969)
Death in Ptarmigan Forest (1970)
Death on the Motorway (1973)
Murder by the Lake (1975)
Murder Beneath the Trees (1979)
Prisoner on the Dam (1982)
Prisoner on the Run (1985)
WRITTEN AS TOM FERRIS:
Espionage for a Lady (pub. Hale 1969)
WRITTEN AS ANDREW ARNCLIFFE:
Murder after the Holiday (pub. Hale 1985)

WRITTEN AS NICHOLAS RHEA:
Family Ties (pub. Constable 1994)
EMMERDALE TITLES:
WRITTEN AS JAMES FERGUSON:
A Friend in Need (pub. Fontana 1987)
Divided Loyalties (pub. Fontana 1988)
Wives and Lovers (pub. Fontana 1989)
Emmerdale Book of Country Lore
(pub. Hamlyn 1988)
Emmerdale Official Companion
(pub. Weidenfeld & Nicolson 1988)
Emmerdale's Yorkshire
(pub. Weidenfeld & Nicolson 1990)
The *Constable* series pub. Hale
WRITTEN AS NICHOLAS RHEA:
Constable on the Hill (1979)
Constable on the Prowl (1980)
Constable around the Village (1981)
Constable across the Moors (1982)
Constable in the Dale (1983)
Constable by the Sea (1985)
Constable along the Lane (1986)
Constable through the Meadow (1988)
Constable at the Double (1988)
Constable in Disguise (1989)
Constable among the Heather (1990)
Constable beside the Stream (1991)
Constable around the Green (1993)
Constable beneath the Trees (1994)
Constable in the Shrubbery (1995)
Constable versus Greengrass (1996)
Heartbeat Omnibus I (1992)
Heartbeat Omnibus II (1993)
Heartbeat – Constable among the Heather
  (pub. Headline 1992)
Heartbeat – Constable across the Moors
  (pub. Headline 1993)
Heartbeat – Constable on Call
  (pub. Headline 1993)
Heartbeat – Constable around the Green
  (pub. Headline 1994)
Heartbeat – Constable in Control
  (pub,. Headline 1995)
Heartbeat – Constable along the Lane
  (pub. Headline 1995)
Heartbeat – Constable versus Greengrass
  (pub. Headline 1996)

Heartbeat:

Constable in the Dale and Other Tales of a Yorkshire Village Bobby

Nicholas Rhea

HEADLINE

First published in this edition in 1996
by HEADLINE BOOK PUBLISHING

10 9 8 7 6 5 4 3 2

ISBN 0 7472 5403 6

Typeset by CBS, Felixstowe, Suffolk

Printed and bound in Great Britain by
Cox & Wyman Ltd, Reading, Berks

HEADLINE BOOK PUBLISHING
A division of Hodder Headline PLC
338 Euston Road,
London NW1 3BH

CONTENTS

Constable
in the Dale

1

'Here, there is plenty of gooseberries which makes my mouth watter.'
Marjorie Fleming 1803-11

Very few agricultural shows are devoted entirely to gooseberries. Those which do specialise in this useful and wholesome fruit (*Ribes grossularia*) live in a world of bulging berries and boosted bushes, and they are given to fierce competition spiced with awesome claims about the size of their specimens. Perfection is their goal, and the bigger the better. It was Mrs Beeton, in her famous cookery book, who said that 'the high state of perfection to which the gooseberry has here been brought, is due to the skill of the English gardeners, for in no other country does it attain the same size and flavour.' She added that, when uncultivated, the gooseberry is small and inferior.

Had she visited Aidensfield to view the fruit of a very select band of berry growers, she would have regarded their special fruit as colossal, and those of her proud gardeners as small and inferior. One sometimes wishes she had lived to view these supreme examples of *Ribes grossularia*.

It is berries of this kind that prove beyond doubt that gooseberry-growing is an art; the monsters produced by the gooseberry societies around England are staggeringly handsome by their shape, size and quality. Each is a true work of art, and to view a modern Aidensfield berry in its natural habitat is indeed a sight to be treasured. Each berry is grown upon a specially nurtured bush, and, when ripe, is about the size of a domestic hen's egg. Some are larger than golf balls, with pulsing veins prominent against their tender and taut skins. When such enormous berries dangle upon their slender stalks, they threaten to topple the tiny parent plant. These bushes are the strong men of the fruit garden, sturdily bearing their precious loads in defiance of weather, wasps and wind.

It is not easy to define the area of greatest gooseberries. There are about eight other societies, most of which are in Cheshire but a strong claimant to be the leader in the field must be the North Yorkshire village of Egton Bridge, a beautiful place lying deep in the Esk Valley. There, the Egton Bridge Old Gooseberry Society was established in AD 1800, and I am privileged to be a member, where I was known as a maiden grower until I produced a berry worthy of display among the champions. The annual meeting continues to be held on Easter Tuesday every year, and the annual show of berries is held on the first Tuesday in August, once the day after Bank Holiday. Since the Government messed around with the calendar, Show Day is now held on an ordinary Tuesday. It may be an ordinary Tuesday to many, but it is a very important Tuesday for berry growers.

Before daring to show a berry, I had to familiarise myself with the rules. For example, it is stipulated that all berries handed to the weighman must be sound and dry. Twin berries are defined as those which are two on one stem, grown naturally, and they must be distinctly twins. Furthermore, a pair of twins cannot be split; either both are shown, or none.

The heaviest berry takes the premier prize of the show, and if that happens to be the work of a maiden grower, then he also takes the maiden prize. There are first, second and third prizes for the heaviest twelve berries, and for the heaviest six; the four colours, yellow, red, green and white, attract their own prizes, and hairy ones have their place too.

The rules which govern the taking of berries from other persons' trees are stringent, but the prize-winning fruit are wonderful to behold. A recent winning berry weighed over 1½ ounces; there would be about ten of these berries to a pound. Indeed the World Champion gooseberry was claimed by Egton Bridge for over thirty years, the world champion grower being Mr Tom Ventress, president of the local society. The World Championships have been held at Egton Bridge for nearly 200 years, although the society records only date to 1843. This must surely be the doyen of all gooseberry shows, and it competes with those in distant places like Derbyshire and even Brighton. They are always in the background, while Egton Bridge hogs the stage – that was the situation until the Aidensfield Old Gooseberry Society was founded.

No one quite knew how it started, but reliable sources suggest that someone crept into Egton Bridge one very dark evening and stole several show bushes from the garden of a noted grower. The story says that these were smuggled across the moors and planted in a quiet cottage garden at Aidensfield, where they were fiercely guarded and brought to maturity in secret behind tall fences and a crop of well-regulated nettles.

The story is quite feasible because in Yorkshire it seems that only the Egton Bridge berry bushes are capable of producing the gargantuan fruit so necessary for show purposes. This meant that if the Aidensfield Growers wished to knock the Egton Bridge men off their prickly pedestals, they would require bushes with the same inherent qualities. Such plants rarely grace the *market overt*.

Sometimes, I wonder if those rumours of berry-bush smuggling were circulated to discredit the Aidensfield trees, for it is fair to say that the Aidensfield Society did boast such grandly named trees as Lord Kitchener, Lord Derby, Blücher, Thatcher, Woodpecker, Surprise, Princess Royal and Admiral Beatty, all top names in the gooseberry world. This is quality – it would take a good thief to steal such gems. I suspect it is just a nasty legend.

From those first trees, therefore, by whatever means they arrived, the Aidensfield Society flourished, each new member taking cuttings off the first of its type until a select number of village gardens boasted a veritable forest of thorny competitors.

During the formative years of the Aidensfield Society, the presence of those bushes was a closely guarded secret and it was not until they were producing colossal fruit that they were revealed to an astonished world. It came with the shock announcement that one berry from Aidensfield would be competing in the forthcoming World Championships at Egton Bridge.

The fact that no one, not even the experts, had heard of the Aidensfield gooseberry caused a furore among the other growers. Even those experts from distant parts of England had never wrested the World Championship from the noble Eskdale village, so the first showing of an Aidensfield berry was earth-shattering in its audacity. It was akin to a learner driver in a mini-car competing in the World Motor Racing Championships and I happened to be village policeman at Aidensfield during the run-up to this grim competition.

It transpired that seven residents of Aidensfield owned trees. Every one of them had bush ancestors in the Egton Bridge locality, and each of those seven people had for years protected their berries against unauthorised attention. Their secret had been brilliantly maintained until it was time to execute the coup de grâce.

The President of the Aidensfield Society was Joe Marshall, a retired railwayman who lived in a beautiful cottage along the lane at the eastern edge of Aidensfield. His home stood close to the highway, with an extensive garden behind. It was in the seclusion of that garden that Joe nurtured his berries, and he hailed me from there one fine July day.

He was a stocky man who habitually wore brown corduroy trousers, a grey sports jacket and black hob-nailed boots. In his late sixties, he sported a flat cap which never left his head, indoors or out, so I never knew whether his iron-grey hair covered his entire head or merely sprouted below the rim of his headgear.

'Mr Rhea,' he announced solemnly, removing a smoking briar pipe from his mouth. 'Ah'm right glad to find you.'

''Morning Joe,' I greeted him. 'Trouble, is it?'

'Nay,' he said slowly in the manner of a Yorkshireman, 'not trouble. Help, Ah think. Guidance, mebbe.'

'Right,' I said. 'How can I help or be of guidance?'

'Thoo'd better come in,' and he led me into the smart, sunny kitchen of his home where his wife worked. Mrs Marshall was a shy woman who rarely went out, except to the post office for her pension and to the shop for groceries, but she smiled at me and Joe said, 'Tea, Mr Rhea?'

'Thanks.' It was a warm afternoon, and a drink was welcome, even if it was a hot one. The kettle sang on an open fire, and within minutes, the silent Mrs Marshall in her flowered pinny produced a brown, earthenware teapot and some china cups. She poured delicious helpings of hot tea, and found a plate full of scones with fresh butter and strawberry jam to smother them. It was marvellous.

During her careful ministrations, Joe chattered about the weather, the animals in the fields and a host of other incidental things, and I allowed him to 'waffle on', as we say in Yorkshire, until he came to the point of his request.

'Mr Rhea,' he said eventually, 'Ah'll come straight to the point,' and he drew on that smelly pipe. 'It's about them gooseberries of mine.'

'Gooseberries?' At this stage, I was blissfully unaware of the forthcoming competition.

'Aye, thoo knaws!'

I didn't know, and the expression of my face must have told him so. 'What gooseberries?' I asked, looking at Joe and his wife for guidance.

'By gum!' he almost shouted. 'Thoo must be t'only feller in these parts that dissn't knaw!'

'Sorry!' I apologised. 'Am I missing something?'

'Thoo'll knaw aboot yon gooseberry show across at Egton Bridge?' He put the question in the form of a statement.

'Yes,' I said, but I didn't inform him that I was a member who qualified as a maiden grower. Obviously, he didn't know about my Yellow Woodpeckers.

'Aye, well, we've set up our own society, and we're gahin ti beat them Egton Bridgers. We've been growing berries for a few years, allus waiting until our bushes and berries were just right. And now, they are. This year, we're gahin ovver t'moors wiv oor berries, and we'll come back here wi' t'World Championship!'

'Does anybody else know about this?' I asked.

'Nay,' he said. 'Nobody, except us seven. Ah was joking, when Ah said thoo should have known. There's just us seven.'

'You seven?' I raised my eyebrows.

'Ah, there's seven of us, all members of this Society. We've kept things very secret because we want to catch them Egton Bridgers napping.'

As he spoke, a feeling of impending horror crossed my mind. As a member of the opposing Society, I could be considered a spy! I was one of the dreaded Egton Bridgers and he didn't know! And he'd laid open his soul to me in a moment of deepest trust. I wondered how the *News of the World* would treat the revelation of a gooseberry spy in Aidensfield.

'What do you want me to do?' My voice quivered as I put my question.

'Guard oor berries,' he said. 'When you're out on patrol, we all want you to look to our bushes.'

'Nobody's going to nobble them, surely?' I put to him, wondering if he'd received some intelligence reports from the Esk Valley.

'Ah wouldn't put it past 'em,' he said, shaking the stem of his pipe at me. 'Ah wouldn't that! If they know we've a world beater on our hands, they might send troops out to stick pins into our fruit, or knock 'em off t'bushes. Ah can't take that sort of a risk, thoo sees, there's a lot at stake.'

My intimate knowledge of the Egton Bridge growers assured me that they would never stoop to such ploys to beat the opposition. Their inbred confidence and growing ability, plus the secret ways they had with gooseberry bushes, meant there had never been any serious threat to their unique position in the gooseberry world. No one from beyond that lovely village could beat an Egton Bridge grower by fair means. The Eskdale berries would always beat the world, and I knew that the Egton

Bridgers would let the Ryedale berries grow in peace. They had no reason to do otherwise – the Egton Bridgers were invincible. Or were they? I dismissed any lingering doubts as pure fantasy!

I tried to convince Joe Marshall of that fact, but knew I was facing a losing battle. He was convinced his berries would be nobbled, so I was compelled to do my duty in the protection of his property, and I re-assured him that I would patrol diligently past his gooseberry patch from time to time. I would keep an eagle eye cast for signs of illegal attention to his maturing fruit, and those of his colleagues.

Throughout July, therefore, I maintained my vigil, and I also paid close attention to the six other growers in the village. No one nobbled the growing fruit, and towards the end of July, Joe called me into his home.

'Mr Rhea,' he said, 'Ah's fair capped that thoo's seen fit ti keep an eye on them berries o' mine. They're coming on grand, real whoppers they are. Ah reckon one of 'em might just get that title away from Egton Bridge. Ah'll settle for t'World Championship.'

I didn't like to disappoint him, but none of his berries was anything like the necessary size to achieve that distinction. Certainly they were gigantic by the standards of those seen in any fruit shop or market stall, but by Egton Bridge standards, they were by no means remarkable. 'Nobbut middlin" as they would be described.

'What does thoo think of 'em, then?' he put to me, his pipe issuing thick fumes of astonishing pungency.

'Nice berries,' I said, for I could not say otherwise. Indeed, I had half a dozen on my own bushes which were bigger than any of Joe's. I couldn't deflate the poor old fellow; I let him ride on his wave of optimism.

'This 'ere pipe,' he said, removing it and brandishing it around, 'This 'ere pipe keeps t' wasps off. Ah blows smoke across them berries every day, and it puts a lining on t'berries. It makes wasps keep clear; if they can get near, Mr Rhea, they'll punch a hole in t'fruit to get at t'juice, just like a needle gahin in, and Ah doesn't let that happen. This tobacco smoke keeps 'em off.'

I knew of that trick and I also knew that pigs' blood and cow muck were ideal for manuring the bushes. Joe didn't seem to use those – by his methods trees were surrounded with fireside ashes which he'd spread last autumn to prevent this year's caterpillars climbing up the trees. Some growers put coal dust around the roots in the early spring as a substitute for spraying and there were other tricks too. Joe appeared to know most of them.

He told me how he made little umbrellas of linen to place over the huge berries to prevent heavy rain knocking them off, or causing them to burst by swelling too rapidly. He also fed them with a mixture of sugar and water. Sometimes, when a truly colossal berry made its appearance, the grower would fashion a tiny hammock to sling beneath it. This was to give the straining stalk some relief from its continuing effort to support the bulbous fruit, a sort of berry brassiere.

Joe spent a long time with me. He told me most of his secrets and explained how he'd learned these surreptitiously from a boastful Egton Bridger who had failed to realise that Joe was a future competitor. I wondered if Joe knew my secret . . .

My own berries were coming alone fine. My little colony of six Yellow Woodpecker bushes was in a sunny but sheltered place in my hilltop garden. Upon them, I had lavished great care and attention of the kind outlined by Joe, expertise I had gleaned from generations of prize growers. My own berries were astonishingly beautiful and round, certainly worthy of the show.

The Egton Bridge show was the day after Bank Holiday Monday; my entry was authorised because of my membership of the Egton Bridge Old Gooseberry Society, but my competing berries must come from my own trees. That presented no problems. They had to be with the weighman before two o'clock on the afternoon of the show, and would remain on the table until seven-thirty that night.

Having been privileged to see the size of Joe's specimens, I began to contemplate entering my own. I did not believe I had a World Champion among my little charmers, but I might just get into the prize list with the heaviest six, or even a single heavyweight in yellow. I began to muse over the possibility. With the end of July, the day of the berry show was almost upon us.

I had to work on that Bank Holiday, performing a motorcycle patrol throughout Ryedale from ten o'clock in the morning until six that evening. My duties entailed stopping the bike in villages to undertake foot patrols, as well as keeping an eye on holiday traffic, seeking thieves who stole from cars in beauty spots and youngsters who used the holiday as an excuse to drink themselves into oblivion in the local hostelries.

All day, my mind was far away, over the moors in Eskdale, thinking about gooseberries. I could not miss the final opportunity of making a cheeky inspection of Joe's berries, so I parked the faithful Francis Barnett in Aidensfield, close to the village hall, and donned my flat cap instead of my motorcycle crash helmet. I began one of my routine foot patrols; it was mid-afternoon on a hot, sticky August Bank Holiday Monday.

I was in shirt sleeves and hadn't realised how clammy the day had become; the wind from my motor-cycle had kept me blissfully cool and unaware of the heat. As I walked along the lane to Joe's house, I felt like sipping a long cool glass of orange squash. The heat was intense.

But Joe didn't believe in such drinks. When he saw me heading towards his garden wall, he called me in and his silent wife produced a mug of her instant tea. I drank it, and the sweat poured out as he walked me about his garden. He still wore his corduroys, jacket, boots and flat cap.

'Just thoo look at yon berries, Mr Rhea,' he eyed them with pride. 'Thoo's done a grand job, protecting 'em like you have, Ah'm grateful.'

'It's all part of the service, Joe,' I said, closely inspecting the berries. One had burst, I noted, and none of the others was up to Egton Bridge standard. I realised I had not seen any of the opposition, except my own little clutch, so perhaps this was a poor berry year? Were the Egton Bridge whoppers smaller than normal?

We would all know tomorrow. I went home and booked off duty. That night I decided to enter the Gooseberry Show.

Next morning, having allowed the hot sun to dry my Yellow Woodpeckers, I picked the largest single berry I could find, and followed with a further six. I packed them gently in an open box of cotton wool, and began the long drive across the spectacular heights of the North Yorkshire moors. The scenery must be seen to be believed; I once met a Londoner who thought the moors were flat, and I wondered if he also believed the moon was a green gooseberry!

I drove into Egton Bridge, parked near the gigantic Catholic Church of St Hedda, and entered the building next door. Many years ago, this used to be the church but it is now the village Catholic School where I learned my reading, writing and arithmetic. On Show Day, it is converted into an arena for displaying monster berries.

I was off duty, of course, and clad in Berry Show clothing which really meant a good suit because members enjoy dinner afterwards, at the curious hour of half-past five, in a local hotel.

I located the small queue near the weighman and joined the growing number, clutching my seven Yellow Woodpeckers in their cosy bed of cotton wool. Each man's berries were carefully weighed and documented before being placed on the table for exhibition, and my large single Yellow Woodpecker weighed in at 20 drams 11 grains, a very useful fruit, but far short of the World Record of 30 drams, 9 grains. The six accompanying berries weighed a total of six ounces, 5 drams and 20 grains, but I would not know whether I was included in any prize list until all had been weighed and catalogued. The beautiful scales used for the ceremony are serviced regularly and they are so delicate that the tiniest feather affects them. The difference between a champion berry and a second best is minuscule in terms of weight, but enormous in terms of prestige.

I turned to leave the weighman's table and bumped straight into Joe Marshall; he stood in the queue bearing a little box which he shielded with his big hands.

'Ah, Joe!' I beamed at him. 'Is that one of your champions?'

'Noo then, Mr Rhea,' he smiled slyly at me. 'Nice day.'

'It's a lovely day, Joe.' I eyed the box, but he kept it covered. 'Is that the world champion then?'

''Appen,' he said.

He was very reticent about revealing the gem he cosseted so carefully, and I suspected something was afoot.

'Summat wrong, Joe?' I asked. 'Has your berry burst, or something?'

'Nay, lad,' he beamed. 'This is a cracker, mark my words,' and he graciously opened his box to reveal a colossal Lord Derby of magnificent proportions.

'By, that's a rare beauty!' I spoke with genuine surprise. 'Is it one of yours, Joe?'

'Aye, lad, it is that,' he sounded very smug. I wondered why I had not seen this fruit on any of his Aidensfield trees, and I must admit that I suspected skulduggery of some kind. Had Joe Marshall and his mates done the very thing they'd expected of the Egton Bridgers? Had he raided an Egton Bridge bush to steal this giant?

'It looks like a winner,' I had to admit, for it was certainly bigger than my Yellow Woodpecker.

'Mr Rhea,' he whispered confidentially, 'sorry about this . . .'

'Sorry for what, Joe?' I was puzzled.

'The secrecy about this big 'un.'

I didn't understand his remark because my brain was racing to anticipate his next statement.

'Go on,' I said, as others brushed past us to weigh in.

'We cheated thoo a bit,' he admitted. 'We knew thoo was a chap frev this area, and that thoo grew berries for showing.'

'Go on.' I folded my arms and looked steadily at him.

'Well, thoo sees, we reckoned that if we persuaded thoo to look to our bushes, thoo'd see t'quality of oor berries, and then thoo'd tell t'Egton Bridgers they were no good.'

'Go on,' I instructed the crafty character.

'Well, dissn't thoo see? We kept this big 'un very, very secret. Thoo was allowed ti see all oor middling berries, and we reckoned thoo wad tell these folks over here how small oor berries were, then they'd nut bother aboot growing very big 'uns this year . . .'

'Joe!' I said, pretending to be hurt. 'You didn't . . .'

'Aye, well, we wanted this big chap to be a surprise, thoo sees, to win t'Best in t'Show award . . .'

I gazed at the massive berry. Unless someone from Egton Bridge produced a bigger one, Joe's berry might win this year's award. Then I smiled at him.

'Joe,' I said, 'I didn't tell a soul. I didn't report back here – there's no need. These chaps don't stoop to terrible things like nobbling their competitors' berries! They fight true. In fact, I've entered one of my own.'

'Thoo has?' It was my turn to surprise him.

'A Yellow Woodpecker,' I said proudly. 'It's been weighed in, it'll be on the table now.'

He blanched. 'Thoo can't beat this 'un o' mine?' he gasped.

'No,' I smiled. 'But there's more to come from Egton Bridge.'

He weighed-in his prize fruit and it scaled at 25 drams 9 grains, a large berry, and, to be honest, large enough to win the prize for this show, albeit not to gain the World Championship. He had beaten me, but would he triumph over this village of champions?

'Joe,' I asked when he came back to talk to me. 'Where did you grow that berry?'

'In a spot not far from my house,' he smiled. 'Ah kept it very secret, and shall yet. Next year, thoo'll see, Ah'll grow a real big 'un . . .'

He checked the time. The latest for weighing-in was two o'clock and it was five minutes to two as we waited. An air of expectancy descended as the final moments ticked away. I could see Joe's crafty face growing redder and redder as he visualised himself walking off with the Champion berry prize for this year. But at the last moment, in walked a pretty woman clutching a jewellery box. She ran across to the table and smiled at the weighman.

'Am I too late?' she oozed at him.

'Nay, lass, thoo's just made it in time,' said the man, accepting her box.

Out of it, she produced a colossal Yellow Woodpecker, and gasps of astonishment filled the room. The crowd surged forward as the enormous fruit was placed delicately on the scales.

'It's from your own tree, is it?' The question had to be asked.

'Yes, my dad gave them to me and I've grown them myself. This is my first try, though, and I don't know if it's any good . . .'

As she twittered on, he announced the weight, and the clock struck two.

'Twenty-seven drams, fifteen grains,' came the verdict. 'This is the year's Champion Berry . . . Miss Jean Ferris . . .'

'She's from Egton Bridge.' I leaned across and smiled at the unhappy Joe. 'You'll have to try harder next time, Joe.'

'I used a recipe given to me by my dad,' said the young woman, 'but he said not to tell anyone what it was . . .'

Loud applause filled the busy room, as the doors opened to admit the sightseers, and I wondered if she was the first woman to win a berry championship. Maybe she'd try for the World Championship next year?

But as a maiden grower, she'd upheld the reputation of the berry village of the North Yorkshire moors.

If Joe Marshall's dream was to win the World Championship for gooseberries, then Hubert Mitford wanted to raise his status by winning the Best of Breed with his Large White pigs at the Great Yorkshire Show.

Hubert's pigs were certainly noted in Aidensfield, if only because their presence was confirmed by the strong smell which rose from their sties, and by the continuing grunts of satisfaction which filled the evening air at feeding time. Occasionally, one of them would escape to gallop in joy along the main street, or else to sample the culinary delights of the cottage gardens en route to freedom out in the big wide world. One frisky piglet got into the pub where it scattered the bar stools and terrified a barmaid in its wild thrashings as it was chased by the assembled drinkers.

But such incidents apart, Hubert's litter of beautiful white pigs was one of the prides of Aidensfield. He carted them to all the local agricultural shows, and came back with rosettes and cups; be bred lovely little pigs and handsome large pigs, and he knew them all by their first names. It seemed they all knew Hubert too, and there was undoubtedly a firm bond of affection between man and beast at Brantgate Farm.

Every time he won at a show, Hubert would visit the Brewers Arms and buy drinks for everyone, local and visitor alike, consequently it was in the interests of the community to ensure Hubert's pigs were the best in Yorkshire. And indeed they were; they thrived on an expert diet of excellent food, personally supervised by Hubert. Among their treats were many delicacies from proud villagers, and he even named his best sows after some of the village ladies. I'm not sure whether they knew that. Everyone wondered who 'Cuddles' really was, for she had beautiful eyes, a fine rump and shapely rear legs with juicy, milky white thighs.

Hubert's popularity in the village and the good will he generated through his wonderful animals led to the vicar deciding to buy a pig. He did so in the belief that his activities would draw people to him as they were drawn to Hubert and thus he would fill his empty pews.

I received my first hint of this when the Reverend Roger Clifton hailed me as I patrolled along the village street.

'Mr Rhea,' he greeted me formally. 'I was hoping to catch you.'

'Yes, Vicar?' I liked him; he was a friendly man who worked hard to preach his faith.

'I am contemplating the purchase of a pig,' he said seriously, 'and wondered whether I need a licence of any kind.'

'You will need a movement licence to bring it from the place of purchase,' I answered, 'so the Ministry of Agriculture can trace its movements should it catch Swine Fever or some other notifiable disease.'

'And where do I get such a licence?'

'From the place you buy the pig,' I said. 'Usually, there is a policeman at the market to issue pig licences.'

'And that is all?'

'So far as I know,' I had to admit. 'Where will you keep it?'

'There are six disused sties at the vicarage,' he said. 'They are very sound and fully enclosed with a brick wall. I'll use those.'

I did not know whether any recent legislation had imposed conditions about keeping pigs on private premises, and advised him to discuss this with the Ministry of Agriculture or the local council. After talking about the village and its flock, he went on his way rejoicing, and I popped into the Brewers Arms for one of my routine official visits.

Two weeks later, the Rev Roger Clifton journeyed along the village street, beside the driver of a Landrover which towed a trailer. In that trailer was a beautiful Large White sow. The parish had acquired a pig.

The Parochial Church Pig was one of his undoubted hits. She was christened White Lily, which means purity and modesty, a fitting name for an unmarried sow. As the lovely creature blossomed in the fullness of her youth, and flourished on her diet of holy scraps with lashings of mashed potato, she found herself being used as the basis for many sermons. All kind of parallels were suggested from the pulpit, and the swine of biblical times became succulent meat for the Rev Roger Clifton.

I think Mr Clifton, in truth, had rejected any suggestion of ever killing the fat pig because he often quoted those parts of the Scriptures where the meat of the pig was not to be eaten because it was considered unclean. This was not a nice thing to say of White Lily, and he reminded his congregation of the Hebrews' views on the subject when he said,

'It is said they had the flesh of this animal in such detestation, that they would not so much as pronounce its name, but instead of it said, "The beast, that thing".' The village felt he did this to gain sympathy for White Lily, and so it became evident that the vicar had no intention of killing Lily or of selling her on the market. So, instead of White Lily helping to swell the Parochial Church Funds, she became another mouth to feed on the Parochial Church Income.

One village gossip, a voluble lady, who felt the church shouldn't subsidise a pig, said that the Hebrews and Phoenicians only abstained from pork because there was none in their country, but the vicar retaliated by quoting from the Book of Proverbs, Chapter 11, Verse 22, where it said, 'As a jewel of gold in a swine's snout, so is a fair woman without discretion.' No one really understood it, except that it meant the church pig was not for sale.

I think it was another villager's quote from Matthew, Chapter 8, Verse 30, about a herd of swine feeding, that gave the vicar an idea. He would keep the sow and breed from her. He would produce a litter of swine, and sell the little ones. That would satisfy his critics, for church funds would swell to enormous proportions. At least, that was the Rev Clifton's theory.

By chance, some time later, I was in Hubert Mitford's farmyard, leaning on a pigsty wall with a coffee in my hand as the Reverend Roger arrived. He had come to discuss the possibility of breeding a litter of pigs from White Lily.

At that stage, I had no idea of his plan, but his blushing hesitancy suggested he wished to talk about a delicate matter.

'I'll go,' I said, diplomatically.

'No, Mr Rhea, don't go on my account.' He shook his head vigorously. 'I'd like you to hear my plans.'

'Summat good, is it?' smiled Hubert, revelling in the Reverend's shyness.

'That sow of mine, Hubert,' the vicar took a deep breath and spoke his piece. 'I'm thinking of breeding from her.'

'Ah!' beamed the farmer with an evil glint in his eye. 'Then that'll be more pigs for t'church to keep.'

'No,' cried the vicar. 'No, it won't. You see, I will keep White Lily, and sell her piglets. I was wondering whether this was feasible . . . I don't know much about pig-breeding, you see . . .'

'Ah've a smashing awd boar,' came in Hubert. 'Nobbut a tenner a time for serving a sow. If that's what thoo's come for, Vicar, Ah'm your man. Ah'll soon fix yon pig and she'll give nice little piglets that'll sell like hot cakes at Thirsk Mart.'

'Is there a special time, then?'

'Well, noo, there might be and there again there might not,' smiled Hubert. 'Ah'll tell thoo what, Vicar. Ah'm summat of an expert in these matters, so Ah'll pop around to see the pig o' thine, and we'll soon get her fettled up.'

The vicar looked at me.

'Well, Mr Rhea? Do you think it will make money for my church?'

I had to be honest and say I did. Many folks who had taken to breeding pigs had made money, so I gave my considered view that the church at Aidensfield was about to prove yet again that where there's muck, there's money.

It would be three weeks later when I saw the Reverend Roger taking his pig to be served by a boar. In the manner of a medieval monk, he had a long piece of rope tied to one of White Lily's hind legs and she was ambling down the street, sampling the growth of the verges and causing ladies to leap for safety into houses and gardens. This contented pig grunted and rooted until she arrived at Hubert's farm.

There, with the aid of Hubert's skill, she was driven towards a cosy pen for a hectic session of love-making with one of his prize boars. There could be no doubt that White Lily's litter would be beautiful and valuable, and in that sense, Hubert was doing more than his bit for the church.

As I was there, I helped to drive White Lily through the gate, and was a witness to the next, and most important, part of proceedings.

Hubert brought the boar from a sty; he was a massive, ugly creature but he must have been a prince in a white suit in the eyes of the waiting maiden because she grunted with gleeful expectation as the scent of his ardour reached her nostrils. Hubert opened the gate and the willing boar needed no further guidance; he was beside his loved one in a trice, sniffing with pleasure at the perfume she wore.

Hubert shut the gate. They were alone.

At this stage, the pink, embarrassed complexion of the Reverend Roger turned a brilliant red. He had, by some mischance, positioned himself very close to the marital bed and was clearly embarrassed by the opening sounds and visions of pleasure coming from the happy couple.

'Er, Hubert,' he said, 'I've never been in this position before . . . I mean, do I have to observe the actual . . . er . . . the . . . coupling . . . I mean, it is parish funds that are being used for this . . . er . . . enterprise . . . Do you think I should wait and see that they . . . er . . . do it properly?'

'Aye,' said Hubert, 'thoo'd better, 'cos thoo won't have time to marry 'em.'

And so the story had a happy ending. The pigs got married and lived happily for a few minutes, and in time White Lily produced eight lovely piglets. The parish was happy at this event and brought even more food for their pigs. I believe the church made a handsome profit from its first year of breeding. Today, if you go down the side of the vicarage, you can still hear the descendants of White Lily and her various beaus, as they grunt and snuffle around the vicarage gardens, raising much needed funds for the faithful of Aidensfield.

But for Hubert, things did not work out quite so well.

Through his important contacts in the pig world, and due to his standing in the village, Hubert decided to offer himself for election to the Rural District Council. He sincerely felt he had a great deal to offer society in general, and the folk of Aidensfield in particular, and so he sought, and achieved, nomination as the official candidate for that ward. But there was one terrible problem associated with his nomination. He had decided to stand as a Liberal.

This was shattering news. Never in the political history of the area had a Liberal emerged from anywhere to stand at any election, national or local. Horror was expressed at his decision; Hubert's standing slumped and there were fears about his sanity. Indeed, there were also fears about the future of the church's pig-breeding enterprise. Could a Liberal be allowed access to this capitalist venture? For years, nay centuries, the folk of this blissful rural area had always voted Conservative; Churchill and his men were for Britain, and any other political adherent was deemed a dangerous subversive.

Heavens knows what might have happened if Hubert had opted for Socialism, for there would have been worries about nationalisation of the pig-breeding enterprise or whether the Red Flag would be sung in church. As he had opted for Liberalism, however, such events were unlikely, but his new-found creed meant that no one really knew what he stood for. This meant he could canvass around the district without fear of contradiction, and this lack of contradiction made him believe his policies were acceptable. The truth was that no one argued because no one understood his policies.

Inevitably, election day arrived. The school was used as the polling station, and I had to perform a long day's duty, from seven o'clock in the morning to the close of polling at 10 p.m. My duty was to ensure there were no election offences or breaches of the Representation of the People Act, 1949. I had to make my presence obvious around the polling station, looking fierce and making sure no one used undue influence or threatened any force during the voting. I had to ensure that no bribery was used and that no one voted in the name of any other person. Order had to be maintained throughout and I made friends with the Returning Officer because she was pretty and had brought a kettle.

After my early start, the day wore on, and I noticed that Hubert had really immersed himself in the occasion. He wore a massive yellow rosette and had decorated his old car with yellow banners as he trundled it around outlying farms and houses to convey his supposed voters to the polling booth. I knew they wouldn't vote for him; a free ride was fine, but voting Liberal was something no one would do.

But I had to admire Hubert. He never gave up. He chattered to potential voters, made countless trips in his car, and gave yellow rosettes to everyone. And all the time he tried to convert rock-hard Conservatives to his new faith.

At ten o'clock, prompt, the polls closed and my job was to oversee the sealing of the ballot boxes, following which I had to escort them to a collecting centre at the council offices. There, the count would take place. *En route*, we collected many more boxes from other villages and I signed a form to say none had been tampered with.

I got home around quarter past midnight, and was just sitting down for a hot goodnight drink when my telephone rang. Mary dashed through to answer it before it roused the children, and said, 'It's Hubert, he sounds upset.'

'The results won't be out yet!' I remarked as I trudged through to the telephone.

I picked up the handset. 'PC Rhea,' I announced.

'Mr Rhea, thoo'll have to cum quick. Real quick.' I recognised the urgency in Hubert's voice.

'What's matter?' I put to him.

'It's my pigs,' he said. 'I reckon they've caught summat real bad, and wondered if it needed reporting. They look terrible . . .'

'Have you called the vet?' I asked.

'He's not in yet, he's out at Brantsford with a calving cow.'

'I'll be there in five minutes,' I assured him.

Not knowing a great deal about contagious diseases of animals, I nonetheless knew that I would have to do something quickly, so I gulped down my cup of cocoa and hurried on foot towards his farm.

When I arrived, his car, still bearing the yellow banners and flags, stood in the foldyard. Several placards in dazzling yellow stood around the walls, but on the ground the mud was brown and thick. I splodged across to his sties and found him standing near the end wall, looking dejectedly at the pigs inside. As I approached, he heard my squelchy arrival.

'Ah, Mr Rhea, thoo's come then.'

I halted at his side.

He shone a powerful torch into the sty, and there, grunting in the dazzling light, were a dozen growing pigs. They looked terrible.

'Are they all like that, Hubert?' I asked.

'Aye,' he said sadly.

Then I laughed. 'Hubert!' I almost cried with laughter, 'They're not ill! Somebody's turned them all into little Liberals, that's all!'

Every one of them had been sprayed with a bright yellow paint.

Next day, it was announced that Hubert had polled four votes, and we never knew who'd perpetrated any of those deeds.

2

'Ah, when will this long weary day have end,
And lend me leave to come unto my love?'
Edmund Spenser 1552-99

This is the story of a man called Soldier, and because he spent some of his time in prison I will refer to him by that name alone. He was known affectionately as Soldier during his incarceration, and although he lived at Brantsford I first met him at a police station on the south coast of England. It happened like this.

Sergeant Blaketon rang me late one evening at the latter end of summer, and said, 'Rhea, there's an escort job for you. Catch the first train from York tomorrow morning, and go to Brighton. There's a prisoner to fetch back. Foxton will go with you. He's got the money for your fares, and warrant and something for a meal on the way. I've rung Brighton – they're expecting you. Make sure the fellow is handcuffed to one of you all the way back. He's for court at Eltering later this week.'

Sergeant Blaketon gave me the prisoner's name, and rang off. I called Alwyn Foxton at Ashfordly Police Station and confirmed what the sergeant had told me. It seemed our train left shortly before seven o'clock, and we had to travel in civilian clothes in order to be very inconspicuous. Alwyn would collect me in the morning at six o'clock and would have the necessary warrant to secure Soldier's arrest by our good selves. There were times when such formalities were necessary.

Everything was arranged, and so I rose from the warmth of my marital bed at quarter past five next morning to make myself a cooked breakfast. I didn't disturb Mary or the children as I went about stocking my body with hot food, and I had the sense to make sandwiches and provide myself with a flask of coffee for the long trip. Police know from bitter experience that it is wise to arm oneself with food and drink when away from one's usual source of supply. Prompt at six, Alwyn arrived in the official car, and we drove through the wilds of Ryedale to York's famous railway station.

Alwyn Foxton was a jolly, red-faced policeman of indeterminate age, whose thick grey hair and stock figure made him something of a father-figure, even to young constables like myself. Easy-going and affable, he had never sought promotion and was happy to let the big wide world pass gently by. On a long, boring train journey like this, he was good company as he reminisced about his life in the force, and offered words of home-spun wisdom to his youthful colleague.

We reached Brighton before lunch, tired and hungry, and decided to buy some food in town before presenting ourselves at the local police station to collect Soldier. I liked Brighton, except for the beach whose stony slopes are like river beds, and on impulse bought a postcard depicting a pretty part of the resort and posted it home to my mother. I learned afterwards that when she received this missive, bearing the words 'Having a lovely time, Nick,' she thought I'd abandoned my wife, family and career to run away to a new life in the deepest south. Such is the penalty for warped senses of humour, however light the act! We spent some time in the town, rather than wait with a prisoner for our return train, and eventually Alwyn and I entered the door of the police station and made our identities known to the sergeant. It was late afternoon by this time, and we had seen the delights of this lovely town.

The sergeant had difficulty understanding our strange tongue, but after showing him the magistrates' warrant and our warrant cards, he realised we had come to relieve him of Soldier.

He spoke to us in a strange accent and waved his arms,

which we interpreted as a request to follow him into the cells. This we did, and Alwyn passed me the handcuffs.

'He's yours,' he said, and I accepted the handcuffs before I realised what responsibilities I had thus acquired. If Soldier escaped, I would be responsible and liable to disciplinary action.

'Cell Number Two,' chanted the sergeant, and we halted at the locked door. He rattled his bunch of keys in the lock and the heavy studded door swung open on well-oiled hinges to reveal a tousle-haired man sitting on the wooden platform which was his bed.

He stood up as we entered.

'Great!' he said. 'Now I can get home.'

'Listen first,' the sergeant ordered him. 'These officers have come to arrest you for failing to answer to your bail.'

'I know,' the man said, 'and I'm not arguing. I just want to go home, that's all.'

'Read the warrant to him,' the sergeant ordered, and Alwyn began a pompous recital of the obscure wording of the document in his hands. In simple terms, it ordered us to arrest Soldier and take him to Eltering Magistrates' Court where he would be dealt with for an offence of housebreaking, committed many months ago. Soldier listened, and shuffled uneasily, wanting only to be out of the cell.

He was a tall man in his middle twenties, with brown hair all tousled and curly; his face, with its hint of freckles and dark brown eyes, bore that unmistakable aura of mischief, and yet it was a friendly face. He was casually dressed in grey trousers and a matching sweater, but his other possessions were in a locker labelled 'Prisoner's property'.

We walked him from the cell into the charge room, where the sergeant formally handed over his belongings, for which he had to sign an official form. There was a small amount of cash, a roll of bedding tied around the middle with a leather belt, a small suitcase and an overcoat.

Our train left at shortly after five and after a farewell cup of tea for us all, the sergeant arranged a car to convey us to the railway station. I asked Soldier to stretch out his arm, and promptly fastened the handcuffs upon him. Having seen that he was right-handed, I fastened the cuffs around his right wrist, so they linked with my left. And so we were handcuffed together with this small, but often valid, precaution. Alwyn folded the warrant, endorsed it as being executed and slid it back into his pocket.

Soldier, and indeed ourselves, were now ready to return to Yorkshire.

We found an empty compartment on the train and jostled ourselves into a comfortable position on the seat, with me sitting by the window and Soldier linked to me by the handcuffs. Since leaving the police station, he had not spoken a word, nor had he offered any resistance. He sat by my side, as good as gold, and watched the passing scenery of Sussex as we gathered speed on our long, tiring journey to the north.

Alwyn sat opposite; he had bought a few magazines and paperbacks for us, offering a glossy magazine to our prisoner. Soldier accepted it with a ready grin, and bowed his head to read.

I did likewise. Within minutes, we found it necessary to reach a neat reading arrangement because, at first, every time he moved his hand to turn a page, I had to lift mine to go with him, and the reverse happened when I wanted to turn a page. We soon got a system working, as Alwyn sat unmoved with his book. Then Soldier began to speak.

'Now we're out of that bloody place,' he said, 'I can talk. You are Yorkshiremen, aren't you? I like Yorkshiremen, coppers or not.'

'We are,' I spoke for both of us.

'Good, then you'll see sense. My name's Soldier. They called me Soldier inside, 'cos of the way I walk. Soldier this, and Soldier that. I did the tobacco baron bit inside, fixed things for the others, you know. Got the screws to unbend a bit, made life easier. They liked me, the others did. Captain of the cricket eleven I was, just because I come from Yorkshire. They don't know how to play cricket do they, those who live outside Yorkshire? I taught 'em a thing or two, with my googlies and off-breaks . . .'

And so he rambled on, spilling out the words in a rich tapestry of mixed prison jargon and a Yorkshire accent. I listened enthralled, but Alwyn pretended to continue reading, although I knew he was listening. But Alwyn was not going to admit being tricked into anything ridiculous like listening to the half-truths of a convicted prisoner. But I found myself warming to this voluble man.

'What are you in for?' I asked.

'Passing dud cheques,' he grinned. 'Lots of 'em. I had a real time, I tell you.'

'In Yorkshire was it?'

'No, all over. Well, you know how it is, Constable. The job got me down, there's the wife and a kid and no money. All work and worry . . . it just got me down. So I nicked a cheque book and had a bloody good spend.'

'They caught you?'

'In time. I nicked a few more cheque books and stayed at posh hotels. Bought a car an' all, and sold it. Easy money it was, Constable. Dead easy. Better 'n working. Too easy, really. I got daft.'

'What is your job – when you're working?' I put to him.

'Labouring. Building sites and that. Mucky work, heavy sometimes.'

'So they caught you. Who caught you?'

'Liverpool police. I was in this flat, and they found out it was me. Raided the place and caught me with the cheque book. I got sent down for eighteen months. I've done a year, behaved myself, so they've let me out.'

'And now you'll be going straight?' I smiled.

'I am, honest. No, I mean it. You know what I wanted in there? All that time?'

'No.' I let him tell his tale.

'A tea party at my own house. I wanted to get home, see the wife and my little lass, and have a proper tea with a white cloth and nice cups. That's what I've wanted all along. Tea like that, done proper.'

'And your wife? She'll be waiting for you?' I visualised the happy domestic scene.

'Yeh,' he said with some nonchalance. 'Yeh, she will. I wrote you see, said I was coming home today and told her to put a white cloth on.'

'Did she say she'd look forward to it?' As we chatted, I warmed to this likeable fellow.

'She hasn't replied.' There was a suggestion of sadness in his voice. 'Mind you,' he added, 'she wouldn't have time to write back. I mean, they didn't tell me I was going home till a couple of days back, and then I wrote straight away so she'll have just got my letter . . .'

'But this arrest? You knew we'd be coming?'

'Oh, aye, I knew that. I didn't answer bail for something way back – housebreaking I think – and the screws said you fellers would be waiting with that warrant. They brought me here. I didn't mind – I mean, I get a free trip home under arrest, and I was going anyway. I'm dying for Yorkshire, you know, I really am. Just dying to see my wife and our kid . . .'

'And that white table-cloth?' I smiled.

'Aye, and that.'

Unwittingly, we had caught a slow train to London, and during that journey, Soldier chattered to us like a friend. He was so open, so friendly, so in love with his wife and child, whose name I learned was Susie. He told us of his wishes, his loves, his pranks and dodges in prison, and his escapades with the stolen cheque books. As he chattered, Alwyn Foxton joined in, now relaxing in his role as senior police officer in charge of our prisoner.

'I'm not going to run, you know,' Soldier said eventually. 'You can take those cuffs off.'

Automatically, I glanced down at the chromium plated chain that linked us. There were no passengers in our compartment and Alwyn sat opposite. Soldier's only way of escape would be to jump through the window and risk death by falling on to the line or alternatively to make a dash for the corridor. Both were unlikely.

I made the decision to release him.

'No funny business then!' I said rather inanely.

'Don't be bloody silly, Constable,' he said, 'I'm going home. I want to go home, don't I?'

I didn't answer, but located the handcuff key in my pocket and loosened the cuffs. I removed them and slid them into my pocket. Alwyn looked askance at me, but said nothing. After all, Soldier was my responsibility. He rubbed his wrist and said, 'Now that's better. I'm not going to run, you know. I won't – honest. There's no need.'

Somehow, I believed him. He produced a paperback from his bag and began to read.

'Agatha Christie,' he said. 'Good stuff, eh?'

And he lapsed into a long reading session. At various stations along the route, people entered and left our train, some joining us in the compartment but none guessing we were two police officers escorting a prisoner north for a court appearance.

Due to the slowness of our train, we were very late arriving at Victoria, and as we slowed at the end of that part of the journey, Soldier put his book away and asked the time.

I remember telling him, although I cannot recall the precise time save to say that Soldier said, 'Then we've twenty minutes to get across London. Our train home goes in twenty minutes, Constable. If we miss it, we won't get home until the early hours.'

'We can't make it across London in twenty minutes!' Alwyn cried.

'We can – I know the way!' chirped Soldier.

'There's tickets to get at the tubes,' I said, 'there's always a queue at the windows . . .'

This was before the days of those handy ticket machines, but Soldier said, 'You don't need tickets in the tubes if you've got British Rail tickets. Just show ours – they'll do.'

'Will they?' I asked.

'Course!' he cried. 'Bloody hell, Constable, you've not been around, have you?'

'No,' I admitted. 'Not a lot.'

'Then leave it to me . . .' he said, 'I'll get us on to that train.'

'I'll have to handcuff you through Victoria,' I said.

'No need,' he assured me, 'I'm not leaving you blokes. You've got my ticket, remember?'

'I can't let you walk through London without them!' I began to worry about this.

'Walk? Who's going to walk, Constable? Run you mean, run like hell. We run like hell, me leading and you chasing. If you don't, we miss that bloody train home, and I don't want to wait until the early hours. I want my bed tonight, and my wife and little girl, and that white tea cloth . . . I'm going to get all that, mate. All of it. And soon.'

The train was slowing on its final yards and Soldier was on his feet, waiting at the door and clutching his belongings.

'Come on!' he said. 'There's no time to hang about. Keep with me, and don't get left behind. If I lose you,' he said, 'I'll see you at King's Cross barrier . . . I can get through the tubes all right . . . don't need tickets if you know the ropes . . .'

'I'd better just put these on . . .' I pulled out the cuffs and dangled them before him.

'No time,' he said. 'Come on, lads, run!'

And as the train slowed to its grinding halt, he opened the door and leapt on to the platform before the train halted. He was galloping towards the ticket barrier, shouting for us to follow him, Alwyn was coughing and spluttering and I was dithering.

'You've done it, Nick!' he cried. 'That was a bloody stupid thing to do . . . he's away . . . he's a con man, you know . . . that's you and me for the high jump . . .'

But I was already jumping from the train in advance of the other passengers and galloping after Soldier. He saw me, waited a moment, and waved urgently.

'Come on!' he shouted. 'Don't hang about.'

Alwyn gathered his wits and we all passed through the barrier together, flashing our tickets. Soldier darted off again, rushing through the crowded station at Victoria and heading for the nearest tube. We followed, Alwyn puffing with advancing age and me desperately trying to keep Soldier in view.

He kept looking behind and waiting for us; he knew exactly where he was going, and we had no alternative but to run with him. Already, he could have escaped and ruined our careers, so we simply galloped through London's crowds with my eye on the back of his bobbing head.

To this day, I cannot remember which way we took. Not being accustomed to London, its web of tube stations and the crowds of stolid faced humans, I simply followed Soldier and shouted at Alwyn to keep pace. Barrier after barrier was crossed, escalator after escalator was galloped up or down, crowds were parted and people apologised to, and then, as if by magic, we were rushing across the platform at King's Cross.

'Two minutes to go,' Soldier smiled. 'Not bad.'

We hurried along the platform, seeking an empty compartment, but every one was full. People were even standing in the corridors, and as the guard looked at his watch, we opened the nearest door and leapt aboard, panting and perspiring.

'My God!' said Alwyn. 'I never thought we'd all get here.'

'Me neither,' beamed Soldier, 'I thought you blokes were going to let me down.'

We laughed, and settled down for a long haul home in a crowded corridor. The guard looked at his watch.

'One minute,' grinned Soldier, and at that precise instant, a newsvendor walked down the platform with one or two papers still in his satchel. Like lightning, Soldier dived for the door, opened it and leapt on to the platform.

'Get him!' shouted Alwyn.

But I couldn't move. There was a fat woman directly in front of me, and the guard was shouting and blowing a whistle. I watched with horror as our prisoner galloped up the platform, but he halted before the newsvendor, handed over a coin for a paper and raced back to the open carriage door. Even as the train began to move, he leapt inside, slammed the door and gave the two-fingered sign to the harassed guard.

'Sorry about that,' he said. 'I like a read when I'm on a train,' and opened the London *Evening Standard*.

I breathed a sigh of relief, but daren't look at Alwyn. My poor heart must have missed many beats.

At the first stop, seats became vacant, and we took our places in a crowded compartment, Soldier remaining silent as he studied every word in the paper. I grew increasingly tired and felt like dropping off to sleep, but knew I must not do so. After all, I did have responsibilities.

It was a long, tiring and boring journey with many halts. Soldier solved his boredom by falling asleep but left his paper to be shared by Alwyn and myself.

We were due into York around midnight, so far as I remember, and we were all tired, hungry and travel stained. As we neared the city, I nudged Soldier into wakefulness.

'Come on, Soldier,' I said. 'Get ready to leave. We're coming into York.'

'Then you'd better handcuff me,' he said. 'The sergeant wouldn't like to see me loose like this, would he?'

'No,' I said, thankful he'd reminded me. Having organised ourselves for disembarkation, I slipped the heavy cuffs around his wrist, locked them securely, and smiled at the reaction of our travelling companions. I didn't offer any explanation – they would come to their own conclusions about us, I'm sure.

At York, we left the train and walked sedately along the platform where the tall, gaunt figure of Oscar Blaketon awaited. He looked grim and forbidding, but relaxed as he noticed our little party.

'Ah, Foxton and Rhea. You made it then?'

'Yes, Sergeant,' I said.

'No problems with him?'

'None, Sergeant,' I confirmed.

'Right, the car's waiting outside,' and so we were marched

through the final barrier. Soldier and I climbed into the waiting police car to be driven home by Oscar Blaketon while Alwyn brought the other car home. Sergeant Blaketon seemed to think there was safety in numbers.

Until this point, Soldier had not spoken to the sergeant, but once we were settled in the car, handcuffed together in the rear seat, Soldier asked, 'Is my wife waiting for me, Sergeant?'

'Wife? No,' he said, expressing surprise at the question.

'Didn't she come to say she'd be surety for me, for my bail?'

'No,' said Blaketon equally bluntly, 'nobody's been.'

'You'll go and ask them for me, won't you?' he addressed the sergeant, leaning forward from the rear seat.

'Rhea can go round when we get to Brantsford.'

Without a surety for bail, he would have to spend his time in our cells until his court appearance. I could see his world beginning to crumble. I could see his precious dream fading, and felt terribly sorry for him.

We arrived at Brantsford Police Station and placed him in the cells. It would be just after one o'clock in the morning, but I went around to his home address to see if his wife was there.

I knocked but got no reply. I peered through the windows, but the house looked deserted. And there was no white cloth on the table.

I had to go back and break the news.

'Sergeant,' I said, 'could I act as surety for him?'

'You, Rhea? Don't be silly,' was Blaketon's response, and so I went home.

Next morning, Mary listened to my story and said, 'Well, bring him here for tea. I'll put a white cloth on.'

I found an excuse to visit Brantsford Police Station that afternoon, and learned his case was due for hearing at Eltering the following morning. Among the other outstanding crimes, he was to be charged with yet another case of false pretences, and I went to see him.

I stood at the cell door, where I spoke through the small square hole in the heavy woodwork.

'Any luck?' I asked.

'No,' he said. 'She's not been.'

'You can come to our house for tea,' I said. 'When this is all over, give me a call, and my wife will put a white cloth on for you. I mean it, Soldier. I owe you a favour.'

'Thanks,' he said, and I noticed the merest hint of a tear in his eye. 'Yeh, thanks. I will. They'll send me down again, you know. I'd have done it willingly, if I could have spent last night at home . . . with the wife . . . and Susie . . .'

'I know,' I said. 'Sorry.'

'Nice to have met you, Constable.'

'I'm at Aidensfield,' I said. 'Rhea's the name.'

'I'll look you up, honest,' he said.

And I left.

He was sentenced to another twelve months imprisonment for his outstanding offences and he never called for his tea. To this day, I do not know what happened to him, but I never saw him at his own house, nor did I ever see his wife and child.

But I will never forget that gallop through London, hard on the heels of my prisoner. So much could have gone wrong, but everything went right because a Yorkshireman wanted a cup of tea and cakes on a white table-cloth with his wife and baby.

There is little doubt that hardened law-breakers do respond to thoughtfulness and kindness from police officers. I was given a perfect example of this late one Saturday night during a noisy dance at Ashfordly Town Hall.

The dance attracted many lively youngsters from neighbouring market towns and villages, and I was drafted into Ashfordly that night to increase the strength of the local force. My presence made it two constables on duty that night – two against about 250 revellers.

There was the usual noise and loud music from the hall as

the dance was in full swing, but little or no trouble. If there was to be a problem, it would start as the local pubs turned out, when young men, full of fiery liquid, attempted to show who was the best at whatever caught their fancy. Much of it would be a show of bravado richly combined with stupidity, for such antics generate a lot of noise but little else. High spirits at this level can be tolerated.

As the pubs closed their doors, therefore, Alwyn Foxton and I separated and patrolled the town to reveal the presence of our dark blue uniforms in strategic places. In those days, the police uniform was respected, and it did not encourage trouble; many of the noisy youths simply continued their noise but did not reduce themselves to fighting. Instead they formed a modest procession from the pubs into the dance hall, filling it almost to capacity.

Once they were inside, we could breathe a sigh of relief. When the majority were indoors Alwyn and I slipped into the caretaker's office for a welcome cup of tea. It was now 11 p.m.; the dance ended at quarter to midnight, and we reckoned to have the market square clear by the stroke of twelve.

We did not prolong the cup-of-tea break; within ten minutes, I was heading for the stairs which climbed to the dance floor, my purpose being to poke my nose through the door of the hall to show the uniform yet again. Such periodical displays of our dark blue suits did achieve results. These dances generated very little trouble.

But as I climbed the stairs, a pretty girl of about twenty in a delightful blue dress called me and her voice had a note of urgency.

'Mr Rhea.' She knew my name; I recognised her as a girl called Sandra who worked in a local shop. 'Mr Rhea, quickly, up here.'

She turned and raced up the stairs, her slim legs and swaying body being enough to make the most sluggish of hearts miss a beat or two. I followed, trotting in her wake until she paused outside the gents' toilet.

'In there,' she said.

'Trouble?' I asked, panting after my race up the stairs.

'My boyfriend,' she said. 'He's hurt.'

And as I entered the toilet area, I noticed large drops of blood on the wooden floor. Fresh blood. I could see a trail of it along the landing and into this toilet; it led from the rear staircase. I had no idea what to expect.

Inside, I found him.

A scruffy, long-haired and rather surly youth was sprawled across the two washbasins, one of them taking his weight while the other, with its running cold tap, was full of brilliant red blood made brighter because it was mixed with the flowing water.

He was alone; only this girl hovered outside as I approached.

'Now then,' I said inanely. 'What's happened?'

'Oh,' he stood up, clutching his wrist with the uninjured hand. 'Oh, I fell,' he said. 'It's cut bad.'

He kept his bleeding hand over the washbasin as the swirling water carried away the lost blood; the fact that it was bright red blood stirred memories of my First Aid training and I knew it came from an artery, not a vein. He was bleeding profusely and this was no ordinary cut. I noticed the display of agony and worry on his pale face.

'Let me see.' I took hold of his wrist and turned his hand palm upwards so that I could see it, making sure it did not spill on to the floor. Due to the blood welling from the wound, I could not see it clearly, so, gently I returned his hand to the tap to wash away the fountain of blood. And there, right across the palm of his hand, was a long, clean cut almost like a slash from the blade of a sword. It was a clean, but deep and severe wound.

This would need rapid treatment; it required more than first aid or the botched-up bandaging of an amateur of any kind. This lad required urgent and professional medical care.

'You said you fell?' I said, attempting to stem the flow by finding a pressure point.

'Yeh,' he said, assuming something of a cocky air.

'Where?' I was desperately trying to find a pressure point

in his arm, searching in the requisite places beneath his biceps or near his wrist.

'Down the steps,' he said vaguely. I knew he was lying. No fall could produce such a clean cut, unless he had fallen on to a knife or some glass. But there was no time to waste investigating his claims; I had to find a doctor. I don't think the lad realised the danger he was facing as his life-blood was being swilled down that sink, being pumped out of his body by his youthful heart.

'Stand still,' I said. We were now attracting an audience. Some of his friends had arrived, and his girl still hovered near the door, her face showing genuine concern but her upbringing keeping her out of the gents' toilet.

'You all right Kev?' asked a huge, unruly looking ruffian.

'Cut hand,' said my patient. 'Leave us be, the cop's doing his best.'

'You're not taking him in, are you?' came the question.

'I'm taking him to a doctor,' I said. 'This cut needs expert attention.'

'All right Kev?' His pals sought Kev's agreement to my course of action.

'Yeh,' said Kev, and they slowly dispersed, leaving the worried girl, and myself with the pale youth.

'Ah!' I had found the pressure point beneath his biceps and squeezed tightly. 'Can you hold your own arm there?' I asked him.

'What for?'

'To stop that blood coming out of your hand. You can do it better than me, because we're going to the doctor. Just grip your arm like this,' and I demonstrated the correct method, 'and that'll stop the blood gushing out.'

Holding his injured hand in the air, Kev searched until he found the pressure point, then squeezed hard. He was a fit youth, with the powerful hands of a labourer, and his left hand gripped his own arm and he watched with some fascination as the blood ceased to flow.

'Have you a clean handkerchief?' was my next question.

'I have.' Sandra had now ventured into the toilet and she produced a large white handkerchief from her handbag.

'Good. Now, Kev,' I used the name I'd heard his pals call him. 'I'm going to put this over the cut, right? Just close your fist lightly, and hold it in place. Don't squeeze. Got it?'

His hand closed over the rolled up handkerchief which rapidly changed colour to a brilliant red, and with Kev holding his own brachial pressure point, I escorted him out of the building. Sandra came with us, worried and anxious about him, but I now reassured them that the matter was under control.

As we walked between the cars parked in the market place, he regained much of his confidence and said, 'I did fall, Officer, I did, you know.'

'I'm not arguing, Kev,' I said. 'If you say you fell, then you fell, although my natural curiosity asks how you managed to get a cut of that sort just by falling. But my concern is to get you fixed, and to get it done by a doctor. There's a surgery just opposite, over there,' and I pointed to a large green door in a building with a brass plate bolted to the wall.

He said nothing as our little procession halted outside the imposing door. It was nearly twenty minutes to midnight and the whole house was in darkness. I ventured up the alley alongside, but there was no sign of a light. The doctor was in bed.

The bell-pull was one of those old-fashioned knobs with a cable attached and I hauled on this to produce a loud ringing sound within the huge house. I rang several times to produce what I hoped to be an indication of urgency, and in the meantime looked at the pale Kev beside me.

'Release the pressure for a few seconds,' I advised him. 'We don't want to cut off your whole arm's supply of blood. The handkerchief will stop it spurting.'

He smiled briefly and nodded.

'Maybe he's away,' said Sandra.

'I hope not!' I murmured, hauling once again on the strong bell-pull. This produced lights. I rang the bell again to confirm my message of urgency, as behind me the first rush of dancers began to leave the hall. Suddenly, the market place was full of laughing, chattering people, getting into cars and hurrying home, some alone and some with their evening's conquest. I hoped the doctor didn't think the bell ringer was a late-night reveller doing it for a prank.

But more lights came on, and I could hear the deep grumbling tones of Doctor William Williams, a fiery Welshman, as he unlocked the large door.

'Pressure point on?' I smiled at Kev.

'Yeh,' he said, clinging to his arm. Sandra had an arm about his waist and I could see the shock beginning to affect him. He was starting to quiver and his face grew deathly white.

'What the hell . . .' began the doctor as the huge door swung open. 'Oh, the police!'

He was dressed in a large green dressing gown and slippers, and he looked unkempt. Undoubtedly, he'd been in a deep sleep, but the sight of my uniform made him realise the bell hadn't been ringing for frivolous reasons.

'This boy is badly cut,' I said. 'He needs treatment, Doctor.'

'Does he now? Well, then, bring him into the surgery. Come in, all of you.' His musical Welsh voice sounded odd in a North Yorkshire market town, and I knew his burly, aggressive appearance concealed a warm heart.

We followed him along the passage and into the surgery where he pointed to a chair. 'Sit down,' he said to Kev. 'Now, let me see.'

Kev slowly opened his hand and Doctor Williams removed the blood-stained handkerchief. He studied the cut with care and tenderness, before saying, 'My word, a nasty one here, isn't it?'

'I'll leave now,' I offered.

'Can I stay?' asked Sandra.

'I think you'd better, girl,' smiled the doctor as he rolled up the sleeves of his dressing gown. 'Thank you, Constable, this does need treatment. Now son,' he said, 'just let go of that muscle of yours and let's see how the blood is flowing . . .'

I left them in his tender care, closed the big door behind me and resumed my patrol of the market square. Alwyn spotted me and said, 'I'll do a quick recce of the council estate. Can you look after the town centre until one o'clock?'

'Sure,' I said, breathing in the clean fresh air.

Less than five minutes later, I was walking past the side door of the King's Head Hotel when I spotted the landlord standing at the door.

He noticed me at the same instant and said, 'Oh, hello Constable. Got a minute?'

'Of course,' and he took me into the inn, along the passage and into the gents' toilet. 'Just look at that!'

One of the small windows was broken, with a large hole apparently punched through the middle of the glass, and there was blood all over.

'I wouldn't mind if they'd come to tell me – that can't have been an accident . . . nobody would be daft enough to shove a hand through there . . .'

'What would it cost to replace it?' I asked him.

'Not much. Thirty bob or so.'

'If I get the villain in question to fetch the money, would that settle the matter?'

'You know who did it?'

'I've a good idea,' and I told him of the sequence of events at the dance.

'That fits what the locals said,' he confirmed. 'They said a lad with a bleeding hand rushed out of here, down the yard and out.'

'I'll see what I can do,' and I left the pub. Sure enough, the light of my torch showed a trail of blood from the yard door near the broken window, and it led the few hundred yards to the town hall, entering via the rear door.

I saw no more of the injured youth that night, but as I left the quiet market place at one o'clock that Sunday morning, the lights of Doctor Williams' surgery were still burning.

It was the following Thursday evening when I next met Kev. He was walking through Ashfordly Market Place with

Sandra on his good arm, and they spotted me standing near the monument. I was on duty, and clad in my flat cap and summer uniform, making a routine patrol of Ashfordly town centre.

The couple came towards me, with Sandra smiling broadly. She looked a picture of happiness, but Kev looked rather bashful and surprisingly shy.

'Hello.' Sandra broke the ice. 'Thanks for helping Kev last Saturday. Dr Williams was good to him, he bandaged the hand and gave him an injection.'

Kev, his pale face now showing signs of its normal colour beneath his neglected hair, looked at his arm and hand. His fist was swathed in rolls of bandage and he had his arm in a sling.

'Yeh,' he shuffled uncomfortably before me, 'yeh, he was good. Look . . .'

I waited for his speech. He was clearly not accustomed to speaking to a policeman in this way and I didn't want to dissuade him from the effort. I smiled at Sandra.

'Well,' said Kev, his feet still shuffling upon the surface of the market square. 'It's like this. I mean, no copper's ever done anything for me, not ever. Not like you did, I mean. Help. That sort of thing . . .'

'It was the least I could do, Kev,' I said. 'You were hurt and it was my privilege to be able to help you. You've Sandra to thank, you know, she called me in.'

'Yeah, she's great, isn't she? Too good for me, that's true. Too good. I'm a layabout really, no bloody good to anybody. Nothing but trouble . . .'

'There's good in everybody, Kev,' I said. 'Anyway, thanks for your kind words.'

'I'd like to do summat to help . . . I mean . . . I didn't deserve help at all . . .'

'You could give the landlord of the King's Head the price of his broken window,' I suggested. 'Thirty bob.'

'You know?' He lowered his eyes in shame and stared at the ground.

'There was a trail of blood – your blood – from the window into the Town Hall. I knew that cut wasn't done in a fall – it was too clean.'

'Sorry about that, Officer. It was an accident – my mate shoved me and I fell, put my hand clean through that window, I did. Then I ran . . . he did, an' all.'

'Thirty bob will square the whole thing. I want no more to do with the window – the landlord won't push for any more action if he gets the damage paid for.'

'Oh well, in that case . . . I mean . . . it was my fault wasn't it? For fooling about . . .'

'OK. Well, it's all over, Kev. Are you off work?'

'Yeh, till the hand's better. Look, Officer, like I said before I'm not good at saying things and I'm a right villain really, allus fighting and things . . . well, I mean, I don't help the law, me nor my mates. Never. But, well, if there's trouble in any of the dances and you're needing help, well, like, I'll be there. With you, I mean. Helping you to sort 'em out. That's a promise, honest. I'll help you.'

'Thanks, Kev.' I knew what this offer must mean to him. It meant as much to me, and I made a show of attempting to shake his bandaged hand. I simply touched his right arm and wished him luck in the future.

At several of the local dances in the months that followed, I saw Kev and Sandra, and he always came across for a quiet word with me. We talked about nothing in particular, and I do know that he paid for the damaged window. But the sincerity of his promise was never tested, for I never experienced bother at any of the subsequent dances.

Nonetheless, he did attend them all, and this gave me a strong feeling of security. It still does.

3

'No sound is dissonant which tells of life.'
Samuel Taylor Coleridge 1772-1834

I am not really sure how I came to be a member of the Aidensfield String Orchestra. Perhaps, during some off-guard moment in a casual conversation, I let it be known that I played the violin, or it may be that some other person who knew me as a child let it be known that I could produce a tune from a battered old fiddle.

Whatever the source of the tale, I was approached by our local auctioneer, a Mr Rudolph Burley, who had heard of my doubtful prowess. He informed me there was a vacancy for a second violin in the village orchestra. I protested that I had not put bow to string for many years, and that I was as rusty as a bedspring on a council tip, but all my protestations were in vain. By the following Monday night, I was in the village hall partaking in a practice session of *Eine Kleine Nachtmusik*.

It is fair to say that the noise was awful, and that the acoustics of the hall did not help; the village piano was out of tune, and our conductor, the said Mr Burley, seemed unable to co-ordinate all sections of his 30-piece orchestra. I was never sure of the real purpose of these weekly gatherings because we attempted to play impossibly difficult pieces like Brahms' Violin Concerto and finished in the pub to discuss our errors. I began to wonder if it was just an excuse to visit the pub.

Because most of the practice sessions were littered with wrong notes, wrong timing, flat and sharp faults and almost every other kind of musical disgrace, the entire orchestra spent a lot of time in the pub. There were deep discussions on the best way of righting all our wrongs, and at length it was deemed the only true solution lay in two parts. The first was to comprise lots of diligent practice, and the second was to have some objective in mind, like a concert or public performance.

It was therefore decided to hold a concert in precisely one year's time. It would be in aid of village hall funds, and it is pleasing to record that this decision injected the orchestra with a new enthusiasm. Now, we had a goal; the fund for modernisation of the village hall had been stagnant for years, and had lately lacked the necessary impetus to commend it to the community. Our tuneless practice sessions, plus the publicity we began to stimulate were responsible for generating a necessary new desire to achieve something.

Fired with a fresh zeal, the rate of orchestra practice sessions was increased to two nights a week, Mondays and Thursdays. Although this put pressure on the key instrumentalists and the conductor, it did help those like myself with family commitments and duties at odd hours. Even by attending once a week, my rusty skill would be renewed.

Early that spring we started in earnest and our objective was to produce a full orchestral concert in the village hall by the following Easter.

Quite soon, the anomalous collection of people with their equally anomalous collection of instruments began to behave in a disciplined way. Our noises began to sound like real music, and I began to think that even great composers like Mozart or Chopin might have found something of interest in our enterprise. We tackled pieces like the Violin Concerto, but eventually decided that the concert would comprise: Mozart's *Divertimento in D*; Holst's *St Paul's Suite*; Dvorak's *Serenade*; Handel's *Concerto Grosso*; Tchaikovsky's *Serenade for Strings*; our favourite *Eine Kleine Nachtmusik*; the *Introduction and Allegro for Strings and String Quartet*, and Dag Wirren's *Serenade for Strings*.

Looking back on those halcyon days, the Aidensfield String

Orchestra possessed a remarkable cross-section of the village, most of whom had delved under their beds or climbed into their attics to produce ancient violas, cellos, or double-bass, several violins and even a harp. The initial idea had come from Rudolph Burley, and it was his drive and enthusiasm that welded the group together. He could be a bully at one moment and a cajoling charmer the next, but he got results. He was a one-man committee, the sort that achieved success without the hassle of open-ended and fruitless discussions marked with opinions of great stupidity.

Rudolph was a character. He lived with a shy wife in a big house on the hill overlooking the west end of Aidensfield, and was in his late 40s. A successful auctioneer, he sold household junk by the ton, and also conducted business at cattle marts in the area, managing to make his rapid-fire voice heard above the squeak of pigs, the bellowing of bulls and the bleating of sheep. His stentorian tones were an asset when conducting the Aidensfield String Orchestra – when unwelcome sounds emanated from the music makers of the village, he could quell them with suitably loud advice.

He looked like a successful auctioneer. He had a thick mop of sandy hair which was inclined to be wavy and always untidy, and this was matched by a set of expressive eyebrows which fluctuated according to the volume of his voice. Those heavy brows lowered dramatically when he spoke softly, but when he raised his voice high enough to lift the roof of the hall, his eyebrows appeared to rise in an attempt to muffle his tones. When he was conducting, they behaved in a similar manner, rising during the crescendos and falling during the diminuendos.

His bulky figure tended to sway rhythmically during the romantic moods and jerk up and down spasmodically when things got exciting. I felt that music was bred in him even if he did stand before us in his tweed jacket, cavalry twill trousers and brogue shoes, while shouting like a salesman at a horse-market. Somehow, he coaxed sweetness from that motley collection of re-discovered musical instruments.

The double-bass player was another character of charm and fascination. His name was Ralph Hedges, and he was a retired lengthman, a man whose working life had been spent in the maintenance of our highways and byways. He was a stocky fellow with simple, grey clothing and black shoes, always clean and well kept. His rounded face was the picture of health, and he peered short-sightedly through thick spectacles during our practice sessions; turned 70, he was dependable in that he came every practice night, and he knew most of the pieces by heart. This could be a problem at times because he played them at his own speed, but Rudolph gradually tamed him.

His double-bass was ancient but its tone was mellow and beautiful and he could pluck its thick strings in a way that showed remarkable empathy between man and instrument. His strong fingers, hardened by years of working with a pick and shovel, coped easily with the powerful strings of the bass and possessed an agility that was remarkable in a man of this age. Everyone loved old Ralph.

Lovable though he was, Ralph had one very distressing habit. By this, I mean it was distressing to other, more sensitive members of the orchestra. Try as they might, they never did grow accustomed to it, for it was a habit which meant he had to be placed at the rear of the orchestra, nicely beyond the sight of any audience, and well away from those who were distracted by his noisy effusions.

The problem was that he spat on the floor as he coaxed such lovely music from his double-bass. Furthermore, he did this in time to the music, the result being that, to the count of four, the orchestra would be complemented by the sound of Ralph's spittle positively smacking upon the polished wooden floor. At times, when the pace increased, or when it was a particularly exciting piece of music, Ralph would increase his rate until he sounded like a distant herd of cows, all dropping juicy pats in time to the prevailing beat.

The snag with Ralph's problem was that if he ever dried up and failed to produce his unique, well-timed sound, there would be a vacuum in the minds of the musicians. This could cause them to miss a note, or to turn their heads away from their scores to see if the ageing Ralph was still alive. The disruption could be catastrophic during a concert.

It was suggested that the orchestra subscribed to a spittoon for him, with a never-ending supply of sawdust. The idea was rejected because, although this would save the caretaker some unpleasant work after band practice, it would not produce the particular sound of Ralph's special blend of music. He was therefore allowed to continue, and his spitting noises were accepted as part of the orchestra's stylistic tones.

I learned that several older members were pleased to tolerate his spitting as a sign of good fortune. The custom had been practised among the ancient Greeks and Romans, and even Pliny believed it averted witchcraft. Local farmers would spit on their hands before shaking over a deal, and a large number of rural businessmen continue to spit on the first money of a deal. I think we all came to regard Ralph's musical spitting as a harbinger of good fortune for the village hall and our fund-raising efforts.

One of the orchestra's embarrassing members was the Honourable Mrs Norleigh, Rosamund to her friends. A lady of noble ancestry, so she told us, she had married plain Mr Norleigh because she loved him dearly, and the fact that he owned a chain of hotels and shops might have contributed to her romantic climb down the social scale. Embarrassing as she was, she was a valuable member of the orchestra because she played the cello with some skill, having been nurtured on the instrument in her native Surrey.

Now in her late forties, she had been rejuvenated musically and, it was rumoured, she'd also had a facial and a nose-job because of the limelight into which she was about to be thrust. She had a figure which was as exciting as a southerner's attempt at making a Yorkshire pudding and a face which did a lot for the cosmetics industry. Her noble features were rarely seen in a natural light because they were always swathed in pounds of powder and many liquid ounces of make-up. The result was something like a walking waxwork of very indeterminate age, while the clothes she wore were indicative of a lady approaching the autumn of life but who steadfastly believed she was in the eternal spring of youth.

Her most embarrassing feature was her choice of knickers. For some inexplicable reason, Rosamund always wore bright red flannelette knickers of the *directoire* type which came down to her knees, and for a cello player this was hardly the recommended dress. When she opened her legs and spread her skirts to accept the formidable breadth of the cello, she displayed yards of bright red which caused amusement or embarrassment according to the viewer's understanding of 'entertainment'.

The diplomatic Rudolph had tried positioning her to the left, to the right, in the middle row, back row and even behind the piano, but from whatever angle she was viewed, Rosamund's red knickers were visible. The only way to conceal them was to sit her facing the rear of the stage, but this was not wise because she would be unable to see the conductor. Rudolph decided the audience would have to suffer her propensity for showing off whatever she had, or for proving she'd hidden whatever she wished to hide.

The pianist, young Alan Napier, was interesting because he couldn't read a note of music. He was a farm labourer, more accustomed to milking cows and digging ditches than making music, and yet those heavy, scarred fingers could coax the most wonderful music from a piano. Even complicated pieces like concertos or major orchestral items did not deter him. For simple pieces, he would ask for them to be played through just once, and for the difficult scores, he would acquire a gramophone record. At home, he would listen to the record and the next time he came to practise, he could play the entire piece by ear.

The lad was a born musician, but maintained he was not interested in the piano as a career; he liked to play for fun. Alan was about twenty-five years old, a single man who lived with his parents, and he had a handsome, dark face with curly black hair. Music was in him, and yet he could not sing a note, nor would he agree to being schooled in the finer art of piano-playing. He did not want his piano-playing to become a chore.

'Let me hear it, and I'll soon play it,' he would say. And he did.

This collection of country musicians, aided by a further two dozen assorted players, formed the Aidensfield String Orchestra, and there is no doubt they enjoyed their music-making. I did too; it was quite surprising how we changed from making a mess of lovely music to producing a passable piece of entertainment. It was all due to Rudolph's patience and drive.

After several months of hard but productive practice, Rudolph called for silence at one of the sessions. I was there, off duty, and was pleased to have a rest during the hard-working rehearsal.

As we paused with our instruments resting on our laps or on the floor, Rudolph wiped his brow. 'In five minutes,' he spoke gravely, 'the Colonel is going to speak to us.'

As one, we turned to look at the door behind us, but the Colonel had not arrived.

After our murmur of gentle surprise, Rudolph's loud voice quelled the speculation as he said, 'Now, I've no idea what he wants to say, but he did ask if he could address the entire orchestra tonight. He said it was a matter of importance and forthcoming pride for Aidensfield.'

More mutterings filled the room, and Rudolph halted them by emphasising some of our more noticeable weaknesses. However, he did express pleasure because our faults were fewer and our music stronger and said we were beginning to sound like a real orchestra and not something rushed together for a charity concert. We enjoyed an atmosphere of pride.

Then came the sound of the door crashing open followed by the tramp of heavy footsteps, all of which heralded the arrival of Colonel Partington and his Dalmatian. The Colonel's Christian name was Oswald and his dog was called Napoleon for reasons we never understood. Man and dog advanced into the room, and at an almost inaudible command, Napoleon sat on the floor just inside, then lay down to watch the proceedings.

The Colonel was the epitome of a retired army officer in rural Britain; stoutish in build, he bristled with belief in his own efficiency and sported a moustache which was greying like his hair. He stalked everywhere rather than walked but no one seemed quite sure where or when he had been a colonel. We assumed his friends all knew because everyone called him simply 'The Colonel'. He lived in a big house called Beckford Hall on the outskirts of Aidensfield and I suppose he occupied the unofficial position of squire to the community.

'Good evening, Colonel,' greeted Rudolph with a large smile and a loud voice.

'Good evening, Burley.' The Colonel called everyone by surname. 'A nice turn-out, what?'

'We've maintained an excellent attendance record,' beamed Rudolph like an RSM on parade. 'I'm proud of our members.'

'And their music, what? How's that coming along?'

'First class. We've mastered *Concerto Grosso* and by the date of our concert, we'll have studied and conquered enough music for a two-hour programme.'

'Good. Well, that's why I'm here. To talk to them all, what? I believe in telling everyone, not keeping things hushed up, you know.'

We waited for his news.

'Burley, you said you had planned a concert for the spring?'

'Yes, Colonel.'

'Any chance of making it a firm date, what? Say Saturday the fifteenth of April?'

'Fifteenth April?' Rudolph looked at us all for guidance, but the date meant nothing to anyone. I carried a pocket diary and checked the date – I had no private engagements that day, but it was too far in advance to know whether I'd be committed on duty.

'I'm free, subject to the exigencies of the service,' I spoke in a formal manner.

'Thank you, Rhea,' beamed the Colonel. 'What about you others, eh?'

There was some discussion among them, and it seemed that any date was suitable. There were no particular objections to a performance on Saturday 15 April, and we had time to rehearse fully before then.

'So can we make it a firm date, what?' he asked, addressing his proposal to Rudolph. I could see that Rudolph was somewhat reticent about committing himself to a date without knowing the reason, but the Colonel's status in the community did carry a certain persuasion.

Because no one made a formal objection, Rudolph Burley agreed.

'That is marvellous,' beamed the Colonel. 'Now I can confirm it with No. 10.'

At first, no one reacted to his reference to No. 10, and I must admit the phrase did not alert me in any way. In the moment's silence that followed, Rudolph took the initiative.

'No. 10?' he asked the Colonel.

'Downing Street,' he smiled. 'The Prime Minister is my house-guest that weekend, and I thought it would be nice to fetch him to the concert. Perhaps we should officially open the renovated hall the same evening? I'll ask him to do the honours, what? And we can entertain him with a salad supper or something, and music from this orchestra. How about that?'

'The Prime Minister?' cried Rudolph.

In the excitement, Ralph spat twice in rapid succession and Rosamund's red knickers flashed as she wondered what to do with her cello. I was aghast – for me, there would be no music that night. I'd be up to the neck with security worries, and there'd be the Chief Constable, the hierarchy from the County Council, Special Branch officers, CID and a veritable entourage of officials and social climbers to cater for. I wondered if Rudolph realised the work, worry and problems he'd created by his acceptance of the Colonel's suggestion.

But he had agreed and that was that. The orchestra was so

excited that everyone raised a cheer and the dog barked in happiness.

'Marvellous for the village, what?' beamed the Colonel. 'We can put on a good show for him, can't we?'

News that Aidensfield String Orchestra was going to play for the Prime Minister flashed around the village, and I thought I'd better tell Sergeant Blaketon about it. The very next day I motor-cycled into Ashfordly to discuss it with him.

I located him in his office where he was working hard on a report for the Superintendent. He bore my interruption with dignity.

'Yes, Rhea? What is it?'

'A visit by the Prime Minister to Aidensfield, Sergeant,' I said, hoping to surprise him.

'Ah, yes, he's friendly with Colonel Partington. When's he coming?'

I told him, and explained about the village hall and its modernisation scheme, following the orchestra's role in the occasion. Having satisfactorily explained all this, I then mentioned my part in the orchestra's violins.

'No chance, Rhea. On that day, you'll be officiating, on duty, in uniform, on behalf of the North Riding Constabulary. There'll be no fiddling time off that day, Rhea,' and he chuckled at his own joke.

'Thanks, Sergeant.' I smiled ruefully, knowing deep down that this must be the only course of action. 'What about the administrative arrangements for the Force during the visit?'

'I'll have words with the Superintendent. No doubt we'll be given official notification of the visit, and that will set the administrative wheels in action. On a visit of this kind, there are all kinds of official papers to worry about. But none of that's your concern, Rhea. Just be available on the day, that's all, for police duty.'

And so it was deemed that I would not play my violin for the Prime Minister and I was sure he wouldn't notice my absence. Whether he would have appreciated my skilful A flats and pizzicato expertise is something I will never know, so my only way or proving myself worthy to stand in his gaze was to make a good job of policing Aidensfield on the big day.

Even though I was not going to play before the Prime Minister, I continued with rehearsals and found it stimulating. I was privy to the arrangements on the police side, seeing them intensify as time progressed, and I was also aware of the band's internal problems. In many ways, I was the liaison officer between the orchestra and the police, and found myself advising on the best position for the conductor to stand, the route to be taken from Colonel Partington's home to the hall and sundry other practical details.

As time went by, the event gained in stature. The occasion started to acquire people who wanted to be part of the accepted guest list. Before we realised what had happened, the vicar had persuaded the Archbishop of York to say a few words prior to the concert, then the local parish council, district council and county council all felt they should be represented, and so did a party of obscure gentlemen who reckoned they'd belonged to the Colonel's old Regiment. The British Legion, Women's Institute, Parochial Church Council, Meals on Wheels, Black-faced Sheepbreeders' Association, Catholic Women's League, Ryedale Historical Society, Ashfordly Literary and Philosophical Society, the League of Rural Artists, Country Landowners' Association, the Labour Party, and sundry other organisations all wanted to be part of the act. The poor Colonel had the devil's own job fitting everyone in because all the officials reckoned they deserved seats with their names on, all at the front, and all next to the Prime Minister.

The poor people of Aidensfield found themselves being thrust further and further into the background as fewer and fewer seats became available for them – in their own village hall. There were the inevitable complaints and grumbles, but as the official wheels began to turn inexorably, there was nothing any of them could do. Officialdom, plus its tail of petty politics, had, in all its horror, come to Aidensfield, and it was the last thing anyone wanted or needed.

Like everyone else, I was acutely aware of the upset this had caused, and I knew there was nothing anyone could do about it. Or was there? Officialdom, once it takes over, does not cater for the wishes of the real people; it caters for society types in high positions and minor politicians, and because the PM himself was to grace our hall with his presence, every petty official for miles around began to wheedle his or her way on to the guest list.

I'm sure the PM would not have wished this to happen; I'm sure that when Colonel Partington honoured us by suggesting the great man visited our concert, he visualised the PM taking a seat like anyone else in the village, without any formalities and fuss.

But it didn't work out like that. The chairman of the parish council had to make a formal speech of welcome, following which the Archbishop would make an address, and then countless other minor officials and local politicians wanted to say their piece. All this was written down in an official programme, and even if everyone took only two minutes over their individual speeches, the programme would be prolonged by nearly forty minutes.

The affair was out of hand. I had no doubt about that, and when I received my formal copy of the approved programme, I saw that the final speech, before the concert started, was a *second* address by the Archbishop of York who would say the Lord's Prayer. As the 'Amen' sounded from the assembled mass of officials and few villagers, my job was to raise the curtain on stage and signal the band to commence with our beautifully rehearsed *Introduction and Allegro for Strings*.

My task on stage, albeit behind the scenes, was allocated to me for several reasons. First, there was the question of security on stage during the concert, and I could keep an eye on the rear entrance; secondly, I was familiar with the orchestral pieces and could maintain a liaison between the orchestra and the Colonel, who in turn would inform the PM if there was a break for him to 'retire' as it is nicely phrased; and thirdly, I was to act as liaison between the audience, the official programme, and the conductor. My role was therefore of considerable importance.

My most important duty of the night however, was personally to raise the curtain as the Archbishop said his final 'Amen' after all the speeches, the signal to start the concert. I was to alert Rudolph seconds before doing so, so that he could prepare the orchestra: as the curtain rose, the hall would be filled with the music of the Aidensfield String Orchestra.

The final days passed in a blur of activity, and the hall looked resplendent in its coat of new paint, fresh curtains, polished woodwork, scrubbed floor, carpets in strategic places and flowers inside and out. Half an hour before the PM was due to take his seat, the place was packed and from my vantage point on stage behind the curtain, I could see the rows of petty officials who had wormed their way into this place, to deprive many villagers of their moment of pride and pleasure.

Rudolph knew of my anger. He felt the same. Together, we peered through a gap in the curtain as the hall buzzed with anticipation.

'I'd like to kick that lot out!' he said vehemently. 'Look at them – sitting there in their posh hats and new suits, just because it's the Prime Minister . . . This was a village concert, Nick, not a bloody excuse for ingratiating themselves with him . . .'

As we stared at them, an awful scheme entered my mind. At first, I tried to dislodge the notion, but he more I tried, the more feasible it seemed.

'We could cut out all those speeches, Rudolph,' I said quietly.

'Could we?' Even his loud whisper almost deafened me at this range. 'They're all in the bloody programme! We can't cut them out . . .'

'If I cut half an hour off those introductory speeches, can you fill it with music before the finale?'

He grinned wickedly.

'We can. We've rehearsed enough for three concerts.'

'Right,' I said. 'I'll take responsibility for this. I'll have an accident . . . Can your members all be on stage and ready to go by the time the Archbishop has finished his *first* speech? Not the prayers?'

'Just leave it to me!' and off he went.

At seven-thirty, everyone was in position. The hall was full, and prompt on the stroke of the half-hour, the Prime Minister, to polite applause, entered Aidensfield Village Hall and took his seat. I was behind the curtains, with my hand on the handle which would raise them at the right moment, and I was peeping through the gap, watching the proceedings in the hall. On stage, Rudolph and the orchestra were ready. He was poised in his evening suit, baton at the ready, and he had warned the players about their earlier than scheduled performance.

I waited as the chairman of the parish council, the chief citizen of Aidensfield, officially welcomed our distinguished guest. This was an important part of the ceremony, and he spoke well. The Archbishop climbed on to the steps before the stage and welcomed the PM, as Head of Her Majesty's Government, to the Diocese of York. Having made his speech, he prepared to dismount, and his place was to be taken by the first of a long line of mini-officials, all with boring words to say.

This was my moment.

I raised my hand.

Rudolph saw it; he brought his orchestra to a state of readiness, and before the next speaker could reach the foot of the steps, I pressed the lever and the curtain rose. There was a long pause before the hall erupted into an explosion of applause, and Rudolph was already bringing the orchestra into the first notes of the *Introduction and Allegro*.

From my place behind the scenes, I saw the looks of apprehension and disappointment from the assembled minor officials, the smiles of glee on the villagers seated behind, a look of pleasurable anticipation on the Prime Minister's face, and happy smiles by all players in the orchestra. Old Ralph was spitting bang on time, and Rosamund's knickers were in full view of the Prime Minister, so tonight she wore blue ones.

Afterwards, when it was all over and he'd opened the refurbished village hall, the Prime Minister came backstage to thank us all. Rudolph introduced me as the man whose duty it was to raise the curtains at the start, and who was in charge of security backstage.

The Prime Minister looked at me quizzically, asked if I'd had any security problems, and then said, 'You got us off to a flying start, PC Rhea. Well done.'

But I still had to face the Superintendent and Sergeant Blaketon.

Colonel Partington accompanied the Superintendent as he followed in the official party and when he reached me, the Colonel said, 'Rhea, the PM says you did a good job tonight, getting us off to such a flying start. He's asked you to take sherry with us at my home tomorrow before lunch. Do join us, Rhea.'

'It will be a pleasure, sir,' I smiled, and the Superintendent said nothing, therefore Sergeant Blaketon maintained his silence.

4

'Life itself is but the shadow of death.'
Sir Thomas Browne 1605-82

Very furtively, and with utter contempt for rules and regulations, Patrick Hughes set about establishing a caravan site on a patch of scrub land at the extremities of his ranging farm near Elsinby.

Being an astute businessman, who saw money in this useless earth, Patrick recognised the potential profits to be made from tourism, albeit on a minor scale, and so he purchased half a dozen second-hand caravans. Using his Landrover, he towed these shabby vehicles one by one from their point of purchase, and installed them on his lumpy piece of unprofitable land, known locally as Alder Carrs.

To be fair to Patrick, the land in question had no possible use in agriculture because it was very rocky in places and riddled with deep hollows full of marshes and reeds. It could never be ploughed or cultivated. It simply existed on the other edge of his farm, well away from the village and hidden from the road. The caravan-site idea was typical of Patrick's desire to earn money from every square inch of his land.

He positioned his six caravans around Alder Carrs so that each had an extensive view across Upper Ryedale, and it must be said that he worked hard to make this new enterprise a success. He wanted his visitors to have as many home comforts as he could muster and he saw his site as the Mecca for a new breed of discerning caravanners.

He painted all the vans in a pleasing shade of tan so that

they merged with the surrounding countryside, and gave each the name of a flower – a charming idea, I felt. Thus we had Primrose, Bluebell, Buttercup, Daisy, Violet and Snowdrop and I did wonder if this was to baffle any tax man who might inspect his accounts, because these were typical of the names given to cows.

No one seemed to question his choice of nomenclature, and having beautified his vehicles by painting a picture of the appropriate bloom upon each one, he built a small area with a rubble base for a car park. Next, he installed rubble paths to all the vans, and even erected a double-seater flush toilet in a secluded place, with a small shelter adjoining the latter sporting two cold taps and a drain. Waste and sewage from Alder Carrs Wash Room, as he called it, and from the toilets of both the caravan site and the farm itself (i.e. the house and outbuildings), flowed down the hillside in pipes to a sewage pit which had been a feature of the farm for many years.

The pit was necessarily a long way from the village and from Patrick's domestic quarters because the merest hint of warm weather made it somewhat mephitic. When the wind was in the wrong direction on a hot day, Elsinby's patient villagers would get a whiff of the effluvium but as it was not much stronger than Patrick's muckspreading activities, no one complained. Agricultural fumes of varying potency are generally accepted as part of rural life, and so the sewage pit remained to satisfy the needs of Alder Farm and the local fly population.

It was a deep pit, very sensibly positioned, and it had been adequately fenced right from the moment of its construction; that fence was inspected by Patrick before his first intake of campers and he decided that it was adequate to deter children and adults from running headlong into his pit of feculence. He reasoned, in a typical countryman's way, that if any children or adults were daft enough to climb over the fence, the very smell and appearance of the place would deter them from venturing further.

Having established his site in what he considered a very

professional manner, Patrick set about attracting some visitors. He advertised in papers local to the big cities and called his site The Garden of Ryedale. The little paths about the site were called Leafy Ways, the shed with the cold water tap was Water Lily House, the car park was Forget-me-Not (because he hoped people would never leave their vehicles unlocked – a nice touch, I felt), while the toilet block was appropriately named Meadow Sweet.

Milk, eggs and vegetables could be purchased from Patrick's wife at the farmhouse and he agreed to let them use the telephone upon payment. In all, it was a worthy enterprise, its only failing being that it did not have the blessing of the appropriate authorities such as the Rural District Council. They did not know it existed and Patrick felt that application for permission was a waste of time because it might be refused.

Like the Council, I knew nothing of the Garden of Ryedale until I received a telephone call just after eight-thirty one Wednesday morning in June.

'PC Rhea,' I announced.

'Is that the policeman?' came the distant voice of a man who sounded worried.

'Yes,' I acknowledged.

'And is Elsinby under you?' the voice continued.

'Yes, it is on my beat. Can I help you?'

'Well, it's my son and his wife. They're in a caravan at The Garden of Ryedale Caravan Site and I want a message getting to them. I don't know the name of the proprietor. I wondered if you could possibly deliver it for me – it's urgent and it's family.'

The delivery of such messages was a regular feature of my work as a rural policeman, especially when so many isolated homes did not have a telephone. It was a worthwhile service because it brought me into close contact with the people in a helpful way. This particular call was destined to bring me into very close contact with the Garden of Ryedale Caravan Site and Patrick's smelly sewage pit.

My caller was a Mr J. C. Hicks, and his son was called

Alan. Alan and his young wife, Jennifer, were caravanning there for two weeks, and the news was that Jennifer's mother had collapsed in Birmingham. She was in hospital in a serious condition. I told Mr Hicks that I had never heard of the Garden of Ryedale Caravan Site, but in a small village like Elsinby it would not be difficult to find. I set off immediately, hoping to catch the young couple before they left on a day's outing and said I would get Jennifer to ring Mr Hicks, senior, at a number I obtained from him.

I told Mary where I was heading, and said I'd be back for lunch around twelve-thirty. I decided to spend the morning in Elsinby after carrying out this humane duty, but my first job was to find The Garden of Ryedale.

This was comparatively easy because I simply called at Elsinby Post Office and asked Gilbert Kingston, the local postmaster, if he knew where I could find it.

'Aye,' he said readily. 'It's on Patrick Hughes' farm – Alder Farm, you know,' and he pointed in the general direction.

'Is it a big site?' I asked, wondering why I hadn't come across it before.

'No, only half a dozen caravans. Patrick's only just got it established, Mr Rhea. I think his first customers arrived at Easter.'

'Thanks, Gilbert.' I smiled my thanks and left his premises.

I arrived at Alder Farm less than ten minutes later, and found Patrick working in the foldyard. He was an amiable man in his mid-forties with a head of thick grey wavy hair, and several days' growth of beard on his face. His eyes were warm and brown, while his face shone with the ruddy colour of a man who spends his days in the open air. His clothing comprised a pair of heavy corduroy trousers, black wellingtons and a battered brown sweater with holes in the sleeves. On his head was a flat cap which went everywhere with him, and he had a heavy muck-fork in his hands.

As I parked my motor-cycle against the wall of an outbuilding, he ceased his work and strode towards me, a big smile on his face.

'Now then, Mr Rhea, thoo's out and about early today?'

''Morning, Patrick. How's life?'

'Grand. Very pleasant, especially on a summer day like this.'

He was right. The countryside was at its best, and the warm June breezes were filled with buzzing insect life and caressing sunshine.

'Patrick, you've a caravan site they tell me?'

'Aye, it's down on Alder Carr. Nowt wrong, is there?'

'No.' I knew nothing of any rules or regulations governing the establishment of such sites, for the enforcement of such rules and regulations were not within the scope of a police officer's duty. I was ignorant of the fact that Patrick had never made formal application, and indeed, such a lapse on his part was no concern of mine.

'Oh,' he said. 'Down there then, Mr Rhea.' He pointed to a gate at the bottom of the yard and I saw the new track of rubble and gravel.

'Thanks,' and to put his mind at rest, I explained the purpose of my visit.

'Hicks? They're in Primrose,' he informed me. 'T'names are on t'doors and there's a primrose on t'van.'

'Primrose, eh?' and I decided to walk down his new road. It was very uneven, but within five minutes I was standing in the centre of his little site, looking for Primrose. I found it, and could see a young woman busy in the tiny kitchen. I approached and she noticed me; there was surprise on her face, then alarm. As I reached the door of her caravan, she had already opened it and was looking down at me with her pretty face creased in worry.

'Mrs Hicks?' I asked.

She nodded, drying her hands on a towel.

I gave her the information I'd received from her father-in-law and she asked if I knew anything more. I said I did not, but felt sure Patrick would allow her to telephone her relatives and the hospital from the farmhouse.

'My husband's gone for a walk near the river,' she said. 'I'll leave a note in case he comes back while I'm at the farm.'

She had difficulty in finding a pen, so I loaned her mine and waited as she scribbled the message, then accompanied her to the farmhouse. Patrick was still forking in the foldyard and readily agreed to help, so we waited together at a discreet distance as the girl made her calls. She emerged from the house looking white and anxious.

'It's my mother,' she said. 'She's been taken into hospital. I must go to her, she's critical. I'll go back to the van for my husband . . .'

Patrick smiled at her. 'Look, luv,' he said kindly. 'Just leave everything here if you want to be off. If you decide not to return to finish the holiday, let me know and I'll knock summat off. You see to your mam, that's your first job.'

Smiling her thanks, she hurried back to locate her husband.

'Thoo'll have a coffee, Mr Rhea?' Patrick looked at his watch, 'It's gittin' on for 'lowance time.'

I joined him and his wife in the large kitchen of their comfortable house. Mrs Connie Hughes was a large, angular woman with a mop of black hair tied back in a rough bun, but she was kind and amiable. She produced a plate of cakes and a mug of hot, steaming coffee for us all. This kind of hospitality is enjoyed by all rural bobbies, and we chatted about life in the area, and about Patrick's new venture. Connie said she enjoyed the companionship it provided because Alder Farm was a lonely place, especially when Patrick was at market or away on business.

None of us could have known that at this precise moment, Miss Fiona Lampton was heading towards the farm on her hunter. He was a large chestnut horse called Apollo. If we had known, it would not have mattered a great deal because there was a public footpath through the bottom of Patrick's land, not far from Alder Carrs, and it was regularly used by people on foot and by horse riders. The picturesque path twisted and turned among the trees beside the river banks, and would undoubtedly be used by visitors to The Garden of Ryedale.

Fiona Lampton was a very horsey lady approaching forty

summers, and she had a private income. This allowed her to indulge in her passion for keeping horses and she had several, but it had never attracted a husband for her. If her money was attractive, her horsey appearance and demeanour could be a little off-putting for anyone not closely associated with the pastime. Not even horsey men appeared to find her romantic.

Due to having considerable periods of spare time, therefore, she found herself involved in lots of village affairs at Aidensfield where she lived in a cottage, and one of her passions of the moment was conservation of the countryside. She had become involved with many groups who worked to keep the countryside free from all that would destroy it; she happened to believe that caravans were a growing menace, which explained her presence near Alder Carrs that morning. It seemed that when word of Patrick's enterprise reached her ears, she had decided to carry out her own inspection before deciding what action, if any, she should take.

And so it was that Miss Fiona Lampton aboard Apollo approached The Garden of Ryedale just as I was enjoying a coffee with Patrick and his wife. At exactly the same time, young Mrs Hicks was running about, urgently trying to trace her perambulating husband who was somewhere in the same vicinity.

The precise sequence of events is not very clear, but having talked to all the participants, I believed they occurred rather like this.

Mrs Hicks, knowing that her husband was likely to be away for another hour or so, resorted to a device they'd employed while camping in tents. If one of them wished to attract the attention of the other, while away, they would seize the frying pan in one hand, and a large tablespoon in the other. By thumping the bottom of the frying pan with the spoon, considerable noise can be generated, and this can be reinforced by persistent shouting. Young Mrs Hicks therefore decided to adopt this husband-tracing technique by standing on top of one of Patrick's rocky outcrops on Alder Carrs, and clouting the frying pan for all it was worth. She reasoned that the sound would carry to all corners of this peaceful glade.

There is no doubt it seemed a good idea at the time, particularly as the din *did* reach the ears of the wandering Mr Hicks. He recognised the urgency of his wife's summons, and at the time, had been standing on a high boulder in the wood, stretching his neck to inspect a nuthatch's nest high in a dead tree. Upon hearing the significant tones of the frying pan, followed by his wife's call, he had leapt off the boulder, crashed through the broken twigs and rubbish, and then galloped out of the trees towards the woodland path.

In so doing, his movements were rather noisy; it was somewhat akin to an elephant dashing through the jungle, and he was shouting too. The noise startled Miss Fiona's nervous mount. She had difficulty controlling Apollo during those hectic moments, and he almost got away from her; he jumped and bucked with alarm at the crashing noises and raucous human voice which came out of the trees, but managed to work his nervous way along the path. Fiona had him under control, a tribute to her skill.

But just as Miss Fiona had calmed the anxious beast, horse and rider turned a bend and there, in full view, was Alder Carrs; at that moment, the horse saw Mrs Hicks standing aloft on a pinnacle of granite and belabouring the frying pan for all she was worth. She was shouting too, and behind was the crashing in the wood. These curious noises and waving arms were all too much for the nervous Apollo.

He bolted. Ears laid back in terror, he opened his powerful legs and moved across the land as if his heels had wings. Aboard, Miss Fiona shouted, kicked and hauled on the reins but Apollo was having none of it. He wanted to be free from these weird noises and sights and no amount of horsemanship would persuade him to remain.

Unfortunately, his flight path led towards the tidy fence which surrounded Patrick's sewage pit.

Rather as one would expect from Pegasus, the legendary winged horse, Apollo soared over the fence quite heedless of the pervading smells. Just as Pegasus had kicked Mount

Helicon to create the fountain of the Muses, so Apollo kicked the surface of the stinking pond to create a fountain of the messes. But unlike Pegasus, Apollo was not able to fly across the waters. He landed in the middle with Miss Fiona still on board and he immediately sank amid a colossal spray of foul-smelling effluent.

When the evil spray settled like the canopy of a parachute, it enveloped both horse and rider as they sank into the horrible depths; Apollo began to fight for his survival, while Miss Fiona clung to his neck because there was nothing else to cling to and besides, she couldn't see anything due to the coating of slime which bathed her face. She lay along his broad back and shouted, as he fought to climb out of the slurry.

But the more he fought, the more he sank, and the more he sank the more he fought. The slippery ooze threatened to remove Miss Fiona's grip and its thick texture prevented Apollo from swimming through it. It was too fluid to provide any kind of platform and he sank until his feet touched the bottom. Only his head and neck showed, with Miss Fiona clinging to these life-saving parts of him. Gradually, he became very still; exhaustion caused him to give up the battle and he sensibly allowed things to settle about him.

Miss Fiona dared not dismount; she could never swim through this mess and if she dismounted, she would sink over her head anyway. So she sat as still as a mouse, waiting. She wiped her eyes, her aquiline nose twitching at the awful stench that assailed her, and she began to shout for help.

Fortunately, the couple who were the cause of Apollo's sudden gallop were on hand to witness his sticky end, and they quickly sized up the situation. Mr Hicks shouted for Fiona to sit still and said he'd call for help.

That's how I become involved.

Leaving the Hicks couple to rush off to Birmingham, Patrick rang the Fire Brigade and explained the situation, then we both went down to the sewage pit to see what could be done. There was nothing we could do, but the flies were having a super time, dive bombing and tasting the delicacies so fortuitously presented to them.

'She'll etti sit tight, Mr Rhea,' advised Patrick. 'If she tumbles inti that crap, she'll vanish for ivver.' Then he shouted, 'Hold on, Miss Fiona. Sit tight. That awd gallower o' thine'll sit tight if thoo lets him . . .'

And so we waited for the Fire Brigade.

The Fire Brigade, with the expertise of its members for coping with peculiar situations, is beyond compare and it seems that our local brigade were quite accustomed to rescuing cows which got into this sort of difficulty. When they arrived, it was a remark by Patrick that reminded me of this skill, when he said, 'Thoo'll be used ti gitting coos oot o' spots like that?' His use of words did cause me to wonder about his opinion of Miss Fiona, however.

The Fire Brigade team used equipment they had brought, and, with the grateful help of Miss Fiona, they attached a harness to Apollo, with a sling around his rump, and simply hauled him from the mess. He emerged with a hollow sucking noise, kicked his legs in delight, and whinnied his happiness. Fiona slid off him with a squelching sound, thanked the firemen from a safe distance, them mounted Apollo to ride home. She was accompanied by cheers from the gathered assembly, which now included some caravanners, and a fair selection of flies and assorted muck-living insects which escorted her home in the form of a happy cloud.

'Thoo'll have a cup of coffee, you fellers?' suggested Patrick, and the firemen accepted. After swilling off the muck, they drank their coffee in his farmyard, and the senior man present said, 'We'll have to make our usual report about this.'

The significance of that remark escaped both Patrick and me, but three weeks later it resulted in the Public Health Inspector visiting the farm to inspect his hitherto unknown caravan site. And he promptly closed it down until the sewage disposal arrangements were made satisfactory.

As Patrick later said of Miss Fiona, 'That bloody woman's gitten a drastic way of doing things.'

I had to agree.

* * *

It was George Eliot in *Mr Gilful's Love Story* who said, 'Animals are such agreeable friends,' and this was personified in the partnership of Mr Aaron Harland and his dog, Pip.

Aaron was a retired quarryman, a widower who lived alone in a terrace cottage at Thackerston. He kept the place as clean as the proverbial new pin, and in his retirement went upon long walks around the countryside. He was a friendly man, very quiet and thoughtful, and his round, clean face bore thick spectacles which always needed cleaning. I often wondered if he thought his home was covered in dust; he spent his life peering through it, and it occurred to me that this was probably the outcome of a life-time's work in the dust of quarrying. Perhaps he thought the world was in a dust cloud.

His dog, Pip, was a Jack Russell terrier, a small pert dog with a short tail and two black ears. Its coat was tough and wiry, and it stood little more than a foot in height.

Man and dog went everywhere together. The little terrier was never restricted by a leash, and spent its time investigating rabbit warrens, hedge backs, holes in barn walls and other places where rats, mice and possible prey might lurk. And if creatures did hide there, Pip would flush them out and enjoy a rapid scamper across the countryside in pursuit.

Jack Russell terriers are essentially working dogs, and they are good at ratting which makes them popular with countrymen. They're also an asset in fox-hunting because they will enter the fox's earth and will bark when they discover the whereabouts of Reynard. These quick, lively little dogs love to work and revel in exercise, but they are small enough to be a companionable house pet as well. There is little wonder many countrymen keep them.

I would often meet Aaron and Pip as they went on their perambulations around Thackerston, and we always stopped for a chat. Sometimes, if Aaron was working in his tiny garden, or was on his way home from the post office, he would invite me into the house for a cup of tea and a chat, a pleasant diversion for me. On the occasions I did pop in, Pip would sniff suspiciously at my legs, look me over once or twice, and then settle down on an old rug which Aaron placed near the fireside. His short tail would pump with happiness for a few seconds before his bright, alert eyes closed in what appeared to be a nap.

Aaron would invariably tell me about the quarry where he'd worked for most of his life, digging out limestone by the ton, and he would tell me all about the district too. When his wife died over twenty years ago, Aaron took to studying the history of the district and became quite an authority, but he never wrote it down.

There were many times during our fireside talks when I pleaded with him to write down his memories and findings, but he never did. One day, I hope he will – the last time I saw him, he was approaching eighty and was still talking of his researches, still discovering more of Thackerston's past and still keeping a Jack Russell terrier for companionship.

Pip died some years ago, but it was his adventurous spirit that caused an upset one April.

Aaron and Pip had embarked on one of their long walks, and because the April sun was bringing the countryside to life, they walked a little further and a little longer than usual. Aaron had, in fact, walked to his former place of work, Thackerston Quarry, which lay well over a mile from the village.

It was now disused; the floor was full of discarded rubble and abandoned machinery. There was rusting metalwork everywhere, yards of miniature railway lines, old trucks, winding gear, diesel engines and a host of forgotten equipment. Where men had once scraped a living from the steep sides of stone, there now flourished willow herbs, wild briars and a multitude of rock plants, while large pools of dusty water stood in hollows about the quarry floor. An old hut, battered by the weather, occupied a corner site and there was a tiny brick-built office near the entrance, with a table and chair inside. On the table was a dirty old teapot and three mugs, relics of someone's last tea-break.

In Aaron's day, this place had been a hive of activity, with teams of wagons coming to cart away the work of the day, and the quarry had played a social role in the village. The workers and their families had become a close community, while the owner of the quarry had looked after them as best he could. He had provided aid for housing them, occasionally giving them a bonus based on the profits earned and striving to keep them in work by finding more outlets for his quarried material. Aaron had retired from the quarry and now lived on his savings and a pension, but soon after he'd left, the quarry had closed. Now, it was like a deserted wild-west scenario, a haven for animals and plants where the sound of insects had replaced the rumble of busy machines.

For Aaron, that return to the quarry must have produced happy memories; he must have heard again the voices of his former colleagues and friends, the noise of the machinery and the crumple of explosives as new paths were made into the solid walls of the quarry. He must have experienced anew the unmistakable scents of the place, the chatter of the men, the hooter telling them it was break time, the constant presence of rising dust . . .

For Pip, on the other hand, the quarry was a haven of different delights. There were fascinating holes to explore, animals to hunt, smells to investigate and things to cock his leg against. Pip scurried around the quarry in a frenzy of canine activity, uncertain which of his many options to follow.

As Aaron shuffled about the floor, kicking old buckets, handling old equipment and thinking of old friends, Pip darted into a crevice in hot pursuit of anything that might live there. There could be rabbits, rats, foxes, mice, almost any living creature. In he went, tail wagging, on what for him was an exploration of delight.

But he never came out.

For about half an hour after Pip's entry, Aaron continued his journey into nostalgia, completely oblivious of his little friend's exploration. Finally, having wallowed in his memories to a state of satisfaction, he looked at his watch and decided it was time to go home for tea.

'Pip?' he called as he always did, expecting the game little dog to bark its response.

But there was no response.

'Pip?'

Poor Aaron stumbled about the uneven floor of the quarry calling for his dog, but Pip never came. We will never know what passed through Aaron's mind during those awful minutes, but I do know that he went home to see if Pip had returned for any reason. There being no Pip at the house, he returned to the quarry to see if he was there. Many times, he did this and each time the outcome was the same. There was no Pip at either place to bark a welcome and wag that stumpy tail.

With all his quarrying experience, and with his knowledge of Jack Russell terriers, Aaron feared the worst. Pip must have entered one of the countless crevices in the limestone, and was now trapped underground. It had happened many times before with dogs; dogs hunting foxes had become trapped or lost in endless burrows and some had never been seen again. Old quarries were always a source of trouble for inquisitive dogs, and there is nothing more inquisitive than a hunting Jack Russell.

Bravely, Aaron kept his awful secret until next morning. He spent an overnight vigil in the quarry, repeatedly calling for Pip and shouting his name into all the crevices and cracks, hoping against hope for that single distinctive bark in response. Jack Russells did bark when they found anything, and this one barked at the sound of its own name.

Why on earth Aaron failed to tell anyone we shall never know but I reckon it was his Yorkshire canniness coupled with a belief that he could solve his own problems. I should imagine that he didn't want to be embarrassed in his sorrow and that he did not want to put others to any trouble on his behalf. For all those reasons and more Aaron Harland kept his lonely vigil during that April night.

Next morning, I was on early patrol, starting at six o'clock on my Francis Barnett to tour the outlying villages and communities. These early tours were a regular part of my work – we performed one late and one early each week, and they were a way of showing our presence at unusual hours.

On this occasion, my first port of call was the telephone kiosk in Thackerston where I had to make a point at 6.40 a.m. While travelling down the gently sloping incline into the village, I noticed the weary figure of Aaron trudging homewards. There was something not right about him, and for a moment, I couldn't decide what it was.

I pulled up ahead of him, and sat astride the machine until he reached me. He looked terrible. His face was ashen and unshaven, and his feet and hands were covered in limestone grime and mud. His hair and clothing were dusty too, and he was almost exhausted.

'Aaron!' I must have sounded alarmed. 'What's the matter?'

He shook his old head and I could see the beginnings of tears in his eyes; then I realised what was not right about him. Pip was not by his side.

'It's Pip,' he said. 'He's gone.'

'Gone?' At this stage I had no idea how or where he'd gone.

'Up in t'quarry,' he mumbled sorrowfully.

'Has he fallen over the cliff?' I asked, struggling to get the full story from him.

He shook his head. 'Nay, lad, I think he's gone into the quarry face, up on one o' them fissures. Jack Russells do that, go into spots seeking foxes and rabbits.'

'When?' I asked, and he told his story, explaining how he'd searched everywhere outside the quarry too, and how he knew, in his heart of hearts, that Pip had got lost in the labyrinth of cracks underground. He told me about the qualities of limestone, and how it lent itself to long fissures which could stretch for miles beneath the surface of the earth, sometimes opening up as colossal caves or underground lakes. No one knew what lay deep behind that disued quarry face.

'Won't he find his own way out?' I asked.

'He might,' Aaron shrugged his shoulders. 'Nobody can tell.'

'Is there anything I can do?' I asked, relying on his experience as an ex-quarryman.

'Nay, lad, there's nowt. I'll just etti wait and see.'

'How long can he last without food?' I put to the old man.

'It's hard to say.' He was honest. 'Four, five days, mebbe, even longer. He might have found summat under there, mind. Rabbits, mice and things, and water. He'll need water, Mr Rhea.'

'So if he's not injured, he could live for a long time in there and come out safely?'

'Aye, he could,' and his final word was filled with uncertainty.

I knew that Aaron wanted his little friend to be found safe and well, and there seemed so little anyone could do for him. The agony was in the waiting, and the waiting was full of imponderables.

'Jump on the pillion,' I said. 'I'll take you home.'

Aaron obeyed, clambering stiffly on to my motor-cycle, and I carried him the final half-mile to his little house.

'I've got a point to make, Aaron, but I'll be back in ten minutes. You get yourself some breakfast, then we'll talk about it.'

I watched him enter his house, a shade of his normal, happy self, and felt that something should be done for him. But what could be done? How could anyone help? As luck would have it, Sergeant Bairstow made one of his rare visits to me at my 6.40 a.m. point and asked,

'Anything doing, Nick?'

I told him about Aaron and his missing dog, and Sergeant Bairstow said, 'Poor old bugger! Has he been out all night?'

I explained the full situation, and Sergeant Bairstow agreed with me. Something must be done and he believed he had the answer. He said he would meet me at my 7.10 a.m. point which was in Ploatby, but in the meantime, he advised me not to build up the old man's hopes. It was necessary to fear the worst.

While I went for a cup of tea with Aaron, Sergeant Bairstow drove away in the official car upon his mystery mission; I asked Aaron not to go traipsing around the countryside searching for Pip, and promised I would visit the quarry regularly this morning to see if he had emerged. Aaron appeared content with this – at least, his problem was now shared, but I did not tell him about the sergeant's discussion.

Twenty-five minutes later, I drove across to Ploatby and waited outside that telephone kiosk at the appointed time, and sure enough, Sergeant Bairstow turned up. He was smiling.

'Great news, Nick,' he greeted me as he stepped out of the vehicle. 'Today, we're gong to attempt the rescue of that dog.'

'Are we?' I asked. 'Who, exactly?'

'Jim Fairburn, to be precise. He owns Chaffleton Quarry. You know it?'

'Yes, I do.' It was a large, busy concern just off the road to Malton.

'Nice chap, is Jim,' Sergeant Bairstow said, 'and he owes me a big favour. I've told him about the dog and he's sending his men up to Thackerston this morning to blow that old quarry to pieces.'

'What about the dog?' I cried.

'He'll cope with that, he's not daft,' said Charlie Bairstow with confidence. 'The explosions will clean the face away, but leave the underground intact, so he says. It's all done by experts. He owns Thackerston Quarry, by the way; he bought it when it became exhausted, and says he's been thinking about examining the limestone to see if it is workable. Today will serve two purposes – hopefully, we'll find that dog, and he'll have an excuse for working the old quarry to see if it is viable. It could do us all some good.'

'What about Aaron?' I asked. 'Should he be there to see it?'

'That's a tricky one. What do you think?'

I tried to put myself into Aaron's shoes. It wasn't easy. All I could say was, 'I reckon he'd want to be there. If we did find Pip, or if the dog got killed in the work that's going on, I'm sure he'd want to know.'

'OK. Go back and tell him. They'll start about half past eight, after Jim's ferried the men and the equipment up from Chaffleton. If Aaron wants to watch, he can, but he'll have to do as he's told by the foreman.'

'He's been doing that all his life.' I smiled, and then I remembered something else about Aaron. I caught Sergeant Bairstow in time.

'Sergeant!' I called after him. 'Forget what we said about Aaron witnessing the rescue. We'd better not tell him it's a rescue attempt, and then he won't be disappointed if it fails. Besides, he's an independent old cuss and would hate to think *he* didn't find Pip.'

'Fair enough, so what do we tell him?'

'Just that Jim Fairburn is doing some exploratory work in Thackerston Quarry today; we'll say he's been told about the dog, but his real reason is to examine the old quarry to see if it is workable.'

'Good idea. I'll brief Jim about that and you can tell Aaron. If Aaron wants to come along, then that'll be fine. Let's hope it works, Nick.'

And so the plot was prepared. I returned to Aaron's house after making a second point at 8.10 a.m. at Thackerston telephone kiosk, and gave him the news. He looked at me through those dusty spectacles, and said, 'If they kill my dog with their new-fangled quarrying, I'll nivver forgive 'em. These new fellers aren't quarrymen, they're explosives experts, nowt else. They know nowt about quarrying, none of 'em. Aye, Mr Rhea, I'll go and see they keep my dog from getting blown to bits. I'll keep an eye on 'em.'

I conveyed him there, complete with some sandwiches and a flask of coffee, so he could spend the day observing events in Thackerston Quarry.

I did not stay because I had other duties to occupy me,

although I did pop in from time to time. The place was a hive of activity with lorries, a crane, mechanical diggers, JCBs and a host of other heavy and light equipment. Dust was flying and I realised why Aaron's glasses were always dirty – it was a state of normality for him. Already, heaps of fallen rock lay about and men were busy on the cliff face. Every fifteen minutes or so there was an explosion as more rock was blown into small fragments, and I could see the anxious figure of Aaron hovering on the periphery of the work.

I found Jim Fairburn and asked, 'Any luck?'

He shook his head sadly. 'Nothing. Not a sign, and not a whimper. I reckon his dog's gone miles underground, Mr Rhea; it might take days to come back here, if it ever makes it.'

'It's good of you to do this for him.'

'Think nothing of it. It was a job we had to do anyway, and we can use the stuff we've moved today. It'll cost me nowt – in fact, I might even make a bob or two and it's a change for the lads. If we find Aaron's dog, that'll be a bonus for us all.'

'Do the lads down there know what's going on?'

'Aye, they do. I needed summat to stir 'em into working away from the usual spot. They won't tell awd Aaron though.'

My last visit that day was just before five o'clock, and the men were packing up. Aaron was talking to Jim Fairburn as I approached them.

'Any luck?' I asked Jim, a question that was open to more than one interpretation.

'Nowt,' he said, turning to Aaron. 'That dog o' yours must be well away under that limestone, Aaron. We've not seen it.'

'Are you working here tomorrow?' Aaron asked Jim.

'Aye, we've a lot more testing to do; I reckon this quarry's got a lot of good stuff left.'

'I allus said it had,' beamed Aaron. 'I said this quarry was one of t'best in this district, workable for years to come. Can I come tomorrow?'

'Sure, you'll be welcome.'

I took Aaron home and he was dejected.

'Them young fellers know nowt about quarrying,' he said speaking almost to himself. 'It's all blast and ignorance these days. No skill. I could show 'em a thing or two, but yon boss feller said I had to keep away. If you hadn't told 'em about Pip being in there, Mr Rhea, I reckon they'd have blown the whole bloody cliff-face down.'

'They've got to assess the depth of the usable stone,' I tried to sound convincing, 'but they're being very careful about it, because of Pip.'

'Aye, they are. I appreciate that, Mr Rhea.'

'You'll be going tomorrow?' I put to him.

'Aye, I will.'

I left him and promised to give him a lift in the morning, but he said he would walk. I decided to pop into the quarry anyway, and made several visits during the day. The work continued and, in my inexperienced eye, it was exactly like a normal day's quarrying. The layman would not have guessed they were seeking a little dog, and I wondered if the modern techniques were sufficiently changed to confuse the old man.

But at the end of the second day, Pip had not been found. I walked into the quarry at five o'clock and found Jim Fairburn closing the day's work. Aaron was deep in the workings, just standing and staring at the quarry face.

'I reckon that dog's dead,' Jim said. 'We've not heard anything, Mr Rhea. Jack Russells will bark, you know, if they hear anything. That dog's gone, I reckon. There's not been a whimper.'

'You'll not be coming back tomorrow?'

'Sorry. We've done all that we can – I've had the lads blast open all the routes we can find, and it's served my purpose. There's a bit of quarrying left here, but not a lot. Maybe a year's work for us, no more, but it would need equipment being here all the time. I've done what I wanted, Mr Rhea, but I haven't found old Aaron's dog. I'm sorry about that – we all are.'

'You couldn't have done any more.'

'You'll take him home?'

'Yes,' I promised.

I had my own car today because I was off duty, and gave Aaron a lift to his front door. He never spoke during that journey, and I knew he feared the worst.

'There's hope yet, Aaron,' I said as he left me.

'They've shifted more stuff in two days than we could in a week,' he sniffed, 'and still he's not come out. He is in there, Mr Rhea, I'm sure of it.'

'I'm sure you're right, Aaron, and if those men didn't find him dead, then there must be hope. He could live off things he finds – rabbits and so on.'

'Aye, but he would have barked, you know. He's bred to bark.'

'Maybe he was too far away for us to hear? You said those cracks went for miles underground.'

'They do, they do, Mr Rhea. Look, thanks for what you've done. Do you think I should write a letter to that Mr Fairburn, to thank him for looking?'

'I think he would like that, Aaron,' and he went indoors, closing the door behind himself. I felt sad; he had lost a friend, but dogs had survived longer than this underground. There was still hope.

Two days later, I saw him walking up to the quarry, his knapsack on his back, and a long stick in his hand. I stopped for a brief chat, and discovered he was going to shout into some of those cracks and fissures, just in case. He was going to spend the day there, he said. It was now half past eight and I was on my way to Malton for a meeting with the Superintendent; it was the quarterly meeting for rural beat constables and would take all day.

I returned past the quarry at about quarter to five, and decided, on impulse, to see if Aaron was still there. I guided the Francis Barnett down the rough road and leaned it against the office building. Aaron was positioned in the floor of the quarry, sitting on a large lump of rock, and he was eating a sandwich.

'Hello, Aaron,' I said. 'Any luck?'

His face told me the obvious answer. He shook his dusty old head and I said, 'Come along, I'll give you a pillion ride home.'

'No, Mr Rhea,' he said. 'I'll stay till dark.'

The tone of his voice indicated he had made up his mind, and I knew better than suggest any alternative.

'I'll bring a flask for your supper then,' I laughed.

'He's still in there, Mr Rhea, you know. Alive. I can feel it.'

'I hope you're right, Aaron,' and I left him to his vigil.

As dusk was falling that night, I returned to the quarry with a flask of Mary's coffee and a round of ham sandwiches. I was in my own car this time, and drove it into the quarry floor. Even now, it was almost dark, and I could see the dim figure of Aaron Harland on the rock in the centre of the floor. I walked across with the food and drink, and his face revealed his gratitude.

'Anything?'

He shook his head.

'Here,' and I pushed the sandwich at him. He thanked me and ate it as I sat beside him, holding the flask.

'I'll drive you home, Aaron, you can't sit here all night.'

'If he is down one of those long cracks, Mr Rhea, he might hear us, but we might not hear him, on account of his good hearing, eh?'

'Yes, I'm sure you are right, Aaron. I'm not sure how sound travels along underground passages.'

'It echoes a bit – come, I'll show you before I go home.'

Leaving the flask on the rock, he took me to one of the large fissures and said, 'This is a new one, those fellers uncovered it with their blasting,' and he leaned into it, cupped his hands about his mouth and produced a piercing whistle.

There must have been a huge hollow chamber a long way inside, because his whistle echoed as he said it would. It was a faint, distant echo.

'If those chaps had blasted right back, we might have discovered a new cave system, Mr Rhea. There are caves hereabouts, you know.'

'Yes, I know. This place is riddled with tunnels and caves – I'd love to explore this area underground.'

We turned to walk away and in a moment of lovely silence, I heard the whimpering of a dog. It was faint, but it was there echoing down the passage. Aaron, with his ageing ears, had missed it.

'Aaron!' I halted him. 'Sssh . . .' and I held up my hand.

'What is it?'

'Listen!' I pointed to the gaping entrance of the fissure, but there was nothing. I waited with my heart pounding, and then I said, 'Whistle again, like you did.'

'It's the whistle I give when he's a long way off,' he told me.

'Fine, just do it!'

He produced the same piercing whistle and together we waited. And then, deep from the black recesses, we heard the unmistakable whimper of a dog.

'He's there, Mr Rhea, he's there . . .' and the old man jumped up and down and clung to me, with tears unashamedly tumbling down his cheeks.

'Keep whistling,' I pleaded. And he did.

The whimpering continued, but it grew louder. We waited a long time. The darkness was almost complete so I went to the car for a torch, and shone it deep into that ragged fissure. And there, hauling himself towards us, bruised, battered and dirty, was the unmistakable figure of Pip.

'There he is, Aaron,' I cried.

Aaron called him, and the gallant little dog literally dragged himself by his forelegs along the uneven, rocky floor of that crack. But he was alive . . .

Three days later, I called again. Pip was lying on the rug near the fireside, and he looked clean and well. His bright eyes surveyed me and his tail thumped the rug.

'The vet says he'd been in a fall of rock, Mr Rhea, and got badly bruised about his back end. He'd not eaten either. He's got a few cuts and bruises, but he'll mend. The vet reckoned another day down there would have fettled him.'

'I'm pleased you found him then.'

'Nay, them fellers who did the quarrying, they found him. That was a new crack he came along. I reckon if they hadn't opened it up, I'd have lost him.'

'It doesn't matter now, you've got him back.'

'Aye, I have, Mr Rhea. Isn't life grand?'

'It is,' I agreed, 'and you'll not be going back to Thackerston Quarry in a rush!'

'I am!' he said. 'I'm going up there tomorrow with my shovel and I'm going to block the entrances of all them cracks. I don't want any more dogs getting stuck in there.'

'It'll be just like going back to work, eh?'

'Aye,' he said, 'It will, but Pip's not coming this time! He can stay and guard the house instead. He can work at that for a change.'

I left him caressing the velvet black ears of his happy friend.

5

'He is a portion of the loveliness
Which once he made more lovely.'
Percy Bysshe Shelley 1792-1822

It was in the 1950s that litter gained publicity as a problem in the countryside. This coincided with the discovery of beauty spots by motorists and the post-war fetish for putting things in near-indestructible plastic wrappings and containers. When this kind of perpetual rubbish is abandoned in picnic areas, woods, fields and hedge-bottoms, it is destined to remain for eternity, if it is not eaten by a cow.

If a cow attempts to eat a plastic bag, it will probably block the cow's windpipe and kill it; if a hedgehog gets a plastic carton stuck on its head, it cannot feed and will die of starvation, and if an animal cuts its feet on a broken glass bottle, it may survive for a while in acute agony. Apart from many reasons of this kind, rubbish is unsightly, messy and a confounded nuisance to country people.

It cannot be disputed that some visitors to the North Yorkshire moors and dales do cause little problems; some of their rubbish is little more than discarded orange peel or cigarette packets, but others leave behind the offal of their riotous weekends in caravan or tent, and there are awful types who drive to the country for the sole purpose of depositing unwanted domestic junk. Things like old refrigerators, mattresses and settees have been left in our woods and glades, and the snag is that these lovely areas belong to some unfortunate person who is left with the problem of removing the stuff.

It is akin to a countryman dumping his unwanted and rusting machinery in a suburban garden, or casting his waste animal matter into someone's semi-detached rockery. It is a sad reflection on life that even today, many townspeople do not know how to conduct themselves in a rural environment, and some regard a National Park as nothing more than a glorified car park. Indeed there are times when countryfolk feel they are being penalised for living and working in these picturesque areas, but in spite of such anti-social habits many opt to suffer these penalties rather than exist in a wilderness of concrete and bright lights.

Litter is a product of carelessness, rudeness and a lamentable lack of consideration, so in an attempt to counteract this unsocial trait, several organisations began to think in terms of a Best-Kept Village competition. The countryside needed some form of publicity if the flow of junk was to be halted, and this movement coincided with the passage of the Litter Act, 1958. This statute forbade the dropping of litter in the open air and reinforced its provisions with a staggering fine of £10.

As a village police constable, I was notified of the new Litter Act and was exhorted to reinforce it when people threw cigarette packets out of cars, cast chip papers into gardens or dropped beer bottles in the street. The snag was that the Act gave no power for the police to demand a suspect's name and address, nor did it give us a power to effect an arrest if such a person was non-co-operative. It was really a toothless tiger.

What the Act did achieve, however, was that it drew the attention of public-spirited people towards the litter problem. From this, a crop of Best-Kept Village competitions spread across the countryside and all kinds of official organisations and magazines like *The Dalesman* arranged their own contests. Our village was not going to be left out, and so it was decreed by the elders of Aidensfield that the village should compete in a local competition.

In keeping with the prestige of such events, a committee was formed whose duty was to encourage active participation by village people of all ages and groups, but especially organisations like the Women's Institute, Parish Council, British Legion, Boy Scouts and the Parochial Church Council. For that reason, a representative from all the parish organisations was co-opted on to the committee, and I found myself nominated because of my law-enforcement expertise. It was reckoned I would know a little about the Litter Act of 1958, and I would have the ability to crack the proverbial whip when slackness was observed.

The competition for villages in our district was organised by the Ryedale Village Communities Association which expressed a desire that all villages in the area should compete. The prize would be a colourful trophy made in metal and positioned on top of a tall oak post. That trophy, plus a plaque for display in the village hall, would be awarded to the Best-Kept Village in Ryedale. The trophy and the plaque would belong to the village for all time.

It was stressed that the competition was for the *best-kept* village and not the prettiest or the most beautiful, thus a very ugly place could win first prize if its residents kept it neat and tidy. The word was passed around the villages, nominations were sought, committees elected and a programme of judging established. We were told about it in February and discovered the judges would tour the competing communities in July and August. The winner would be announced during September, hopefully before the school holidays ended.

Our first meeting was in Aidensfield Village Hall on 10 February, which is Umbrella Day, a time for Englishmen to carry umbrellas in commemoration of the public's acceptance of this article. It was publicised by Jonas Hanway in the eighteenth century and he had the devil's own job to get the object taken seriously. I don't think the choice of this day was significant, but I never really knew.

The Chairman was Rudolph Burley because of his loud voice, and other members of the committee included the vicar, the Rev Roger Clifton; the farmers' representative, George Boston; Joe Scully from the British Legion; Mrs Virginia

Dulcimer of Maddleskirk representing local Women's Institutes; Joe Steel from the shop and me from the law, with one or two local folks to keep the villagers interested and involved.

Rudolph was a fine chairman, just as he was a good conductor of the String Orchestra, and after outlining the purpose of the meeting, he asked the committee to decide formally whether Aidensfield should enter the Best-Kept Village competition. Everyone agreed it was a good idea, and he suggested the vicar be appointed secretary to carry out our enrolment, and to fulfil future clerical duties. We all agreed.

'Right,' he said in resonant tones. 'I reckon we'll need one person to be responsible for each aspect of the contest. For example, the condition of the churchyard, and any burial grounds and chapel gardens is one of the judging points. I think the responsibility for that must rest with the vicar?'

He turned to peer at Roger Clifton who gave his consent.

Rudolph continued, 'Right, I'll list the points that will be examined, and if you wish to make yourself responsible for supervising one or more of these, please give your name. If I get no volunteers, I'll appoint someone.'

He paused to allow his words to take effect, then announced the first point.

'Absence of litter. Now,' he said, looking around the gathering, 'this is vital, of course. PC Rhea? It strikes me this could be your forte – you could always threaten miscreants with the Litter Act and the fierceness of our local magistrates!'

'I'll do it,' I volunteered and he wrote down my name. I found I was also expected to supervise the tidiness of the parish tip and other refuse dumps.

'Next,' he smiled, 'condition of the Village Green, Village Centre, and Main Street.'

Joe Steel from the shop felt this was within his province, especially as he walked the street daily to deliver his groceries and newspapers. He was also asked to supervise fences, walls and hedges, to ensure they were kept in good repair and in the case of the hedges, neatly trimmed. Joe was asked to make sure the residents kept their gardens tidy, painted their doors and windows, and removed junk from any shed windows which faced the street. Joe was also asked to be responsible for gardens and sheds which were within public view, although the judges would not enter private property. But whatever they could see would be considered part of the contest.

George Boston, being a farmer, was given the duty of chasing up the local farmers and their wives with a view to ensuring all farmyards were neat and tidy, with shovels, picks and all other implements carefully stored away or kept in graceful arrangements. Haystacks and rusty implements could be a problem, he was reminded.

Rivers, streams and footpaths on the outskirts were allocated to Joe Scully and he was asked to ensure that no beds were concealed under the bridge, and that old tyres, tins and rubbish were removed. The chairman did say he had noted a frying pan and three oil drums in Maddleskirk Beck and had noticed a nest of sticklebacks in a bean tin just below the stepping stones. The river must be as fresh as a mountain stream.

Mrs Dulcimer, who represented the Group WI, said she and her members would see to the village hall and other public buildings, including the War Memorial, and they would also attend to the orderliness of advertisements upon local noticeboards. The Chairman pointed out that one notice in the ante-room of the village hall was still announcing the village's Coronation arrangements, and suggested it be stored in the County archives.

Every member of our committee was exhorted to co-opt the assistance of neighbours and friends and to use groups like the Boy Scouts and British Legion. We decided to adopt the slogan, 'Make Aidensfield Tidy', and make it the aim of everyone in the village.

There is no doubt that the enthusiasm of the Tidy Committee, as we became known, infected the villagers. In no time at all, the schoolchildren could be seen picking up rubbish on their way to and from the classroom, men in the pubs cleaned the streets as they walked home, farmers tucked in stray pieces of straw when they flapped upon their barns and old ladies talked old gentlemen into painting their doors, windows and fences.

Someone painstakingly picked the moss out of the lettering on the War Memorial and changed the poppy; the ivy around Ivy Cottage was trimmed, and Home Farm's milk-shed windows were cleared of their generations of spiders' webs and emptied of disused bottles of cattle medicine. The names of cottages were smartened up and their windows cleaned; door steps were given a coat of white when they abutted the street, and the shops arranged their notices in a tidy, artistic manner. One farmer even trimmed his horses' tails, and another painted a scrap plough because he couldn't be bothered to remove it. Milk churns were made to gleam and the parish seat was given a new set of wooden rails which were painted a pleasing green.

It is fair to say that the whole village worked very hard, more so because we learned that Maddleskirk, Elsinby, Ploatby, Briggsby and Crampton had all entered. We couldn't sully our reputation by letting any of them beat Aidensfield. But the work did produce its arguments, differences and examples of rural slyness.

In my role as the official Litter Eradicator, I made regular foot patrols about Aidensfield, trying to jolly the people along and constantly nagging at visitors and careless locals about the heavy fines for unlawfully dropping things in our tidy street and clean public places. It was during one of these foot patrols that I chanced to look into Ryedale Beck where it flows beneath Aidensfield Bridge.

To my horror, tucked neatly under our bridge, was the framework of a huge double-bed complete with rusty springs and an old mattress. It had been very carefully positioned because it was impossible to see it from the road, and it was by the merest chance I had noticed its reflection in the clear water.

I had to speak with Joe Scully, our man in charge of rubbish in streams.

'It wasn't there last week, Mr Rhea,' Joe assured me. 'I checked – I inspected every bridge in our parish. They was all clear, honest, so somebody's put it there! I'll bet it was the Elsinby lot!'

'Elsinby? That's a rotten trick!' I shouted.

'They're like that down there,' he said grimly. 'They'll resort to anything to get us to lose this contest. If the judges had spotted yon bedstead, we'd lose points, Mr Rhea. Points *and* the contest would go.'

'We'd better have it shifted then,' I said.

'Leave it to me!' He winked. 'I'll have it taken back to Elsinby at the dead of night. I'll cap 'em.'

'They'll know who's done it, won't they?' I reminded him. 'Then they'll only fetch it back when it's too late for us to move it.'

'Then leave it to me, Mr Rhea. I'm in charge of streams.'

I did. I saw him four or five days later and asked, 'Well, Joe, you managed to dispose of that old bedstead for us?'

'Aye,' he grinned. 'I took it down to Crampton and stuck it under one of their bridges.'

'I meant you to take it to the tip,' I laughed, 'not nobble the competition!'

But the deed was done, and I reported to the committee that saboteurs were abroad, and so we must maintain constant vigilance. I did not tell the committee about the bedstead or its destination, but left a question mark in the air by saying I had received the tip-off about saboteurs from one of my reliable sources.

Our next piece of trouble came from Rufus, a golden labrador dog with a lust for emptying dustbins. In the time I had been at Aidensfield, Rufus had been the catalyst of many fierce arguments because of his urge to push off the lids of dustbins large and small in order to scatter their contents over a wide area. Unfortunately, he continued this game during the run-up to the Best-Kept Village competition, and his owner had an awful time with him. Rufus got blamed for every piece of spare rubbish in the village.

The worst came one Wednesday morning. I received an irate telephone call from Mr J.C. Roberts, who occupied a bungalow almost opposite the house where Rufus lived.

I walked down the village to see the cause of Mr Roberts' complaint and when I arrived, I discovered a large sheet of newspaper stuck to his coalhouse door. The paper had clearly contained fish-and-chips at some stage of its history, and it was not a pleasant piece of rubbish. Also stuck to the same door was a margarine wrapper, a bread wrapper and a crumpled up piece of tissue paper containing some unmentionable goo. The finished result was a terrible example of modern art – 'Papers on a coalhouse door'.

'Look at that!' bellowed the irate Mr Roberts. 'It's that bloody dog again!'

'Rufus?' I asked innocently.

'Who else? He's upturned that dustbin at the house opposite, and last night's wind has blown those filthy papers on to my new paint. I'd just painted that door, Mr Rhea, ready for the judging and look at it now . . .'

It meant another trip to see Rufus's master, who made his usual apologies, and I knew my efforts were wasted. I pleaded with him to keep the animal in close custody during the final days before judging. As it began next week, these final days were invaluable. Promises were made; Mr Roberts repainted his door and I hoped things would subside.

But they didn't. The next complaint I got was from a Mr M.C. Argument whose name was a perfect portrayal of his personality. He rang me at home one Sunday morning, and fortunately I was on duty. I called on him at ten o'clock that morning and he took me down his garden.

'Just you look at that, Mr Rhea!'

And there, in the centre of his lovely lawn was a huge pile of rubbish, clearly the contents of someone's dustbin. There were ashes, bottles, waste cartons, orange peel – in fact, a whole week's waste from a typical kitchen, all piled in the centre of his lawn.

'It's not yours, I assume?' I said inanely.

'It most certainly is not!' he affirmed with some feeling. 'It's that neighbour of mine. I've had nothing but trouble from him; he throws all sorts into my garden – weeds, junk . . .'

'But never a full dustbin?' I asked.

'No, that's why I have called you in, Mr Rhea. This is the end. I've done my best for the Best-Kept Village competition, and this really is the limit. I have taken immense pains to get rid of my own rubbish and to keep my garden and house tidy – and then this!'

'I'll have a word with him,' I promised.

I walked around to the bungalow next door and knocked.

A pretty young woman with her hair all tousled and dressed in a housecoat opened the kitchen door and her pretty face crumpled into a puzzled frown when she saw me.

'Oh, I thought it was the papers,' she blushed.

'Mrs Fletcher?' I asked.

'Yes?'

'Is your husband in?'

'No, he's gone fishing,' she told me. 'Is something wrong?'

'Somebody has tipped a dustbin full of rubbish on to Mr Argument's lawn,' I said in what I hoped was not an accusatory manner.

She began to giggle and then clapped her hand over her mouth as she fought to control herself.

'Really?' she chuckled, showing good firm teeth and a marvellous sense of humour. 'Who?'

'Your husband?' I ventured, smiling with her.

'Oh!' she came out of the house in her slippers and pottered around to a point beneath the kitchen window. 'It's gone!'

She pointed to a space on the concrete beneath the kitchen window and there was the circle of damp where the bin had recently stood. It had gone. I searched her small garden, and peered over the wall into the adjoining allotments, but there was no sign of the dustbin.

'Somebody's stolen our dustbin!' she began to giggle. 'Oh dear, whatever next. Why would anyone do that?'

'I'll bet it's one of the Elsinby lot!' I chuckled with her. 'They're desperate to win this Best-Kept Village trophy.'

'Do I have to report it officially?' she asked, clutching the coat about her slim body.

'Wait until your husband comes home,' I advised. 'He might know what's happened to it. He won't have taken it fishing, will he?'

She giggled again, prettily, and said, 'It was a brand new bin too, Mr Rhea.'

'I don't think this is one of Rufus's pranks,' I said, wondering if she knew of the dog's delight, 'but I'll keep my eyes open.'

I left Mrs Fletcher and retraced my steps to Mr Argument where I acquainted him with the truth. When I explained that someone had apparently stolen the Fletchers' new bin and had dumped the contents on his lawn, he saw the funny side of it and laughed it off. I never did get a phone call from Mr Fletcher to make an official report of the theft, although I did keep my ears and eyes open for the phantom bin pilferer. He or she was never traced, and that mystery remains.

Another event during the run-up to the judging involved a weekend caravan family and a farmer called Derek Lightfoot. Derek farmed an expansive patch along the road between Aidensfield and Elsinby and at one point his land stretched well over a mile at both sides of the highway. He had several fields down there, one of which had a pleasing copse on top of a small mound, and this pretty area attracted passing campers and caravanners.

Derek had no objection to them camping there; often, it meant sales of eggs and milk, with a modest rental for the site. Some of his regulars came year after year, visiting the site over many weekends during the summer. But, in those final days as the Best-Kept Village contest produced its most hectic session of clearing the countryside, a man and his wife arrived in their caravan. They asked if they could park on this lovely little site for the weekend, Friday afternoon through to

Sunday lunchtime. Derek agreed; he charged his few pounds in rent, sold them a dozen eggs and three pints of milk, and expressed a wish that they enjoy themselves. The man paid by cheque for everything, and thanked Derek profusely for his kindness.

During that weekend, Derek travelled past the site several times and saw the caravan parked half-way up his tree-covered mound. By tea-time on the Sunday it had gone. On that Sunday evening, Derek went for a walk with two of his dogs, and his route took him through the very same area. To his dismay, there was an enormous pile of household rubbish which had not been there on the Friday before the arrival of that family. It was more than a weekend's caravanning rubbish – it looked like a fortnight's kitchen waste.

It seemed they had loaded their surplus junk into a large plastic bag to bring here for disposal. There were empty soup and fruit tins, newspapers, a cracked bowl, a broken radio, several beer bottles, an old pair of trousers, two brassieres, fruit waste like apple cores and orange peel, paper, ashes and other household junk. It was a dustbin-sized heap and more, and it was attracting the undivided attention of the area's flies. Furthermore, tins with jagged lids and broken bottles were a hazard to both the wild and domestic life. Poor Derek stood there, with his anger rising. It was a terrible manner by which to repay a favour.

Even if the contest had not been running, this would have angered anyone, and Derek stormed home to ring me. Sympathetic though I was, I did not feel that the provisions of the Litter Act extended to private premises. It catered only for the dumping of rubbish in any place in the open air to which the public had access without payment. Derek's caravan site was not open to the general public, but only to a section of the public, and furthermore, he made a charge for its use. This meant I could not hope to bring a successful prosecution against the ghastly couple; in any case, it would not be easy to prove they had left it. Regretfully, I had to inform him that the rubbish was his problem.

'Aye, right ho,' he said. 'Ah'll deal with it.'

I saw him the following Friday as he trundled a tractor load of manure through the village. I stopped him to ask whether he'd sorted out his litter problem.

'Aye, Ah did, Mr Rhea. Ah capped that lot,' and he smiled knowingly.

'What did you do?'

'Well, they paid by cheque, Mr Rhea, and the bloke's name was on it. It was a funny name, with three initials. F. W. P. Oliphant, it was, and his bank was at Middlesborough. Now there's not many blokes of that name, so Ah looked in t'telephone directory and found him. Ah rang him just to make sure it was t'same feller who'd camped on my land, and it was. Ah said he'd left summat behind, and seeing Ah was coming to Middlesborough on Wednesday, Ah'd fetch it. So, you see, Ah went to Middlesborough last Wednesday, Mr Rhea, and found his house.'

I began to guess what he'd done.

'Go on,' I grinned.

'Well, it was one of them neat little semi-bungalows, with a garden like a postage stamp. All neat and tidy, it was. Ah'd gitten all this stuff on my trailer and a good deal more besides, Ah might add, and Ah just tipped it all into his little garden. A whole trailer load, Mr Rhea. Mine, his and a fair bit from Aidensfield added in for good measure.'

'What did he say?'

'Nowt, Mr Rhea. He said absolutely nowt, and Ah just left. He can't take me to court under t'Litter Act, either, 'cos his is private land, like you said. Ah reckon more farmers and landowners should do this. Ah felt better after it, an' all.'

Unorthodox though it was, I had to admire Derek for his initiative and said I'd tell the story around the village, in the hope that others would take similar action against litter louts.

Then it was judging time. We knew the judges would arrive without warning and without identifying themselves, and so we worked hard to make our village spotless right through July and August. The schoolchildren helped by organising themselves into Keep Aidensfield Tidy groups during the holidays, and they set a wonderful example to their parents. It kept them occupied during the holidays too, and we maintained our tidy, litter-free condition well into September.

It was towards the end of September that Rudolph, in his capacity as chairman of our Best-Kept Village committee, received a letter from the organisers. It listed the points we had lost and gave the reasons, but then said we had won!

Aidensfield was declared the best-kept village in our area, and we were to be awarded the tall oak post with its lovely plaque on top. There was also to be a framed certificate to display in the village hall.

We had won by a narrow margin, beating Woodthorpe into second place. Woodthorpe was not on my beat, but it is a beautiful village on the east of Malton, on the way to Scarborough.

Needless to say we all celebrated, and then the big day arrived. The trophy was to be formally presented, and the committee decided it would be erected at the junction of the village street with the Ashfordly-Elsinby road. At that point, there is a small rising portion of land from which the sign would dominate the village and remind all-comers of our success. The chairman of the Ryedale Village Communities Association intimated he would make the formal presentation on 8 October, a Saturday afternoon, and Rudolph was asked to make the necessary arrangements. All necessary publicity, and notification to the local Press, would be undertaken by the Association.

And so the great day dawned. Rudolph had organised a suitable hole for the pole and it was neatly squared with cement. Men from the village ceremoniously dropped the post into the hole and secured it, and then the speeches were made. There was a lot of cheering and pleasurable sounds from the assembled people, and I was pleased to see our triumph had attracted sightseers and villagers from far away.

By four o'clock, the ceremony was over, and everyone adjourned to the village hall for tea and cakes. I remained to guide a few visiting cars from the parking area, and as the last person left the scene, I noticed scores of ice-cream cartons, oceans of sweet papers, crumpled and discarded programmes and masses of empty cigarette packets which littered the area around our new trophy. There was rubbish everywhere!

Now that we were famous, visitors could come and drop their litter!

Unless it was the Elsinby lot dropping litter in pique . . .

So if you come to Aidensfield to see our trophy and admire our tidiness, please use the bin we've provided for your rubbish. It's the one marked 'Keep Aidensfield Tidy'.

One interesting outcome of the Tidy Village contest was the devoted attention paid to the churchyard. Before the contest, the churchyard had been neglected. There was no other word for it. The prolific grass between the graves was allowed to grow without hindrance, whilst many of the older graves had suffered total neglect. New graves did receive attention from relatives of the dearly departed, lots of them being attractively maintained and regularly replenished with fresh flowers. But as memories faded, so did the interest in these final resting places.

When a large area in a churchyard is neglected, the feeling is that the whole place needs attention, and for many years, this had been a problem for the Rev Roger Clifton. He was too busy to spend his time wielding a scythe and his spasmodic band of volunteers cut the grass with enthusiasm for a week or two, and then became too busy themselves. The families of the recent and uncomplaining occupants of the graveyard tended their graves, and this resulted in a tiny, if changing, portion of the place being neat all the time, thus making the remainder look even worse.

It was the Best-Kept Village competition that changed the situation. In order to win, the churchyard must be groomed; the vicar did achieve great things on the run-up to judging because the grass was as smooth as a billiard table, and all the graves were neatly trimmed and supplied with fresh flowers. I do know that we received a very high mark for the quality of our churchyard.

The secret lay in ten sheep. They were black-faced moorland ewes owned by one of Roger Clifton's parishioners, Sam Skinner, and Sam had suggested there was nothing better than grazing sheep for keeping grass trimmed. He had volunteered their services free of charge, and had even offered to surround the churchyard's walls and hedges with wire netting to keep them in. During the first exploratory visits by the ewes, the fresh flowers were removed from new graves so that these highly efficient grass-cutters could get down to their real mission of shearing the thick grass.

There is no doubt they did an excellent job. Within a remarkably short time, the grass in Aidensfield Churchyard was shorn until it was velvety smooth, and even surplus weeds around the perimeter had been disposed of. Another of Roger Clifton's willing parishioners had built some wire netting cages, comprising sheep netting and wooden stakes, and these were placed over the new graves to safeguard the flowers and other graveside augmentations. These allowed the sheep to graze freely.

So successful were the sheep that it is fair to say they helped the village carry off the Best-Kept Village prize, although there had been some misgivings about the ethics of using sheep in such a hallowed place. The vicar rapidly side-stepped these misgivings by constantly alluding to shepherds and sheep in his sermons, saying these dumb animals were the Lord's favourite. The fact was the graveyard had never been so neat and tidy, and so it was decided that the sheep would remain at work after the contest.

And remain they did. Their presence kept the grass very neat, and the animals appeared to be content with their vital role in a human society. The local folks who had new graves to tend made good use of the portable, ewe-proof grave shields, and there were no further complaints.

Then at seven-thirty one Tuesday morning, my telephone rang. I was still in bed, having worked late the previous evening, and it was a struggle to stagger downstairs to take the call. But I made it, and in the meantime the whole family was aroused.

'PC Rhea,' I muttered into the mouthpiece.

'Roger Clifton at the Vicarage,' the voice said. 'Have I got you out of bed, Nicholas?'

'I was just getting up,' I lied easily. 'What's the problem?'

'My sheep. I mean the church sheep. Someone's stolen them.' He sounded very agitated.

'Stolen them?' I repeated his words in disbelief. 'Who'd steal ten sheep?'

'Lots of people get their sheep stolen,' the vicar remarked, and he was right. Sheep stealing was a profitable crime, especially on the moors where many animals were spirited away for handsome profits paid by unscrupulous butchers and hotels. Sometimes, a single animal was taken; sometimes dozens. I groaned at the news. A case of sheep rustling from the churchyard was the last thing I wanted.

'I'll be there in an hour,' I promised. There was little urgency with this. If the animals had been stolen, they'd be lumps of unidentifiable meat by now, and if they hadn't been stolen, they'd turn up somewhere else. I could afford to treat this alleged crime with a lack of desperate urgency.

I made myself a hearty breakfast before journeying down to the vicarage and I walked to give myself some exercise. I knocked on the vicarage door, and Roger Clifton answered. He was dressed in a casual sweater and light trousers, looking most unlike a man of the cloth.

'Come in, Nicholas,' he invited. 'Coffee?'

'No thanks, I've just finished my breakfast.'

We went into his cosy book-lined study and he seated me before his desk. I took out my notebook to record the details of this dastardly crime.

'Right,' I smiled. 'Tell me about the country's most recent case of sheep rustling.'

'You could be hanged for this, you know,' he said in all seriousness. 'Not many years ago, a man was hanged on the moors above the village, for stealing one lamb!'

'Nowadays, they take you to court, tell you to be a good man, and give you money from the poor box!' I agreed. 'So what's happened, Roger?'

'I checked my flock last night just before eleven,' he said. 'All ten were there. I counted them, as I always do.'

'To make you sleep better?' I said, but he failed to see the joke.

He continued as if I'd not spoken. 'And this morning, I went to unlock the church at quarter past seven, and they'd gone. I checked the whole place, in case they'd sheltered under one of the yews or even got into the boiler house, but there's not a sign of them.'

'Was the church gate open?' I asked.

'No,' he was adamant. 'No, it was closed.'

'There are no other means of exit from the churchyard?' I put to him.

'None,' he assured me.

'Did you hear vehicles in the night? Sounds of animals being moved?'

'Not a thing,' he said. 'There was nothing different this morning, except the animals had completely vanished.'

'"Go rather to the lost sheep of the house of Israel",' I quoted from St Matthew.

And Roger replied, smiling, '"I saw all Israel scattered upon the hills, as sheep that have not a shepherd".'

'Touché,' I said. 'So they've been stolen, you think?'

'What else can I think?'

'Let's take a close look at the fencing around the churchyard.' I had to say this. We police officers seldom take anything for granted, and I knew that a tiny gap in the wire was sufficient for these silly animals to stray through. And if one went, the rest would surely follow.

With Roger Clifton hard on my heels, I began my examination near the gate and turned right, thereafter following the line of the boundary around the large churchyard. Whoever had wired this before the judging of the Best-Kept

Village contest had done a good job, for the wire was securely anchored to thwart adventurous ewes. As we carefully examined the western boundary, there was a tremendous bellow from the road behind us.

'Vicar?' came the shout. 'Are you there?'

That voice was unmistakable. It was Rudolph Burley, our loud auctioneer.

'Here, Rudolph, behind the second yew tree, with PC Rhea.'

We could hear the squeak of the gate as it opened and the crunch of heavy footsteps on the path. We waited until the bulky figure of Rudolph appeared.

'Ah, there you are! Are you looking for your bloody sheep, by any chance?'

'Yes,' smiled Roger Clifton. 'I think they've been stolen.'

'Stolen my Aunt Fanny! They're all in my garden, every one of those bloody silly animals, and they've eaten all my beans, my sprouts and most of my flowers!'

'Your garden? How . . . ?' spluttered Roger.

'I don't know how. I just know they're there, and I want them out mighty smartly.'

'Oh dear, I'll have to get Sam Skinner. They're his really, you know, just on loan to the church, and he'll drive them out. He has a good dog, you see . . .'

'There must be thick end of fifty quid's worth of damage to my garden, Vicar, and it's getting more expensive by the minute!' and he stormed away to protect his produce.

'You go and phone for Sam,' I advised Roger, 'and I'll check this fence right round. Somebody could have put them there for a laugh, you know.'

'Nobody would do a thing like that, would they?'

'Wouldn't they?' I smiled. 'Off you go.'

While he was telephoning Sam, I found the gap. There was a point where the wire had to negotiate some rocks and this created a fold in the wire; the fold produced a gap, which one of the sheep had located. It had widened the wire with its snout as it ferreted for fresh greenery, and very quickly had made a hole large enough to push through. The adventurous ewe had found herself at the other side of the hedge, the rest had followed, and all had made for some available and succulent greenstuff, which happened to be in Rudolph's extensive and beautiful garden. By first light, they had reduced part of his garden practically to the prime state of the churchyard, not a pleasant sight for a carefully cultivated corner.

'He's on his way.' Roger Clifton returned and we went around to Rudolph's to await Sam and his sheepdog.

Sam Skinner was a retired shepherd who kept a Border collie and several sheep as a form of active interest rather than for making money. He was an expert in all matters relating to sheep, and I watched as he entered Rudolph's garden, with his little dog at his heel and a long crook in his hand. As the dog saw the sheep, its ears pricked up and it looked at his master for guidance.

Sam gave a low whistle and the dog sat on its haunches, waiting for the next command.

'Where d'yer want 'em, Vicar?' called Sam.

'Back in the churchyard, Sam,' Roger Clifton said. 'With as little mess as you can make.'

'One of you ho'd this feller's gate oppen, and t'other ho'd t'choch gate wide,' he said. 'My dog'll do t'rest.'

As we went about our part of the operation, I heard Sam start to count the animals, and he used the old-fashioned North Riding dialect method of totalling them.

'Yan, tan, tethera, methera, pimp, sethera, lethera, hovera, dovera, dick.'

That was ten, and fascinating to hear. He waved the crook over their heads and whistled; the dog, with its head low, began to circle the assembled sheep and gradually rounded them up. Soon, they were a tidy group on the lawn of Rudolph's lovely garden, with the dog crouched flat beside them, waiting.

Sam checked that both gates were open, and with more whistles accompanied by the occasional gesture from his hand, he began to move the group, almost as one animal. They went towards Rudolph's gate as Roger waited, standing as still as a ramrod. The sheep hesitated before going through, but once one had made the break, the others would follow. Sam's dog encouraged the first to do this and seconds later, all were through and being guided along the lane towards the churchyard.

I held the church gate wide open and did my best not to alarm the oncoming flock. Man and dog, working beautifully together, guided the first through my gate, and in a matter of a few seconds, every sheep was back inside the churchyard. Very quickly, they lowered their heads and began to graze.

Roger came towards Sam and me as we waited at the gate.

'Thanks, Sam,' he smiled his gratitude. 'We couldn't have done without you.'

'Thoo'll nivver keep 'em all in there, Vicar, not now they've gazed all that grass off. There's nut enough for 'em all. You could do wi' only half that lot.'

'Is that so? Is that why they got out?'

'Could be.' Sam was non-committal. 'Maybe they were seeking summat fresh and juicy, like Rudolph's flowers.'

'Look, if you think five would be enough . . .'

'Ah do, and ah'll tak five away right now,' and he whistled once more. The dog scuttled into the churchyard once again, and by using a complicated system of whistling, Sam ordered it to separate five sheep from the others, one at a time, and he gathered these in a corner.

'Ah'll away with them five,' he said. 'Mak sure that wire fence is sheep-tight, or they'll be out again. Who's going to pay Rudolph, then, Vicar? Me or you?'

'Oh, it will have to be the church,' agreed Roger Clifton, nodding his head quickly. 'Definitely the church.'

'Then you'll be holding a bring-and-buy sale for church funds, eh?' beamed Sam. 'Come, Rex.' At a further whistle, Rex brought five puzzled sheep out of the churchyard and Sam walked down the street, a happy man as the dog followed behind with yan, tan, tethera, methera and pimp.

It did occur to me that an outsider hearing him count the sheep might believe those curious words were the sheep's names. In fact, it is a very old system. The ancient Greeks counted in this way: 'Hen, duo, treis, tessares, pente, hex, hepta, octo, ennea, dekem', while the Red Indians went, 'Eem, teen, tether, fether, fip, sather, lather, gether, dather, dix'.

As I pondered old Sam's skills, the Reverend Roger Clifton leaned over the gate and said, 'You know, Nicholas, it is a long time since we had a bring-and-buy sale for church funds.'

'Why not sell anything that's made from wool?' I suggested. 'Have a wool sale.'

'Nice idea; I might even get Rudolph to auction some of the garments!' he chuckled. 'He'd be very keen to raise as much as possible!'

'You could do worse.' I left him to this thoughts, and wondered how the shepherds of old counted up to fifty or a hundred. One day, I would ask Sam.

6

'Blake is damned good to steal from!'
Henry Fuseli 1741-1825

It was one of those beautiful April mornings when no one in the world should have worries or cares. The sun was shining with more than a hint of the summer warmth to come, and the sky was a rich blue between the puffy white clouds which hurriedly crossed from one horizon to another. The countryside in Ryedale was a rich fresh green, with new foliage on the boughs and young buds desperately wanting to show off their blooms. There was a strong feeling of spring, both in my mind and in the song of the birds about me.

I was riding my Francis Barnett motor-cycle across the hills into Ashfordly. I was not going upon any specific business, for it was one of those days when there was a lull in my daily routine. I had served all my summonses, seen all my farmers about their stock registers, checked all the firearms certificates that were due for renewal, and completed all my written work, including files on two traffic accidents and one case of housebreaking.

In my panniers, I had two reports which I was going to drop into Sergeant Bairstow's tray this morning, and then the rest of the day was mine. It was the perfect time to wander in bliss about the countryside. I would collect any incoming mail from Ashfordly Police Station – there might be some enquiries to make, or people to interview, but failing that I was free to tour the exquisite patch of England which formed my beat. I could explore new areas of my patch and meet new people, both vital to a village policeman. Local knowledge is so important, so this Thursday promised to be very enjoyable.

Ashfordly Police Station was deserted when I arrived. I let myself in with my official Yale key, put on the kettle for a cup of coffee, and set about removing my motor-cycle suit. I would spend ten minutes here, sifting through official orders and instructions and checking the mass of crime circulars which came from neighbouring police forces. By the time I had removed my ungainly suit and dropped my correspondence into Sergeant Bairstow's tray, the kettle was boiling. I made a cup of typical awful police station coffee, flavoured by the powdered milk we used, and settled down at the counter with the file of recent legislation.

Then the telephone rang. Telephones always ring when one is at one's most leisurely, and I must admit I was tempted to ignore it. For one thing, Ashfordly wasn't on my tour of duty for today, so whatever the call was about, it was really the problem of the local duty officer.

But on the other hand, it could be Mary making efforts to contact me, or it could be somebody in need of urgent help . . .

I put down my file, took a quick sip at the hot coffee and picked up the mouthpiece.

'Ashfordly Police,' I announced.

'Is that the police station?' demanded a loud voice. It was a woman and I got the impression she wasn't accustomed to using a telephone. By the sound of her voice, she didn't need one!

'Yes,' I said. 'Can I help?'

'My egg money's getting pinched,' she shouted.

'Egg money?' I groaned inwardly. Here was the report of a crime, so my planned carefree day had evaporated in a loud conversation.

'Aye,' came her stentorian reply. 'Egg money. Ah put it in my kitchen drawer and somebody's pinched it.'

'When?' I asked.

'Since yesterday afternoon.'

'And how much has gone?'

'Five pounds,' she shouted.

'And who is that?' I need these facts for the initial record of this crime report.

'Blake,' she said. 'Mrs Blake, Laverock Farm, just out o' Gelderslack.'

'And your first name, Mrs Blake?'

'You want a lot o' personal stuff, Mr Policeman,' she bellowed. 'There's nut monny fooalks knows my name. I'm not one for gitting personal wi' fooalks.'

'I need it for my official report,' I shouted back. 'Then I'll come and see you.'

'There's no need to shout, Ah's nut deaf,' she said, following which there was a long pause before she added, 'Concordia.'

'Concordia,' I repeated, writing down the name.

'Aye, that's what Ah said.' She sounded embarrassed. 'But Ah'd rather be just Mrs Blake if you don't mind.'

'That'll do me. I'll come and see you about it. What time would be suitable?'

'Anytime will do me, Mr Policeman, Ah's allus about the place. If there's no reply from t'house, come and shout about the buildings. Will it be this morning?'

'Yes, within the hour,' I said.

'By gaw, that's quick,' and the phone went dead.

After completing my office work, my reading and my coffee, I re-dressed in my motor-cycle suit in case of April showers and locked the office. I didn't know Gelderslack too well, but enjoyed the journey because it took me from the floor of the dale high into the surrounding hills. Here, the countryside changed dramatically from the sylvan beauty of the valley to the rugged and rocky heights, replete with heather and bracken made happy by the song of the skylark. I had to stop at a cross roads to consult my Ordnance Survey map for the location of Laverock Farm, and found it along a lofty, rough moorland track.

The farm buildings nestled in a miniature valley of their own where the grass was green and the moor had not made any inroads. Mr Blake, and Laverock Farm's many occupants before him, had struggled over several hundred years to claim this piece of land from the moor, and it would be a never-ending battle to keep it green and free from bracken. If that farm was ever abandoned, the creeping bracken would envelop the cultivated patches and conceal them for ever. But now, it was a veritable oasis in this wild region, a memorial to the farmers whose work had produced it.

As I negotiated my motor-cycle along the tricky route, I was not looking forward to this enquiry. It had all the hallmarks of what we call an 'inside job', more so when one took into consideration the isolated location of the farm. The theft of egg money was scarcely the work of an opportunist thief out here, and the disappearance of cash must therefore throw suspicion on everyone who either worked there or lived there. Crimes like this always left a nasty feeling. The moment I began to ask questions, everyone would be under suspicion; they would suspect one another too, and I think it is fair to say that every police officer detests the thief who steals in this way. They are detestable because they steal, of course, but also because they cast doubts upon the honesty of everyone else in a small community or organisation.

I had to negotiate three gates before reaching the farmyard, not an easy task when struggling with a motor-cycle on a track of this kind, but by eleven o'clock I was hoisting the machine on to its stand on a concrete area outside the Dutch barn. I removed my helmet and gloves, placed them on the pillion, then walked across to the house.

Although the whole complex was a little shabby and weather-beaten, I could see that it was clean and the fabric was sound; a coat of paint would have transformed the whole outfit, but its location in this tiny valley of the moors was delightful. As I walked towards the house, I could see the rim of the moors above me on all sides, while the sloping fields and bank sides beyond were rich with silver birch trees and conifers of various kinds. Somewhere out of sight, I could hear a stream rapidly flowing over jagged rocks, and a skylark sang in the sky above. Here was true tranquillity.

I knocked on the green door of the farmhouse and waited. There was no reply, so I opened it and shouted inside. Again, no reply. I remembered Mrs Blake's advice to shout in the buildings, and therefore began a tour of the farm, shouting her name.

She was in the missel, the local name for the cow-house, and responded by shouting, 'Aye, Ah'm coming.'

She met me in the doorway of the missel, a surprisingly small and compact lady with iron grey hair tightly curled about her head. She was barely five feet tall, with a fresh round face, and bright clear blue eyes. She was dressed in an old grey working jacket, known as a kytle in North Yorkshire, beneath which was a well used grey skirt and a colourful Fair Isle pullover. She appeared to be wearing lots of other skirts about her waist, but I think one garment was a hessian apron, known as a coarse apron, and another was her daily house skirt. I don't know why she chose to wear such a volume of skirts.

Thick brown stockings covered her legs, and on her feet she had ankle length wellington boots and short, heavy socks.

I guessed she would be in her early forties, in spite of the grey hair, for she had a neat figure, from what I could see of it, and her eyes were youthful and very pretty. I tried to imagine her out of her rough, working clothes and guessed she would be very, very pretty, but I doubted if anyone would ever witness that event. I wondered if her husband had ever seen her in a pretty dress.

'I'm PC Rhea,' I announced myself. 'You rang me at Ashfordly.'

'Aye, that's me,' and she wiped her hands on a piece of rag before emerging into the daylight. 'Come in ti t'house.'

Off the telephone, her voice was surprisingly quiet, and she almost ran across the yard, with her little wellies twinkling at her rapid pace. She opened the door and went straight in, never halting to remove the dirty boots or any of her outer clothing.

'Sit down,' and she pointed to the plain scrubbed table.

I obeyed by pulling out a chair, and with no more ado, she set about making tea in a large brown pot which stood on the Aga in the corner of the kitchen. Then she produced a plate of scones and cakes. She placed all these before me, never asking whether I wanted anything to eat or drink, and I knew this was customary on the moorland farms. Any visitor, at any time of the day or night, was expected to partake of such hospitality.

Eventually, she sat in front of me, and smiled. It was a pretty smile, and beneath the rough exterior, there was a lovely woman. I wondered if she knew how pretty she could be?

'By, you got here quick!' she smiled. 'Ah'd hardlings got yon telephone put down when Ah heard that bike o' yourn.'

'Luckily I had no other commitments,' I said. 'Now, you are Mrs Blake?'

'Aye, that's me. And none o' that Concordia thing, think on!' She blushed just a little. 'If anybody calls me by my first name, it's Conny, nowt else. Just Conny.'

'I think Concordia's a nice, unusual name,' I commented.

'Well, you might, but Ah don't.' She picked up a scone and started to eat. 'Now, what do you want to know, Mr Policeman?'

'This egg money, where did it go from?'

'This drawer, right here,' and she pulled open one of the drawers in the table we were using. From my seated position at the other side, I could see it contained a good deal of cash, as well as bills, receipts and other bits of paper.

'You mentioned five pounds,' I reminded her.

'Aye, that's the one Ah'm sure about.'

'And when did it vanish?' I took out my notebook and began to tabulate the facts I needed.

'Sometime yesterday.'

'Morning or afternoon?' I tried to localise it a little more.

'After eight in t'morning and before tea-time – half-past four.'

'You're sure?'

'Ah's positive!'

'And it was definitely five pounds? Was it five one pound notes, or a single five pound note?'

'Five separate pound notes, Mr Policeman. I know, because I put a pencil mark on their corners, all five of 'em.'

'Then some money's gone before?'

'Well, Ah wasn't exactly sure about that. Ah've been having a feeling for a week or two that my egg money's been going, and my husband said he wasn't helping himself, nor was that lass who works here.'

'Your husband? He's out today, is he?'

'Aye, he's gone across to Thirsk mart with some cattle. And this lass comes three days a week, Mondays, Wednesdays and Fridays, to do the house and a bit of work outside.'

'Who is she?'

'She's called Katy. Katy Craggs.'

'Is she a local girl?'

'From Whemmelby. Her husband has a small spread up there at Foss End, and she comes to work for me, to earn a bit. Two kids, she has, an' all.'

'How old is she?' I asked.

'Middle twenties, Ah'd say. Nice lass, a good worker.'

'Honest?' I had to ask.

'Oh, aye, dead honest. She's never done owt that would cause me to worry, Mr Policeman.'

'And your husband? Would he take any money for the mart, or his expenses?'

'Not without leaving a note in here, or telling me. Ah've asked him about this and he's not got it. If he had, he would tell me. He said Ah should call you fellers in.'

'Does anyone else work here?' I put to her helping myself to another buttered scone.

'No, just us.'

'And regular callers? Do folks call here?'

'Not a lot. Hikers pass along that ridge near where you came down, and sometimes we get a salesman or two.'

'Neighbours then?'

'T'nearest must be half a mile away, and he allus comes on

a tractor, so Ah'd know when he came.'

'Before I start making enquiries,' I adopted my official tone, 'I'll have to be certain, in my own mind, that the money is being stolen.'

'Ah wouldn't have troubled calling you if it wasn't,' she said solemnly. 'Ah wanted to be certain in my own mind first.'

'You've told your husband of your suspicions?' I asked.

'Oh aye, he said Ah should call in your chaps.'

'And the girl?'

'Katy? Nay, Ah've never voiced anything to her, not about getting t'police in.'

I paused, knowing that the girl would have to be interviewed, either to ascertain whether she was the thief, or whether she had seen strangers or indeed anyone else around the farm on Wednesday. The other alternative was to say nothing to the girl, and to set a trap.

My pause for thought caused Mrs Blake to look at me carefully, and then say,

'Now, Mr Policeman, don't say you suspect that lass!'

'I don't suspect anybody in particular,' I said, 'I was just wondering which was the best way to tackle this.'

'There must be somebody out there who creeps in when Katy's doing upstairs or cleaning the milk things,' was Mrs Blake's assessment.

'I think a trap is the answer,' I said after hearing this remark.

'What sort of a trap?' I could see the horror on her face and realised she'd be thinking in terms of rat-traps or rabbit snares, or even those huge, iron-jawed mantraps that were so popular in Victorian times.

'I don't mean anything that will hurt the thief!' I stressed. 'We can coat the money in the drawer with a powder that reacts to fluorescent light. If it is stolen, we can examine all the suspects and see if their hands have touched your money.'

'Oh, Ah see. Aye, well, Ah reckon that'll be all right. When would you want to start?'

'If the money's been going each Wednesday, we'll have to come next Tuesday and set it up.'

'Ah'll be in.'

'Don't tell a soul about this, except your husband,' I added as an afterthought. 'Once that money is marked and put in the drawer, neither you nor he will have to touch it.'

Conny Blake said she understood, and I promised to return to the farm the following Tuesday, with a detective to begin our operation.

We arrived about four thirty that afternoon, and enjoyed more scones, cakes and tea before planting twenty pounds in the drawer, in mixed notes, all of which were recorded in our notebooks by their serial numbers. Each one had been treated with magic powders provided by our Criminal Investigation Department. If anyone touched the money, the powder would transfer to their hands, and under the searching rays of an ultra-violet light, the powder would show upon their hands, even after several days of washing. The suspect would never know the evidence was upon him. This simple but effective method is used to trace thieves who prey on their fellow workers or who rifle jackets or handbags in toilets and changing rooms. It is ideal for trapping petty thieves who operate from the inside.

We left Conny and her strong silent husband that Tuesday evening, with instructions not to tell a soul; they must not touch the money, and were told to ring me on Wednesday night if the notes had disappeared.

They didn't tell a soul, and the money did disappear. Another five pounds in £1 notes vanished sometime on Wednesday, so Conny rang me at home.

My first job must be to interview Katy Craggs. She must be seen, if only for elimination purposes. I did not tell Conny of my immediate plans but said I had a little initial enquiry to make and would visit them later in the evening.

It took me three-quarters of an hour to ride the Francis Barnett from Aidensfield to Foss End at Whemmelby, and as I parked my motor-cycle against the drystone wall which bordered this smallholding, a young, dark-haired woman was hanging baby clothes on the line, to dry in the fresh mild breeze of these pure heights. She smiled as I approached, and waited happily in the garden as I opened the latch gate. I was not going to like this interview.

'Hello,' she smiled, as fresh as the April breeze which caressed my face. 'You're new, aren't you?'

'I'm from Aidensfield,' I told her, trying not to be over affable at this stage. 'I'm PC Rhea. Are you Katy Craggs?'

'Yes?' She was a lovely girl with jet black hair and eyebrows, and very dark brown eyes set in a pale, smooth face. She was well built if a little on the sturdy side, and had surprisingly large hands with rough fingers. I noticed these as she stood before me, clutching a bag of pegs and some tiny blouses.

'Look, this is not easy,' I began, standing at the gate. 'Is your husband in?'

'Terry? No, he's gone down to Brantsford to get some petrol. Did you want to see him?'

'No, it was you,' I began. 'You do work for Blakes at Laverock Farm?'

She nodded. 'I go there three days a week, yes. Scrubbing out, cleaning the bedrooms, looking after the dairy and working about the house.'

'You were there today?'

'Yes; is something wrong, Mr Rhea?'

'Yes, there is. Some money has been stolen.'

That awful look of discovery on her pretty face will haunt me for years. At first, her eyes and cheeks showed no sign of guilt, but within seconds her dark eyes had misted over and tears formed in the corners, to spill over and run down her cheeks. And her lovely, pale face coloured to a deep blushing pink. I knew she had taken the cash – now I had to prove it.

I continued, 'I must ask you if you have taken any money, without authority, from Mrs Blake's kitchen drawer?'

'You'd better come in,' and she wiped away a tear, using the child's blouse clutched in her right hand.

I ducked as I entered the low door of the cottage, and she led me into the kitchen. It was small and dark, for it was located at the back of the house in the shadow of the hill, but it was clean and tidy. She almost collapsed on to a kitchen chair, so I took the washing from her and placed it on the draining board.

I sat down beside her.

'Well?' I asked, not wishing to take advantage of the situation to make the girl feel any worse than she did.

She nodded.

'Look,' she said, 'I had to, for the children. I only get £2 a week from Terry . . . two pounds to feed the bairns, clothe them, buy groceries . . . I went to work to earn more, but he takes it off me for the car and his nights out . . .'

She broke down and told me everything. The children were in bed, and I think her husband must have remained in Brantsford to have a drink. I obtained a long, signed statement from Katy who admitted stealing £5 a week from Mrs Blake's egg money over some six weeks. I also included the reasons for her thefts and made sure the statement contained details of the money from which she had to feed and clothe her little brood. At that time, a reasonable week's wages was around the £15 to £18 region.

I took possession of today's five £1 notes, and gave her a receipt for them; there had been no need for the fluorescent light test, although I felt the sergeant might want to put these notes under the light to prove they had come from Laverock Farm, and that Katy had taken them, should she later retract her confession.

I cautioned Katy in official tones and told her she was not being arrested, because there was no need. I would proceed by summons instead; in due course, she would receive a summons to attend Eltering Magistrates' Court, when she would be charged with stealing £5 from Laverock Farm.

'What will happen to me?' she sobbed.

'It's hard to say, but I think you'll be put on probation,' I said. 'Now, I think you need assistance and advice. I will ring the local probation officer tomorrow, and get them to come and see you. Will you be in?'

'Yes, the children will be here . . .'

'I'll tell Mrs Blake next.'

'She'll sack me . . .'

'I'll tell her the reason. Look, this is not the end of the world, Katy, and there is a lot of professional help and advice available. Now, what about your husband?'

'He'll probably half kill me!'

'Shall I stay and tell him?'

'No, thanks all the same. I'd rather do it myself.'

She was gathering herself together, and I said, 'If you'd asked Mrs Blake, she'd have loaned you the money . . .'

'I don't borrow, it gets people into debt and needs repaying . . .'

'Are you going to be all right if I leave you?' I asked, knowing that some women would resort to tablets or other drastic solutions in a situation of this kind.

'I'll be all right,' she said, and because I believed her, I left the house.

Mrs Blake was horrified. The news hit her terribly hard, and she said if she'd thought it was Katy, she wouldn't have called the police. She'd have talked to the girl, to see if she needed help.

'Look, Mr Policeman, can this be stopped? Ah mean, does she have to go to court?'

'I'm afraid she does,' I said. 'Once a crime is officially reported to us, we must follow the procedure which is laid down. I am going to ring the probation service about Katy, because she does need help.'

'Ah've a few friends in high places too, Mr Policeman, and Ah'll get her sorted out. Ah'll go and see her tonight; her job's safe, by the way. She's a grand lass is that, and she shouldn't let that husband of hers ruin her like he has.'

'I agree entirely,' I said.

To complete the story, Katy appeared at Eltering Magistrates' Court, charged with larceny of £5 from Mrs Blake, and Mrs Blake came to speak in defence of the girl. The probation service was represented too, and told the story of her hardship; her husband bravely came to court in his best suit and said he had no idea housekeeping cost more than the money he'd been giving her. He now gave her £10 a week, and paid the electricity, the coal, the rates and the rent of his smallholding.

After hearing the case, the Magistrates wisely gave Katy a conditional discharge for the larceny, the conditions being, (a) that she repaid the £5 which was no trouble because the money was available after being shown in evidence, and (b) that she agreed to being placed on probation for a year. She agreed to both conditions.

I watched them leave court, Katy, her husband and her employer, all friends, and all wiser through Katy's offence. There is no doubt it was totally out of character, and that it was her cry for help. In her case, it succeeded.

I saw her several weeks later, shopping in Brantsford, and stopped her. She looked very sheepishly at me, but when she saw my mission was one of concern, she smiled.

'We're all fine, thank you, Mr Rhea. My husband is lovely to me now, he is, honest. He really cares, and Mrs Blake took me back.'

'You've a nice future to look forward to,' I said, not being able to think of anything else. As I strode back to my motorcycle I thought of the words of John Gay, who wrote, 'One wife is too much for one husband to hear.'

It had taken drastic measures to make Terry Craggs hear his wife's call, but when he had been compelled to listen, he had responded. He deserves credit for that.

It would be around the same time that another theft caused us a few headaches. I went into Ashfordly Police Station around half past nine one Sunday morning because I had been instructed to patrol this lovely market town for a couple of hours. Sergeant Blaketon was away on a week's holiday, and PC Alwyn Foxton had caught a dose of influenza. Because the town was therefore short-staffed, I was brought in for the morning, and Sergeant Bairstow said he would cover during the afternoon.

But when I arrived at Ashfordly Police Station, Sergeant Bairstow was already there, and he looked very worried.

'Nick,' he asked in a very confidential manner, 'when did you last see the county bike?'

I couldn't answer immediately because I had not used the huge black bicycle for months, and then only once to rush into town to catch the post.

'It must be seven or eight months ago, Sergeant.' I knew it was a vague answer, but it was the best I could muster.

'It hasn't gone for repair, has it?'

'If it had, it would go to Watson's in Church Lane. It's the only place that does cycle repairs.'

'When you are out this morning, pop in and ask if he's seen our bike, will you?'

He dropped the subject at that stage, and within the hour, I popped into Watson's. Even though it was a Sunday, the small garage was open and a mechanic was lying beneath a car, doing something to its exhaust pipe.

'Morning.' I smiled at Mr Jack Watson, the boss of this busy but small business.

'Hello, Mr Rhea. Quiet, isn't it?'

'For a Sunday, yes,' I agreed, 'but the trippers will start soon. The market place'll be full of buses and cars by lunchtime.'

'So long as they call here for petrol, I don't mind. Well, what brings you here? Pleasure or business?'

'It's always a pleasure to drop in,' I smiled, 'but this time our sergeant has asked me to make a little enquiry from you.'

'Summat serious, is it?'

'Very,' I said sternly. 'Have you got our bike? The official one?'

'No,' he said immediately. 'Should I?'

'I don't think so. Sergeant Bairstow asked me to see if it was here for repair.'

'Nay, Mr Rhea, it's not been here for months. The last time we had it in was when t'back wheel needed straightening up, and that was nigh on a year ago.'

I returned to the police station at 11.30 to make a point there, in case anyone called from Divisional Headquarters, and Sergeant Bairstow was sitting with the cycle's record in his hand.

'Well?' he asked urgently as I entered.

'It was there about a year ago, Sergeant,' I told him. 'A job on the back wheel.'

'It's logged on the card,' he said, 'and the last time it was used, according to this, was eight months ago. It hasn't been returned to HQ for scrap, has it?'

'If it had, that card would have been marked accordingly,' I told him.

'I've talked to everybody else about it,' he sighed. 'Alwyn was the last to use it, and he put it back in the garage, beside the car, and it was in good condition then. And that was eight months ago.'

'That garage is often left open when we're out in the official car,' I said. 'Maybe someone's borrowed it?'

'Who?' he asked. 'There's one at Brantsford, one at Eltering and two at Malton. We got rid of one a year ago, because we're motorised and you lads have motor-bikes. That bike was kept in cases of emergency, like a broken-down car.'

'Are you saying it's been stolen, Sergeant?' I put the question to him.

'Now, Nick, dare I suggest a thing? Who is going to make an official report to acknowledge we've been careless at Ashfordly by letting somebody steal our official bike? Just imagine what fun the Press would have – to say nothing of other police forces!'

'Maybe it's just been borrowed?' I tried to sound hopeful.

'Without permission? We can't go lending official bikes without permission. Besides, if it was someone local, we'd have seen it around the town, wouldn't we?'

'What are you going to do? Shouldn't it be reported?'

'I'm not reporting it, Nick. Not me! I'm too long in the tooth to go around raising hares like that. Just pass the word among the rest of the lads and I'll do the same. We might see it up a back alley, or hidden in a field or something. Then we can sneak it back without anyone knowing.'

'Will you tell Sergeant Blaketon?' I asked.

'Would you?' he put to me. 'If old O.B. gets to know, the balloon will well and truly go up. You know what he's like with his rules and regulations. Everybody will be under suspicion of pinching it, or selling it to make money. He'll have the CID in to make a full-blooded investigation, and all our lives will be miserable. No, Nick, for God's sake don't tell him.'

'He's bound to find out,' I said.

'Then let him. Let him be the one to make the awful discovery, and let him have the problem of deciding what to do about it.'

And so the matter rested, at least for a few days. All of us who used Ashfordly Police Station as our Section office spent our spare time seeking the elusive black police cycle, with its distinctive colour and size. Large black bikes, with POLICE written in white on the crossbar, are not easily overlooked, but we failed to recover this one.

One thing I could not understand was how its loss had never attracted the attention of the ever-vigilant Sergeant Blaketon. His eagle eyes and passion for checking every detail of his working environment must surely have revealed this loss. But he was away, and we could not, or would not, ask him.

On market day the following Friday, I was again in Ashfordly, doing yet another of my patrols due to the absence of other officers, when the station telephone rang. It was the police at Eltering, our Sub-Divisional Headquarters.

'Vesuvius here,' came the distinctive gruff tones of PC Ventress. 'How's life, Nick?'

'Fine,' I said. 'It's market day here, so there's a bit happening.'

'Well, I've some information for you. There's more about to happen. Is Sergeant Bairstow with you yet?'

'No, he's due any minute now.'

'Well, tell him to be sure to be at Ashfordly Police Station at 12 noon, will you? The Inspector's coming over to check the station inventory and wants Charlie Bairstow there to sign it.'

'Right,' I said and after some domestic chatter, I replaced the telephone.

When Sergeant Bairstow arrived, he exuded cheerfulness and pleasure, but this rapidly turned to misery and anxiety when I told him the news. 'Never mind patrolling the town, Nick, find the list and help me check it. And what about that bike, eh? What's the Inspector going to say when he finds out it's missing?'

I was unable to reply. I just did not know the answer. With Sergeant Bairstow, I carefully checked everything else, from typewriter to official car, and all were present, or could be accounted for. Except the bike. And it was eleven-fifteen now. Forty-five minutes to zero hour.

'Nick,' Charlie Bairstow said to me confidentially, 'before half-past eleven, you must acquire a bike. I don't care where it comes from, or how long we can keep it, but just get one. Right?'

'But, Sergeant . . .'

'Bike, Rhea,' he said in a very official voice.

'Yes, Sergeant,' and I walked out on my errand of mercy.

There wasn't a great deal of time left to find a suitable replica of the station bike, and as I walked into the town I didn't know where to start. Then I remembered Watson's Garage and its cycle-repair business.

Jack Watson greeted me with a wry smile. 'Now then, Mr Rhea, still looking for that bike o' yours, eh?'

'No,' I said. 'Another one, just like it.'

'Have we a thief with a liking for black bikes, then?'

'Who said anything about stolen bikes, Jack?' I laughed. 'Now, do you know anybody who's got a big black bike like ours? I want to borrow it.'

'Oh, is that it? Well, I haven't any, but the Council chaps have.'

'Council chaps? Which Council chaps?'

'Round at the Highways Depot. They bought one off me years ago, a big black Raleigh like yours. It was supposed to be used by the lengthmen as they inspected their bits o' road, but it didn't really get used. It'll need a lick o' paint, I should think, but it was t'marrow o' yours.'

'Jack, you're a life-saver!' and I hurried around to the Council Depot. In the office, I found a man who lived in Aidensfield; I knew him as John Miller, and he was a quiet, shy man who kept himself very much to himself. In fact, this was the first time I knew where he worked, although I'd often seen him around both Aidensfield and Ashfordly.

'Hello, Mr Miller.' He looked at me and his face bore that look of apprehension that greets most uniformed police officers. 'So this is where you work?'

'Oh, er, yes, Mr Rhea. Yes, this is where I work.'

'I'm here on a peculiar mission,' I said to put his mind at rest. 'Have you got a large black bike here?'

'Black bike? Er, yes. It's very old and it's not used a lot.'

'That doesn't matter. Can I borrow it for the morning please?'

'Well, it's got flat tyres, Mr Rhea, and is not in very good condition. Rusty, you know. Lack of use.'

'That's fine, so long as it's a big black bike.'

'A clean-up would do wonders, Mr Rhea, an oily rag or something.'

'Could we borrow it then?'

'Well, you'll have to ask the foreman; he's in the yard, but I don't see why not.'

'We just want to show someone what a police bike looked like, and yours is like the ones we use. Ours are all at Divisional Headquarters now.'

'Oh, well, I'm sure it will be fine. Yes, I'm sure it will.'

I went into the yard, found the foreman, and presented him with my proposal.

'Aye,' he said readily. 'Take it. Keep it, Mr Rhea, if you want. Nobody bothers with it here, we never use it.'

'No, that would not be allowed. It's Council property,' and

I went across to the lean-to which housed the cycle, along with other machines and implements. It was certainly in an awful state, and I half carried it out.

The foreman ambled across to me. 'Where's thoo taking it, Mr Rhea?'

'Round to the police station. We're just borrowing it for the morning.'

'Stick it in that dumper, I'll run it round. Hop on yourself.'

I looked at the cycle. Its tyres were flat, the chain was rusted and the spokes looked unsafe. I would feel a real idiot pushing this dusty, rusty monster through the streets on market day, and so I accepted his offer. We lifted the rattling cycle into the square, dish-like container of the dumper, and he started the engine. I climbed aboard the little yellow machine and we sailed out of the yard in fine style.

We chugged through the town at walking speed, the strong motor causing the dumper to throb and jerk as it progressed, and the ancient cycle rattled in the carrier. I stood beside the driver's seat, and we must have looked an odd outfit; within minutes, we pulled up at the police station and I lifted out the bike.

'Thanks!' I shouted above the noise.

'Think nowt on it; give us a buzz when you want us to fetch it back.'

'Thanks,' and he was gone.

I half-carried the cycle into the garage, and was placing it against the wall in the position normally occupied by the official bike, when Sergeant Bairstow came in.

'Was that you aboard that thing, Nick?'

'It was, Sergeant, and I have found us a bike.'

'Is that a bike?' he laughed as he pointed to the rusty thing.

'I'll clean it up, Sergeant.'

'I think you'd better. Is this the best you could do?'

'It's the twin sister of ours,' I informed him. 'It'll pass the inspector's casual gaze.'

'I hope it does,' and he left me to find a rag. I started to polish the framework, and after twenty frantic minutes, no one would have recognised this as the junk I'd brought from the Highways Department. The ironwork had been covered with a thick layer of greasy dust and this had protected the frame; the wheels were the same and were soon restored to a fine chrome which glistened in the morning light. I oiled the chain, and borrowed a pump from the man across the road. My hectic session with rag and polish had transformed it.

Ten minutes before the inspector was due, Sergeant Bairstow came to examine my handiwork, and was pleased. The inspector came, did his tour of the premises, accepted what he saw and signed the record of our inventory. Off he went to Brantsford to do the same, and we all breathed a sigh of relief.

That afternoon, I took the bike back to the foreman. Now I was not worried about my appearance when wheeling it through the town, and he was delighted.

'By gum, Mr Rhea, thoo's made yon bike shine for us. Thoo can borrow it anytime!'

'Thanks,' I said, not thinking I would ever have to accept his offer.

But less than a month later, I was once again in the office at Ashfordly, when Sergeant Blaketon loomed above the counter. He looked bronzed and fit after his holiday.

'Good morning, Sergeant.' I stood up to greet him. 'You look as though you enjoyed your holiday.'

'I did, Rhea. Yes indeed. It was excellent. We took one of those chalets, a self-catering place, on the Cornish coast. Very cheap and very nice.'

'I must do the same sometime.' It wouldn't be easy, taking all our youngsters to such a place.

'Do that, Rhea. I can recommend it. Now, down to business. When I left that holiday chalet, I had to check its inventory with the owner, item by item.'

'That's done in a lot of those places, isn't it?'

'It is, Rhea, but it reminded me that I have not checked the inventory of this station for some time. I thought I would remedy that defect today. Now, I have an appointment at the

Council Offices in twenty minutes, and I expect to be there an hour.'

'Yes, Sergeant.' My heart was thumping. Of all the things to decide to do! And with our bike missing . . . he'd spot it. Even if we substituted the Council bike, old O. B. would notice. Nothing escaped his eagle eye.

'Right, then. Get things organised for when I return. Say eleven thirty.'

'Yes, Sergeant.'

I had hoped, as I'm sure we all did, that Oscar Blaketon would return from his holiday feeling in a benevolent mood, but it had only made him more chillingly efficient. I could imagine him sunning himself on the Cornish coast, and thinking of new schemes for Ashfordly Police Station and its members. But there was no time to lose. I needed that bike again.

I waited until he walked around to the Council Offices, which were fortunately several streets away from the Highways Depot, and then hurried around to my friendly foreman. Once more, I borrowed the bike, and once more he ferried the machine and me back to the police station.

It did not require a great deal of cleansing this time, but I gave it a cursory rub for luck, then positioned it where the official bike should be. Having done this, I went into the office, made sure all the objects and equipment were present, and waited.

Sergeant Blaketon came back from his meeting looking happy and efficient, and said, 'Right, Rhea. Inventory!'

I passed him the piece of paper which listed all our equipment. He set off at a fast gallop, touring the station and its curtilage and ticking off the articles as he found them in order.

Finally, it was the turn of the garage. My heart began to thump and I tried to anticipate his line of questioning when he found the replacement bike. He ticked off the car, the bucket for washing it, and the hose-pipe. He checked the tool kit, the spare wheel, the first-aid kit and fire extinguisher, and went carefully through his list, ticking off the items.

I felt sure he would hear my heart pounding, as I waited for our ruse to be discovered. I closed my eyes as he turned to examine the contents of the rear of the garage, but he saw the bike, looked for it on the list and said,

'Bike. Here.'

And he ticked it off the list.

As he turned back to me, I saw a strange expression on his face. It was practically indescribable; I could not decide whether it was a look of utter pleasure and relief, or whether it was one of surprise. Sergeant Blaketon was not noted for showing emotion, and later, as I thought about it, I think he was very, very relieved to see a bike there.

If one had not been there, there would have been all kinds of questions and accusations for him to answer as officer-in-charge of Ashfordly Section, and I think he guessed there was some sort of skulduggery because he did not closely inspect it. That was contrary to his usual practices; he did not, for example, check to see if POLICE was painted on the crossbar, nor did he inspect the serial number.

For once in his lifetime, I felt he'd taken the easy way out, although I could never be sure.

But on the way from the garage, he said, 'You know, Rhea, I think you ought to be put in charge of the station bike. Then, when we have an inventory check either by me or by the inspector, you could make sure the bike is clean and well-maintained. Do you think that is a good idea?'

'Yes, Sergeant.' I couldn't say anything else.

Afterwards, it did occur to me to ask the Council foreman if we could keep the cycle at the police station, for safe custody of course, and then he could ask for it if his bosses ever wanted to carry out an inspection.

7

'At once on all her stately gates
Arose the answering fires.'
Thomas Macaulay 1800-59

Police officers spend a proportion of their time near fires, either watching the fire brigade extinguish them, or warming their cold posteriors in moments which are stolen from the critical gaze of the general public. By this means, they discover the truth of the old saying that 'If you wish to enjoy the fire, you must put up with the smoke.'

From their back-side warming moments, many officers steadfastly confirm the old legend about Noah sitting on a leak in his ark. If you don't know the story, it attempts to explain why men enjoy standing with their rumps on offer to a blazing fire. The story is that Noah's Ark sprung a leak, and one of the two dogs on board attempted to stop the leak by sticking its nose into the hole. That brave act has since been commemorated by all dogs, because they all have cold noses. However, the leak became so large that the puny nose of the dog was too small, and so Noah offered to sit on the hole. And so he did; his stern endeavour kept the water out and since that time it has been the misfortune of male members of the human race to suffer from cold bottoms. For this reason, men love to stand with their backs to a fire. Some fires, however, are too large for this to be done in comfort.

Of the unexpected fires attended by police officers, some are the result of arson, some the outcome of carelessness, some arise from accidents and many occur through sheer stupidity. The sources of some blazes remain unknown, or they arise through natural causes, but it is a fair comment to say that the discovery of an unwanted fire prompts urgent action by those who find it.

Here in rural North Yorkshire however, the definition of 'urgent action' is relative. What is urgent to a city man is not necessarily urgent to a countryman, and I had a wonderful example of this at Eltering Police Station one sunny afternoon.

I had attended court during the morning to give evidence in a case of careless driving. The sitting, with its list of miscellaneous offences, had stretched until lunchtime without hearing my case, so I enjoyed a quick sandwich and my flask of coffee in Eltering Police Office, as I waited my turn in the afternoon.

The office is neat and modern. It is part of a new complex of official buildings comprising the Fire Station, Ambulance Station, Court House and Police Station. All are housed within this pleasantly built and conveniently situated block of buildings with its tree-lined forecourts and tubs of geraniums.

It follows that there is a good deal of coming and going by members of the public. One pleasing fact is that visitors regularly pop into the police station for nothing more than a chat or to pass the time of day. It is a friendly place. The officer on the counter is content to while away his hours in the same way, there being little else to worry him. Such is the pace of life at Eltering.

That lunchtime, therefore, I was seated at a small desk at the rear of the enquiry office, and Vesuvius, the gentle giant of Eltering Police Station, manned the counter. As I munched my lettuce sandwich, he was gazing out of the window, contemplating life.

'Hello,' I heard him say to himself. 'There's awd Reuben Tempest on his tractor.'

I paid slight attention to his remark, for I did not know Reuben Tempest, nor did I know why his presence on a tractor was worthy of comment. Soon, the air was filled with the throbbing notes of his tractor as it pulled up directly in front of the police station where Reuben switched off the engine. A few moments later, the office door opened, ringing the bell to announce the arrival of a customer, and a ruddy-faced farmer presented himself at the counter.

'Now then, Reuben,' greeted Vesuvius, rising from his chair. I didn't know which of them was the untidiest, for Vesuvius' uniform was crumpled and his shoulders were covered in dandruff; this new arrival was clad in an old yellow sweater with mud and dirt all over it, and his long, straggly fair hair was protruding at all angles from beneath his grimy flat cap.

'Now then, Alf.' The farmer addressed Vesuvius by his Christian name; his real name was PC Alfred Ventress.

'Grand morning,' returned Vesuvius.

'Aye, not bad for t'time of year,' said the farmer, looking at the day through the office windows. 'This year's passing along nicely.'

'You'll be farmed up, then?' asked Vesuvius.

'Coming along. Aye, Ah's coming along. Ah've gitten that 100 acre cut and dried and my turnips howed ovver. Mind you, Alf, there's a lot to do. There's allus a lot to do on a farm.'

'Nay, you fellers mak it all up. You're nivver busy, allus just pretending. You spend all your time at marts or sales, and get other folks to do t'graft.'

Reuben grinned. 'It's neea good keeping a dog and barking yourself, is it?'

'Nay, I'll agree to that. Anyway, what's up? It must be serious if you've rushed here on that tractor.'

'Well, Ah don't know whether it's summat I should rightly trouble you with, Alf.' The farmer pursed his lips and rubbed his chubby cheek. 'But my missus is out at Scarborough, and Ah didn't know who to ask for advice, so because Ah needed a drop o' diesel for that awd tractor, Ah thought Ah might as well pop into Eltering, and see you chaps at t'same time.'

'Summat serious, is it?' asked the policeman.

'Aye, we've a fire at our farm.'

At the word 'fire' my ears pricked up; this was serious. But

for these characters, it wasn't serious enough to panic them
or to rush into frantic action.

'What sort of a fire?' asked Vesuvius.

'It's a grass fire,' the farmer told him.

'A big 'un, is it?'

'Oh aye, there'll be a few acres burning.'

'Do you want it putting out or summat?'

'Aye, well Ah think it might be best. Ah've been to have a
look and it's on t'railway side, along yon cutting at t'bottom
of my land. There's a wood doon yonder that might be at risk,
and some buildings of Harry Tordoff's – he's away on holiday
– and then there's them corn fields o' mine. Now, if yon blaze
got among my corn, it would mak a mess of my harvesting.'

'You've got your hay in though?' asked Vesuvius.

'Oh, aye, in and stacked.'

'It would make a mess o' them stacks then, if it got close
enough?'

'It would that!'

'How long's it been blazing then?' asked Vesuvius.

'Nay, now Ah've no idea. Ah spotted it when Ah was having
my dinner, so Ah went and had a look, and saw it was pretty
bad, so Ah came here.'

'All of a rush on your tractor?'

'Aye.'

They paused in the middle of this remarkable conversation,
and then Vesuvius said.

'Did you ring t'Fire Brigade, Reuben?'

'Nay, Ah didn't. That's why Ah'm here. Ah thought Ah'd
cum and ask if you thought Ah should.'

'It's nut a bad idea when there's a fire, Reuben. Those
fellers are pretty good at putting 'em out if they're told about
'em.'

'Well, Alf, thoo sees, Ah've heard they've got to cum all
t'way from Northallerton or somewhere. Noo that's all of forty-
five miles and it's a long way . . .'

'Nay, lad!' soothed Vesuvius. 'Just because we ring 'em at
Northallerton, doesn't mean they cum from there. When we

ring 'em at Northallerton, they ring bells and things at Eltering, then our local lads turn out. Their spot is right next door, here, just along t'path.'

'Oh, that's how it works, eh? So if Ah'd telephoned from my spot, it wad have gone through to Northallerton, and they'd have rung t'lads here, and these lads would come and fettle my fire?'

'Aye,' nodded Vesuvius.

'Right, well Ah'll get away home and give 'em a ring. Ah'll etti be sharp because it's gittin a strang hold, is yon fire. It's moving pretty fast.'

'Noo, there's no need to panic, Reuben.' Vesuvius was already lifting the receiver. 'Ah'll ring Northallerton now.'

Reuben stood by and watched with something bordering on amazement as Vesuvius used our private line to dial direct into the Fire Station; as Eltering Fire Station is manned by part-timers, his call went automatically to Fire Brigade Headquarters at Northallerton.

'By that was quick!' admired Reuben, as Vesuvius spoke.

'Hello, yes, Eltering Police here. I've a Mr Reuben Tempest with me. He's from Low Marsh Farm, Eltering.' He paused as the operator made a note of the name and address, then continued, 'There's a fire on his farm. A grass fire, and it's moving fast, and is threatening his crops.'

And Vesuvius replaced the telephone.

'Now, Reuben,' he said, 'get yourself round to next door and wait for t'lads to come. They'll be there in a jiffy; tell 'em exactly where yon fire is, and then follow on.'

'Have Ah time to get my diesel, then?' asked the farmer.

'Nay, thoo has not!' Vesuvius said firmly. 'By t'time thoo gets around next door, them fire brigade lads will be there, anxious to be off. So get thyself there sharp.'

As he turned to leave the police station, the siren sounded above the town, and Reuben's ears pricked up. 'Is that it?'

'That's it, Reuben. That's Northallerton calling 'em to your fire, but they need an engine first, full o' watter.'

'And that's in t'garage next door to you, eh?'

'It is.'

'By gum, Alf, things is getting very official,' and he left.

I saw him pottering along the footway towards the doors of the Fire Station, and even as he left us the first fireman hurtled past on his bicycle. Within seconds, others arrived by taxi, car and motor-cycle, all half-dressed in their uniforms, and all desperately anxious to beat their previous best time for getting mobile.

Within two minutes of the siren's awful notes fading into the summer air, the gleaming red fire appliance, with its bell ringing, tore out of town on its way to Reuben's grass fire.

I saw him climb on to his tractor, then turn in the opposite direction.

'He'll be going for his diesel,' said Vesuvius, returning to his books.

I learned that the fire was safely extinguished before it damaged any of Reuben's crops or buildings, although it left its mark on the grass embankment of the railway line. For Reuben, it was a moment of drama in his day, and I doubted very much whether he'd tell his wife about it when she came home. He'd probably tell her he'd had a few problems getting his diesel oil.

It is worthy of comment that in those days, every part-time fireman had a bell in his house. The bells rang to call them to the station, and these were supplemented by the noisy siren in town. When those noises occurred, the local police knew it was vital to keep clear the route from each fireman's home or place of work, for they knew that half-dressed men would soon hurtle through the streets aboard any kind of transportation they could find. To stand in the way of those dashing men was both dangerous and frustrating, and so the call of the siren meant the town's people froze until the fire engine was safely at its destination.

But modern technology has caused some problems. Now, each fireman has a bleeper, and this makes a personal noise to inform him that his presence is urgently required at the fire station. The snag with this system is that no one else knows.

The siren doesn't sound any more, and so the people are unaware of this impending stampede.

The result is, quite without warning, towns like Eltering are full of half-dressed men in cars and on bicycles hurtling through the streets on missions that appear bewildering.

One outcome of this new procedure is an increase in the number of traffic accidents in towns like Eltering, as people and firemen collide. As a form of communication, the old-fashioned siren had a lot to commend it – it ensured that everyone knew what was happening. And in a small community, that is important. But I often wonder what Reuben thinks of the new system – he probably thinks modern firemen arrive by telepathic means.

In that same summer, two old men of Aidensfield caused something of a panic when a henhouse caught fire.

The henhouse was totally destroyed, but because the blaze occurred during the daytime, all the hens were outside, pecking to their hearts' content in the small enclosure provided for them. The hens, and their ruined home, belonged to Arthur Poskitt who was one of the old men in question. The other was his life-long friend, Sam Crowther.

Friends though they were, the two old men, both well into their seventies, used to argue and fight over trivialities. This long-standing battle continued in their homes, in their neighbouring gardens and in the pub during an evening when they went for their pints of refreshing medicine.

The destructive henhouse fire was the outcome of such an argument. Long before I was posted to Aidensfield, Arthur Poskitt had owned a henhouse on the same site. It had been a smart construction of timber, well saturated with creosote for the purposes of preservation and for water-proofing, and it had a sound roof of equally waterproof material. Inside, there had been double perches, and nest boxes so that six hens could lay at the same time. In this comfortable abode, therefore, Arthur had kept a dozen Rhode Island Reds.

Then one fateful day, during a summer of long ago, Arthur's

henhouse had ignited. The hens had been saved because they were outside at the time, and those who'd been inside were wise enough to flee the place as the flames licked their feathers. Most of the village thought this old fire had been forgotten – but it hadn't.

It was a heated argument over that first fire which caused the second. The second one occurred during my period of duty at Aidensfield, and the story happened something like this.

It was a long, hot summer day in July, when the whole of Europe, including Aidensfield, was basking in a heatwave of remarkable intensity. All over the place, girls in scanty costumes pleased the men by displays of beauty seldom seen in rural areas, and the men sat around hoping that the heat of the sun would not burn the hairs off their chests. It was one of those summers when it paid to remain in England, for the suntans here were better than those obtained at great expense in France or Spain.

Around twelve noon on the fateful day, the two old men were sitting in deckchairs just beyond Arthur's henhouse, with handkerchiefs draped over their heads, and braces supporting ancient corduroys which were rolled up to the knees. They were not asleep, although a passer-by would have had to be very alert to discern any sign of wakefulness.

The two old characters had been sitting in this semi-comatose position for several hours, when Sam spoke.

'This is like the day when your henhouse caught fire,' he said.

'It wasn't as hot as this,' came the reply.

'It was hotter,' Sam affirmed. 'Much hotter!'

'It wasn't as hot as this when my henhouse caught fire,' retorted Arthur. 'Nowt like.'

'I remember it well,' returned his friend. 'It was a damned sight hotter than this, because you needed two handkerchiefs over your head and you had sunglasses on.'

'That wasn't because it was hotter. It was because my eyes were tender, and my head was sore.'

'You never told me your eyes got tender, or your head got sore?'

'Why should I tell you? If my head gets sore, it's nowt to do with you.'

There followed a lengthy pause, after which Sam renewed the attack.

'You remember that day, then?'

'What day?' answered Arthur.

'That day your henhouse caught fire.'

'Remember it? Aye, of course I remember it. It cost me enough to build this new 'un.'

'It was your own fault.' Sam now scored a triumphant hit.

'My fault?' Arthur sat bolt upright in his chair, his old eyes blinking against the sun. 'Who said it was my fault?'

'They all did.'

'Who's "all"?'

'Folks in Aidensfield. They all said it was your fault. You put your pipe in that long grass, on a day like this, and it caught fire.'

'It was kids what did it!' snapped Arthur, reclining once again.

'What kids? We were here, both of us. You and me. The kids were at school. It was before t'summer holidays. There was no kids, just us two, sitting here, and all that dry grass.'

'Well, it wasn't me. My pipe would never have done a thing like that. You don't set grass on fire with pipes!'

'You can! All you want is a pipe full of hot ash, and a bit o' wind, and dry grass'll catch fire like nowt.'

'Well, it didn't set my grass on fire, nor my henhouse.'

'There was nowt else!' Sam continued his attack. 'Summat must have set it alight. Henhouses don't catch fire themselves.'

Arthur sat upright in his chair once again and glared across at his reclining friend.

'Are you trying to tell me that my pipe will set fire to grass?'

Sam didn't move as he said, 'Aye. Remember – it was long, dry grass, nearly like hay, and there was just a touch o' breeze. You put that pipe o' yours down when you went in for a glass o' watter, and when you came out, yon grass was well away. Ah knew that and t'whole of Aidensfield knew.'

'Then you must have told 'em. There was only you and me here.'

'Then you admit it? You admit it was your pipe?'

'I admit nowt! All I'm saying is that a pipe full o' hot baccy isn't strang enough to set fire to growing grass, no matter how dry it is.'

'Cigarette ends have set fire to forests before today,' Sam said with a nod of his head. 'And they've set fire to settees and houses, an' all. If a cigarette end can do that, then a full pipe can set fire to growing grass – and henhouses.'

There was another long pause before Arthur struggled to climb out of his deckchair.

'I'll prove it!' he said. 'I'll prove that a pipe full o' hot baccy can't set fire to growing grass. There's growing grass there,' and he pointed to a length of dry grass which grew beneath the hedge. 'I'll fetch my pipe and show you!'

'You do that!' and Sam waved a finger at his pal.

Arthur went indoors to find the pipe he hadn't smoked for years, and emerged with it, plus a box of matches and some ready-rubbed tobacco. He sat on the edge of his deckchair and studiously filled the pipe, pushing the dried tobacco deep into the bowl in readiness for its test. Then he lit a match, applied it to the pipe, and inhaled as only a smoker can. Even though he'd rested from his pipe some time, he soon had the bowl glowing like a furnace, and clouds of sweet smoke circled above his head.

'That's a good pipe!' smiled Sam.

'Not one of my best,' Arthur told him, 'but good enough for this.'

'Good enough to set fire to a henhouse, eh?'

'Good enough for a test like this!' snapped Arthur, removing the pipe from his mouth and peering into its bowl. 'It's ready.'

'It'll be only right if you do today what you did last time you set your henhouse on fire.' Sam could not resist the gibe.

'This is to show my pipe couldn't have done it; now that

time, I set it down and went in for a glass o' watter . . .'

'Then we'll do t'same this time, and I'll come with you, just to make sure you do everything . . .'

Arthur's pipe was glowing nicely and he carefully set it down in the long grass, just as he had all those years before; it sat steadily between the dry stalks, a tiny glow of dangerous red among the tan colours of the weathered growth.

'Just like that, Sam,' beamed Arthur, pleased that his faithful pipe had not fallen over. 'Now, then, a glass o' watter . . .'

Together, the pair of them marched in step towards Arthur's kitchen where Arthur, re-living as best he could the events of long ago, reached into the cabinet, found a glass and filled it with water from the tap.

'I think my missus asked me summat, but I can't remember what it was,' he said, sipping heavily. 'Then I went outside . . .'

And he stalked back through the kitchen, round the corner of the brick cottage, and there, blazing furiously, was his patch of dry grass.

'It's afire!' he shouted. 'Sam, the bloody grass is blazing again! Git some watter!'

But old men are not as agile as they believe, and in the confusion and delay of those precious seconds, the searing flames were fanned by a fresh breeze which blew between the cottages. In a matter of seconds, the entire area of dry grass, which grew long and thick beneath the hedge, was ablaze and roaring towards the henhouse.

'Watter, watter!' shouted Arthur. 'Sam, ring for t'brigade . . .'

'You ain't a phone!'

'Try t'Post Office!'

And so the pair of them tried to bring about an air of calmness and efficiency as they worried what to do next. As Arthur tried to find a bucket, and as Sam rushed off to telephone the fire brigade, I noticed the pall of smoke rising from behind the village street.

At first, it meant nothing special. The folk here lit many fires in their gardens to burn their rubbish, and this fire had all the indications of such a blaze. There was the thick grey smoke coupled with the scent of burning vegetation, and even from my vantage point in the street, I could see that the seat of the fire was well away from the houses.

It was only when Sam came rushing out of the gate, shouting, 'Fire,' that I knew something was wrong.

'What's up, Sam?' I asked.

'Fire, Mr Rhea, in Arthur's garden. Send for t'Brigade, sharp.'

'What's on fire?' I asked.

'Grass,' he said, 'but it's blowing towards his henhouse!'

I was torn between two immediate courses of action. At that moment, I knew nothing of the history of this event, nor did I know the geography of Arthur's garden, but I recognised the alarm on Sam's face.

'Right, Sam, I'll fetch a fire engine. You go back and try to put it out.'

The nearest fire brigade was a private one at Maddleskirk Abbey. It was run by the monks for the protection of their own premises and it comprised one Green Goddess and lots of pipes, all staffed by an enthusiastic band of monks who donned firemen's uniforms for the occasion. They liked nothing better than a local opportunity to practise their fire fighting craft. Besides, they'd be there a good half-hour before the part-time Ashfordly Brigade, and those minutes could be vital if Arthur's henhouse was at risk.

I rang the Maddleskirk Abbey Chief Fire Officer, otherwise known as Brother Laurence, and gave him brief details.

'Lovely, Mr Rhea, we'll be there in a jiffy.'

I marvelled that Brother Laurence had been selected as Chief Fire Officer, when his namesake, St Laurence of Rome, was invoked by religious folk everywhere to protect them against fire. St Laurence was roasted alive on a gridiron to suffer a martyr's death, and I hoped Brother Laurence would not come to a similar fate in Arthur's henhouse.

I hurried back to the scene and entered Arthur's garden through his small gate.

The two old men were using everything possible to extinguish the running fire which threatened the henhouse. The hens, in the meantime, had been cast out of their run, and the gate had been opened to permit entry by the fire brigade. I ran to them, grabbed a spade and started to beat the glowing grass, hoping to kill the flames. It was like fighting a forest fire – the tall grass was riddled with new seats of flame, and as fast as we put out one tongue, another erupted elsewhere. The three of us were kept busy, but it was no good. The running fire, fanned from behind by the strong warm breeze, had crept along the back of the part we were tackling. Those flames were concealed by smoke and vegetation, and were already licking the creosoted walls at the rear of the henhouse. None of us noticed them until it was too late.

Suddenly, the henhouse was roaring as the flames ate into the wood which was so richly fuelled for them; the dry timber, with its creosote coating, was a gift from the gods, and the blaze roared across that rear panel in a split second.

'Arthur!' I shouted, but it was too late. The ferocity of the blaze was frightening, and as we stood back from the searing heat, brother Laurence and his fire-fighting monks arrived at the scene. To their credit, they had responded with remarkable speed, and were completely professional in their approach, but the fire had gained a firm hold. They managed to save part of the floor, and a couple of nesting boxes. The rest was burnt to the ground.

'Sorry, Arthur,' apologised Brother Laurence unnecessarily. 'We couldn't do a thing.'

'Nobody could have done more.' Arthur sounded dejected, but he spoke the truth. 'It was all Sam's fault!'

'My fault!' cried Sam. 'I didn't light a pipe and lay it in that grass!'

'What's this about a pipe?' I asked, and it was then that the story came out. Brother Laurence chuckled over the yarn, and said he'd found the exercise extremely valuable for his team; real fires, produced in real places under real circumstances, were far better for his men than those created artificially for training. He thanked Arthur for his fire, retrieved all his equipment and drove away through the little gathering of spectators.

My next duty was to complete a Fire Report, and I decided to write this one off as 'Accidental – No suspicious circumstances', for I dare not include the fact that Arthur had deliberately laid his glowing pipe in the grass to see if it would destroy the henhouse. That could raise all kinds of questions from Sergeant Blaketon, so I simply wrote that hot ash had accidentally fallen from his pipe into the grass, and the wind had fanned it into a blaze which had swept towards the tinder-dry henhouse. The value was about £25, as near as I can remember, and no lives were lost. The hens were without shelter for several days afterwards, and laid their eggs all over the place, but the incident provided Aidensfield with a lovely talking point.

It would be eight or nine weeks later when I popped into the Brewers' Arms and saw the irascible pair at a window table.

'That fire wae all your fault, Sam,' Arthur was saying. 'If you'd never doubted me, it would never have happened.'

'Doubted you? What do you mean? You did the first one with your pipe, and you did the second in exactly the same way! What's it got to do with doubting?'

'Friends aren't supposed to doubt each other,' Arthur was saying. 'If you'd believed my word, I wouldn't have lit that pipe and put it where it could fall over . . .'

'Arthur, you old sod, you set fire to your own henhouse and it's no good blaming anybody else.'

'When that grass grows again,' he said, 'I'll show you . . .'

'Then we'd better get Brother Laurence standing by right from the start!' laughed Sam. 'It might be your own house that goes up in smoke next time!'

'My house is too well built for that sort of fire to catch hold!' said Arthur.

'It's not!' argued Sam. 'Fires can burn stones and bricks,'

and I left before they could dream up any more of their dangerous schemes.

Police Constable Michael Sealifant transferred to the Eltering Sub-Division of the North Riding Constabulary from Birmingham City Police because he was sick of urban grime and suburban attitudes. He wanted to find himself, to be close to nature, and to live in a countryside free from pollution and the threat of the atomic bomb.

In those days, the transfer of individuals between police forces was fairly common, especially at constable rank, but if higher ranks wished to transfer to fill a vacancy in a new force, there was opposition on the grounds that the incoming man of rank was denying a local man promotion.

But when constables made application, they were favourably looked upon because there was always a shortage of men, especially those with experience, and it was felt that officers with police experience in other areas could bring untold benefits to our small force.

And so it was with Police Constable Michael Sealifant, aged 29, married with two children. His parent force wrote a glowing account of this man and his potential, but such reports are always regarded with suspicion on the grounds that if he was so good, why did they want to release him? When someone writes a glowing report about a man wishing to leave, it is usually done to make sure he goes. Even so, we accepted PC Michael Sealifant into our bosom, and the Chief Constable allocated him a rural beat house near Eltering. It was in a village called Fellerthorpe, which lies on the edge of the moors and is graced by wide open spaces, moorland sheep, summer visitors and winter tempests.

Because of its remoteness, no one in the North Riding Force wanted the beat, and so the house had remained empty for seven or eight years. But young Mike, in his desire for rural bliss, reckoned this was the answer to all his dreams. He looked at the house, liked it, and said he would accept the posting.

For the Chief Constable, it represented an additional man, albeit in a very remote area; the beat had remained vacant for all those years simply because it was more important to have officers where there were people who might need them, and not wasting away in the hills. Because Fellerthorpe beat was so remote and unwanted, the Standing Joint Committee had threatened to sell the police house, and this would mean more acres to be supervised by fewer men. The Chief Constable was naturally opposed to this, and because other officers declined the post for domestic reasons (and no one blamed them), PC Michael Sealifant was the answer to a Chief Constable's prayer. It was Ben Jonson who talked of 'Service of some virtuous gentleman', and here was a virtuous gentleman who wished to be of service.

On the day of PC Sealifant's arrival in Yorkshire, I was on duty. The section at Ashfordly was, for once in its lifetime, fully staffed, which meant I was given a motor-cycle patrol which embraced most of the sub-division. That area embraced portions of the Eltering Sub-Division which included Fellerthorpe beat. As was the custom in those halcyon days when a new constable arrived, one of the local men would be allocated to him to help unpack his belongings and generally settle him in. I was therefore told to report to the Police House in remotest Fellerthorpe, there to help the new constable unpack his furniture.

Mike was a real live wire. He was as jumpy as the proverbial nit, always rushing into things and he wanted the pantechnicon unpacked even before its wheels had stopped turning. I introduced myself when he paused for breath, and he said I could help with the heavy stuff, like wardrobes, the settee, his beds and so forth.

He was a very tall, thin individual with a gaunt face and a sallow complexion, topped by a thin thatch of straw coloured hair. His long, slender arms operated rather like windmills, and he continually badgered the removal men to be careful with his crockery, or not to paddle on the bare floorboards. His wife, on the other hand, was a mousey girl who was rather plump, but very nice and open. She brewed copious quantities of tea for us, and managed to rustle up a meal as darkness descended around half past five. It was eggs, chips and peas, and it was gorgeous.

Mike managed to halt himself for this break, and beamed at us all.

'By Jove,' he grinned, his lean cheeks crinkling to show his good teeth, 'this is the life. Look at those moors out there! Listen to the silence . . . and all that space for the children to play . . .'

He went into raptures about the location of his new beat, and in some ways he was right. The house, a stone-built cottage-style structure of the last century, was not a standard police house, and possessed great charm and character. It was spacious, which might cause worries over heating it in winter, and it was very isolated. But Mike and his lovely wife, Angie, seemed totally content. Both were looking forward to their life in rural Yorkshire.

I remained with them after the pantechnicon had departed, and helped them unpack much of the smaller stuff, assisting Mike to position things about the house while Angie bathed the two little boys. By nine o'clock that night, it looked more like home, and the blazing coal fire added a cheery dimension to the house. Showing considerable good nature, the inspector at Eltering had despatched a man over to Fellerthorpe every day for the previous two weeks to light fires in the house, so that it would be aired and cosy for the new arrivals. It was a nice thought, and I know Mike appreciated it.

I took my leave at half past nine. With Mike and Angie at my side, I stood on the front doorstep and we all admired the tremendous views from his porch. In spite of the darkness, we could see the outline of the valley and the dotted lights of houses and villages below were like glow-worms.

'God!' he shouted suddenly. 'What's that?'

His long arm pointed excitedly to a huge blaze somewhere in the valley and a similar one over to the east.

I laughed gently. 'Burning straw,' I informed him. 'When

the harvest is in, modern machines leave lots of waste straw behind. It's literally left in long rows in the cornfields and because recovery is so expensive and difficult, the farmers simply set fire to it. It's an easy way to destroy it.'

'There's another one!' and Angie pointed across to the west, where a smaller fire flickered in the darkness.

'You'll see a lot of those this autumn,' I said. 'Don't worry, they're all under control and they're just one of the features of the countryside.'

'I've a lot to learn about the countryside,' he said fiercely, 'but we're going to learn, aren't we, darling?' and he put his arm around his wife's ample waist. I left them standing at the door as they admired the glorious views from their lofty and lonely home.

As I rode away on my Francis Barnett, I wondered how this couple would cope. Living in exotic, remote locations is not easy, especially in the winter, and winter was not many weeks away. It takes a hardened countryman to live without neighbours, shops and the other comforts of civilisation, and yet this man of Birmingham and his wife seemed determined to give it a try. I gave them credit for their determination.

In addition, the house had not been lived in for years, and it was in need of maintenance. Although the fabric was sound, the exterior needed some paint before another winter and I knew the Police Authority would approve the work. They would probably decorate the interior too – the Chief Constable would exercise all his powers of persuasion and charm to effect these considerations for his new, isolated-beat constable.

Another problem was the garden. Its years of neglect had turned it into a veritable hayfield. Long, tough couch grass had rampaged across the garden to conceal paths, rockeries and agricultural patches alike. It had been joined by many other prolific grasses and weeds, making the garden into a tough, thick wilderness. It would need a completely new start.

I didn't envy Mike in his dream house.

Three days later, just after lunch, Sergeant Blaketon called me into his office, and he seemed very fierce when he rang me. It sounded as if I was in trouble.

I drove down to Ashfordly, parked the machine, obeyed all the rules of parking and knocked on his door. My heart was thumping.

'Come in,' came his loud, angry voice.

'Good morning, Sergeant.' I knew that the tone of his voice demanded the utmost respect from me, but I did not know what I had done to aggravate him.

'Rhea,' he said very slowly, 'what in the name of God did you tell that new man?'

'New man?' I spoke stupidly because I had not the remotest idea what he was leading up to.

'The chap with the funny name who's just come to Fellerthorpe.'

'PC Sealifant,' I said.

'Yes, what did you tell him?'

'Well.' I was flannelling because I did not know the drift of his questioning. What on earth had the fellow done? Got lost? Gone out to work without telling the Sub-Division? Fallen off his motor-bike?'

'Go on, Rhea.' Blaketon's voice was ominous.

'Just ordinary things about his work in the countryside.' I tried to sound confident. 'How to meet people, what the folks up here are like, what they expect of police officers, how to check a stock register and renew a firearm certificate . . .'

'Go on, Rhea,' he ordered me.

'Well, Sergeant, I can't remember precise things. I mean, there's not a lot you can say when you're humping heavy furniture about.'

'What about straw-burning?' His dark eyes bored into me.

'Straw-burning?' His remark baffled me.

'Yes, Rhea, what did you tell him about straw-burning? That is what I asked.'

'Nothing,' I said, and then I remembered our final conversation on the doorstep. 'Oh,' I halted, then continued, 'just before I left him, he spotted several fires in the valley, around Eltering mainly. He thought something was on fire, so I explained what was happening.'

'Ah, so you did tell him about straw-burning?' He sounded triumphant.

'I only put him right about it, Sergeant. I explained what the farmers were doing with their waste straw.'

'You did, eh? Precisely what did you explain to him?'

'Just that when the harvest is gathered in, the modern machinery leaves behind a lot of waste straw. For economical reasons, and practical ones, it is disposed of by fire.'

'That's all?'

'Yes, Sergeant.'

'Did you, or did you not, explain the technical ways of actually setting fire to the straw?'

'No,' I almost shouted, still wondering what had happened.

He slumped back in his chair and scowled at me from beneath those heavy black eyebrows.

'Rhea,' he said in a voice loaded with resignation, 'that new man's a bloody liability.' It wasn't often Sergeant Blaketon swore.

'Why?' I had to ask the question and did so hoping it would lead to some form of clarification.

'You know that confounded garden of his, at Fellerthorpe?'

I nodded and recalled the profuse growth of waste grass and weeds.

'He decided the best way to clear his garden was to set fire to it, just like the farmers did with their straw.'

I felt like laughing, and did not know what to say.

Sergeant Blaketon continued, and I could see the beginnings of tears of mirth in his eyes, accompanied by the start of a wide smile on the corners of his mouth. 'Rhea, that bloody man did just that. But do you know how he got it going? He poured *petrol* on the grass and down the path . . . petrol! And then he threw a match into it.'

'Sergeant! You're joking . . .!' I found myself laughing and he was roaring with laughter too, tears running down his face.

'I'm not joking, Rhea! I wish I was. He had saturated his garden with petrol . . . I mean . . . the whole lot went up like an explosion . . . whoosh . . . all on fire . . .' He was holding his sides now, and laughing until it hurt. 'Door frame, door, kitchen window . . . the stuff had dribbled out of his can, you see . . . from the house . . . all the kitchen's gone . . . he's lost his hair, eyebrows and most of his clothes . . . what a bloody mess, Rhea . . . what a bloody mess . . . the kitchen's gutted . . .'

'Is he hurt?' I managed to ask.

'Not a bit. Scared yes, but hurt – no. We're having to re-house him and his family. They're sending him to South Bank.'

I knew South Bank. In those days, it was in the North Riding, although on a heavy industrial suburb of Middlesborough, and was known for its grime and tough people. Rather like Birmingham, I suppose.

'He won't have learned much about the countryside, Sergeant,' I said.

'I reckon he's learned quite a bit, Rhea,' he chuckled to himself, wiping the tears from his eyes. 'He'll be able to tell 'em all about straw-burning when he gets to South Bank. He might even become their straw-burning spokesman! I'm sure they burn a lot of straw in South Bank.'

And I left him to his thoughts.

8

'Experience teaches slowly, and at the cost of mistakes.'
James Anthony Froude 1818-94

One branch of the police service which has almost slipped into oblivion since World War II is the Special Constabulary. The sturdy folk who join are a supportive arm of the regular Police Force, yet they are ordinary citizens; they rise to the occasion in times of strife and social unrest.

The Specials have a long and interesting history, but came into their own around 1831, the date of the first statute to concern itself specifically with them. In the last century, Specials were used by magistrates during many historic upheavals, such as the Chartist riots, the Rebecca riots, the bread riots, strikes and other type of industrial unrest. As the newly formed regular police forces established themselves, however, the use of Specials declined for this kind of work.

Specials were marvellous as supporters of the police during the two World Wars, and afterwards their role changed. They were not called upon only in times of tumult, but were welcomed as patrolling officers in uniform, when they supplemented the slender blue line by helping out at all kinds of busy times. Examples of their work include first-division football matches, holiday times at the seaside, Saturday night revels, visits by VIPs and the local police station's annual Christmas dinner. When every regular officer wanted to be off duty at the same time, the Specials would take over the town and patrol in their dark-blue uniforms with such efficiency and smartness that few members of the public realised they were not regular officers.

By 1965, their appointment and qualifications were set down in a Statutory Instrument known as the Special Constables Regulations, 1965, which stated that a Special Constable should be not less than eighteen years old, should be of good character and health, and be of British Nationality. There were no height stipulations, although local Chief Constables could determine the height of their own Specials. Few of them accepted men or women who were less than 5 feet 6 inches tall.

A formal training programme was established, with a career structure and pensions for those injured on duty. Specials, however, do not receive payment for their work, although expenses can be approved.

As a consequence, many people with a sense of social duty or vocation, have over the years joined the Specials and have performed useful and dedicated service. To call them hobby bobbies is perhaps unjust, for lots of them serve faithfully as volunteers in other organisations and seem to get themselves involved in almost anything that happens in the community.

Such a man was Maurice Merryman, the undertaker at Ashfordly. He did not fit the usual image of an undertaker, because he was not tall and gaunt, he did not wear black clothes all day and his eyes were not set in deep, shadowy recesses within a skull-like cranium. Instead, Maurice was short and tubby, with a round, pink face and chubby cheeks. His pale grey eyes beamed from behind thick-lensed spectacles, and he wore very smart suits in all his enterprises, although he did wear black for funerals.

Apart from being the undertaker for Ashfordly, he drove the local taxi, sold flowers from a market stall, and ran a fruit shop. He was always busy, always cheerful and constantly available to perform a good turn. Maurice was kindness itself, and that is the reason he became an undertaker. He couldn't bear to think of people being left unburied in cold weather, so he established himself as the local burial expert with a boast that he saw them to their eternal rest in the nicest possible way.

I think he became a Special for similar reasons. He felt that the law could be enforced in a humane way and even believed there was some good in most villains, a belief not shared by the majority of police officers. But Maurice was undeterred by the misgivings of others and set about patrolling the streets of Ashfordly for his stipulated two hours a month. He saw himself there to enforce the law and to do good to the community.

One of his spells of duty occurred during the section dinner. This is one evening out of the whole year when every member of Ashfordly section, including wives and/or girl-friends, is off duty. They go to a local hotel for a good meal and a dance, and it is a social gathering where everyone can meet everyone else. But as the town cannot be left without a police presence, Maurice comes forward on this auspicious night and volunteers for duty. He does more than his required two hours, and happily patrols the streets and supervises the office until normal service is resumed.

One Friday night, therefore, he was performing this duty in our absence and was enjoying a spell in the office where he had made a cup of tea and was reading police circulars. For Maurice, life was good, and he felt very important because during that evening, the law enforcement of Ashfordly lay in his carefully manicured hands.

Around ten o'clock, as he sank his third cup of tea, a car pulled up outside Ashfordly Police Station. It generated more than the usual amount of noise, it braked with some difficulty and parked in what some officers might describe as a haphazard manner. The driver's door slammed as the horn blew accidentally and the lights flickered in unison.

Maurice pricked up his ears and wondered what was to befall him. The metal gate, which led down the police station path, squeaked then clanged against its support, and there followed the shuffling steps of someone heading erratically for the door. Maurice put down his papers and stood behind the counter, waiting.

The heavy door crashed open and in staggered a rounded gentleman. He was enveloped in a cloud of whisky fumes and hiccupped many times as he staggered towards the supportive woodwork of the counter.

'Evening, Officer.' Powerful alcoholic odours enveloped Maurice and his customer as the fellow clung for support. 'Not a bad evening, is it?'

Maurice recognised him as Aubrey Barraclough, a haulage contractor from Brantsford, a man involved in big business and many associated interests. Clearly, the fellow had not recognised Maurice in his blue suit with the shiny buttons; had Maurice been behind the counter of his fruit shop, there would have been instant recognition.

'Hello, Mr Barraclough,' smiled the helpful Special Constable. 'What can we do for you?'

'Oh, it's not the policeman, it's Maurice! I didn't know you'd joined the Force, Maurice?' and he hiccupped.

'I haven't, I'm a Special Constable,' beamed Maurice. 'But tonight, I'm manning the station and looking after things. So what can I do for you?'

'I've come to give myself up,' stated Mr Barraclough. 'I have drunk far too much and feel I cannot be allowed to drive home.'

'Oh,' said Maurice, wondering what he should do with the fellow. 'I'm not sure of the procedures.'

'Well, I will walk home. I am too drunk to drive . . .'

'No,' said Maurice. 'I cannot allow that. If you leave your car outside, and I let you go, then I will be asked awkward questions. I will be asked why I didn't proceed against you, and that could result in you losing your driving licence. I would have to find a doctor to examine you to determine whether you are fit to drive, and there are all sorts of complications. I cannot let you walk home and leave the car.'

'You are the officer in charge of law enforcement, Maurice, so what do you suggest?' Barraclough swayed rather violently and clutched at the counter to maintain his upright stance.

'If you leave your car outside, I will have to formalise things by arresting and charging you. That'll mean a night in the cells, and a court appearance tomorrow, with lots of publicity for you.'

Barraclough shook his head, an action which made him spin rather like a waltzing top which was losing its momentum.

'No, I just wanted to leave the car, that's all.'

'Well,' said Maurice in his kindest mood. 'You drove it here and you are aware of your condition. You talk lucidly, and you are coherent. I believe you are not too drunk to drive it home, Mr Barraclough, so I suggest you go back to the car and drive home slowly.'

'You do?'

'Yes, I do. That would solve all your problems.'

'You really think so, Maurice? You are a very good policeman, Maurice, a very good one. Yes, all right.'

And Barraclough turned and made for the door. He achieved some success and emerged into the fresh air, whereupon he headed, with a little swaying of the legs and much more hiccupping, towards his waiting car.

No professional police officer would have allowed that to happen, but Maurice was a helpful, kind-hearted undertaker with a penchant for wearing police uniform, and he did not appreciate the problems he thus created.

With a monstrous crashing of gears and a blaring horn, Aubrey Barraclough launched his Daimler upon the town of Ashfordly. Being late at night (and ten o'clock is late in those peaceful places) the streets were quiet, which was fortunate, because Barraclough's Daimler performed what can only be described as terpsichorean movements along the highways and byways of Ashfordly. The lovely car waltzed and screeched around corners as it made for the Market Place with the intention of taking the road to Brantsford.

Its meandering journey could not hope to end in success, and one of its prime reasons for failure was a keep-left bollard at the junction with the Market Place and the road to

Brantsford. When driving along the wide road past the Market Place, Barraclough had noticed the illuminated sign and recognised it as the beginnings of his final run home. He therefore accelerated.

His beautiful car collided magnificently with the bollard, and crumped to a halt. This threw him forward into the windscreen and caused the bonnet to burst open like the mouth of a gigantic hippopotamus. It is said that Barraclough hiccupped twice, put the car into reverse and dragged it clear. He stepped outside, slammed the bonnet shut and set off in his intended direction.

After travelling only five hundred yards, he collided with a stationary Morris Minor which was parked harmlessly outside a cottage on the outskirts of Ashfordly, and this time his efforts were spectacularly successful. The Morris, just home after a trip to Malton, was lovely and warm, and when Barraclough's speeding Daimler rammed into it, the petrol tank split wide open and the Morris burst into flames. In a very short time, those flames also licked the thwarted Daimler and within minutes, both cars were wildly ablaze. The surrounding houses flickered in the light, and the heat made the road surface bubble as the tar melted.

Barraclough managed to scramble clear and ran for his life, while the owner of the Morris, just tucking into an apple-pie supper, rushed out to see his pride and joy in an advanced state of incineration. He dashed next door to call the fire brigade and the police, while the distant darkness concealed the unsteady departure of Aubrey Barraclough.

Because the fire brigade at Ashfordly comprised part-timers who were now in the pubs, and as the only police presence was Maurice, it took some time to gather wits and equipment. Eventually, these emergency services arrived at the scene.

By the time they did arrive, the Morris was burnt to a cinder and the Daimler had all the appearances of a cast-off shell. Only its number plates were identifiable, so Maurice stated he knew the culprit.

'It's Aubrey Barraclough!' he cried, and promptly began

searching the remains of the car for the remains of Mr Barraclough, doubtless with some kind of commercial motive at the back of his mind. But no Aubrey or part of Aubrey was found.

'He'll have run for it!' snarled the owner of the Morris ashes. 'He'll want to avoid being done for drunken driving. He's always drunk . . . it's time the bloody police did something about him.'

'I'll make a report about it,' suggested Maurice, not really knowing what he was supposed to do next.

The cunning Aubrey had stumbled down one of the alleys between the cottages, and had found a pedal cycle. Hearing the commotion in his wake, he had jumped on to the cycle with enough sense not to switch on the lights, and with an almost silent swishing of tyres had begun his escape run. By now, he was slightly more sober than hitherto, and knew how to keep his balance; he also knew which way to turn the pedals and the handlebars. As more officials and onlookers began to gather at the scene of the blaze, the dark figure of Aubrey Barraclough, on someone's stolen cycle, moved quietly along the dark road, homeward bound. He could always claim somebody had stolen his Daimler . . .

As he began to craftily calculate the best way of extricating himself from any responsibility for the destruction he had left behind, he felt the soothing wind in his hair and the coolness of night upon his cheeks. His podgy legs pressed the pedals and caused his breath to become heavier and more rapid as time progressed. It wasn't long before he actually began to enjoy this sobering-up exercise; he experienced the exhilaration of youth as the cycle sped along its way.

Those of you who know the road from Ashfordly to Brantsford will recall that it weaves through the countryside in a most interesting manner. Some two miles out of Ashfordly, it dips quite suddenly as the highway races down a slope to cross a stream, and at the crossing place, the road turns quite suddenly to the left, before rising to continue its picturesque way.

In a car, that point can be dangerous, but local people such as Aubrey are familiar with this place; they always cope with it, even when slightly intoxicated.

But Aubrey was more than slightly intoxicated; furthermore, he was not in his Daimler with its wonderful brakes and high-quality headlights. Without any headlights to guide him, he hadn't realised he'd come to this point. He reached the summit aboard a pedal cycle of unknown quality, in darkness, and he was singing blissfully to the stars as he pedalled along.

Almost without warning, Aubrey began to gather speed as the cycle started its descent, and it was quite apparent that the bike was going faster than Aubrey wished. He used the brakes, but they were not as efficient as those of his Daimler, especially when carrying seventeen stones, so the cycle refused to reduce its onward pace.

Very soon it was bouncing along at Daimler pace, and Aubrey took his feet off the pedals. He began to wobble; he began to shout for help, but none was forthcoming. By all accounts, his onward path took him across the grass verge at the bottom of the slope, and the cycle collided with the off-side parapet of the bridge.

The cycle stopped but Aubrey did not. We are told that he became airborne for a short distance before the cold waters of Ashford Gill cushioned his heavy return to earth. There must have been an almighty splash as Aubrey arrived at this point, and it is a well known fact that cold water in abundance has a wonderful ability to aid the sobering-up of most drunks.

It is believed that this water did help to sober up Aubrey, because the abandoned and buckled cycle led to his discovery on the banks of the stream. He was found lying there with his huge belly in the air, all damp and cold, and he was fast asleep. When he was roused, he was very, very sober, and promptly denied everything.

But scientific evidence and eye-witness accounts are marvellous, and within two months Aubrey appeared before Eltering Magistrates' Court. He was charged, among other things, with dangerous driving, malicious damage, failing to report an accident, larceny of a pedal cycle and riding a bike without lights.

For poor Special Constable Merryman, there was the inevitable blasting from the mouth of Sergeant Blaketon, and the unenviable thrill of becoming an object lesson in all future lectures and training sessions, for both specials and regular officers. The Merryman Incident, as it became known, was a lesson in how not to deal with drunken drivers.

But Maurice was retained because of his value on our Section dinner night. We all benefited from his special brand of policemanship.

It was Alexander Pope who produced those famous words 'To err is human', but lots of us forget the words which follow, for they are 'to forgive, divine'.

If the police officers of Ashfordly learned anything from Special Constable Merryman's mistakes, it was that mistakes can occur even if the intention is honourable. Poor Maurice Merryman's intentions were always honourable, and with that knowledge in mind, I found myself wanting to assist the less fortunate. Police officers are constantly meeting those who need help and guidance, and lots of unofficial and unpublicised assistance is given by them. But could such help ever be wrong? Could there be a time when help from a police officer was a mistake? I was not afraid of making a mistake, for mistakes happen to everyone, but could I forgive or be forgiven if I did?

The opportunity to find out came on Sunday morning when I was off duty. I was cutting the lawn outside the front of my hill-top police house when Gordon Murray came to the gate.

Gordon was a young man of twenty-eight who worked as a labourer on building sites. Stocky, with brooding dark eyes and a thick head of wavy hair, he was a good-looking man whose burly figure and cavalier approach to life attracted a lot of women. He had many girl-friends, who fluttered to him like moths to a bright light, but he had never succumbed to marriage.

I had known him a while; he ran an old van which was

always falling foul of the law because of its condition or its lack of tax and insurance. Another of his foibles was to fight everyone in sight after he had enjoyed four or five pints of beer. Sometimes sullen and moody, he was strong and fit, and a good worker when he felt like it. He could also be a thorough troublemaker when the mood took him – he was certainly unpredictable.

During my short time at Aidensfield, I'd had several confrontations with him, many when he was fighting fit on a Saturday night, and fortunately I managed to cool his earthy antagonism; he was good enough to respect the uniform I wore, and sensible enough to take my regular advice to 'get away home before there's any more trouble'. Without me there, he would speedily launch himself into any situation, good or bad, and at times would emerge with black eyes, bruised groins and flattened nose. Sometimes he was the victor, sometimes the vanquished.

Even though I had taken him to court for many motoring offences, and dragged him off umpteen opponents outside dance halls and pubs, there was a peculiar kind of respect and friendship between us. In his sober, upright moods, he would do anything for me; he once saved me from a beating up when some thugs came from Stokesley to do battle with the Ashfordly youths. In return, I always assured him that if he needed the kind of help I could give, he should not be afraid to ask.

And so here he was, standing at my garden gate one Sunday morning. He was casually dressed in a rough shirt and jeans, and his muscular arms were bronzed and firm after working out of doors for so long. He pushed open the gate and approached me. He looked rather nervous, for he was well out of his territory; visiting police establishments voluntarily was not in keeping with his character.

'Hello, Mr Rhea.' He always referred to me in this way, never by my Christian name.

'Hello, Gordon,' I greeted him. 'This is an honour – do you fancy a coffee?'

'Er, well,' this meant he must enter the awesome portals of the police house, but he accepted and followed me into the lounge. I took him there because I was off duty, and because I felt he'd come for reasons which were not official. Mary produced two cups of coffee and closed the door as Gordon sweated over the purpose of his visit.

'Now, Gordon, what's troubling you?'

He played with the cup of coffee, moving it nervously in his heavy hands. He kept his eyes averted from me as he tussled with his problem.

I waited; I had seen this kind of hesitancy before and knew that any prompting from me might cause him to dry up entirely; whatever was on Gordon's mind must be important because it was most unlike him to enter a police house or to make an initial approach of this kind. But I had him cornered – he was not outside a pub where he could walk off; he was here on my settee, in my lounge, with a cup of coffee in his hands.

I sipped my coffee, waiting, and then he looked at me earnestly.

'Mr Rhea,' he began, 'you might have heard about me . . .'

He paused, as if expecting a reply, but I did not know what to say.

'You mean something recent?' I put to him.

'Aye. About me getting married,' he blushed vividly.

'Married?' I cried. 'No, Gordon, that's news to me. Well, is it true?'

He nodded and a shy smile flitted across his features. 'Aye,' he said, 'it's right enough. That's why I've come to see you.'

'Go on.' I inched forward in my seat. 'First, though, congratulations. I think you'll enjoy married life.'

'Aye, well, it's summat I'm not used to, being settled. I've allus gone where I've pleased. I mean, my old mum looks after me, washes my clothes and does my food and things . . . and there's all sorts I don't know . . .'

'About the ceremony you mean?'

'That as well. But everything. Flowers and the church, all that.'

'The vicar will help you with the formalities,' I advised him. 'In fact, I think he's got a little book that tells you step by step how to organise everything from the organist to the reception, even the honeymoon.'

'I've him to see next,' he said. 'Me, seeing a vicar!' and he raised his eyes as if to Heaven.

'Mr Clifton will make sure things are running smoothly,' I assured him. 'Is this why you wanted to see me?'

He nodded, and took a long drink from the mug of coffee, then wiped his mouth with the back of his hand.

'Aye,' he said, 'well, I've done a bit of asking about, to try and find out what I'm to do, and . . .'

He paused again, took another long drink as I awaited his next worry. He was approaching another difficult speech.

'Go on, Gordon,' I tried to ease the problem out of him.

'Well, they say the most important bloke at a wedding is the best man. He's got to make sure things go right, hasn't he? Get the bride to the altar, fix the reception and things. You know, jolly things along, and keep things right, make speeches and all that.'

'Yes, that's true, Gordon. Most men, when they are thinking of getting married, make sure they choose a good best man for that reason. He's got all sorts of jobs to see to – he keeps the wedding running smoothly. Yes, you need a good best man.'

'Well,' he licked his lips. 'That's why I'm asking you.'

At first, his words did not mean a lot; I thought he was asking me for my advice, but it gradually dawned that he was asking *me* to be his best man.

'Me?' I said. 'You're asking me to be your best man, Gordon?'

'Aye, well, none of my mates are up to it, and I've no brothers and no dad, and I do want things to right and real smooth . . .'

'Who's the lucky girl, then?' I had to know this before committing myself.

'Sharon Pollard, she works over at Thirsk in one of the hotels. Lives in.'

I shook my head. 'I don't know her, Gordon. Where's the wedding to be?'

'In Aidensfield,' he said.

'Not Thirsk?'

'No, she's not a local. She's from Liverpool, just working here, and doesn't want to go back there. So she'll live in our house, as a lodger, before the wedding.'

'Well,' I said, 'this is a turn-up for the books, Gordon! You're the last man I expected to see going to the altar. She must be a real cracker to have caught you.'

I paused, and I knew he was awaiting my answer. I knew his earthy background, and his equally earthy relations, most of whom were petty villains of one kind or another. He was from a noted family of local villains. What they would think to a policeman being best man at Gordon's wedding was something I could never guess, but he had asked me as a friend. In some ways, I was very flattered, if a little puzzled by his odd request.

'All right,' I smiled, realising it must have been a difficult request for him to make, 'I'll do it. Gordon, it will be a pleasure. I will be proud to be your best man.'

His face lit up and he leaned across to shake hands with me.

'Mr Rhea,' he said, 'this has made me a very happy man.'

After he'd gone, I told Mary the news.

'You've what?' she gasped.

'I've agreed to be best man for Gordon Murray,' I repeated.

'Why?' she demanded.

'Because he asked me,' I answered. 'He came specially to ask me, and I agreed. I think it's a great honour.'

'You must be stupid!' she said flatly. 'If a man like that asks a policeman to be best man, you can bet there'll be a catch in it.'

'I owe him a favour.' I tried to justify my actions. 'He says none of his relations or friends is capable . . .'

'They'll all be drunk, that's why,' she said. 'You should hear the gossip about the Murrays in the shop. They're a right lot – there's that cousin of his who's a scrap-dealer and always in court for stealing, there's that other cousin from Eltering who got fined for dealing in drugs, and another who steals cars . . . Nicholas, what have you let yourself in for?'

'I am going to be best man at the wedding of a friend!' I said. 'And that's final.'

I must admit that Mary's misgivings had given me cause for concern, and it was probably wise to keep this assignment from the eyes and ears of Sergeant Blaketon and the other officers at Ashfordly. Later, when Gordon confirmed the date and time of his wedding, I applied for a day's leave and it was approved. Over the weeks that followed, Gordon came to the house a good deal, and he accepted his new responsibilities with remarkable aplomb. I liked him in these moods; he was affable, courteous and very anxious that his wedding day would be a success.

Mary grew to like him too, for she kept us supplied with coffee, and when the official invitation came, she was included as a guest. Gordon readily accepted the practices governing the bride's parents, her family and guests, and those of the groom, and I could see he was genuinely looking forward to his new state of matrimony.

Some six weeks before the May wedding, Sharon arrived at his mother's house, and Gordon brought her to the police house to meet us. She was a pretty girl, extraordinarily thin with long black dull hair and a pale smooth face. She had the slender figure of a model, and the unmistakable accent of a Liverpudlian. Her clothes were on the dowdy side, her shoes down at heel and her finger-nails black with dirt. But Gordon loved her.

Mary brewed the inevitable coffee, and Sharon played with our children as we made small talk about weddings, bridesmaids, honeymoons, and that sort of thing. Sharon did not talk about her background, other than to tell us her father was dead, and there were seven of them in her family, she being the youngest. She had come over to Thirsk for work, because there was so little in Liverpool; the Thirsk job had come to her notice through one of her father's old Army friends.

I was pleased to meet Gordon's chosen bride, and when they'd gone, Mary said, 'She's pregnant.'

'Never!' I chided her. 'She's too thin . . .'

'She is pregnant, Nicholas,' Mary affirmed. 'I can tell – any woman can tell. It's the skin and the eyes . . . Gordon's going to be a dad, and this is obviously a rushed job. She's nice, though, isn't she, even if she's a bit scruffy.'

'She'll be good for Gordon.' I believed that to be true. 'He was telling me they've been allocated an estate cottage at Briggsby, so that'll get him from under his mother's feet.'

As the weeks passed, I began to appreciate that Mary's diagnosis had been correct. Sharon did look a little more plump around the waistline, but it was not a plumpness which would be noticed by a casual observer. I did not hear any other hints of her condition during my patrolling, nor did I seek any clarification on that point. The fact was that Gordon loved her, which he told me several times, and it was evident that Sharon loved him. I believed it would be a fine match, if a little volatile at times.

On the night before the wedding, Sharon's mother and two of her little nieces arrived in Aidensfield and were accommodated in a holiday cottage, rented for the weekend. There was no room with Gordon's family, and the cottage was an ideal solution. So that Sharon's mum could take her rightful part in the ceremony, it was arranged that the taxi would collect Sharon from the cottage, together with the bridesmaids, so that it would appear as if she was leaving the family home. One of her brothers was to give her away – he would drive over on the morning of the wedding.

The great day arrived. The wedding was at eleven o'clock in the parish church, followed by a reception in the village hall, the food and drink being supplied by the Brewers' Arms. Gordon had hired a nice car for his honeymoon in the Lake District, but he had concealed this arrangement, and the car, from his boisterous friends who wanted to find it and tie old

tins to it, then smear it with shaving cream. As the time for
the ceremony approached, I kept him calm; I had the ring, I
had fixed all the taxis, got money for the vicar and organist,
supervised the reception, ordered flowers and drinks and
arranged for the telegrams to be delivered . . .

I spent the final minutes soothing his fevered brow and
then took my place at his side in the front pew. Gordon stood
close to me as we awaited the blushing bride. She came two
minutes late to the familiar strains of *Here Comes The Bride*,
and everyone turned to admire her.

Sharon really did look beautiful; the flowing skirts of her
white dress concealed any evidence or hint of little things to
come, and she had a glow of happiness about her. Her tattiness
had gone too. Beside me, Gordon was looking his best; his
suit was new and smart, his hair had been neatly cut and
washed, and he cut a very fine figure. He'd even cleaned his
shoes.

Behind me, on his side of the church, I could identify the
unmistakable scent of premature celebrations, for I knew the
menfolk had been to the Brewers' Arms for a quick one or
two before the ceremony. On the bride's side there were similar
scents and many hiccups. But all this was behind me as Sharon
moved with considerable grace down the aisle. She had
shampooed her long black hair and it glistened in the lights, a
pretty contrast to her white gown. The vicar was waiting with
a smile on his face, and the congregation was hushed as Sharon
took her final dainty steps to the altar.

At that moment, someone burst into a noisy bout of
weeping, and I turned to see it was Sharon's mother. She was
holding a handkerchief to her face as the tears cascaded down
her plump cheeks. Apart from this, the church was silent as
the Rev Roger Clifton opened with those famous words,
'Dearly beloved, we are gathered here in the sight of God,
and in the face of this congregation, to join together this man
and this woman in Holy Matrimony . . .'

My part in the ceremony was not over-taxing, but the
service and its non-musical, watery accompaniment by

Sharon's mum caused the time to pass rapidly and before I knew what was happening, I had handed over the ring, Sharon and Gordon were pronounced man and wife, and everyone was filing outside for the photographs.

There was some boisterous noise and rather physical jockeying for position in the photographs, through which Sharon beamed beautifully and Gordon looked every inch the handsome groom. Being best man, I did a lot of cajoling, pleading and ordering about; I started to fix the line-ups for the cameraman and brushed dust off Gordon's suit. I did a lot of running about, but as the hustle of the photographic session continued, I became vaguely aware of some unrest.

At first, my ears were not attuned to sounds beyond my immediate duties, and I associated the loud voices and frequent shrieks with happiness, euphoria and general high spirits. The truth was that other spirits were at work, such as gin and vodka. Sadly, they were acting upon the ample figure of Sharon's mother, who wanted to be in all the photographs with two fingers raised to the heavens.

At first, her insistence on being in every photograph was something of a chuckle, but when she raised her two fingers in what was definitely not a Victory sign, it was evident she had some kind of chip on her shoulders or a massive grudge of some kind. It dawned on me, as I'm sure it had already dawned on the other family guests, that Mrs Pollard was determined to cause trouble or embarrassment.

The photographer did his best to arrange some pictures without her, but it was becoming impossible; even when he arranged a line-up of bridesmaids, she would hustle in just as he had focused his camera, and dislodge the line by charging at them like a raging bull. If there can be an analogy, she was like a cow in a china shop.

Had I been a policeman on duty and distanced from the soul of the ceremony, I would have recognised the onset of trouble because that would have been part of my work, especially at a wedding with such characters as the chief actors. Because I was best man I was heavily committed with the internal arrangements and was not aware of the simmering brew being brought to the boil by Mrs Pollard. I learned later that she had had two half-bottles of gin in her ample handbag, and had been sipping these in church and afterwards, all the time working herself up to a pitch of antagonism.

When I found myself thinking like a policeman instead of a best man, I sought guidance from Gordon. Having caught his eye, I took him to one side as the harassed photographer tried to arrange a picture of both mothers.

'What's her game, Gordon?'

'Trouble,' he said. 'She is out to cause trouble, the bitch!'

'I can see that, but why?'

'Because I put Sharon up the stick, and because she doesn't like me.'

'She was all right in church,' I said. 'If she had any objections, she could have made her case known before coming here.'

'She did, that's why Sharon left home to live here. Mrs Pollard's a real bitch . . . she was supping gin in church, Mr Rhea, to get herself worked up for this.'

'She's going to ruin things for you, and there's the reception to come yet, and wine and more drinks. You don't want that ruined, do you?'

'No,' he said, looking at me steadily. 'She's out to make a mess of my wedding day, Mr Rhea. Sharon said she would.'

'Then we'll have to stop her. Is there a useful heavyweight woman on your side?'

'No, Mr Rhea, that's not the way to do it. Anybody from my side would only stir up her lot to fight back. They'd all join in. You need somebody from her side to sort her out.'

'But they'll be sympathetic to her, won't they? And they're all from Liverpool, aren't they? They won't want Yorkshire folk sorting them out, will they?'

'No, Mr Rhea.'

I could sense the beginnings of embarrassment. All around were roughs and toughs from two warring, insensitive families, and the centre of the problem was the troublesome Mrs

Pollard. Even now, she was thrusting herself before the camera with two fingers in the air, and lifting her skirts to reveal long green knickers as she did an awful rendering of the can-can. Her family laughed; Gordon's snarled, while Sharon clung to Gordon, not knowing whether to laugh, cry or fade away somewhere.

Their happiness was rapidly degenerating into something uncontrollable; our peaceful village was about to experience the warlike enjoyment of Liverpool's back streets combined with the skills of some of the toughest scrappies and layabouts in Yorkshire. I was off duty, too, in civilian clothes; I was a real pig in the middle.

I had to do something, not only for my sake, but the sake of Gordon and his bride, and for the village. Then, fortuitously, I caught Mary's eye; she was behind a gathered knot of chortling fools who were encouraging Mrs Pollard to kick her legs higher as the poor photographer tried to get Gordon's family group on file.

I signalled to Mary to move aside, and indicated that I wanted to talk to her. She recognised the concern on my face, and inched away from the ogling crowd.

Where there is a focal point for trouble, one solution is to remove that focal point; on this occasion, it meant neutralising Mrs Pollard in some way. She was the catalyst; she was playing to the audience of the Liverpudlian admirers and causing everlasting embarrassment to her unfortunate daughter. Gordon's relatives wouldn't stand for much more.

Desperate tactics were needed and as I moved aside to talk with Mary, a dreadful scheme crossed my mind. Even as I reached Mary, Mrs Pollard had kicked the camera's tripod over and was trying to dance with the photographer, as her grinning clan stood around and clapped like natives during a ritual dance. For my plan, Mary was neutral; very few knew who she was.

'Mary,' I whispered as she reached me. 'Go to the pub and ask George to remove every drop of liquor from the reception, quickly. Have a bottle of wine ready for the top table, for the bride and groom, but tell him, from me, that there's going to be trouble if this lot have more to drink. Replace the guests' wine with bottles of tonic water or something non-alcoholic. I'll take the responsibility for that. Tell him also, I think he'd better close his pub before the reception. We don't want this lot getting tight in there. Tell them they're likely to wreck his bar for the fun of it.'

'Will he do all that?' she asked.

'Tell him what's going on, then I'm sure he will. Then, while I create a diversion here, ring the office and get a police car to patrol the street. There will be one in the area, it'll be patrolling my beat in my absence. Tell them from me it's important. If there's a double crew, then that will be better. Got it?'

She looked at me slyly and I knew what was going through her mind.

'Best man, eh?' she grunted. 'Gordon's no fool . . . now you know why he asked you!'

'Rubbish!' I snorted, and returned to the mêlée as she hurried about her mission. I began my diversion. I took the harassed photographer to one side, and said we needed the bride and groom photographed while shaking hands with each of the guests. I knew this would take a long time, and it might placate some of them; I spoke to Gordon and Sharon who agreed, and so the marathon began. Sharon was viciously cursing her mother who tried to pop up behind the groups, two fingers raised, and the langauge from the others was boisterous, rude and crude. But this part of the ploy was working.

The buffet could wait while everyone was pictured, and thanks now to the antics of Mrs Pollard, it was taking a considerable time. This suited me – I needed time. Then I saw Mary pushing through the throng, and she was smiling.

'I've seen George, and he's going to move the drinks out. He thanked you for the warning. He says the waiter will produce a bottle of wine for the groom and bride when it's needed – if it's left on the table somebody will pinch it. He'll close the pub now, he says.'

'Good. Now, did you find a car?'

'Yes, Sergeant Bairstow was in the office when I rang, and he's coming right away.'

'Good. I must talk to him without this lot seeing me. When he comes, look out for him, and ask him to drive into the garage. I'll ring him there from the pub's phone.'

'You're being very devious!' she said, with a worried frown.

'We're dealing with a very volatile and devious bunch,' I said. 'Just look out for the Ashfordly car, please.'

Ten minutes went by; Mrs Pollard took another long swig from a bottle she pulled from her handbag, and she paraded before the admiring Liverpudlians to raucous guffaws and loud hand-clapping. Gordon, I felt, was very patient; his poor little wife spent her time in an embarrassed silence.

Eventually, above the heads of the crowd, I noticed the police car enter the village and glide smoothly along the street. I did not acknowledge it. From the corner of my eye, I saw Mary detach herself from a little mob and talk to Sergeant Bairstow, who then drove onwards and turned on to the garage forecourt. He vanished from view; Mary raised her hand and I recognised the signal.

'I'm just going over to the pub,' I called loudly to Gordon, 'won't be a tick. I want to check the buffet.'

He nodded, but the others who heard my words did not react.

I began to feel a little happier as I tapped on the front door which George had already locked, and he let me in.

'Can I use your phone please, George. It's important.'

'They're a rough bloody lot, Mr Rhea,' he said. 'We don't often see weddings like that here.'

'We don't George. Now, I'm going to prevent trouble – I hope.'

He led me to the telephone and I rang Aidensfield Garage, only a few yards up the street, and asked if Sergeant Bairstow was there. He was, and he was brought to the phone.

'PC Rhea,' I announced. 'Good morning, Sergeant.'

'What's all the fuss, Nick?' he laughed. 'I see you've got a right shower here today!'

'It's the bride's mother, a real troublemaker. She's going to stir up something . . . she's drinking herself into a stupor and it seems she intends wrecking the wedding reception; she'll get the backing of those louts for whatever she does. I fear for the reception. I've moved all the booze away.'

'And you want rid of the old lady?' he anticipated my request.

'Yes.'

'Any ideas?' he asked me.

'She's called Pollard, and she's one of a rough family clan from Liverpool. They're all villains, I reckon, and she's obviously the ring-leader.'

'Go on.'

'I thought about having her arrested for something, like suspicion of being wanted on warrant for non-payment of a fine, or anything. Conduct likely to cause a breach of the peace even. Just to keep her out of the way until the reception's over, and the bride's left for her honeymoon.'

'Very devious, young Nick, very devious and highly improper!'

'But very practicable and a means of preventing crime,' I retorted. 'If she stays, they'll do something bloody awful. She's out to make the groom suffer.'

'If we go in there, in uniform, to lift her, we'll start a riot!'

'I will bring her here, to the garage. All you do is take her away for a couple of hours.'

'You say this lot are the Pollards from Liverpool?' he said.

'Yes, Sarge.'

'Then they are a right set of villains. Right, Nick, you're on.'

I was surprised he knew of their reputation. I replaced the telephone and returned to the fray. There was more loud singing and bawdy shouting, and I saw Mrs Pollard stagger to one side as someone tried to dance with her in the street. I approached her.

'Mrs Pollard,' I whispered, 'I'm the best man.'

'I seen yer, mister best man . . .'

'We've arranged a special picture session for you, in colour,' I whispered. 'As a treat, for the bride's mum. But I don't want the others to know.'

'Colour? Me?' and she lifted her skirts to show off those green pantaloons.

'Sssh!' I hissed. 'Just come with me . . .'

She stooped low, as if ducking under low arches, and we crept away from the crowd; someone shouted after her, but she put her finger to her lips and indicated silence. The man withdrew, and I breathed a sigh of relief. The walk to the garage was about a hundred yards, and soon we were out of sight.

'It's a studio down here,' I said, clutching her arm.

I took her into the office of the garage, and there Sergeant Bairstow and PC Alwyn Foxton awaited.

'Jessie Pollard?' he asked, and the sight of the uniform sobered her immediately. I was surprised when he used her Christian name.

'Bastards!' she hissed. 'You bastards!'

'Jessie Pollard,' chanted Sergeant Bairstow, 'I am arresting you for failing to answer bail this morning, when you were ordered to appear today at Liverpool Magistrates' Court on a charge of shoplifting . . .'

Her reply was unprintable, and she fell to the ground, shouting and swearing, kicking her legs in the air and generally creating a mini-riot all of her own. But Sergeant Bairstow and Alwyn between them were able to cope, and bundled her into the rear seat of the two-door car then sped off in the opposite direction to avoid her family.

I returned to the gathering, and saw that the photographer was having some success. I waited until everyone had been pictured, and then shouted over their heads that it was time to eat.

It is not necessary to recount the progress of the reception, except to say that I stood before the gathering and apologised for the lack of alcohol by saying the hall was a temperance hall. The only alcoholic drinks permitted were those for the bride and groom. There was a lot of muttering and shuffling of feet, but as the reception got under way, the good food kept both sides happy.

I also announced the absence of the bride's mother by saying we had arranged a surprise for Mrs Pollard, a special photographic session in Malton, and so she could not attend the reception. Actually, it was true, because her photo would be taken in the cells. She might be back to see the departure of the bride and groom, I said, and everyone cheered. George's food was splendid, and the drinks he had supplied seemed to placate the turbulent crowd. The speeches were well received, and by two o'clock, it was time for the bride and groom to leave. Two o'clock was also the official closing time for the local pubs, and so another little crisis was averted. The pub was officially shut.

Gordon and his happy bride got away safely and I was pleased. Mrs Pollard's real moment of triumph, whatever it was going to be, had evaporated, and she spent the rest of the day in Malton Police Station awaiting an escort from Liverpool Police. She was not going to miss her court appearance a second time.

Two days later, when I saw Sergeant Bairstow, I said, 'Thanks for coming to the rescue, Sergeant. You saved the day.'

'No; thank you, Nick. That woman *was* wanted for jumping bail in Liverpool. She was Jessie Pollard.'

'Was she?'

'Not long before your wife rang with that weird message, we received a call from Liverpool to say she'd jumped bail. They knew she was attending her daughter's wedding somewhere near Ashfordly, and suggested we knock her off after the wedding. We checked with churches and register offices in the area, and the Aidensfield wedding was the only one. We were going to sit and wait until things were over, then move in and arrest her for Liverpool. She's a right villain, they say.'

'So if she had not jumped bail, you might not have come to my rescue?'

'That's an academic question, Nick old son,' he grinned.

But I wondered how many grooms had commenced their married life by getting their mother-in-law arrested.

9

'And they are gone; aye, ages long ago,
These lovers fled away into the storm.'
                        John Keats 1795-1821

Irene Hood was a shy, bespectacled girl of around nineteen
when I first became aware of her existence. She was not the
prettiest of young ladies but she had a lovely personality and
charming manners, each made more attractive by her modest
behaviour and quiet life-style.

Every morning, she would push her red pedal-cycle down
the grassy track beside the large house in Aidensfield where
she lived, and would ride along the leafy lanes to Maddleskirk
Abbey where she worked in the kitchens. I was never quite
sure what her duties were, but it was something fairly mundane
like looking after the vegetables and laying the tables for the
daily turn-over of 120 meals. This undemanding work kept
Irene content and her meagre earnings enabled her to buy
sufficient clothes for her needs, and helped her to maintain
her bicycle and save a little in the Post Office.

Her mouse-like existence came gradually to my attention;
sometimes when I was on early patrol, I would park my Francis
Barnett near the telephone kiosks either outside Maddleskirk
Abbey or near Aidensfield Post Office. If I chanced to be at
either place between twenty minutes to eight and ten minutes
to eight, I would see Irene on her polished bicycle heading
towards the Abbey.

In winter, she rode with her head down against the
fierce winds which drove through the valley, and she wore a

khaki-coloured anorak with a hood which concealed her face. On her feet would be sensible rubber boots and thick leggings, so that the figure beneath all this clothing remained rather a mystery.

By the time summer came, the same bicycle bore a young lady with short sandy hair, heavy spectacles and a working smock of dark green which covered sensible dresses and legs which wore thick brown stockings and flat shoes. The face beneath the spectacles was pale and slightly freckled, and she had grey/green eyes, nice sound teeth and, when the mood took her, a pretty smile.

Each working morning therefore she rode this cycle to work and each evening at four-thirty she rode it back to Aidensfield. My regular trips along the lane between the Abbey and Aidensfield made me aware of the girl's journeys, and I mentally logged this information as a piece of my growing store of local happenings, which might or might not one day be of value. At that stage, I did not know the girl's name, or where she lived.

As time went by, I sometimes noticed her pushing her cycle up the grassy path at the side of a long, low house built of brick. At the time this knowledge meant nothing to me, but as the weeks and months passed, I learned that the brick house was owned by a Miss Sadie Breckon, and that the quiet girl was Irene Hood, her niece.

At least, everyone said it was aunt and niece. Some persistent gossip hinted the girl was the natural daughter of Sadie Breckon, and that she had been adopted with a changed name for appearances' sake. Whatever the history of the two women, they kept themselves very much out of village activities, and Miss Sadie's only trips were to the post office for stamps and to the shops for her groceries. Where they bought things which would not be obtained in the village, no one knew, unless they resorted to catalogues for their clothes and furniture.

Sadie Breckon did not have a job, and I do not know how she supported herself; the house was huge and was probably paid for, but there were running expenses, rates and heating plus the day-to-day living costs of the two women it sheltered. Irene's income would barely support her, so I guessed that Sadie must have a private income.

Over the following months, I observed that young Irene had become unhappy. Although it is no part of a village policeman's duties to make unhappy girls happy I was a little concerned; my observations were born of regular sightings of the girl, and of the telling change in her facial appearance. Instead of the open, placid face I associated with my early sightings of Irene, there was now a morose appearance. I hoped it did not herald some unpleasant work for me – young girls with problems were liable to do awful things to themselves, but I felt Irene was too sensible to behave stupidly.

On several occasions, I passed her in the street when I was walking along the footpath. She would pass by with a sad smile, but would never speak unless I bade her 'good morning' or 'good afternoon'. Then she would smile her quick reply before scurrying off, head down, into Aunt Sadie's long brick house. I got the impression of a lonely, unhappy teenager.

I think it is fair to say that these observations were made in passing moments; they were fleeting impressions of a young girl without sex appeal. A mouse. Almost a nonentity. A girl who never mixed, and whose life-style behind those brick walls was of no interest to anyone. Probably, I would have forgotten all about Irene had it not been for Andrew Pugh.

Andrew drove the bread-van which called at the Abbey's kitchens every day around eight-thirty; it came from Scarborough on a regular run, and I used to see it entering Aidensfield, where it called at the shop, and then went along the lane towards Maddleskirk Abbey. I never had cause to talk to the driver or to become acquainted with him, and it was some time later that I learned of Andrew's name and job.

It seemed that after Andrew had unloaded a massive daily order of bread, teacakes and buns at the Abbey, he would chat to the shy girl who brewed him a quick coffee. That girl was Irene. From those morning chats there developed a stronger liaison, and it wasn't long before Irene found herself deeply in love.

Andrew, it seems, had also fallen head over heels in love with this shy country lass. She was so refreshingly different from the loud, forceful girls he knew at home, and he became spellbound with her calm face and smiling eyes. But he lived at Scarborough which was an hour's drive from Aidensfield. He did possess a motor-cycle, but that was not the solution to his problem. The snag was that Sadie wouldn't let Irene out of the house after work. If Andrew wanted to see her other than during his quick morning coffee break, he had to drive out of Scarborough on a Sunday morning and park in Aidensfield. He knew that Sadie and Irene walked side by side to the little Methodist chapel at 10.30 a.m. and back again at 11.30 a.m. each Sunday morning.

But cups of coffee in a monastery kitchen, and sly casts behind Aunty's back near the chapel railings, are no way to conduct a romance. This was the reason for Irene's misery. There must have been love if Andrew bothered to drive nearly forty miles on a Sunday morning for little more than a glimpse of his beloved in her best clothes.

I am not quite sure when I was made aware of these facts, but they are the kind of information that a village police officer assimilates during his day-to-day contact with the people. I had never been inside Sadie's large brick house, nor had I ever spoken to Aunt Sadie; indeed, other than my formal greetings on the footpath, I had never held a conversation with Irene.

And then, by one of those peculiar flukes of circumstances, two motor-cars collided in Aidensfield village street just as Sadie was heading towards the post office to buy some stamps. She saw everything, and one of the drivers had the foresight to take her name before reporting the accident to the police.

This singular act meant that I had to call upon Aunt Sadie to take a written statement from her. I needed her account of the accident because she was the only independent witness. As I walked up that grass path to the rear door of the long, interesting building, all these little facts of Irene's life registered in my mind.

It was a Tuesday evening when I knocked, a late spring evening with darkness yet to come. The back kitchen door needed a coat of paint; it was black and the old paint was peeling off; following my knock, I heard footsteps and Irene answered.

'Oh, hello,' I said in recognition. 'Is Miss Sadie Breckon in?'

'It's my aunt, I'll bring her,' and she dipped indoors in a trice, vanishing into the dark interior and leaving me on the stone doorstep.

Soon, the lady of the house arrived and smiled at me, albeit with some concern on her face.

'Miss Breckon?' I asked. 'Sadie Breckon?'

'Yes, is it about the accident?'

'It is,' I said. 'I believe you witnessed it.'

'Yes, I did. Come in. It's Mr Rhea, isn't it?'

'Yes, we haven't met,' and I stepped into the dark house, removing my cap as I did so, and then I shook hands with her. She led me through the back porch, where I noticed a stock of coal and Irene's bicycle. We entered an old-fashioned kitchen where there was a Yorkist range with a coal fire blazing cheerily in the grate. The timeless picture was completed by a kettle singing on the range, a floor of flagged sandstones and several clip rugs scattered about the room. It was like stepping back half a century or more, but the place was beautifully warm and snug.

I passed the scrubbed wooden table, stepped down into the next room and found myself in another old-fashioned area. There was an old horsehair settee, lots of rugs and plants about the place, and ancient pictures on the walls, many depicting long-dead ancestors. It was a veritable museum. Irene was standing in front of one of the chairs.

'This is my niece, Irene,' and I smiled at her.

'Yes, we pass each other most mornings, don't we, Irene? I'm pleased to meet you,' and the girl shook my hand delicately, her eyes not meeting mine as she blushed. Her cheeks turned a bright red and she knew this was happening, so she sat down and buried herself in a book.

'She reads a lot,' her aunt said. 'Romances, gothics, that sort of thing, filling her head with all kinds of notions.'

'There's not a lot for a young girl to do in the village,' I sympathised with Irene.

'They can get into trouble anywhere!' snapped the aunt, and I had no idea what lay behind that remark.

Now that we were in the room, as it was termed, she settled me on the horsehair settee and smiled. 'Well, tell me what you want to know, Mr Rhea.'

I reminded her briefly about the circumstances of the collision and she nodded in agreement. 'Yes,' she beamed. 'I saw everything. Such a silly man. I wrote his number down,' and she disappeared into an adjoining room to locate a piece of paper. I looked about the room and smiled at Irene who caught my eye with a shy glance before Aunt Sadie returned flourishing a piece of paper. It was a comparatively simple task to get the statement written down in chronological order, and she was quite happy to add her signature at its conclusion.

That short visit was my first to this strangely old-fashioned home, but it did enable me to speak to the shy girl whom I saw most mornings. Thereafter when she passed, she would hold her head high and smile at me, sometimes returning my wave of greeting. I did notice, on Sundays, the youth with the motor cycle who parked near the chapel railings, as the congregation left. Sometimes, I noticed the surreptitious glances or signs that passed between him and Irene, and felt sorry for the restricted life of this pleasant girl.

I had no idea how restricted it was until she halted one morning with tears in her eyes. I was sitting astride my machine, doing little more than while away five minutes before making a point at Maddleskirk Abbey telephone kiosk. Irene halted her bicycle in the manner adopted by so many lady riders – she didn't use the brakes, but allowed her left foot to scud along the ground until the bike was compelled to halt beside me.

I smiled.

'Good morning, Irene. How's that aunt of yours?'

I saw tears in the girl's eyes, and immediately wished I hadn't sounded so jovial.

'I don't care!' she said. Her calm face had a sullen pout and an air of utter misery.

'Something wrong?' I wondered why she had stopped to talk to me.

'I don't know who can help me,' she wept gently. 'I was always told by Aunt Sadie that policemen are there to help people . . .'

'Yes, we are. If it's something I can help with, I'll be only too pleased to listen. Do you want to talk here?'

'There's nowhere else.' She wiped a tear from her eye. 'Besides, I mustn't be late.'

'Well,' I spread my hands in a gesture of openness, 'here I am.'

'It's Aunt Sadie,' she said. 'She . . . well, Mr Rhea, she's so old-fashioned . . . you see, I have met this boy . . . and . . .'

I finished the sentence for her, 'And she won't let you meet him?'

Irene nodded.

I continued, 'Is that the young man who comes on a Sunday, with his motor-bike?'

'Yes, I'm not allowed out to meet him, you see, not at all, never. He sees me at work, when I make his coffee . . .'

She explained about the bread deliveries and I began to understand. She told of the tribulations in her sheltered life, and I felt very sorry for her. I began to wonder if Aunt Sadie was really the girl's mother, and whether Aunt Sadie had experienced some unfortunate love affair in her sheltered past . . . perhaps this was her way of protecting this quiet girl from a similar fate?

I listened carefully, and realised it was beyond my powers; although I had every wish to see this girl happy and content,

I felt it was not part of a policeman's duty to interfere with domestic arrangements. Yet I did not like to tell Irene this; she had come to me seeking help.

When she had finished her catalogue of sorrow, she said, 'And now, Mr Rhea,' then burst into a flood of tears, 'Andrew says he will not come to see me any more, not after chapel, and not for coffee . . . he'll bring a flask, unless I meet him after work, or take him home . . .'

'I can understand him saying that, Irene,' I said. 'He drives an awful long way just for a glimpse of you on Sundays, and if his only chat is over a quick coffee, with folks standing around, I'm surprised he's been so persistent and faithful to you. Many lads would have given up weeks ago.'

'Yes, I know, but he loves me, you see. He honestly does.'

'I don't doubt it for one minute, Irene. But have you told your aunt about him?'

'Told her? Oh, no, I daren't do that! She's never let me go out alone, and if she knew I had a boyfriend she might stop me going to work . . . she's very funny about boys . . .'

'You're telling me!'

'Mr Rhea, you must help me. Please. Can't you just ask her to let me see him?'

'It must have taken a lot of courage for you to approach me?'

'There's nobody at work, they'd just laugh at me. They don't understand. I thought about the minister at the chapel, but he's friendly with Aunt Sadie and, well, you are a policeman, aren't you?'

'Yes, I am.' I was thinking fast. 'Look,' I said, 'will you be at chapel this coming Sunday?'

'We never miss.'

'And Andrew? Can you persuade him to ride out once more?'

'I think so. Have you something in mind?'

'I was thinking. I have to see your aunt about a small query in that statement of hers. It's just a question of clarifying a small point. I could catch her outside the chapel on Sunday, and you could walk on and talk to Andrew. I'll discuss my point with her, and then I'll tell her what a nice lad you've found. I'll do my best to break the ice for you. How about that?'

Although my bland assurances cheered her immensely, I knew I was treading on very thin ice. If things went wrong, I could be blamed for all sorts, but I am a sucker for a pretty face with problems.

'Tell Andrew, won't you?' I said. 'If a policeman turns up when he's parked there, he might think he's going to get moved on or something. If he drives away, our plans will be ruined.'

She smiled and wiped away a tear. 'Yes, I'll tell him this morning.'

On Sunday, some twenty minutes before chapel was due to finish, I drove down the village in full uniform and parked near the railings. Andrew was already there. I removed my helmet, approached him and we shook hands. He impressed me as a very genuine lad, tall and confident with a head of carroty-coloured hair and a ready grin.

'Hello, you must be Andrew,' I said.

'And you are Mr Rhea. It's good of you to try this for us.'

'I only hope Aunt Sadie gives a little. You've an uphill battle there, young Andrew,' I warned him. 'She's a peculiar old thing, you know.'

'I know, Irene's told me all about her.'

I went over the plans and asked him to keep his fingers crossed. We occupied ourselves with small talk until the first of the congregation emerged. Aunt Sadie came out with Irene following closely, almost hiding herself as if to avoid the confrontation that must surely follow.

'Right, Andrew?'

'Yes, Mr Rhea,' and I walked away from him.

'Miss Breckon?' I called loudly for I wanted her to see me leaving this lad's presence; I wanted her to know I had been talking to him, the suggestion being that I knew him.

'Oh, Mr Rhea!'

'I'm sorry to bother you just after chapel, but I have a

small point to clarify in your statement. I have it here . . .' and I began to delve into my uniform pocket for the necessary papers.

Out of the corner of my eye, I saw Irene walk away from her aunt and move steadily towards the waiting Andrew. I kept her occupied. 'The problem is the car number you quoted,' I began. 'You said it belonged to the green Vauxhall, or the green car as you said, whereas both drivers state that the number you wrote down belongs to a tan car, a Hillman it was. Can we check it, please? You've got your piece of paper?'

This was the genuine enquiry which I was using to its ultimate; as I spoke, I saw Sadie's eyes follow Irene, so I said, 'I've just been talking to that young man. He's very nice and says he knows Irene from work.'

'She didn't tell me she knew any men!' she retorted.

'Oh, it's just an acquaintance,' I said. 'Do you mind if they chat while we check this number?'

She looked at Irene, now smiling at Andrew, and I knew I had confused her.

'Yes, you'd better come in, Mr Rhea. Irene,' she called, 'Dinner is at twelve.'

It was now half-past eleven. Was this a clear half-hour for Irene, or a reminder for the girl to come indoors and help with the preparation? But I strode inside with her and she had kept the piece of paper with the car number; it was tucked behind the tea caddy on the mantelpiece. She had written several snippets of information on it, and the car number was quite clearly recorded. It said 'green' beside it.

I saw Aunt Sadie screwing up her eyes as she tried to recollect the precise sequence of events, and she said, 'No, you are right, Mr Rhea. The word "green" refers to the driver's jacket. A green jacket, not a green car.'

'In that case, I'll need a supplementary statement to correct the first one. Can we do it now?'

She looked out of the window; Irene and Andrew were in full view; I had suggested this to him – 'Don't go out of her sight!' I'd warned him.

It took only five minutes to complete my formalities and I took my leave of her. The Sunday dinner was cooking and its lovely smell filled the kitchen.

'That smells good!' I said. 'You're making me feel hungry.'

'I believe in good food, Mr Rhea, and a good life,' at which she looked out of the window again.

'Miss Breckon,' I asked, following the line of her gaze, 'would you allow Irene to meet that boy again if she wanted?'

She looked at me steadily, and her eyes went moist, just a shade.

'If she must!' she stammered. 'But I want no trouble . . . none. Not from lads . . . I know what they can be . . .'

'Perhaps if he always came when you were here too . . .'

'Well, of course that would be all right. I mean, that's how things were done in the good old days, before all this permissiveness. Girls introduced their beaux to their parents and there were always chaperones on hand . . . besides, Mr Rhea, it is not the duty of a girl to invite a man to her home. It is the duty of the *man* to call and seek permission from the parents or guardians, if he wishes to escort a girl . . .'

'If that young man called here, could he walk in the village with Irene?' I put to her, surprised at her old-fashioned views.

'I should consider it, Mr Rhea,' she said pertly.

'You will not be angry with Irene for talking to him alone, now?' I asked, tongue in cheek.

'No, if that young man is an acquaintance at work, then it would be discourteous to ignore him. I can see they are behaving in a perfectly proper way, and I have no objections.' She spoke rather stiffly, I felt, as she paid great attention to the old-fashioned rules of courtesy.

'Shall I tell Irene to come in when I leave?' I asked.

'I think the young man should make himself known to me,' she stated. 'I think that is his primary duty.'

I wondered where she had unearthed these Victorian ideas, but it seemed she was agreeable to Irene's courtship in condition it complied with those outmoded guidelines. How on earth Irene was supposed to know those old rules, or how Andrew was supposed to equate with them, was something they would have to learn for themselves. But the ice had been broken.

I left the house and walked over to them. Both smiled at me, Irene with a definite look of apprehension on her face.

'She's fine,' I said, 'but she's living by some Victorian book of etiquette, I think. Andrew, this all depends on you. She will allow you to walk out with Irene, if you make a formal request. That means going to the house now, introducing yourself, and behaving like a gentleman of a bygone age. You must ask the guardian of Irene – that's Aunt Sadie – for permission to meet with her and walk with her. After that, you're on your own.'

'She'll see me now?' He seemed amazed.

'She's fine,' I said, 'but she's living in a different world from us. Once you can understand that, you'll get on with her. Right, get yourself over to that front door and tell Aunt Sadie who you are, where you are from, and tell her you'd like to escort Irene. That's how it used to be done.'

Irene smiled. 'Come along, Andrew, or should I call you Mr Pugh?'

'He's Mr Pugh for the time being!' I laughed, and left them to their new role. As I started my motor-cycle and turned it around, I saw them crossing the road towards Aunt Sadie's red-brick house.

Next time I saw Irene, she stopped her bicycle and smiled at me. She looked relaxed and happy.

'That Sunday, Mr Rhea, well, Aunt Sadie invited Andrew to stay for dinner. She allowed him to walk me up and down the village because he'd knocked on the door and asked. We had Sunday dinner together, with her as chaperone. It was quite nice, and we all went for a walk in the afternoon.'

'So she was better than you thought eh?'

'Mmm, much better. In fact, she's taken a liking to Andrew. He can come every Wednesday evening and Saturday evening to walk about, and we can meet after chapel on Sundays. She says he can have Sunday dinner with us and we walk out in the afternoon.'

'Well, let's hope things work out for you. You're lucky to find such a nice lad, Irene.'

'I know,' and she blushed as she remounted her trusty bicycle and pedalled off to work.

Over the following few months, everything seemed fine with Irene and Andrew. He did not object to his visits being arranged and supervised by the watchful Aunt Sadie, and seemed happy to accept this as a condition for seeing Irene. I did not visit the house any more, although I would have welcomed an opportunity to view the entire premises. It was more like a Victorian museum than a modern household and as I passed from time to time, I noticed the aspidistras in the windows, and a pair of green witch globes dangling from a curtain rail. Truly, it was a house of the past.

But if the house and Aunt Sadie were relics from a past age, Irene and Andrew wanted to live and love in accordance with the norms of the twentieth century. This must have presented considerable difficulties and I wondered if Aunt Sadie abided by the words of Robert Browning when he wrote, 'All's love, yet all's law.'

But if Aunt Sadie's strict rules about love frustrated their lives, I have no doubt that the happy pair were fortified by words from Sadie's own Bible which said, 'Many waters cannot quench love, neither can the floods drown it.'

As the weeks passed from spring into summer, their friendship and love grew stronger. The virile Andrew, who must have been a man of infinite love and patience, wanted to spend more time alone with his Irene. And Irene, being a blossoming girl, wanted to spend time alone with Andrew.

Aunt Sadie contrived to frustrate this event; she was a chaperone to beat all chaperones, one who could not be dodged or avoided, and one whose duties were clearly fixed in her old-fashioned head.

I wondered what the outcome would be; if Andrew had been any other modern youth, he would have ditched poor

Irene weeks ago, not because of the girl but because of the overbearing supervision from Sadie. But his love never faltered.

At least, not until one evening in late September.

It was quarter to ten and the night was dark with the onset of autumn; there was a definite chill in the air, and the leaves were beginning to flutter from the trees. It was a clear night, however, with a full moon and small white clouds puffing their way across the sky. It was, beyond doubt, a night for romance. As my clock struck quarter to ten that Wednesday evening, I pulled my crash helmet over my head and prepared for my final tour of duty, a motor-cycle patrol around my beat until 1 a.m. We called it half-nights; I'd been on duty since 5 p.m. and the patrol had been joyous, if peaceful and lacking in incident.

But as I made for the door after kissing Mary farewell, the telephone shrilled in the office. I hurried through, picked it up and heard the typical tones of a call from a kiosk. I waited as the caller pushed the money into the box. 'Aidensfield Police, PC Rhea,' I announced.

'Oh, Mr Rhea,' came the panting tones of a woman. 'It's my Irene and that Andrew, they've run away . . . you must find them . . . quickly.'

Although no name was given, I knew this was Miss Breckon and said,

'I'll be there in one minute,' and hurried from the house.

By the time I arrived at the curious house, she had returned from the kiosk and was waiting in the front doorway where she was framed in the light of the interior. She was wringing her hands and fidgeting with anxiety.

She did not speak as I followed her inside and closed the door.

'Thank goodness I caught you!' she panted. 'Really, those young people . . . they are trying . . . and I thought he was such a nice young man . . .'

I removed my crash helmet and tried to calm her. I sat on the horsehair settee, and my action caused her to settle in a chair opposite.

'Now, Miss Breckon.' I spoke slowly and looked carefully at her. 'Let's start from the beginning. What's all this about Irene running away?'

'They've gone . . . both of them . . . on his motor-bike . . .'

'When?' I asked.

'Just a few minutes ago . . .'

'Hold on,' I raised my hands, 'are you sure? Could they have gone for a spin in the moonlight? I see nothing sinister or worrying in a young man taking his girl for a motor-cycle ride.'

'No, no . . . no, it's not like that, Mr Rhea, you must believe me . . . they've run away . . .'

'Miss Breckon, Irene is not a juvenile any more, nor is Andrew. He's over twenty-one, and she is nineteen, and that means they can go for rides like this without the police being called in. If you're worried about her, then I could search – that's if you're really concerned for her safety, maybe thinking harm might befall her . . .'

I was trying in vain to make her understand that the police aren't concerned about girls of 19 having a quick cuddle or even going the whole way with their chosen boyfriends.

'No . . . no . . .' she was weeping now, 'they've run away . . .'

I paused, wondering what had prompted this drama, and said, 'Miss Breckon, what has happened?'

She did not reply immediately, but sat in the chair quietly allowing tears to run down her cheeks.

'They have run away,' she sniffed. 'She's gone . . .'

'Was there an argument?' I sensed an atmosphere; it was difficult to define but something had happened between Aunt Sadie and the youngsters. Maybe the long-suffering Andrew had cracked at last?

She hung her head a long time before answering this question, and her lack of response told me the truth. There had been a dispute of some kind.

Finally, she said, 'Yes, Mr Rhea. I did remonstrate with them.'

'And they walked out?'

'Yes, and they went off on his motor-cycle.'

'Can I ask what the argument was about?'

'I caught them misbehaving, Mr Rhea, in this house! I will not tolerate such behaviour, and I told them in no uncertain terms . . . there are standards . . .'

I held up my hand. 'Just a moment, how were they misbehaving?'

'I caught them in an embrace, kissing one another . . .'

'Go on.' I wanted to hear this. It looked as if Andrew hadn't wasted his opportunity.

'Well, he came into the house this evening, Mr Rhea; he asked if he could speak to me and I allowed him in, in spite of the lateness of the hour.'

'And then?'

'He asked if he could take Irene home to meet his parents, on Sunday afternoon after chapel. He proposed to pick her up on his machine, take her to Scarborough for Sunday dinner, and return her in the early evening . . .'

'I think that is a perfectly normal thing – and it was good of him to seek your permission.'

'Well, Irene's never been to a big city like Scarborough . . . anyway, Mr Rhea, I had once been to Scarborough, long ago, and my mother had some photographs of me near the Spa. I wanted them to see me there. Well, I went upstairs to find the album and in those few moments, he and Irene . . . well . . . they kissed and embraced . . .'

'And you were angry?'

'I felt insulted; I felt let down. The moment my back was turned they started misbehaving . . .'

'This is not misbehaving in a modern society.' I tried to explain but knew it was useless. 'Anyway, what happened?'

'Well, as I remonstrated with them, Andrew grabbed his things and rushed out, saying I was a stupid old woman . . . and Irene ran after him . . . then they disappeared on his bike and . . .' She burst into a fit of sobbing. I felt sorry for her although this was of her own making.

'Miss Breckon,' I said firmly, 'domestic disputes of this

kind are not a police matter. You ought to know that. Irene is old enough to go out with boys and I know she's a sensible girl and that she won't let you down . . .'

'She has . . . she kissed that . . . that horrible youth . . .'

I ignored this remark, as I continued, 'But because of your concern, I will radio my Control Room and ask our patrols to look out for Andrew's motor-bike. It can't be far, and I will ask him to bring Irene back. The radio is on my motor-cycle outside.'

I had little hope of finding Andrew and Irene, for it was impossible to know where they'd gone, but miracles do sometimes happen and within half an hour, the radio on my motor-cycle alerted me and I responded. I learned that Andrew had been traced to a fish-and-chip shop in Eltering, but Irene was not with him. According to him, she had not left on his motor-cycle; that was the message I received, and Control Room said that Andrew was now heading back to Aidensfield. The drama had produced an unexpected twist.

'This alters things, Miss Breckon,' I said. 'If she's not with Andrew, where is she?'

Her answer came in a flood of tears. 'I don't know, I don't know . . . I thought she'd gone with him . . . they went out . . . tore out . . . and I heard the motor-bike go . . .'

This put me in something of a dilemma. All kinds of possibilities flashed through my mind – was Irene bent on committing suicide? Or was she running headlong into the night? Or had she gone for a quiet think somewhere? Maybe there was a friend in the village she wanted to talk to? What had been the last words between Andrew and herself? Should I begin a localised search, or did the circumstances justify a full-scale hunt? Girls in love were prone to acting in odd ways. The answer was that I did not know what to do – I believed she would return if we left her alone, but I could be wrong. There were so many imponderables.

'I think I'd better wait for Andrew,' I decided. 'I must hear what happened between them after they left the house.'

'You don't expect me to welcome that man back into my

house, after desecrating my niece, do you?' Her eyes flashed at me.

'I'll speak to him outside,' I made a rapid compromise.

There followed an embarrassing silence, so I went outside and sat upon the saddle of my stationary motor-cycle to await the return of Andrew Pugh. This also gave me the advantage of being able to look up and down the village street in case Irene decided to reveal herself before coming home.

The door remained open, and I could hear occasional movements of Miss Breckon inside, but she never emerged to enlighten me further about the events which precipitated this action. After nearly half an hour, Andrew arrived and parked near me. He hurried over, obviously very worried and said, 'What's happened, Mr Rhea? The policeman said Irene had run away.'

'We thought she was with you,' I said.

'Did she say that?' and he pointed at the house.

'She thinks it is true.' I spoke in defence of Miss Breckon.

'Silly old besom!' he spat. 'I've never come across anybody like her, honest. I lost my rag, Mr Rhea.'

'What happened? Can you throw any light on it for me? It might help us to find Irene. Where in the name of God do we start to look? I just don't know.'

'Well.' He put his crash helmet on the tank of my motor-cycle, and loosened his jacket. 'You know what she's like?'

'I do,' I sympathised.

'I wanted to ask Irene over to our house next Sunday, so I knocked on the door and was invited in. So far so good. When I got on about Scarborough, she said she loved Scarborough and wanted to show us – me and Irene that is – some photos she'd had taken there years ago. So she went upstairs to find them. Well, Mr Rhea, I mean, that was the first time . . . the first bloody time we'd been alone . . . so I gave Irene a cuddle and a kiss. You know, arms around her waist and a kiss on the lips . . . she responded . . . we've been waiting for bloody weeks for just a few minutes like that, alone . . .'

'And she caught you?'

'She's drilled bloody holes through the floor boards, Mr Rhea! Just you have a look. In that room, that living room ceiling which is all beams and floor boards, there's bloody great holes drilled through. Peep holes, all over, so anybody up there can peep down . . .'

'You saw them?'

'I did! She had the light on up there, seeking her photos, and I looked up and caught her . . . I saw this beady bloody eye staring down at us, and so I gave her the old two-fingers and gave Irene a right bloody snog!'

I laughed. 'You're not serious, Andrew?'

'Just you have a look next time you go into the room.'

'What happened then?'

'Well, she came storming downstairs and went berserk. She accused me and Irene of being immoral, said Irene was a slut and sex-mad and, well, I thought she'd blown a gasket. I lost my rag; I said I was standing no more of this and stormed out. I got on the bike, revved up and cleared off.'

'And Irene?'

'I dunno. I thought she'd be kept in.'

'You didn't look behind as you left?'

'Not likely. I was going to write to Irene, or see her in the kitchens tomorrow, just to say I loved her . . . but that silly old . . .'

'That's a new one on me,' I said, 'spy holes in the floor, but it seems Irene ran out after you. Obviously she didn't catch you and the old lady thought you'd both run off. Now, Andrew, think hard. Did you and Irene talk about anything that might give us a clue where to look?'

He thought hard. 'We talked about going for walks in the woods,' he said, 'if we were allowed to be alone. But wherever we went, away from the house, Aunt Sadie came. We talked about going walking alone, Mr Rhea, or going for a day out somewhere, like Whitby or across the moors.'

'Did she know any walks in this area?'

'Oh yes, apparently when she was little, she and Aunt Sadie

would spend hours walking the woods and fields.'

'Had she a favourite?'

'Yes,' he pondered, 'yes, now you mention it. There's a place called Lover's Leap, where you can sit on a bench and look down a cliff into the river . . . apparently two lovers jumped off long ago . . .'

'God!' I swore. 'Andrew, could she have thought you were running out on her? I mean you roared off . . . leaving her to face Aunt Sadie . . . Now, if she thought you'd given her up . . .'

'Where is this place?' he cried.

'I know it. Start your bike – I'll come with you on the pillion. I'll tell Sadie to stay here with the door open, in case Irene comes home.'

Minutes later, we were bumping along the footpath which ran beside the river, rising through the dense woodland with its beeches and oaks, and all the time keeping our eyes open for the fleeing girl. Andrew's driving was skilful on very narrow and difficult terrain, and his headlight picked out the trees, the rocks, the tumbling river with its rapids and black whirlpools. We did not speak, except when I guided him left or right as we roared towards the towering cliff known as Lover's Leap.

'There she is!' Suddenly, I could see her on the rustic seat which overlooked the ravine through which the river ran.

'Irene!' Andrew shouted. 'It's me . . .'

I don't know whether she could hear his voice above the roar of the river or whether the noise of the oncoming motor-cycle unsettled her, but she stood up and began to walk towards the edge of the cliff.

'God Almighty!' he shouted, accelerating wildly. 'Look at her! Irene!'

Seconds later, he swept to a standstill before Irene, who stood in the moonlight in her summer dress with tears streaming down her face.

'Go!' I hissed in his ear. 'I'll look after the bike.'

I saw her fall into his arms as I kept my distance.

'I'll see you two back at the house,' I said, turning Andrew's motor-bike around. 'It's a good hour's walk if you take your time.'

And I drove away.

Back at the house, Aunt Sadie emerged when she heard the motor-cycle, and showed surprise when I clambered from it. I went indoors, and closed the door behind me.

'We've found her, and she's fine,' I told her. 'She's walking back with Andrew; they'll be about an hour. She'd gone for a long think about things.'

'Is she all right?' was her first question.

'Yes, she's fine,' I was pleased to tell her.

She walked into the living room and I found myself looking at the ceiling. Half-inch holes had been drilled through the floor boards in dozens of places, each giving a sneak view of anything that occurred below. She saw me examining them and began to cry.

'Andrew told me about the upset,' I said gently.

'I . . . it wasn't me . . . I didn't put those holes there,' she said. 'My mother did. She drilled them to spy on me . . . and . . . I daren't bring boyfriends in . . . she watched us . . . and . . . well, it made me go all secretive . . . and . . .'

'You rebelled and have regretted it ever since?' I said.

'Mr Rhea, I'm sure you must know that Irene is my daughter, born late in life . . . I knew nothing of life . . .'

'But Irene will head the same way if you force her. You must see that . . .'

'I do, I do . . . I'm trying to protect her, and I do love her so, and don't want to see her harmed . . .'

'Then trust her. You've got to win back her trust, haven't you, after tonight? She is a lovely girl, and she loves you,' I said. 'Now, she has found a boyfriend in a thousand, a real nice boy. Don't let her lose him, Miss Breckon. Let her go to Scarborough for Sunday lunch; let him stay here one weekend . . . trust, Miss Breckon. It's needed on both sides. It is cruel not to trust,' I added, dragging part of a quote from Shakespeare to the forefront of my mind.

I remained with her, drinking a welcome cup of tea, until I heard the youngsters outside.

'It's time for me to go,' I said. 'Welcome them back, show them *both* you love them. Andrew is right for her, Miss Breckon, I'm sure of it.'

'He's good for us both, Mr Rhea.' She escorted me to the door, smiling, and opened her arms to welcome the young lovers.

Constable
on the Prowl

1

'Good things of day begin to droop and drowse,
While night's black agents to their prey do rouse.'
William Shakespeare – 'Macbeth'

For the police officer, night-duty is a time to reflect upon his duties, to ponder upon the meaning of life and to assess the value of the police service as a career. Alone in the midnight hours with nothing but dead leaves, stray cats and legends of ghosts and ghoulies to accompany him, the police officer goes about his multifarious tasks unseen and upraised. In his solitude, he deals with all manner of incidents and problems, and there is no one to thank him or console him, although if he errs in the smallest way, it can be guaranteed that someone will see him and report his misdemeanour to a higher authority.

Alternatively, the witness will write to his local newspaper about the reduction in police standards or the lack of internal discipline within the Force. This area of injustice is stoically accepted by members of the Force. Perhaps they know the writings of 'Junius' (*circa* 1770) who said, 'The injustice done to an individual is sometimes of service to the public.'

With such dangers at the back of his mind, it is fair to say that every police officer is nurtured upon a diet of nights. In police jargon, Nights is that period of eight agonising hours which stretch interminably from 10 p.m. until 6 a.m., or in some areas from 11 p.m. until 7 a.m. Sometimes the duty is worked a week at a stretch; on other occasions it is worked by performing two Nights, followed by two Late Turns (2 p.m. until 10 p.m.) and then three EarlyTurns (6 a.m. until 2 p.m.).

This involves 'quick changeovers' when one seldom seems to sleep between those spells of bleary-eyed periods of work.

Some police forces try to ease the eternal lack of sleep by starting with Early Turn, then going on to Nights and finishing with Lates. Then there is the sequence Nights, Early, Late or even Late, Early, Nights or in fact any other combination, all of which are designed to ensure the maximum of work is crammed into the shortest period of time with a minimum of hours wasted in sleep.

Another attempt to baffle the policeman's sleeping routine is Half Nights. This is the period of eight hours from 6 p.m. until 2 a.m., or from 5 p.m. until 1 a.m. This duty is often welcomed during a period of full nights because it enables at least some of the night to be spent in bed and is therefore considered a perk or even a devious way of saying 'thank you' for some obscure task, well performed.

Many youngsters start their police career by working three weeks of full nights, broken only by a rest day or two somewhere during that torturous spell. This first session is a long and extremely exhausting affair because sleep patterns of many normal years are interrupted and the constable's endurance is tested by the requirement to remain awake, or at least to have the appearance of remaining awake, in spite of crushing weariness and sore feet. By the onset of Night No 3 the policeman's sleep pattern has adjusted reasonably well to the demands placed upon it. One of these demands is the ability to eat breakfast at 2 a.m., followed by another at 6 a.m. which ought, in the strictest of sequences, to be called lunch, but which never is. There is little wonder that police stations reverberate with strange gastronomic sounds at such mealtimes – stomachs do need to protest from time to time.

A period of sleep follows a night-duty and this lasts until around two or three in the afternoon, which is a time free to bathe one's feet and have a nap. By nine o'clock in the evening, it is back into uniform for a rapid supper. Sandwiches are collected and a flask is filled with hot liquid like coffee, tea or soup, then it's off to the station to parade at 9.45 p.m. in readiness for another period of lucernal duty.

By the time the officer has totally adjusted to his changed bodily rhythms it is time to have a day off. It is then necessary to readjust to a sort of normality, a task which is not difficult after only two or three nights but which is nigh impossible after a long, breaking-in spell of three weeks. Jet-lag has nothing on this period of readjustment, for it requires a total rethink on teeth-cleaning routines and toilet necessities, all aggravated by weakening torch batteries and the absence of all-night torch battery emporiums.

If this long enforced spell of somnambulism appears to be futile, it does have a purpose. The idea is to allow the budding constable to become properly acquainted with his beat before he is turned loose on an unsuspecting public in the full glare of British daylight. It is reasoned that in the wee small hours of the morning he can potter about the town, often accompanied by a seasoned local officer, to learn all about vulnerable properties, to discover places where cups of tea can be obtained at any hour of the night, to know which bakers use police officers to test the quality of their buns and to locate shops which offer discounts. There is the added bonus of discovering windows at which attractive ladies undress without curtains. It is also advantageous to be shown hiding-places where the sergeant never looks, along with a host of other useful information. A lot of experience is gained on night-duty. It is the foundation of future bobbying.

After the introductory term, the young officer is turned out to face his public with his training-school confidence either pleasantly consolidated or totally shattered by the experiences of those three weeks.

It is of such experiences that I now write, for this part of the book relates some incidents which have occurred during prowling periods of night-duty.

I feel that it is prudent from the outset to state that the term 'night' is of considerable academic interest to the prowling police officer. It has so many different meanings within the law of England, many of which affect the performance of the bobby's duty. Although the law has dramatically changed since my early days in the Force, the definition of 'night' continues to be interesting.

I first learned of the legal intricacies of 'night' at my Initial Training Centre where, by flicking through my official issue of *Moriarty's Police Law* I learned that there were several definitions of 'night'; they were as follows:

Night – arrest; Night – billiards; Night – burglary ; Night – disguised with intent; Night – dogs; Night – larceny; Night – lights on vehicles; Night – loitering; Night – malicious damage; Night – offences; Night – old metal dealers; Night – poaching; Night – spring guns, etc; Night – walkers; and Night – refreshment houses. The problem was that the word 'night' bore little resemblance to our night-duty times and indicated something different in most of the indexed cases. In addition, there were other 'nights' like Night – arrest for indictable offences; Night – cafés, offences in; Night – employment; Night – work (women) and finally, as if to clarify it all, an entry entitled Night – meaning of.

For example, 'night' for the purpose of the convention concerning the night work of women employed in industry, meant a period of at least eleven consecutive hours, including the interval between ten o'clock in the evening and five o'clock in the morning. Under the Larceny Act of 1916 then in force, but now superseded by the Theft Act of 1968, the term 'night' meant the interval between 9 p.m. in the evening and 6 a.m. the following day. In those days, an offence committed during the night-hours was considered infinitely more serious than a similar one committed during the daytime, consequently lots of officers patrolled the streets in case something fearsome occurred and lots of emphasis was placed upon things which might go wrong in the night. The officers had to know how to cope with anything that might arise, be it a domestic disturbance between man and wife or an aircraft crash upon the town.

Typical of the things learned was that a licensee with a billiards table must not allow anyone to use a table or instrument between 1 a.m. and 8 a.m., a provision made under the Gaming Act of 1845. Another learnèd gem was that burglary was a crime which could be committed only between 9 p.m. and 6 a.m.; if it occurred at any other time it was known as housebreaking, shopbreaking or by some other suitably descriptive name. The same period of night, 9 p.m. until 6 a.m., was also featured in the Larceny Act for many offences, including the famous Four Night Misdemeanours. These were:

1. Being found by night in any building with intent to commit felony therein;
2. Being found by night and having in his possession without lawful excuse any key, picklock, crow, jack, bit or other implement of housebreaking.
3. Being found by night armed with any dangerous weapon or instrument with intent to break into a building and commit felony therein;
4. Being found by night having his face blackened or disguised with intent to commit a felony.

For the purpose of keeping dogs under control, the period 'night' meant the period between sunset and sunrise, while the laws governing lights on vehicles determined that 'night' comprised the hours of darkness which were specified as the time between half-an-hour after sunset until half-an-hour before sunrise, although under a 1927 Act, it meant, during summertime, the period between one hour after sunset and one hour before sunrise in any locality. The reporting of offenders under such a multiplicity of rules could be hazardous although we were helped by a High Court case in 1899 (*Gordon v. Caun*) which determined that sunset meant sunset according to local, not Greenwich, time.

So many references to 'night' meant that all manner of juicy crimes could be committed, many of which gloried in the realm of felony. A felony was A Most Serious Matter, like *entering* a dwelling-house in the night or *breaking* into homes which was called burglary. It was felonious to lie or loiter in any highway, yard or other place during the night. Other Less Serious Matters, known as Misdemeanours, included old metal dealers who were convicted of receiving stolen goods, making purchases between 6 p.m. and 9 a.m., and prostitutes or night-walkers loitering or importuning in any street.

In addition, there were those villains who set spring-traps to catch humans, although at that time, the 1950s, it was not illegal to set them between sunset and sunrise if it was done to protect one's dwelling-house. Non-licensed refreshment houses must not be kept open between 10 p.m. and 5 a.m., while pubs were subjected to a whole host of rules which we had to memorise.

With all this potential illegal activity, it follows that night-time patrols were full of interest, although it ought to be said that the interesting things were rarely related to any of these statutes. Most of them had grown seriously out of date during the first half of the twentieth century and were ignored to a large degree. None the less, they did exist and they were the law.

Having studiously learned all the necessary definitions of 'night', and having calculated when one was supposed to be on duty, we were exhorted to go out and fight crime. A suitable town was selected by Headquarters, one which was deemed ideal for the operational birth of a budding bobby and it was to such places that we were dispatched. There were several suitable towns in the North Riding of Yorkshire and the one selected as my tutorial community was Strensford. To this peaceful place I was dispatched to quell riots, solve crimes, arrest burglars, catch rapists and report cyclists without lights. It was my time of learning, my period of studying police procedures and of learning the craft of bobbying from seasoned men. It was also a time to appreciate some of the dilemmas into which members of the public managed to get themselves.

No policeman ever forgets those first faltering steps of nights. If there is a time when the public is at its most vulnerable, it is during the hours of darkness, or between sunset and sunrise, or between the period half-an-hour before sunset until half-an-hour after sunrise.

Having been posted to Strensford, I began to learn the craft of being cunning. I began to fearlessly shake hands with door-knobs and learned how to make use of the shadows to conceal myself from everyone, including the sergeant. Hiding from the sergeant was considered good sport, particularly when it was possible to observe him seeking ourselves. Strensford taught me a lot.

I learned never to put my weight upon a door-knob when trying it for security. It could be guaranteed that that particular door was insecure and that it would pitch me headlong into the shop, to land in a tub of rotting tomatoes or a pile of ovenware or other noisome paraphernalia. The alarm created in the bedrooms of nearby slumbering members of the public can easily be imagined, so door-knobs were treated with respect. Back doors were treated with even greater respect because they were frequently left open by shopkeepers or their staff as they rushed home at 5 p.m., trusting to God and the patrolling policeman to save a lifetime's work from opportunist villains. Some door-knobs abutted the street and they were simple to cope with; others were in deep recesses where many a courting couple has disturbed a policeman going about his legitimate business. Some were along paths or alleys and others up rickey steep stairs. One could almost write a 'Constable's Guide to Door-Knobs' after contending with such a range.

The idea of this twice-nightly friendship ritual with door-knobs (once before the meal break and once afterwards) coupled with an examination of windows, was to make sure no one had been burgled. All 'property' as we termed it, must be 'tried'. That was our main role during the night, while the supervisory sergeant surreptitiously prowled in our wake to check that none of us omitted to discover unlocked shops or attacked premises. If we did miss a knob, we were in trouble, although it did occur to me that if the sergeant tried all the knobs in the town, why did we bother? It seemed such an elementary question that I was terrified to ask it in case the answer made me appear a naïve fool.

If we found an insecure place, we had to enter it and face the unknown foe inside. Biting our chin-straps to silence rattling teeth and in pitch darkness, we must search the place for villainous felons, or people with faces blackened by night and other evil creatures. God knows what we would have done if we'd found anyone!

Having found no one, and having noted that the exposed stock appeared untouched, we had then to make our way, on foot, to the office to discover the name of the keyholder. The next stage was to drag him from his bed with the news that he'd almost lost everything that was dear to him.

Some keyholders appeared to relish being knocked up at all hours because they regularly left open their shops, pubs, banks, offices or clubs. For others, however, the appearance of a cold, grim-faced constable at their door at three in the morning was enough to ensure they locked up in future. Others couldn't understand why we didn't simply drop the latch ourselves instead of making such a fuss. Such an action could be fraught with danger. If something had been stolen and its absence discovered after the policeman's visit, all sorts of accusations would be levelled at the patrolling bobby. There are plenty of unsavoury types all too eager to concoct stories too; so we checked insecure premises very thoroughly in the presence of some responsible person.

The simplest way to complete one's allocation of property each night was to ignore it entirely and curl up for a sleep in a telephone kiosk. There were officers who were very able at this; many equipped themselves with portable alarm-clocks to rouse them from their cramped slumbers, happy in the knowledge that the sergeant would make the tour and find all the insecure properties. It meant a lot of telling off but it saved a lot of boot leather, torch batteries and leg ache. Some dedicated constables went on night-duty armed with reels of black cotton. Having checked a property for secure doors and windows, these cotton-toting constables would fasten a length of cotton about chest or knee height across the path or doorway. Any intruder would break the strand, the logic being that the second tour of one's property would not involve extensive walking along paths and through gardens. It would comprise nothing more than shining a torch upon selected pieces of black cotton. If the cotton was broken, someone had been. The trouble was that it might have been the sergeant, it might have been legitimate visitors or it might have been a villain. There was no way of telling, so I did not rely upon the black cotton syndrome. Besides, it was not the easiest of tasks, finding black cotton at night.

One of my tutorial sergeants at Strensford had a nasty habit of finding properties open in advance of the patrolling constable. He would then sit in them, secretly, until the arrival of the policeman. If the policeman diligently found the insecurity, praise was heaped upon his shining cap, but if he did not find it, he was in dire trouble for neglect of duty. It rapidly became obvious when sarge was playing his game because no one saw him around the town. Sometimes, he did not turn up at the station for his mid-shift mealbreak, so we knew he was sitting in a shop, waiting to pounce.

If that was his contribution to crime prevention, ours was equally good. Whenever he was in charge, we would hurry around our beats to check those properties we knew were most vulnerable or in the hands of careless owners. If we found an insecure or open door which had not been burgled or forced, we did not action it immediately. We left it alone.

Sarge would potter along to find the self-same door some time later and would disappear inside to begin his constable-catching vigil. He failed to realise that we knew he was there. We would leave him there until shortly before six o'clock in the morning, when one of us would return to the premises and 'find' the security. Did he praise us? Not on your life; we got a bulling for being late in making the find, but he gradually got the message. After sitting alone all night among objects like sausages, ladies' knickers, fruit, pans and antiques, he decided there were better ways of passing the time.

Another valuable lesson during those early weeks in the Force was the art of concealment at night. The dark uniform lent itself to invisibility and it was easy to stand in the shadows to watch the world pass by. At night, policemen walk along the inner edges of footpaths, close to the walls in order to be unseen, while shop doorways possess excellent concealment properties, as do areas beneath trees and shrubs.

When concealed, it is necessary to pass messages to one another and in those days before we had personal radio sets, lots of unofficial messages were passed with the aid of our torches. One's colleagues would stand in the shadows and announce the pending arrival of the sergeant, inspector or superintendent, or the movements of a suspected person or indeed anything else, merely by flashing a torch. We had a code of flashes for supervisory officers – one for a superintendent which represented the solitary crown of rank upon his shoulder, two for an inspector and his pips, and three for a sergeant with his stripes. Coded messages of this kind could be passed silently over very great distances and we would sometimes take advantage of the reflections in shop windows. This allowed us to pass messages around corners.

All this could be achieved while remaining invisible. In fact, the simple act of standing still often renders a policeman invisible and I've known persons stand and talk to one another literally a couple of feet from me, totally unaware of my eavesdropping presence. That's not possible in a panda car.

It was considered great sport to conceal oneself in a darkened doorway along the known routes of gentlemen who walked home late at night, having been on the razzle or having supped late in a friendly pub. As the pensive gent wandered slowly along his way, the amiable neighbourhood constable would step silently from the shadows immediately behind him and in a loud voice bid him 'GOODNIGHT'. This had the remarkable effect of speeding him along his journey with hairs standing erect and icicles jangling down his spine. The long-term effect was to make him change his route or abandon his lonesome trails.

Once I unwittingly scared the pants off a late reveller. It was a cold, freezing night and my feet were like blocks of ice. About two in the morning I decided to get a little relief by sitting on one of those large metal containers which house the mechanical gadgetry of traffic lights and which are invariably painted green. The containers are about four feet high and rather slender, so I hoisted myself on to the box and sat there, my large cape spreading from my shoulders and concealing the top of this convenient seat. As I perched there, hugging myself for warmth, along came a late-night reveller, singing gently to himself as he came towards me. It was clear he did not know I was there, and he almost ran into me.

I said from a great height, 'Goodnight.'

His glazed eyes raised themselves suddenly to heaven and in a beery breath he cried, 'God Almighty, a bloody bat!' and burst into a staggering gallop. I felt sure he would be sober when he arrived home.

One indispensable accessory to the art of performing night-duty in those stirring times at Strensford, was the Clock. Whether or not the system applied to every police station, or whether it was unique to my first nick, I do not know. It was undoubtedly a very cunning and complicated fabrication where time was altered with the twofold intention of baffling the bobby and thwarting the thief.

The Clock operated as follows. As I have already mentioned, policemen did not possess personal radio sets at that time. Having left the cosy warmth of the police office, they were effectively out of range of patrolling supervisory officers. Furthermore, if anything happened, the constable could not be contacted and dispatched to the scene of any incident. As we had no luxurious methods of communication like police boxes with direct lines to the station, we made use of public telephone kiosks.

We would stand outside selected kiosks at given times, there to await the arrival of a sergeant or a telephone call announcing that horrific things had happened and that our presence was immediately required. We had to stand outside those red-painted boxes for five minutes every half-hour of an eight-hour shift, moving from one to another in a monotonous, regulated sequence – GPO Kiosk, Fishmarket Kiosk, New Quay Kiosk, Golden Lion Kiosk, Laundry Kiosk, GPO Kiosk again . . . and so on. These five-minute waiting periods were known as 'points'.

The situation was that no one dare miss a point. Even if something catastrophic occurred, one must never miss a point – exciting crime inquiries were abandoned for the sake of making points, gorgeous blondes were not chatted up due to the fear of missing points, valuable clues were not examined in case we missed our points. The making of points dominated our lives.

The method of patrolling a beat was therefore along well-trodden paths between points. The town was divided into several beats, each of which had a different combination of available kiosks, with points at differing times. When lots of bobbies were on duty with their points staggered around the Greenwich clock, a policeman could be contacted fairly quickly. A plethora of bobbies might, in a speeded-up film sequence, be seen to be whizzing across one another's paths but never quite making contact. It wasn't a bad system really, but it had one shocking weakness.

If a policeman was at any kiosk at exactly the same time every day then the burglars, housebreakers, robbers, rapists and other sundry rogues would get to know this. They would know the movements of the local constabulary and, having worked out their timings and movements, would perpetrate their foulest deeds while we were busy making points. That was the flaw.

The Clock was therefore designed to beat the villains – it would baffle the burglar, harry the housebreaker and rattle robbers and rapists.

The Clock itself was a circular wooden board attached to the wall of the Charge Office. It was marked with numerals taken from a police uniform and they were spaced around its outer circumference in exactly the same way as the face of a genuine clock, reading from 1 to 11, and with zero where 12 would normally be. The Clock had a solitary pointer which could be moved around the face to indicate one of the aforementioned numbers.

Thus the pointer might indicate five, ten, fifteen, twenty and so forth up to fifty-five minutes. In addition, all officers were supplied with a little book containing the dates of every month. Beside each date was a figure from the face of the Clock. Thus on 10 January the Clock might show twenty. On 26 February it might show five, and so on, for every day of the year, including leap years. It didn't really matter what it showed, so long as everyone knew and worked on the same basis, hence the explanatory book.

If the Clock showed five on a particular day it meant that all points were five minutes later than scheduled. Thus a 12 noon point shown at the GPO Kiosk would be made at 12.05 p.m. If the Clock showed fifty-five, the point would be made at 12.55 p.m., fifty-five minutes late.

When beginning a tour of duty, therefore, it was vital to check the Clock and to make a note of its reading in one's notebook. The sergeant would then allocate us our beats and off we'd go. This meant an entry into one's notebook and in one's memory bank that one was working No. 6 Beat with points normally at quarter to and quarter past the hour, but with today's Clock at fifty-five.

Sometimes beats were worked in reverse. The Clock would also be given a minus quality. Working a beat backwards with the Clock on minus ten was an hilarious affair, especially when everyone else was working his beat in the normal sequence with the Clock on plus five.

If the system was designed to baffle the burglar, it did not succeed because the burglar never got the chance to study the sequence of our beats anyway. They were never fully manned. In the Clock's favour, it certainly confounded the unfortunate office-bound constables who spent their time ringing telephone kiosks in the hope that someone might answer. There were times when the whole town was alive with the sound of bells and many a worker has risen early, thinking his alarm was sounding. And many a citizen has answered the telephone to find a puzzled policeman at the other end asking if he, the citizen, could see a policeman nearby. Policemen are never around when they're wanted.

In fact, it was probably this system which gave rise to that popular legend when in truth, the policemen couldn't find a policeman when they wanted one.

It was with such a wealth of experience in the art of working nights that I was posted to Aidensfield which was considered a progressive station because it did not operate the Clock.

My arrival in this lovely village coincided with that period of change between the old and the new so far as village bobbies were concerned. The old idea had been to place the bobby on a rural beat and let him work the patch at his own discretion. He was never off duty and no one bothered whether or not he worked a straight eight-hour shift. He did his job as he saw fit; if he fancied digging the garden one afternoon then that was fine so long as he coped with any incident that arose.

I came to Aidensfield at the end of that casual but effective era, for the new idea was that even country bobbies should patrol for an eight-hour day on set routes. If anything cropped up after those eight hours or before they began, the duty of attending to it would be passed to another officer who was patrolling the district. That's if he could be found . . .

The result was that, along with my colleagues, I had to work night-duty shifts in a rural area. This was not a very frequent occurrence, certainly not as often as one week in three, the system to which I had become accustomed at Strensford. On average, it worked out that I patrolled a full week of nights once in every seventeen weeks during my term at Aidensfield. One advantage was that instead of using the motor-cycle, I was allowed the luxury of a motorcar in which to patrol. It had no heater and no radio, but it did have a roof and windscreen. It was an ancient Ford of doubtful reliability and it had a well-tested tendency to proceed in a straight line at bends in the road, especially when the driver was asleep.

I wasn't sure whether I would enjoy night-duty on this large rural patch, but one fact was certain – there was no way of avoiding it.

2

'Humour is odd, grotesque and wild,
Only by affection spoil'd.'
Jonathan Swift – To Mr Delany, 10 October 1718

On a late autumn night I left Mary and the infants in bed,
locked the door of my hilltop police house and drove my motor-
cycle four miles into the sleepy market town of Ashfordly. This
quiet place housed my Section Office and as I coasted the final
ten yards into the garage to avoid waking nearby children, I
noticed the tall, ramrod figure of Oscar Blaketon waiting
outside. He was unsmiling and at his most severe.

I parked my machine in the garage and made sure it would
not tumble over before lifting my sandwiches and flask from
one of the panniers and my peaked cap and torch from the
other. Thus equipped, I walked along the side of the police
station and entered the tiny office. Blaketon was already inside,
waiting for me.

'You're late, Rhea! Ten o'clock start, you know. Not quarter
past,' and his fingers tapped the counter to emphasise his
words.

'I booked on at ten, Sergeant, at Aidensfield. It's taken me
ten minutes to get here. I was on duty during those ten
minutes . . .'

'Clever sod, eh? Look son, when I was a lad, policemen
began their shifts ten minutes *before* the starting-time, not ten
minutes after.'

'I did a few minutes in my own office, Sergeant, before I
set off . . .'

'Ten o'clock start means ten o'clock. Here. Not at home. Right?'

'Yes, Sergeant.' It was impossible to argue when he was in this mood.

Having diplomatically settled that point, he went on to inform me of my responsibilities over the next eight hours, not forgetting to remind me of that disputed fifteen minutes. It transpired that I had to patrol the district in the official car and was expected to make points on the hour, every hour, at nominated telephone kiosks. I had to take my meal-break at Eltering Police Station, the local Sub-Divisional Office, a key to which was on the car key-ring. That being the half-way stage, I must then make the return journey via the same kiosks. It seemed simple enough. My eleven o'clock point would be at Thackerston Kiosk, my midnight one at Waindale and my one o'clock at Whemmelby. During the period 1.45 a.m. until 2.30 p.m., I would be in Eltering Police Station enjoying a meat sandwich and a cup of coffee from my flask. After that I had to return via Whemmelby at three, Waindale at four and Thackerton at five. I would book off duty at Ashfordly at six and travel home, bleary-eyed, cold and undoubtedly hungry, to knock off at 6.15 a.m.

'There's a book of unoccupied property.' He shoved a huge leather-bound volume across the counter. 'Check 'em all. Houses, golf clubs, shops – the lot. Poachers'll be abroad, I reckon, and late-night boozers. Don't go to sleep in that car – it runs off the road if you do. There'll be a supervisory rank on duty at Malton – a sergeant or possibly an inspector – and he might pop out to meet you somewhere. So be there. Also, the Malton rural night-patrol will be doing the southern end of the patch – you might meet him at Eltering. The lads usually meet there for a chat – nothing wrong in that so long as you don't exceed your three-quarters of an hour meal-break. Don't abuse the trust I place in you, Rhea.'

'There's no radio in the car,' I said inanely, wondering what the police procedure was if the car broke down in a remote area, or if I needed urgent assistance of any sort.

'True,' he said, turning into his office. 'True, there is no radio in the car.'

Realising that my statement of the obvious would excite no further comment from Oscar, I turned my attention to the Occurrence Book. It revealed nothing of immediate interest, save a stolen car which had already been found abandoned in Scarborough. I noted some unoccupied premises from the leather-bound volume and, anxious to be off, I lifted the car keys from their hook. I checked that the office fire was stoked up sufficiently to remain burning until my return and said, 'I'm off, Sergeant.'

There was no reply.

I dropped the latch as I made my exit, making sure I had my door key to re-enter at six. In the garage the little Ford Anglia awaited me. I unlocked the driver's door and climbed in. It was a very basic car with no trimmings, the only interior extra being the official log-book which had to be completed after every journey. Every purchase of oil or petrol had to be entered and I checked the book to ensure that my predecessor, whoever he was, had complied with that instruction.

Happily, the log was up to date. Before venturing out I remembered another essential check, a visual examination of the exterior. This was done to check whether the vehicle had suffered any damage that might be blamed on me.

During that era policemen seldom drove cars regularly on duty. That was considered a privilege rather than a right and the exceptions were the *crème de la crème* who had been selected for Motor Patrol duty. It was considered a luxury to have the use of a mechanically-propelled conveyance, owned and paid for by the ratepayers. If any of us accidentally marked an official car by reversing into a gatepost or scratching it in any way we were grounded for ever. The result was that policemen who damaged cars never admitted it. The cunning offenders parked in garages or tight corners so that an unsuspecting driver would take out the vehicle without noticing the blemish. Once you were driving the vehicle it was your responsibility, which meant that any scratches, dents, bumps or bruises were deemed to have occurred through your carelessness. No arguments or excuses were entertained. It was even pointless arguing that the car had been damaged in your absence – it was your fault for leaving it in such a vulnerable position. Every driver therefore casually checked every nut, bolt, screw, indicator light, panel, glass etc., before turning a wheel.

Various intellectual giants within the Force considered it wise to bump the night-duty car on the grounds they'd be forbidden to drive for eternity and thus unable to perform night-duty. Even greater intellectual giants felt this was not a wise move because they would have to patrol at night either on foot, on cycle or on motor-cycles. The point was well taken. Apart from the chilliness of the latter possibility, motor-cycle patrols in rural areas at night were guaranteed to make dogs bark, hens cackle, residents to arouse early and poachers to learn of our whereabouts. Being conscientious individuals we were careful with official vehicles.

Primitive though it was, the car was pleasant and undamaged, so I started the well-tuned engine and began to drive from the garage. Suddenly Sergeant Blaketon was right in my path and flagging me down with his torch. I stopped, wound down the window and asked, 'Is there a message, Sergeant?'

'There is,' he said.

I sat in silence to await the words he wished to impart, but he merely stood by the car, immobile and severe. It dawned on me that he wanted me to get out, which I did.

'Oil, water, tyres, lights, indicators,' he said woodenly. 'Elementary. Always check them. Always. Before every journey. It's laid down in orders. You didn't.'

I didn't argue. I knew he always checked such things. He would stride around the car, looking at the aforementioned points before moving off. He performed this ritual every time, so I now did the same. Up went the bonnet and I found the oil and water levels to be fine. Indicators working, tyres at correct pressures . . .

'Goodnight, Rhea,' he said, turning on his heel and

vanishing into the office. I drove off, thinking about him. I remembered watching him reverse the little car from the police station drive a few weeks earlier to allow a visiting inspector to remove his car. Oscar Blaketon had got out of the Ford, performed a fleeting moment's traffic duty on the street to guide out the inspector, and then, before driving the police car back into the garage, he had performed his ritual of checking oil, water, tyres, lights and indicators. Such was his devotion to the rule-book, even though his ten-yard journey had been broken by only half a minute.

With this salutary lesson in my mind, I began my first tour of rural night-duty as Aidensfield's local bobby. The district around Aidensfield is a land of small communities, many of which boast a single shop-cum-post office, their sole business premises. Even these, however modest, must be examined by night patrols and it was a simple process to patrol in the car between the villages and to check their sparse premises before sallying to the next stop. Until 10.30 each night there was the additional task of checking the public houses, but once the night life of the area ended at 11, the world was mine.

Over the next few days a routine developed. I would arrive at Ashfordly at quarter to ten and check the car noisily so that Oscar Blaketon satisfied himself that the task was done. I would then sally forth into the unknown, making my expedition around the telephone kiosks and checking vulnerable properties in between times. One curious fact that emerged was that in every village there was a light burning, no matter what time of night I passed through. I knew there was always someone about, someone awake in addition to myself. It meant the patrolling policeman is never totally alone and this is a re-assuring fact, although it does mean that we have to be careful when we water our horses or enjoy a quick nap in the car.

One continuing problem at night was keeping awake. Even though the car did not possess a heater, warm air blew in from the engine and this had the effect of making even the most alert of occupants drop off to sleep. The solution was to open a window or park up and take a walk. Unfortunately, this remedy often came too late and the little car has frequently terminated its journey in a field or ditch, happily without serious damage. One can appreciate that, after a full week of nights, the chief purpose of the travelling policeman is to remain awake; it is even possible to fall asleep while standing outside a telephone kiosk. When excessively tired, night-duty becomes very, very tedious.

The most welcome place during those tedious patrols was the police office at Eltering. It had a coal-fire which burned all day and all night in a well worn but tidy room and this produced a very homely atmosphere. The chairs were antiques, being old and wooden in the Windsor style, and there was a clean but worn rug before the fire. To spend three-quarters of an hour here during a meal-break on nights was extremely pleasant, if only because it offered companionship for a short time.

My colleagues who patrolled the rest of the Sub-Division also used this office for their meal-breaks and quite frequently the night car from Scarborough, a fast, sleek, black patrol car with a crew of two, would call in for a chat and a meal. It was customary for everyone to meet there at the same time and even the duty sergeant would come to join the chatter, laughter, card school or whatever amusement was currently popular. There could be a domino school, for example, or even a Monopoly contest.

It didn't take long to become acquainted with the men who shared this cosy spot on night-duty. The most fascinating was a huge, grizzle-haired constable whose name was Alf Ventress. He hailed from Malton and his night-shifts came around approximately the same as mine. This meant we often met in Eltering Police Station over our meals. He was far more experienced than I, for he must have completed more than twenty-five unglamorous years in the job. A typically dour Yorkshireman, he rarely spoke to anyone while eating, but sat in the same chair each time to munch his packed meal. His chief mission was to consume his bait and drink his coffee without interruption.

His uneventful career had not given him reason to be polite or smart, and his uniform was never tidy. It always needed pressing, his boots were forever in need of a polish, while his shoulders and upper tunic were constantly covered with a combination of dandruff and cigarette ash. He chain smoked when he was not eating and the other lads tended to leave him alone. It was not policy to interrupt him, because he had something of a reputation for being short-tempered. No one had actually seen him angry, but it was the way he looked at trouble-makers through heavy eyebrows – it made them shrivel with anticipation of a display of anger, yet he never erupted.

For all these reasons he was nicknamed Vesuvius, the name arising from the fact that he was always covered in ash and likely to erupt at any time.

I soon learned he disliked a crowd and, if we were alone, he was good company, reminiscing and telling me yarns about his younger days in the Force. When the Scarborough Motor Patrol crew arrived, however, the office became alive with their chatter as they recounted hair-raising stories of the exploits and exciting dramas in which they had been involved. Their experiences made us foot patrol lads look very mundane.

Vesuvius listened but never tried to compete with them and, over the months, we all became familiar with his routine for eating his meal. His wife, whose name we never knew, always packed a cheese sandwich, two hard-boiled eggs, a piece of fruit cake and a bar of chocolate. His diet on nights never changed and he swilled it down with a flask of steaming, dark coffee.

I can see him now. He would stride into the office, huge and menacing, as if daring anyone to occupy his fireside chair. Having settled his bulk into the seat he would stretch his legs until his feet rested on the hearth and would then open his bait tin. Out would come a clean white serviette which he spread across his lap and he would position his tin on the floor at his side. The flask of coffee stood like a sentinel beside it.

First out were the two hard-boiled eggs. He always held

them aloft, one in each hand, and brought them together in front of him with a loud crack. This is known as egg jarping in the North Riding, and the action broke the shells, whereupon he peeled them and dropped the waste on to the serviette in his lap. He would then consume both eggs very rapidly before tackling the cheese sandwich. His noisy enjoyment was a treat to observe.

One night I was first into the office and within two minutes the two Motor Patrol lads entered. They were called Ben and Ron.

'Vesuvius in yet?' Ben asked.

'No,' I said, 'but he's due at any time.'

He had obviously been in earlier because his bait tin stood on the counter, and so Ron lifted the lid as Ben took two eggs from his own pocket. He exchanged them with those from the bait tin, concealing Vesuvius' eggs in his coat pocket. He closed the lid and waited. Nothing more was said or done.

Five minutes later the big man entered. Without a word he sat down, lifted his bait tin from its resting-place, stretched out those huge legs towards the hearth and smiled. I watched, wondering what was going to happen next. Ben and Ron sat opposite with long, straight faces, talking earnestly about football.

Vesuvius sat back in his chair and covered his lap with the white serviette, licking his lips with anticipation. I watched him take two white eggs from his tin. I was unable to take my eyes from them as he smiled fleetingly, licked his lips again and opened his arms wide with an egg clutched in each fist. He brought them together smartly as he always did.

They were fresh eggs. There was a sickening, sploshing noise as Vesuvius was suddenly smothered in bright yellow egg yolk and streamers of uncooked egg white. His hands were dripping, while pieces of smashed shell clung to his face and hair.

He roared, 'That bloody woman!' and stormed out to wash himself.

Ben and Ron burst into fits of laughter and I joined in

their fun, for it seemed the prank had been played upon Vesuvius many times in the past. On each occasion he blamed his wife for failing to hard-boil his eggs and we often wondered what was said to her upon his return home at six.

As my visits to Eltering grew in number I realised that poor Vesuvius was the butt of many jokes, both in the office and out of doors. I think all were designed to goad him into a display of temper, but all failed. Vesuvius never erupted. I never played jokes on him – deep down I felt sorry for this man who, in truth, had a heart of gold and a gentle word for the most deprived and depraved members of society. His bluff exterior was not a true indication of his gentle nature and he genuinely loved other people.

It was his attitude to others that led him to organise bus outings for old-age pensioners from Malton. Vesuvius would commission a coach to take a load of old folks for a day at Scarborough, or to a theatre or zoo. He'd arrange to visit establishments like York Minster, Ampleforth College, Castle Howard, Thompsons Woodcarvers of Kilburn and other places of local interest.

His kindness led to another prank at his expense. We were in Eltering police office one night when the terrible twins entered. Ben and Ron were happy and laughing as usual as they settled down for their mid-morning break. As Vesuvius entered to perform his egg-breaking ritual without mishap, Ben went into the sergeant's office next door. I heard him lift the telephone and dial an extension number; then our office telephone rang. Vesuvius answered it.

'Eltering Police,' he growled in his deep voice.

And I heard Ben's voice coming from the next office saying, 'This is the Ryedale Coach Touring Company.'

'It must be urgent to ring at this time of day,' Vesuvius commented. 'It's two in the morning.'

And Ben replied, 'It is very urgent, Mr Ventress, very urgent indeed. We've been up all night, working on revised arrangements. I'm ringing about that trip you've organised tomorrow night, to the brewery. We've had to cancel it.'

'Cancel it?' bellowed Vesuvius. 'Why? It's all laid on, supper an' all, for the lads. Forty lads going . . .'

'That's why I'm ringing you now, so you can cancel things. You didn't apply for a licence, you see,' said Ben from the next office. Ron and myself sat enthralled, listening to both sides of this curious conversation. Vesuvius, of course, could only hear the voice on the telephone.

'Licence?' he snarled.

'Licence,' said Ben solemnly. 'You need a Customs and Excise Licence to run bus-trips. It's a new law. It was introduced in the last budget and we forgot to tell you. It means your trip's illegal, Mr Ventress. We've no option, I'm afraid. It'll have to be cancelled. That's why I'm ringing late, before tomorrow, so you can do the necessary. Sorry.'

'Can't I get a licence, then?' he asked, a picture of misery.

'Not in time for this one, but pop into the post office and ask for a Coach Outing Arrangers Licence application form. It costs £10 for a year and means you can organise trips by coach anywhere in England, except the Isle of Man and the Channel Isles. That's extra.'

'I'll have to contact everybody that's booked, and return their money.'

'Sorry, Mr Ventress, but we daren't co-operate with an illegally run bus-trip.'

'Aye, all right,' and the big, unhappy man put down the receiver.

'What's up, Alf?' asked Ron, a picture of innocence.

'Bus company,' he said. 'I've got to cancel my trip tomorrow night. It's a pity. It's a pensioners' outing – the womenfolk are all off to a bingo session, so I fixed up a trip for their husbands. We're off to a brewery in Hartlepool. Seems I need a licence to run bus-trips now. Can't get one in time . . .'

'Aw, Alf, what a shame!' Ben had reappeared and was having difficulty preventing himself bursting into laughter.

I didn't know what to do. I appreciate a good joke but I don't like to see people hurt and this had clearly upset poor old Vesuvius. He produced one of his pungent cigarettes and lit it, casting clouds of foul smoke about the room as he ate his cheese sandwich in silence. I didn't find it easy to be party to this and tried to make intelligent conversation by talking shop with Ben and Ron. Finally, the terrible twins decided to leave the office, chuckling to themselves as they went.

This left me with a great problem. Should I tell him it was all a joke?

'Tell me about the bus-trip,' I began. Gently, this untidy giant of a man explained how he felt sorry for pensioners without cars and without the funds and ability to get themselves around the countryside or attend functions like concerts, pantomimes and shows. He therefore arranged outings for them. He chatted on and on about some of the more enjoyable occasions and I forgot about the time. I found him a fascinating mixture of personalities. He was a stolid, gentle Yorkshire giant with a heart of gold and a softness beneath which was totally concealed by his external appearance. He looked like a perpetually angry man, yet I don't think he had an ounce of anger in him. I decided I liked Vesuvius.

My dilemma was solved before I left because the telephone rang again. It jerked me back to reality and reminded me that I had lots of property to check before my next point. As Vesuvius answered it, I got up to rinse out my flask.

Seconds later, he was smiling all over.

'The bus company again,' he told me. 'That chap's rung me on his way home, from a kiosk. He's just remembered – I applied before the financial year's end, before Budget Day, so I can run trips without a licence that I'd got booked up before April 4th. It's all right, Nick, and in compensation, they're giving me the best bus, the one with the television in.'

'I'm pleased,' I said, leaving him to his new-found happiness.

In the weeks that followed, my talks with local bobbies told me that poor old Vesuvius had been the butt of countless pranks over the years, but not one had caused him to lose his temper, nor had he retaliated violently. There were the

occasional hints of anger, like the outbursts against his wife
during his egg-breaking routines, and I began to wonder if he
really did have a temper. What *would* make him rise to the
bait, I wondered?

I collected quite a repertoire of jokes that had been
perpetrated upon him. Ben and Ron had once put Vesuvius'
private car number on the Stolen Vehicles Register, with the
result that he got stopped and questioned by a police patrol
in Sunderland, while heading forth for a fishing holiday. No
amount of explanation would convince the Sunderland police
that it was his own vehicle until Vesuvius, in his patient way,
managed to convince a sergeant that he was an honest
policeman from Yorkshire. On another occasion, someone
substituted the Superintendent's home telephone number for
the 'Dial a Story' service offered by Hull Telephone Company.
It had to be poor old Vesuvius, alone in the office one night,
who decided he'd like to listen to a short story, and dialled
the number concerned. The Superintendent was not very
pleased to be roused by the familiar tones of Vesuvius at 2.30
in the morning, and he refused to accept that the joke was
not originated by PC Ventress.

If Vesuvius and his placid nature were the butt of
policemen's jokes, they were also a fine target for civilian
pranks. I learned he had once arrested a local scrap merchant
for stealing lengths of copper piping, and the Scrappy
eventually appeared at court to be heavily fined by the
magistrates.

Thereafter, he considered Vesuvius his sworn enemy. Even
though the Scrappy was later arrested by other policemen
and fined even more heavily from time to time, he continued
to hate Vesuvius, seemingly because that had been his first
arrest and therefore the start of his criminal career.

Vesuvius bore the rancour with his traditional calm until
the Scrappy realised that, once every few weeks, poor old
Vesuvius worked a full tour of night-duty. This meant he slept
between 7 a.m. and lunchtime, spending the early part of the
day in pleasant slumbers. Vesuvius lived in his own small, neat

terrace house in a quiet part of Malton, so the virulent Scrappy decided to visit that street whilst Vesuvius slept. He chose to park his horse-and-cart outside Vesuvius' peaceful home and announce his presence by blowing a trumpet.

The notion behind this scheme was that the trumpet would become a trademark and it would announce his whereabouts to those who wished to off-load their rubbish. They could run out of their homes and deposit it upon the waiting cart in exchange for a small payment, a *very* small payment as a rule.

To thwart retaliatory action by Vesuvius, the Scrappy changed his timing and his day. Some mornings, he would arrive at nine o'clock, others at 11 or 10.30, the result being that poor old Vesuvius never had any idea of the impending arrival of the noisy man and his blasted trumpet. He lost many hours of precious sleep because of this, but he never complained either officially or unofficially.

I learned from my colleagues at Malton that the trumpet was the pride and joy of that offending Scrappy. It was very old and very valuable, and furthermore had a deep sentimental meaning in the family, having been passed down from his great-grandfather, who had played it in a local brass band. When played properly its tone was excellent, but the puffings and blowings of this man did little to enhance its reputation. It merely produced a fearful din at his lips.

Malton police did receive complaints from other members of the public and attempts were made to confiscate the trumpet. Somehow, he managed to avoid all patrolling officers and we lacked the necessary hard evidence for a court appearance.

It was dear old Vesuvius who finally put a stop to the noise.

It happened one morning. Vesuvius had finished night-duty early and had taken four hours off duty in lieu of overtime worked. This meant he had finished work at two o'clock. By ten o'clock that same morning he was wide awake and in fact was downstairs tucking into a hefty plateful of eggs and bacon. It was at that time that the Scrappy chose to play the 'Donkey Serenade' right outside Vesuvius' front door, pointing the mouth of the trumpet high at the window above. The poor fellow was carried away by the thrill of his own music, and the notes were long and loud as the unseen donkey was duly serenaded.

On hearing this foul din, Vesuvius opened his front door and was outside before the Scrappy realised what was happening. One massive fist seized the offending instrument and the other clutched the collar of the ghastly musician. Without a word Vesuvius hauled both offenders through his house and into the backyard, where he released his grip of the bewildered scrap merchant.

Then, without saying a word, Vesuvius opened the door of a small brick building and, smiling at the unhappy witness, removed the mouthpiece of the trumpet. He handed this to its owner with a smile on his face, then stepped inside the shed.

Inside stood a huge mangle with ancient wooden rollers, worn hollow in the centre by years of wringing out the washing of generations. Smiling quietly at the waiting man Vesuvius inserted the slender tube of the mouth end of the trumpet between the rollers and began to turn the handle.

I am assured that cries of deep anguish echoed from the horrified scrap merchant as his precious trumpet was drawn into the mangle. He was kept at arm's length by Vesuvius, who used his powerful free arm to turn the handle. Eventually, the trumpet appeared from the other side, flattened like a pancake. Vesuvius took it in his hands, seized the dirty collar again and propelled the hapless character outside. Not a word was spoken by Vesuvius as he led the Scrappy to his horse, tossed the trumpet among the other scrap on the cart, and closed his door on that episode.

The slumbering Vesuvius was never again aroused by trumpet blasts.

My respect for Vesuvius grew as I saw more of him. Due to our shift system we frequently worked nights together and those mid-shift meal-breaks were regularly provided with entertainment by those terrible twins, Ben and Ron. Their pranks upon Vesuvius seemed endless, although it must be said they were all harmless. Vesuvius, on his part, took them stoically and never grumbled or lost his temper. His nickname seemed all the more apt because the violent eruptions of Mount Vesuvius were not very frequent, although it did grumble and threaten from time to time. They were very similar, he and his volcano.

It was nice to get him talking. On those occasions when the traffic lads did not arrive, Vesuvius and I would chat quite amiably. He would tell me of his early service in the Force, when discipline was strict and money was poor, but he was proud to remember the days when the public respect for the bobby was at its height, and when they appreciated the work done on their behalf. A few smartly clipped ears were infinitely better than either court appearances, the advice of social workers or the utterances of bureaucrats who had no idea of how to deal with people, but who were wizards with statistics. Modern law-makers were thinkers, not doers, Vesuvius would say, but he continued to act in his own way, apparently totally contented with life.

He told me the modern version of the Good Samaritan parable one night, relating how a social worker had found a poor man in a ditch. The man had been violently attacked and robbed by a gang of thugs. As the injured man lay bleeding in the street the social worker said, 'What an awful thing to happen. Tell me who did this to you, so that I might find him and minister to him.'

As we grew to understand each other I realised that Vesuvius was highly intelligent. He was far from the slow and dim-witted person he pretended to be, and several little clues led me to this belief. The regular egg-smashing joke was one example of this. From snippets told me when we were alone he knew that Ben and Ron swapped the eggs, although he never allowed them to realise he knew of their pranks. Whenever he was caught by their tomfoolery, he continued to blame his wife for forgetting to hard-boil the eggs, but he craftily told everyone else of his knowledge. The result was that only the terrible twins were fooled by this and although it meant an egg-splattered tunic from time to time, the real fools of the incidents were Ben and Ron. Everyone else was secretly laughing at them and their ignorance. It was this attitude that gave me an insight into the complex character of the stolid, unflappable PC Ventress.

He once told me he was waiting for the right moment to return their jokes; he would wait for months if necessary. When the opportunity did arise, it was marvellous and I was delighted to be present at their come-uppance.

I was in the office at Eltering Police Station, enjoying one of those midnight breakfasts around two o'clock in the morning. It was a summer's night, albeit cool and fresh and the moon shone brightly. Inside, Vesuvius was in his favourite chair, eating his usual pair of hard-boiled eggs with his napkin across his knees. Conversation was non-existent, for he ate in silence, and then the terrible twins entered. There was enough slamming of doors and noise for an army of men as they breezed into the office.

'Grand night, Vesuvius,' smiled Ron, unbuttoning his tunic as he settled into the chair opposite.

'Aye,' agreed Vesuvius, munching his cheese sandwich.

Ben, meanwhile, had gone straight into the toilet. We heard the distinct crash of its door as he rushed inside, followed by the equally distinctive five minutes' silence. Eventually, we heard the flush of the chain and the re-opening of the door, followed by a somewhat anxious re-appearance of Ben.

'The keys!' he cried as he entered the office. 'The bloody car-keys!'

'Keys?' puzzled Ron.

'Yeh, I stuck them in my trouser pocket, like I always do. They must have lodged on the top, on my truncheon strap,' and he indicated the right-hand trouser pocket. The top of his truncheon was showing and its leather strap hung down the outside of his leg. Truncheons have a specifically made long pocket which runs down the inside of the right leg, to the knee, the entrance to which is adjacent to the usual pocket. It was not uncommon for objects to find their way into the wrong pocket, nor was it unusual for objects to get caught on the truncheon when it was in position.

'What's happened?' I asked.

'Well, there I was, sitting on the bog. I got up, my trousers still around my ankles and reached up to pull the chain. And as I stretched up, the car-keys fell into the bowl – right down. They fell in at the precise moment I pulled the chain! I was too late to stop pulling – I saw the bloody things fall in but couldn't stop the flushing.'

'They've gone?' gasped Ron.

'Gone,' repeated Ben. 'I couldn't help it, honest. What can we do?'

'Search me!'

'The inspector will play holy hell! He'll probably book us for loss or damage to county property, carelessness, dereliction of duty or some other trumped-up charge!'

'Don't you carry spares?' I asked.

'We should,' Ron admitted, 'but it's the second time that idiot has lost ours. He lost the other set down a drain when we got out to deal with a road accident. Tonight's keys *were* the spare set.'

'Are you sure they've gone right down?' I asked, trying to be helpful.

'Sure,' said Ben, sitting in a chair and removing his bait tin from his bag. 'They've gone. I've checked.'

Ron and I went to examine the toilet basin and it was totally empty. There was no sign of the missing keys. We searched the floor and the route back to the office, then out to the car and finally we made Ben turn out his pockets. Nothing. No car-keys.

'They went down, I saw them,' he repeated for the hundredth time. 'I saw them fall in just before I flushed.'

'I can get them back,' said Vesuvius quietly, having concluded his meal. He wiped his mouth and replaced the folded serviette in its tin.

'You can?' they chorused, sitting bolt upright with relief evident on their faces.

'Dead easy,' he said, wiping his mouth with the back of his hand.

'Come on, Alf,' cried Ron. 'Give! Put us out of our misery!'

'You know that manhole cover in the middle of the street outside, just in front of the door to the station?'

Ben nodded. It always rattled when a car drove across it, and was a good warning that someone was approaching, like the Superintendent.

'Well,' said Vesuvius slowly, 'the channels from our station toilets go through there. I've been down before, clearing channels, years ago. That manhole is about eight feet deep, and several channels pass through the bottom of it. All you have to do is climb down inside – there's steps built into the wall – and I could flush the chain until the keys are washed through. You'd get 'em back down there. Dead simple.'

Ben's eyes brightened.

'You sure, Vesuvius?' He looked at me and then at Ron.

'I've done it before,' said Vesuvius, standing up.

'Right,' said Ben. 'Let's try it. You show us.'

We trooped outside and I carried the torch. Vesuvius took the poker from the fireplace and the four of us stood around the large metal cover. Vesuvius prised up one end with the poker and lifted it clear, placing it on the centre of the road. Somewhere, a clock struck 2.15. The town was at peace.

'Torch,' someone called and I shone the light deep inside. It was a square-shaped well, clinically clean and lined with white-tiled bricks. A metal ladder was built into one wall and the bottom would be a good eight feet or even more below us. We could see five channels entering the base from different angles, merging into one large exit channel. It was large enough for at least one man to climb inside; at a squeeze, two could make it.

'The one on the left, nearest the exit route,' Vesuvius indicated to Ron. 'That's ours. If we flush our chain, the muck comes flooding down there and it's carried along that other single channel, out of sight. If Ben gets down there, he can catch it as it comes past and get your keys. The tag will help them swim along to this point.'

Ben did not like the idea at all. His face told us that. For him, the entire scheme was distasteful.

'Ben, it's got to be done,' said Ron. 'You lost the bloody things down the hole.'

'Have we any wellingtons?' he asked. 'I could stop the flow with my foot, eh? Stick my foot in that groove to halt things as they come through?'

'No wellingtons here, Ben,' said Vesuvius. 'You could use your bare feet, eh? I've seen council workmen do that. Take your shoes and socks off, roll your trousers up to the knees and stick your foot in that groove. Your toes will catch the keys, eh? And you'll let the other plother float past.'

Ben looked down at his shoes. They were black leather, nicely polished, and he did not intend wasting them. Besides, feet could be washed.

'All right,' he sighed. 'There's no choice. I'll do it.'

Standing at the edge of the hole Ben removed his socks and shoes, rolled up his trousers to the knees and prepared to climb down the cold, damp metal stairs. They would take him to the brown earthenware floor of the manhole with its array of tiny tunnels.

'When I get down,' he said, 'I'll shout when I'm ready. I'll stick my foot in that channel – are you sure it's that one, Vesuvius?'

'Aye,' he said. 'I'm sure. The one on the left, like I said. Stick your foot in it, toes pointing towards our building. When you're ready, give us a shout and I'll pull. I'll keep pulling the chain until your keys are washed through. It'll take a few flushes, I reckon, it's a bit of a distance.'

Ron stood at the top of the hole, looking down upon his pal as he clambered nervously down the ladder. The rusty rungs hurt his feet, but soon he was on the cool, smooth floor.

'This one?' he stuck a toe into the narrow groove, as if testing the sea for the temperature of the water. Vesuvius said, 'Aye,' and Ben therefore planted his bare foot firmly into the channel, effectively blocking it. His toes faced the police station, as suggested.

'Right, I'm off,' said Vesuvius and he went into the police station, asking me to liaise with him. I had to dart backwards and forwards, making sure both parties were ready before the first pull of the chain. The distance between the toilet basin and the foot of that manhole would be some thirty yards or so, and I wondered how much effluent would have to be dislodged before the bit carrying the keys arrived at Ben's big toe.

I called to Ben. 'Ready?'

'I'm ready,' he replied, his face white as he peered up at me.

I rushed inside to Vesuvius.

'He's ready when you are,' I announced.

'Get yourself back to that hole,' he laughed. 'I'll give you ten seconds. You'll enjoy this!'

Puzzled by his final remark I hurried to the vantage-point on the rim and looked down.

'Count ten,' I said to Ben, for want of something more appropriate.

Surprisingly, Ben did.

I heard him counting – one, two, three, four, five . . . all the time staring at his white foot bathed in the light of my torch.

'Nine, ten,' he concluded.

Then I heard the sound of a heaving chain and the gurgle of an emptying cistern. Somewhere in Ben's chamber I heard the whooshing of an oncoming flow of water, and I heard Vesuvius shout, 'First lot coming.'

'First lot coming,' I repeated for Ben's benefit.

Then I realised Vesuvius' ruse.

The pipe from the police station toilets did not emerge at the base of the manhole – it emerged near the top! It was about six feet above the base, dropping its discharges from a great height. It was the oncoming rush of water that warned me – the sound came from a series of pipes which entered the chamber at varying heights. I could see them now, a series of dark holes. And Ben was standing on the floor.

Too late he realised what was about to happen.

With a sighing, almost obscene noise the mess spluttered and rushed from the darkness just above Ben's head and, in seconds, he was smothered from head to toe. I heard him cough and gasp as Ron burst into fits of laughter at the sight of his poor companion, whose uniform, face and hair were plastered with the foulest mess imaginable. He tried to climb out, but another whooshing noise was sounding. The toilet cistern couldn't have filled already, so Vesuvius must have flushed another one. Another ghastly brew was on its way.

Ben did manage to climb out, but only after three of Vesuvius' pulls had discharged their evil contents over him. I didn't know what to do. I laughed alongside Ron, and noticed Vesuvius framed in the light of the police station door.

'Have they come through?' he called.

There was no reply from the sorry man. It was at that moment that the telephone rang, so Vesuvius dashed inside to answer it and I followed. We left Ron to replace the manhole cover after helping his smelly friend out.

'Right, I'll tell them,' he said, replacing the telephone as I entered.

'Malton Office,' he announced to Ron. 'That was Sergeant Colbeck. There's a domestic disturbance in town. You're needed there urgently, both of you.'

'Now?' Ben cried.

'Straight away!' Vesuvius smiled. 'No. 10 Welsh Terrace.'

'We've no keys!'

'Oh, I forgot,' Vesuvius grinned stupidly. 'There's always a spare set kept here, one set for every car in the Sub-Division and for all official cars which regularly call. Sergeant Blaketon's idea, being a belt-and-braces man. I'll get 'em,' and he pottered into the sergeant's office, unlocked a drawer and lifted out a set of keys. They bore the registration number of their patrol car. 'Sorry I forgot about those,' he said. 'It's not every station that has them – I've a bloody awful memory, you know.'

'I'll clean up in the car,' Ben said, the ordure dripping from him.

'You bloody well won't!' Ron snarled. 'You're not getting into the car like that! You smell worse than a pigsty – what a bloody awful mess!'

'Worse than egg yolks, eh?' smiled Vesuvius. 'That call was urgent, lads.'

And so they had to leave. Ben hobbled to the car in bare feet and sat upon one of the rubber mats which he lifted from the floor and placed on the seat. The stench from his appalling bath was overpowering and they drove away with all windows open and Ben dripping ghastly fluids to the car floor.

Vesuvius smiled.

'They're nice lads, really,' he said quietly, and then the telephone rang again.

'Eltering Police, PC Ventress,' he answered. He listened for a moment and replied, 'No, Sergeant. All's quiet here. Nothing doing.'

He replaced the handset and turned towards me. 'Fancy a coffee, son?' he asked.

3

'From ghoulies and ghosties and long-leggety beasties,
And things that go bump in the night,
Good Lord, deliver us.'

Anonymous

Two fears must be conquered by the constable on night-duty.
The first is the fear of the dark and the second is a fear of
ghosts. There are constables who are subjected to one or both
of these terrors, and for them a night patrol is a continuing
test of courage and devotion to duty. Happily, I have never
been afraid of either and was never worried about patrolling
during the hours of darkness. In fact, it was very enjoyable,
even in the town, but the countryside around Aidensfield
offered far more than the streets of Strensford.

The wide open spaces of the North Yorkshire moors offered
little in the way of crime, but they did produce sounds which
could terrify the townsman. There might be the cry of the
vixen, the scream of the barn owl, the cough of a sheep or
cow and the weird sobbing sounds of wild geese flying
overhead. We called the latter 'Gabriel Ratchets' or 'Hell's
Hounds', for the older generations believed they were angels
seeking the lost soul of unbaptised babies, or that they were
the angels of death hovering over houses in which a death
would soon occur.

Policemen, as a rule, care not for ancient legends or the
vagaries of nature, and our patrols were chiefly a crime
prevention exercise. The presence of our vehicle made the
public aware that we were out and about during the witching

hours, and this was comforting to those who considered themselves at risk. For the lonely and the frightened there is something reassuring about the presence of a mobile police officer at night. In some respects he assumes the role of the guardian angel we were taught about in childhood. He is there if he is needed.

With the passage of time every spell of uneventful night-duty conformed to a pattern. For my part, I would book on duty at Ashfordly, spend some time reading the latest horror stories featuring domestic rows, thefts, burglaries, shopbreaking or stolen cars, and having digested that unsavoury menu, I would sally forth into the market town. There I would diligently shake hands with lots of door-knobs. I would make my uniform seen by everyone who was out and about and thus create among the public the cosy feeling that the police were present and acting in their interest. We care about the communal safety of society and must make that care evident to those in our charge.

As the public houses ejected their regulars it was prudent to patrol the market-place looking fierce as drunks fought the effects of the fresh air, but by 11 o'clock the town was usually dead. Only if the Young Farmers' Club or Ashfordly Ladies' Dining Club had organised a function did the routine vary, in which case the home-going was a little later and the drunks a little more entertaining. In addition, the duty became enjoyable for the policeman because lots of pretty girls were in a chatty and romantic mood.

When Ashfordly was finally at peace we patrolled the villages, making points in the manner I have earlier described. To the layman this must seem a mundane sort of existence and it is fair to say that the duty could be boring in the extreme. It could be crushingly monotonous. One old constable tried to cheer me up during such a period by saying, 'T'job's what thoo maks it, lad,' and with his words in my head, I learned that I *could* bring interest to those lonely patrols.

One way of breaking the tedium was to investigate the marvellous range of epitaphs in churchyards. A fear of ghosts and ghoulies and things that go bump in the night meant a wide gap in the education of the sufferers, and I wondered if I could make a collection of interesting inscriptions. Was there sufficient variety to justify this? I discovered that the night flew if I spent some time in the churchyards of my beat, so I took to wandering around each one for ten minutes at a time, ostensibly checking the security of the premises. By flashing my torch on a bewildering array of tombstones, I discovered some gems. There were old ones and new ones, they were carved in marble and in stone, some were ornate, others very simple. There were obelisks and tiny wooden crosses, but all contained sentiments applicable to the dear departed.

My research revealed that the modern epitaph is a plain affair when compared with some of the older ones, and I enjoyed such beauties as:

> *Tread softly – if she waken, she'll talk*

or

> *Underneath this sod lies Arabella Young*
> *Who on 5th May began to hold her tongue.*

Another read:

> *Here lie I, no wonder I'm dead*
> *The wheel of a wagon went over my head.*

In Whitby I found the following:

> *Sudden and unexpected was the end,*
> *Of our esteemed and beloved friend,*
> *He gave to his friends a sudden shock*
> *By falling into Sunderland Dock*

and this one:

> *Here lies the body of John Mound*
> *Who was lost at sea and never found.*

In a village near Malton, there is:

> *For all the pains and trouble from my birth*
> *All that I've gained is just my length of earth.*

High in the Dales one can find:

> *Think of me as you pass by,*
> *As you are now, so once was I.*

> *As I am now, some day you'll be,*
> *So now prepare to follow me.*

Someone, perhaps a night-duty policeman, had added the following:

> *To follow you I'm not content,*
> *I do not know which way you went.*

It could be difficult to determine the most enjoyable epitaph, but this is one of my favourites:

> *There was an old man who averred*
> *He had learned to fly like a bird.*
> *Cheered by thousands of people,*
> *He leapt from the steeple –*
> *This tomb states the date it occurred.*

My real favourite, which is so brief and typically Yorkshire, reads:

> *Beneath this sod lies another.*

It was during one of those epitaph hunts that I stepped into a rather frightening situation in a graveyard. The boots I wore at night were silent and comfortable, and this enabled me to creep about unheard and unseen, a useful talent when shadowing felonious individuals. It also meant I unwittingly surprised other people and, on this occasion, I had decided to pay a short visit to the churchyard at Elsinby. It was about 10.30 at night and I had some ten minutes to kill before moving around my beat. I reckoned a quick perambulation among the tombstones would occupy those spare moments.

The lych-gate was open, which was unusual, and I wondered if there were criminals abroad. Perhaps someone had broken in to steal the valuables? Fearing the worst I crept along the stone-flagged path, alert and ready for anything, even the presence of Sergeant Blaketon. Then I heard voices, speaking in low whispers and they came from behind the church. I did have intruders!

I crept forward with my spine tingling and the hair on the back of my neck standing on tiptoe. In a state of high excitement I rounded the end of the greystone building and, in the deep shadows, I halted. I knew I was invisible if I remained motionless. I listened for more sounds, but there was nothing. I wondered if I had been mistaken, for I was sure I'd heard voices. Then I saw the vague outline of shadowy figures moving stealthily between the rows of memorials. I wondered if I had stumbled upon a coven of modern witches or someone emulating Burke and Hare. I must see more. I waited, trembling slightly, and once again I could hear mumbling voices. Occasionally, lights would flash and silhouetted heads would appear and disappear before the group moved on. I had difficulty counting the heads because of their up-and-down motions, but after a few minutes of careful study I realised I was watching the congregation of the Hopbind Inn.

Gradually, recognisable voices floated across to me on the silent evening air and, having solved that problem, I wondered what on earth, or in the name of heaven, they were doing. It seemed that the entire regular population of the bar was there, creeping among the graves and muttering among themselves. I decided to perform my duty and find out what was happening. I left my place of concealment and strode purposefully to the area where they were still at work.

When I was close to them I halted and in a loud voice demanded, 'What's going on here, then?'

'Oh, it's you, Mr Rhea,' said the familiar tones of Dick-the-Sick, on a visit to Elsinby. 'We're looking for Dr Russell's grave.'

'Dr Russell?' I was puzzled.

'Aye,' chipped in another voice. 'You remember. He lived in Thrush Grange years ago, a big chap who liked shooting pheasants. Died a bit back. Nice bloke.'

'I never knew him,' I had to admit. 'It was before my time. Anyway, why is everybody looking for his grave tonight?'

'We've a bet on with George at the pub. He reckons the doctor died in 1932 and I said it was 1933. Then somebody reckoned it was summer and another told us it was early in the year, March or thereabouts. Well, we all got to arguing so we put bets on. George is behind the bar, holding our money – ten bob a go. Whoever is closest, gets the cash. So we're all checking. Trouble is, no one remembers which is his grave.'

'I said it was March 1932,' chipped in Dick, leaving me as he continued his search. I watched them with interest. Some had candles, one was using a box of matches and several had hand torches. Two of them had oil-lamps or storm lanterns. The less fortunate relied on lights provided by their colleagues and some even trusted the others to shout out the correct date. The combined effect was pretty eerie from a distance.

Eager to learn the truth I began to walk around the graveyard, shining my torch on the dates and at the same time looking for more interesting epitaphs. Together, the little group walked about that deserted place, some thirty stooping figures all shining lights on headstones. I must admit I got carried away with enthusiasm and found myself as keen as the others to learn the correct date.

Then another voice sounded close behind me.

'Rhea? What's going on? What the hell are you doing?'

It was Sergeant Blaketon. He had arrived in the village with the expectation of meeting me at the kiosk, but I had forgotten the time. He now stood tall and majestic beneath the shadows of the church, his brilliant torch shining directly at me. I walked slowly towards him, realising I was in trouble.

'Checking a date, Sergeant,' I said, wondering if it sounded very stupid.

'Date? What date?'

'The death of Dr Russell, sergeant. There's been a discussion in the pub, you see, and they're all checking . . .'

'Friday, 3rd May 1929,' he said with conviction. 'This is his grave,' and he shone his torch on to a tomb not far from the gate. 'Come on.'

'It's here,' I called to the villagers, shining my light on the gravestone.

With no more ado I walked out of the churchyard with Sergeant Blaketon silent and stern at my side. We stood on the kerb as the villagers all trooped past, each checking it for himself before returning to the bar. There would now be a share-out of the money and hopefully, more drinks, although it was after closing-time.

'Are they friends of the licensee?' he asked and I detected the faintest hint of humour in his voice. Friends of the licensee could drink after normal hours, at his expense.

'Yes, Sergeant,' I said, hoping he would believe me and trusting he would not enter the bar to check the validity of that statement.

'Good,' he said affably. 'Now show me the castle.'

We walked away in silence and turned up the long drive that leads out of the village and up to the ancient castle on the hill. 'Sergeant,' I deigned to ask. 'How did you know that date and where to find the grave?'

'Do you read police books, Rhea?'

'Sometimes, Sergeant.'

'Forensic medicine?'

'Now and again.'

'Well, Dr Russell was a pioneer of modern forensic pathology. Clever chap, he was. Wrote a book about the use of forensic pathology in the field of crime detection. Worth reading, Rhea. Surely you've read *Russell on Scratch Marks*?'

'No, Sergeant, but I'll get it from the library,' and I fell into silence as I marched up the drive at his side, perfectly in step with his ramrod figure. Although he said no more about Dr Russell I got the impression from his demeanour that he was letting the village drink late in honour of the long-dead doctor who I guessed was one of Blaketon's heroes.

This incident showed me that the locals of the Hopbind Inn were an imaginative crowd, but the affair of Dr Russell's tombstone wasn't the only event which caused me problems. It is fair to say that the tombstone happening was a very minor hiccup in my parochial patrolling and, in comparison, the laying of the Elsinby ghost was almost disastrous.

Legend assured us that the ghost of Sir Nicholas Fairfax, a long dead occupant of Elsinby Castle, walked the village at certain times. His appearance, clad in the dark armour which was his symbol, occurred only when the midnight full moon coincided with the midnight of the anniversary of his death. The chances of those events happening together were considerably remote and a local mathematician once attempted to calculate the dates when this would occur. He failed because he got drunk on the free drinks supplied at the Hopbind Inn during his attempt.

It was fortuitous that the anniversary of Nicholas Fairfax's death and a full moon happened to coincide during one of my spells of night-duty. I was blissfully unaware of this momentous event and was patrolling the village during the hours of darkness in my usual manner. The inhabitants of the Hopbind Inn, however, had anticipated this accident of history and had been discussing it at length in the bar. One of the customers was Dick-the-Sick who had been paying one of his regular visits to Elsinby from Aidensfield. As had happened on previous occasions the regulars had plied him with drink and had talked him into taking action he would otherwise have avoided.

This background information was later supplied to me, but I include it here in order to retain the sequence of events. It seems that the locals of the Hopbind Inn were relating the stirring deeds of the brave, handsome Sir Nicholas and told how he met his untimely death. In the hushed atmosphere of the pub there followed the story of the ghost which appeared on such rare occasions.

The reaction from the bar was mixed, to say the least. The older customers swore that it happened – they *knew* that the ghost did appear. Newcomers to the area, and young people, pooh-poohed the idea, saying there were no such things as ghosts, let alone one that celebrated its owner's death by the light of the moon. The discussion raged long and fierce over full and frothy pints, and as the night wore on there arose the question of people's fear of ghosts. Among the loud voices raised in the bar that night was the familiar sound of Dick-the-Sick. He swore he was not afraid of any ghost. He didn't believe in them, and he was not afraid of anything which pretended to be a ghost, even if it was a long dead knight clad in black armour who walked by the light of the full moon.

A bold, definitive statement of that kind from Dick was like manna from heaven. As one, the customers turned upon the poor chap and coaxed him into proving his fearlessness. They plied him liberally with a fiery mixture of beer and whisky and persuaded him to prove his valour. His test would be at the ancient packhorse bridge which spanned the River Elsin at a point not far from the approach road to the castle. The ghost of Sir Nicholas crossed it at midnight when it appeared, and the locals told of the ghostly manifestation which walked from the castle towards the field where the bold knight had met his death by the light of the silvery moon. So horrible was the spectre that no one dared go near the bridge to test the truth of the legend.

It was no surprise to the packed bar that Dick found himself volunteering to watch the bridge that night, at midnight. Dick reassured everyone that he would do just that. He would settle the issue once and for all. Loud cheers greeted this announcement and it seemed yet another occasion to justify the unofficial extension of hours. It was the noise of this minor celebration which attracted my attention as I entered Elsinby that fateful evening.

I walked into the situation like an innocent child stepping off the footpath in London's Regent Street. It would be around 11.15 when I entered the village to see the pub lights blazing and the populace in full song. Closing-time was 10.30, so I entered the pub slowly and, like John Wayne might have done, thrust open the bat-wings of the saloon. Everyone fell silent at the sight of the uniform.

I looked at my watch, making the one-armed gesture very slowly as I stared in official distaste at the landlord, George.

'Pint?' he asked.

'Come off it, George!' I retorted. 'You know it's past closing-time. There's no extension. Put the cloth over the handles and let's be having you out, all of you. Everyone go home quietly.'

There followed the inevitable lull and looks of utter disbelief at my words. It seemed almost criminal to close a pub in this village, but George obeyed and draped the dwyles over the pump-handles, the signal that drinking had ceased. Then Dick-the-Sick pushed himself forward with an almost empty glass of evil-smelling fluid in his hands and said,

'Ah'ssh goin to sshoot the ghossht, Misshter Rhea.' He grinned widely at this announcement. 'Old Nick, down at the bridge, tonight . . .'

'What ghost?'

George came to the rescue. 'There's an old legend, Mr Rhea, that the ghost of Sir Nicholas Fairfax walks across Elsinby Bridge at midnight on the anniversary of his death, but only when it coincides with the full moon. That's tonight, you see, because he died by the light of the moon. He walks down from the castle and across the river to the field where he was killed by a rival.'

'Really?' I tried to sound convinced.

My scepticism caused several of the locals to join an attempt to convince me, and in the end George vanished into the private rooms of his inn and returned with an ancient volume. He opened it at a stained page bearing a drawing of an armour-clad knight striding across the old bridge. There was a full moon in the background and the caption supported their yarn.

'Ah'sssh goin' to sshhoot it . . .' and Dick vanished from the inn.

There followed some loud and heated discussion about the veracity of the story, and I must admit we all forgot about Dick and his shotgun. As the controversy raged I realised it was quarter to twelve, and I had a point at the village kiosk at midnight. It was time for me to leave.

'We're all going to watch the bridge,' George told me as I made my move to leave the inn. 'Coming?'

'I've a point at midnight,' I said by way of an excuse.

'The telephone box is just a few yards from the bridge,' he informed me as if I didn't know that already. 'You'd hear it ring if they wanted you.'

'Aye, all right,' I agreed, for it would be an interesting diversion for me.

In typical Hopbind Inn fashion, every customer in the bar emerged and made their way along the dark byways towards Elsinby Bridge. The bridge was little used because it was too narrow for the modern motor car, although foot passengers, visitors in particular, did enjoy its ancient, arched beauty. The track ran alongside the stream and provided numerous vantage-points among the shrubbery and vegetation. I reckoned there must have been thirty customers concealed along that river bank, all squatting in the darkness on stones and grassy areas, watching the hump-backed bridge. I sat on my haunches beside a man whose name I did not know, and in deathly silence we watched the graceful outline.

The bridge rose high above the water, rising aesthetically from each bank to its peak above the centre of the water. The route across was very rough and cobbled, but it was a beautiful construction, the work of many hours of hard labour. As we sat by the side of that bubbling stream, the full moon broke from the dark clouds and cast its green lights across the entire landscape. It was almost as light as day and yet the gloom about the shrubbery totally concealed the ghost spotters.

If the legend was correct, the ghostly knight would step on to the bridge at the far side and cross towards us, *en route* to the grassy fields behind. He must be almost due. I looked at my watch. It was three minutes to midnight, three minutes to the ghost's walk, three minutes to my point time. As I waited I wondered if Sergeant Blaketon or even the Superintendent would pay me a visit. Absence from a point was inexcusable, but I didn't want to leave here, not now. I must learn the truth of the legend. Risking my career, I stayed put.

Behind us, life in the village appeared normal. The occasional courting cat howled and cars passed through with muffled roars, then the peaceful picture was blessed by the cheery sounds of the parish church clock striking twelve. It began to boom out its twelve strokes, laboriously recording the irrevocable passage of time, and as I counted every slow

note, I kept my eyes glued on that bridge. There was not a
murmur, not a movement, from the assembled witnesses . . .
nine . . . ten . . . eleven . . . twelve! Midnight.

As the final stroke echoed and died away, a small cloud
slid across the moon and a dark shadow was cast across the
water. For the watchers it was like someone switching off a
light or blowing out a candle. It was all over and the ghost
had not appeared, although there was a distant eeriness as a
cool wind appeared as if from nowhere and fluttered across
the surface of the stream. Its passage whipped up tiny wavelets
and rustled the grass and leaves. I shivered. Then followed a
long, deep silence as the wind dropped. There was a total,
stifling silence. The tension was indescribable, but why?

'Good God!' breathed a voice behind me. 'Look . . .'

And there in the gloom at the far side of the water was the
dark, ghostly figure of the knight. It moved slowly and with
great precision, a tall, upright figure gliding smoothly and
purposefully from the shadows of the trees and mounting the
rising slope of the bridge. We saw only his top half – the legs
and waist were concealed by the parapets and the cloudy
darkness made the moving spectre very indistinct. But it was
certainly there. No one could deny it.

'I wouldn't have believed it!' breathed a voice close to me.
'I bloody well wouldn't . . .'

Then there was pandemonium.

The spell was broken by the crash of twigs and branches,
accompanied by a nervous shout and immediately followed
by the crash of an exploding twelve-bore shotgun. It came
from the far side of the beck, and the figure on the bridge
instantly vanished. I was aware of a running figure on the
other side of the river, but I got up and ran to the bridge.

Suddenly I forgot about spectres and ghostly creatures,
for I wanted to cross the river to catch the poacher at the
other side. I was sure I'd got myself a poacher, but as I crested
the summit of the tiny, short bridge my waving torch picked
out the figure of Sergeant Blaketon. He was crouching and
quivering with fear behind the shelter of the stone parapet.

'Rhea? Thank God!' he panted. 'I was shot at.'

'Poachers, I think, Sergeant,' I managed to say, panting slightly. I was thinking fast. 'I was on the other side, watching. I don't think he was shooting at you.'

By now the others had materialised from their hiding-places and were gingerly standing at our side of the bridge as I helped Oscar to his feet.

'It's the sergeant,' I shouted at them. 'He's OK. I think that poacher took fright, lads. He's gone.'

George came to my rescue.

'We'll catch the sod one day,' he said. 'Come on, lads. Back home.'

It wasn't difficult to assure Sergeant Blaketon we had been lying in wait to ambush a local poacher, saying we believed it to be a chap from another village. The suspect had eluded police, gamekeepers and residents alike, so we'd joined forces to catch him. Oscar seemed to accept this, because the area around the bridge was noted for its profusion of pheasants which roosted in the trees. We all expressed the feeling that the timely arrival of Sergeant Blaketon had terrified the poachers, who'd run off, accidently discharging their guns, or one of them, as they ran. One could tolerate one's own poachers, but not those from neighbouring areas.

Blaketon and I examined the ground near the end of the bridge and found signs in the earth which suggested a premature discharge of a shotgun at close range. Our theory was thus borne out.

Some time later I learned that Dick-the-Sick had literally taken fright upon the ghostly appearance of Sergeant Blaketon and had run off in terror. In the darkness and in his haste he had tripped over his gun, which had been accidentally triggered off. Blaketon never knew this, of course, and I was thankful for Dick's fear.

When it was all over and the men had dispersed to their homes Sergeant Blaketon and myself spent about an hour searching for the poachers but drew a blank. I felt a bit of a twit, searching in this way, but had little alternative. Finally, we adjourned to his car, where he produced his notebook, patted his pocket and said,

'Blast! My pen! My fountain pen! It's gone.'

'Maybe you lost it on the bridge, Sergeant?'

'Let's have a look.'

We returned to the ancient bridge and, by the light of my torch, searched thoroughly for his fountain pen. He told me it was a present to him when he left his previous job to join the police force years ago, and he was sentimentally attached to it.

Fortunately, I found the pen lying in a gully upon the bridge, very close to where I had found him crouching. I picked it up, handed it to him and said, 'It's been a lucky night for you, Sergeant.'

I meant it.

We turned and walked off the bridge and I was very content. It had been an interesting night. But, as we left, a cool breeze suddenly rustled the leaves and I shivered. It grew very cold and the village clock struck one. At that instant I chose to take a last look at the old bridge and my action caused Oscar Blaketon to turn his head too. In the back of my mind I was wondering how good a target he had been, and he turned to see what I was staring at.

And there, walking over Elsinby Bridge by the light of the moon, was a tall dark figure in a plumed helmet.

He said nothing. Neither did I, although I did wonder what William Willett and our altered clocks had to do with it. I couldn't decide. The intricacies of Greenwich Mean Time, British Summer Time and Central European Time were a little too confusing for me at that time of night.

But I often wonder who walked across the bridge.

Being practical types most policemen are not easily scared by rumour or fact and they treat ghosts for what they are – flimsy creatures who could never harm anyone, other than to send cool shivers down the spine or give rise to legends in pubs. There are exceptions, of course, because some police officers are terrified of ghosts.

Lanky Leonard Lazenby of Eltering Police Station was such a man. He was terrified of ghosts. The mere thought of them caused him to palpitate alarmingly and it was his misfortune to break into a cold sweat at the beginning of every period of night-duty. He had a dread of meeting a ghost during his patrol, a fact which was very evident to the other members of his shift. Some sergeants, however, were models of consideration and would arrange the station duties so that poor Leonard was given office work or alternatively patrolled the town centre, which was illuminated for most of the night. This arrangement was not out of deep compassion for Leonard – it was a means by which the job continued to be done, because a panic-stricken constable is of little or no value, with or without ghosts. It was sensible to allocate him to a duty where he was of some use, instead of being a gibbering wreck all night.

Periodically, however, Leonard's weakness was overlooked when a relief sergeant compiled the duty-sheet. These newcomers were usually ignorant of Leonard's propensity to tremble at the sound of a fluttering leaf, and so it transpired that Sergeant Charlie Bairstow was allocated the task of being night-shift sergeant for the Eltering Sub-Division.

He had often caused embarrassment to me and it seems, on reflection, that he was aware of Leonard's *other* great fear.

If there was one creature that Leonard feared more than a ghost it was the Superintendent. Superintendents of every kind terrified Lanky Leonard Lazenby. This combination of factors coincided one late autumn night when I was on duty in Eltering.

Leonard was also on patrol in the town and I was performing one of my motorised merry-go-rounds in the surrounding landscape. Another happy fact was that Ben and Ron, the terrible traffic twins, were also on night-duty, carrying out their routine motor patrols. That night we sat in the office, munching our sandwiches and telling stories. Sergeant Bairstow took the chair normally reserved for Vesuvius, who was enjoying a rest-day, and Leonard and I listened to the high-spirited pair and the sergeant as they entertained us.

Those night-shift meal-breaks were relaxing and enjoyable, and sometimes extended more than the permitted three-quarters of an hour. On this occasion Leonard had come in for his break at 1.30 a.m., which meant he was due out at 2.15 a.m. I had come in at 1.45 a.m. with Sergeant Bairstow, and the two traffic lads had entered at 2 a.m. Nonetheless, we formed a happy, laughing group.

As 2.15 a.m. approached, Bairstow turned to Leonard and said, 'Well, Len, it's time to go. Do the second half of seven beat tonight, will you? I've heard the Superintendent will be out early. He's doing one of his morning prowls, trying to catch us out, so we'll be prepared for him.'

'Yes, Sergeant,' said Leonard, his face as pale and as fragile as French chalk.

As Leonard worried about this instruction I noticed a sly glance pass between Bairstow and the two traffic men, but failed to read anything significant into it at the time. Like everyone else I knew of Leonard's terror of dark places and of his pathological dread of Superintendents. I realised that seven beat embraced the castle, its ancient chapel and graveyard, and the long winding and dark footpath through dense woodland to a Forestry Commission workman's hut high on the moors. Inside was a telephone, chair and table, with an oil-lamp. There was nothing else. The place was never locked and was regarded as a sort of refuge for lonely or lost folks on the hills, for workmen, for holidaymakers, lovers or even patrolling policemen who had to make points.

To reach this tiny wooden shelter from Eltering it was necessary to climb the steep flight of steps which led towards the castle and then walk through the adjoining graveyard. A stone-flagged footpath twisted among the ancient tombstones and emerged at the far side, where it led straight into the forest and along the unmade road towards the cabin. It was customary for the Superintendent to meet the beat man at the cabin at the weirdest possible hours. He seemed to enjoy the task of keeping us alert to the fact that he was likely to turn up here at any time of the day or night. I have yet to understand why we had to make a point here, but we did. Tonight it seemed as if the Superintendent was going to make one of his check calls.

That thought sent poor old Leonard scurrying along that route at the dead of night. His fear of Superintendents had superseded his dread of ghosts, but had not obliterated it. Thus he had two fears to contend with as he made his silent way towards that isolated point in the forest. I felt a twinge of concern for Leonard as he began his perilous journey.

When Leonard had left the office, Sergeant Bairstow smiled at Ben and Ron.

'OK?' was all he said.

'Fine,' Ben replied, and after another twenty minutes they also left.

I was now alone with Sergeant Bairstow.

'Well, Nicholas,' he said affably. 'It's been a quiet night, eh? No trouble? Nothing stirring.'

'Very quiet, Sergeant,' I agreed.

'You've never been to that hut, have you? The Forestry Commission place?'

'No, I haven't,' I agreed.

'The local foot patrols go there. It's not really on the beats of you lads from rural patches,' he told me. 'You can't get a car far along the track, although the Super sometimes manages. He wouldn't do it if it was his own private car!'

'Does he often meet men there?' I asked. 'It seems a strange place for him to worry about.'

'He's a strange man,' smiled Bairstow. 'Right, let's go. Leave your car – take a walk with me. I'll show you the castle, the ruined chapel and the graveyard.'

'Thanks.' I was looking forward to the break from routine, but puzzled by his actions. Why show me this? It wasn't on my beat tonight and anyway, Lanky Leonard would be braving the dark to cope with problems in that part of the Sub-Division.

I locked the office and allowed the friendly sergeant to guide me to the lonely Forestry Commission hut. We sauntered casually through the deserted streets and chattered in low voices as he led me towards the outskirts of the market town. Finally he took me through a thicket which led into woodland. As we climbed the steep, shadowy path, I could see the gaunt outline of Eltering Castle over to my right. The lighter areas of night sky revealed the battered outline of this interesting place and in true Dracula style a barn owl floated on silent white wings from the ramparts and glided over our heads as we moved stealthily towards the grounds.

'Don't make a sound,' whispered Sergeant Bairstow. 'There's something I want you to see up there.'

I puzzled over this as his measured tread became lighter. He strode ahead of me, tripping through the quiet avenues of trees until we entered the grounds of the ruined castle by climbing over a low drystone wall. I followed, hardly daring to breathe. Whatever lay in here must be very important and interesting because Sergeant Bairstow was creeping silently across the carefully cut turf and heading for the far side of the grounds. I followed as he padded across the emptiness of the ruin and eventually came to a small iron gate. It was closed but not locked, and he opened it. It squeaked faintly as we passed through and I found myself in a graveyard, somewhat overgrown but adjoining an isolated and ruined chapel.

A small church stood beside it and I knew the church did accommodate services from time to time. Certain Eltering families had ancient rights of burial here, for this was their parish church. Some had their own pews too.

Charlie Bairstow led me through the deep grass, weaving between the assorted gravestones which stood at every conceivable angle. Finally we came to rest near a sturdy obelisk mounted on a series of steps and surmounted by a cross.

'All right?' he hissed.

'Fine,' I said, breathing heavily after the tension of trying to be very quiet.

'Just watch,' he bade me, and I saw him lift his torch and flash it once or twice across the graveyard. I was surprised to see an answering beam from the depths of the distant shadows.

'Fine,' said Bairstow with no explanation.

There was a long pause during which he looked at his watch and eventually he whispered, 'See that path through the churchyard, over to your right?'

'Yes,' I could see it.

'It goes down to Eltering and emerges near the bus station. That's the way the bobby comes on his route to the Forestry Commission hut. We took a short cut.'

'Oh,' I said as if understanding his conversation.

'The hut is across to our left, a few minutes' walk into that forest,' and I turned my head to see the tall, slender, pointed outlines of the conifers which formed the forest.

Then there was some movement. He hissed for silence and squatted behind the sheltering base of the obelisk. I did likewise, albeit keeping my eyes on the scene ahead. My sight had become accustomed to the pale darkness and I could see that we were very close to the path which bisected the graveyard before leading into the woods. Beyond, at the far side, were more rows of dilapidated tombstones, some showing white in the darkness, and I was sure the torch flash had come from near one of them. I wondered if I was involved in an important observation exercise, perhaps lying in wait for a criminal? Maybe the local police had received a tip about something unlawful? A visit by a graveyard vandal, maybe? A robber of the Burke and Hare variety? A writer-on-tombstones? Someone hiding loot from the proceeds of crime? The handing over of stolen property? The range of possibilities was almost endless.

It was quite exciting really, waiting in the darkness with an experienced officer at my side and learning first-hand the art of catching villains and ne'er-do-wells. I was looking forward to the outcome of this strange excursion.

Then someone was coming. I heard the sounds. A tall figure materialised over to our right, coming from the direction of Eltering town. The darkness made it difficult to see him properly, but the anonymous person walked very slowly into the graveyard and began to cross it. I waited, my heart thumping. A crook? A night prowler of some sort?

The figure halted. Sergeant Bairstow cursed under his breath and I heard him mutter to himself, 'Go on . . . do it . . .'

A crime of some kind was about to be committed. I knew the value of witnessing the actual commission of a crime, rather than trying to convince a court that the man had attempted to commit something unlawful. There's a world of difference between an intent and an attempt, and another world of difference between an attempt and the full commission of an unlawful act. No doubt Charlie Bairstow wanted this character to prove himself a wrong 'un, then he'd pounce to effect a very smart arrest.

As the sergeant crouched at the base of the obelisk I looked into the gloom, trying to spot anyone else. The torch signal told me that someone lurked out there and I guessed it was the CID, although it could be a uniformed officer from Malton.

Sergeant Bairstow's eyes were still firmly fixed on the figure across to our right. The figure was still motionless. It was stalemate.

As Sergeant Bairstow appeared to be in command of the situation I looked around for other villains, hoping to contribute by spotting the approach of his mates. I looked around carefully and as my glance rested on the gate which led into the woods I saw someone. My heart leapt. There *was* another figure; he was standing very close to the gateposts and appeared to be hiding from the man on the footpath. He was just within my view. I could distinguish the pale face, although his clothing was so dark that it was impossible to see any more of him. An occasional movement betrayed him; sometimes I saw the white of his hand as he examined his watch and I thought about notifying his presence to the sergeant but I felt I should not interfere in this operation. Besides, any movement or noise from me could spoil the whole thing. After all, I was a mere observer in what was clearly a carefully planned police operation. Every detail would have been considered and every participant well briefed about his role.

Eventually the tall, slow-moving figure who was the focal point of the exercise came forward and his confidence was growing. He seemed to accept that he had a nerve-jangling mission to complete and began to stride purposefully across the quiet churchyard, heading for the concealed man behind the gate. The meeting was nigh. I could feel the tension, especially in Sergeant Bairstow. He hardly dared to breath.

When the man reached a point directly in front of Sergeant Bairstow and myself, Bairstow whispered, 'This is it, Nicholas!'

I watched intently, holding my breath. The excitement was electric.

Suddenly there was a ghastly shriek and I saw the earth move. A dim light appeared from the base of a tombstone directly across the path from our position, and I saw a horrible white face rise from the grave. A blood-red light accentuated the eye sockets and nostrils. It was an awful sight.

With a sharp cry the tall figure turned and ran. I saw him galloping the way he had come, and at that point Charlie Bairstow burst into fits of laughter. The tall, running figure vanished through the gate and could be heard crashing his way through the undergrowth towards the town.

Holding his sides with laughter giving pain and pleasure together Charlie Bairstow left his hiding-place and walked across to the scene of the apparition, laughing uproariously. I went with him, shaken but interested in what had happened.

My heart was pounding after the sudden shock but there, before us, were Ron and Ben, chuckling to themselves. Ben's face was smothered in white flour and the two traffic men doubled up with laughter as they saw us.

It had been a well-planned joke against poor Lanky Leonard.

I examined the scene. Covering one of the old graves at the side of the path was a large square piece of theatrical grass, a green mat-like material. It was the kind of stuff used in showrooms or upon the stage to simulate a grassy area and in the darkness looked most realistic. Ron had concealed himself behind the tombstone while Ben had laid full length

upon the grave of some long-dead character. The grass-green
coverlet had hidden him; with his face powdered a deathly
white he had lain there with his hands crossed upon his breast,
clutching the torch. At a shriek signal from Ron he had
switched on the light. With the lens covered with a piece of
red glass the light had shone from beneath the coverlet to
spotlight his horrible face, shining from directly beneath his
chin. Thus illuminated Ben had slowly raised himself into a
sitting position with the green coverlet pinned to his tunic
under the chin.

From a distance it had looked for all the world like a corpse
rising from its tomb and not the ideal sight for a highly nervous
person like Leonard.

Sergeant Bairstow and I had a good laugh, while Ben and
Ron thought the whole episode hilarious. Charlie Bairstow
had done it again – he had deliberately allocated this beat to
poor Lanky Leonard, knowing his fear of ghosts and his even
greater fear of the Superintendent. No one will ever know
the conflict in Leonard's mind as he struggled with his
decisions that night. From his point of view it must have been
horrifying and I must admit to a certain sympathy with him
as he galloped to safety. It transpired he had gone straight
home to report his going off duty, sick – suffering from
diarrhoea.

After the episode Ben and Ron returned to the office, taking
us with them in their police car. Over a cup of congratulatory
coffee we relived the prank which, I knew, would enter the
annals of remarkable police legends.

As we laughed and talked I remembered the other person
who'd been at the woodland gate. Who was that? He wasn't
here, celebrating with us.

'Who was that other chap?' I asked amid the laughter and
gaiety.

'Other chap?' cried Charlie Bairstow. 'What other chap?'

'At the top gate, the one leading into the Forestry
Commission land. He was standing there just before Ben did
his stuff. I saw him.'

'Are you sure?' Charlie asked. 'What was he like? Who was it?'

'I dunno,' I had to admit. 'It was somebody in dark clothing, hiding just outside the gate. I thought it was one of our lot.'

'Bloody hell!' he groaned. 'I wonder who it was?'

We racked our brains before resuming patrol, and I realised I still had not been to the mysterious Forestry Commission hut. There was always another time for that pleasure.

The next night, however, I knew the identify of the mystery observer.

The Superintendent had reported sick, ostensibly suffering from a stomach complaint.

4

'The learn'd is happy nature to explore
The fool is happy that he knows no more'
Alexander Pope – 'An Essay on Man'

The country policeman spends a lot of time walking close to nature and, in the still of the sleeping-hours, there is much to see and hear. Wild animals and birds appear to accept the presence of man at night in a way they would never tolerate during the daytime. Perhaps this is not an accurate assessment, but it certainly appeared to be true during my sojourns into the countryside of darkness. In some ways I was conscious of being an invader in their territory and yet their objections were never more than a mere whimper or a muffled cry of alarm. It is tolerance of this kind which makes one feel very humble and very sorrowful for the way man has treated nature in the past, and the way he will treat her in the future.

Although a good deal of my night-duty was spent in and around small market towns I did spend many hours among the pine forests, moorland heights and green valleys, either performing a routine patrol or engaged upon a specific inquiry or observation of some kind. I enjoyed these very much.

I spent one night, for example, in a draughty barn, keeping observations regarding a potato thief. The farmer, an interesting character called Bainbridge, cultivated a remote place on the outskirts of Briggsby and stored his season's potatoes in a large, open barn. The spuds accumulated there to await collection by a local merchant, but over a period it was clear that someone was sneaking in and stealing them by the sackful. One sack every week was disappearing but unfortunately there was no pattern to the thefts. It was difficult organising observations while engaged on so many other duties away from my beat, although I did deign to spend the occasional overnight stint in his barn. I hoped the potato pincher would enable me to arrest him red-handed.

One chilly night in late autumn, therefore, I informed Mr Bainbridge that I would inhabit his barn from midnight until three o'clock in the morning for the purpose of spud-watching. Thoughtfully, he provided me with a massive sandwich of bread and cheese, an apple-pie cooked by his wife and a quarter bottle of whisky, while I armed myself with my packed supper, a flask of coffee and a torch. It promised to be a long, boring vigil although food would not be in short supply.

Inside the barn I settled among the neatly arranged sacks and found a position out of the draughts, one which provided adequate views of the various entrances. For a time my potato-filled seat was quite cosy, but the chill night air soon began to eat into my bones. I took several short walks to maintain the circulation of my blood, but it was a long, cold duty and I was never cosy.

During my time in the barn I became aware of the intense animal activity in and around the place. Sitting immobile in the darkness, I could hear furtive scufflings and scratchings of all kinds, the sound of tiny creatures running about the dusty floor or investigating the sacks for morsels of food. High-pitched squeaks came from distant corners and I guessed they were mice or shrews. Now and again, I flashed my torch in the direction of those sounds, but seldom spotlighted anything. They were too quick for me.

I discovered a large brown rat which scuttled away as my light struck its eyes, and once or twice I lit upon the scampering figures of mice, busy about their night-time chores. Cats were frequent visitors too, and if anything, they were more alert than the creatures of the wild, scattering into the farmyard outside at the slightest hint of danger. A fox came too; I heard his approach because some nervous poultry in a nearby henhouse clucked their alarm as he sniffed and snuffled around their home. He knocked a bucket so that its handle rattled, but that didn't seem to scare him off as he continued to investigate the flap of the henhouse. I listened and guessed it was Reynard, my supposition being proved correct when he entered the barn.

I noticed his slouching gait as he cautiously entered the open barn, a dark, agile figure against a patch of light in the doorway. Then I flicked on my torch. I caught him squarely and bathed him in the light which highlighted his russet coat, his bushy tail with its white tip and those sharp, greenish eyes which glowed quickly against the beam. In a trice he was gone. He vanished as suddenly as he had come, and I never saw him again.

On one occasion a barn owl flew right across my line of vision, its soft underparts almost ghostlike as it moved silently in one door and out at the other side, doubtless hunting mice and other small creatures. Bats fluttered around too, albeit not many. These were pipistrelles, our smallest resident bat and they would be hunting late-night flying insects and finding their way around the pillars and contents of the barn by their remarkable system of radar. At times the place was filled with their squeaking cries.

In spite of the chilliness and the hours of inactivity it was a fascinating session of duty because nature came so close to me. The problem was that the thief didn't! I spent several nights in that barn but never saw him. Happily, he never came again. Maybe he was a local character who knew of my interest. I'll never know, but it does seem that my vigilance was rewarded because there were no further thefts from that barn, or indeed from the village.

My night-time country walks were equally enchanting. I have observed deer, foxes, otters, rats, mice, insects and a multitude of birds. I have found baby hares squeaking for their mums at my arrival, mother jackdaws nesting in ruined buildings, rabbits with their legs caught in snares and river birds with cruel fishing hooks stuck into their flesh, throats or

feet. I've found nests of baby birds and lairs of baby animals
and I've discovered dead animals of every kind, many having
perished pointlessly at the hand of man. There is little doubt
that man is nature's greatest enemy.

Of all the wild animals that I have witnessed at night Belinda
the badger is the most memorable. I called her Belinda because
I felt she needed a name.

We first met on a lonely and minor road between Elsinby
and Ploatby. I had parked the police car in a small complex of
buildings at the side of the lane in order to enjoy a half-hour
stroll. Such strolls were necessary because the eyes and ears
of a policeman on foot are infinitely better than the headlights
of a car when seeking villains or preventing crime.

That lovely lane is bordered on one side by young Scots
pines and on the other by low-lying fields. It is a long, winding
road, but I could walk into the heart of Ploatby and return to
the car in time to make my one o'clock point at Elsinby kiosk.

My boots had soft crêpe soles and I walked easily and
quickly along the smooth surface of the road, enjoying the
exercise and fresh night air, so full of the scents of the nearby
pine forest. To my left was one of the open fields and as I
approached its gateway I was aware of a creature scurrying
through the corn stubble. Its progress was very noisy among
the short, stiff stalks and I froze, my torch at the ready, waiting.
I was about twenty yards short of the gate.

It was fascinating, watching the outline of the rapidly
moving animal as it neared the gate. When it was very close I
could distinguish the unmistakable white face of the badger,
so recognisable due to the black bars which run the length of
the long snout. Not many humans have been privileged to see
this lovely animal in its natural surroundings, let alone observe
it at such close quarters, and I was enchanted.

The running badger squeezed beneath the lower bar of
the gate and started to cross the road directly ahead of me.
Its next move was to clamber up the steep grassy verge at the
far side of the road, and I could hear its sharp claws grating
against the rocky surface beneath. I now decided to flash my

torch because I wanted to see the badger more clearly and, as I switched on the powerful beam, it caught the fleeing animal like a spotlight.

Its broad, powerful back was a lovely silver grey colour, the effect being produced by a mixture of grey and almost black hair. As it momentarily turned its head towards me I saw two tiny eyes set in that long face, then its short legs carried it rapidly up the hillside towards the sheltering forest. Long body hair almost concealed its legs, making it appear to be running on castors. It moved with astonishing speed.

Still bathed in the light of my torch the badger had difficulty in clambering up the steepening slope, for it was a portly animal, but my presence and my annoying light spurred it to greater efforts. It reached the top and was then confronted by a tall wire fence, topped with two strands of barbed wire. I hadn't realised the fence was there.

The badger leapt at the barrier. I switched off my torch, not wishing to alarm it any further. I had no wish to panic the animal into doing something stupid, and I hoped it would not get its head fast between the top strands. It didn't.

Instead, it managed to get itself marooned across those wires. I did wonder if the barbs had got entangled with its thick belly fur, for the badger was well and truly stuck halfway across the fence. It was balancing on the centre of its stomach, with its head at one side and its tail at the other. Those tiny short legs were battling to secure a foothold upon the wire below, but they failed. They were far too short.

The result was that the badger was rocking to and fro on top of the fence, grunting and panting with frustration as it attempted to release itself from this embarrassing plight. Its long fat body straddled the fence like a sack of flour, and I laughed involuntarily. It was almost like a Chaplin comedy.

I couldn't leave it like that. I climbed the embankment and talked soothingly, as if that would make any difference! Soon I reached a position directly behind and knowing the badger's reputation as a hard biter, I kept well clear of the snapping teeth. With both hands I lifted the rump end and toppled it over to the far side, where it gathered itself, shook its entire body, and waddled high into the trees with never a backward glance or a hint of appreciation.

But that was not the end of our association.

The badger is a fascinating animal and I was delighted to learn that I had a colony of them on my beat. Almost every country dweller finds them interesting, so over the following months I made a point of travelling along that lane many times in the hope of seeing more of my local badger. Badgers are creatures of habit and I guessed that the route it had taken through the cornfield and under the gate to cross the highway had been used for many years by the local badger community.

It is this hard-headed determination to use the same route without deviation that has caused so many badger deaths. If a motorway or main road is built across a badger route, the badgers will continue to use it in spite of heavy traffic. Invariably, this has disastrous results to the badger population, for they are slaughtered by fast-moving vehicles. Some thoughtful highway authorities have built badger tunnels under their roads to preserve this curious animal from further mutilation and death. This is a good example of officialdom catering for the needs of the wildlife of England.

My patience was rewarded and I did see my badger from time to time. I did not make the mistake of shining my torch but allowed it to waddle across the road at its own pace. It always managed to clamber over the fence, achieving this without difficulty when it wasn't harassed into panic movements. I realised that the bulk of the creature was due to her pregnancy. I now knew she was a female, and she grew larger as the weeks rolled by.

My interest in the location of her home grew more intense and I began to enjoy the physical exercise of entering the wood to search for her sett, or cett as it is sometimes spelt. It wasn't very difficult to find because of the well-trodden path to the badger's regular route across the road. I climbed high into the trees and there, near the summit of a small hillock among the scented pines, I located the badger's home.

By any standards a badger's home is a remarkable piece of construction work, for this animal is perhaps the cleanest and most homely of the wild animals of England. This sett was typical, for it bore the tell-tale signs of occupancy by Brock. That is the name we give to the badger in North Yorkshire, a name which features in many place names and farm addresses like Brock Rigg, Brocklesby and so forth.

The entrance nearest to me was about a yard wide and eighteen inches deep, snugly situated beneath the roots of a straggling Scots pine. The area before the hole had been paddled down into a firm, earthen base by the regular comings and goings of the family in residence. Another sign comprised many claw marks on the trunks of nearby trees, the result of badgers sharpening their claws or cleaning them. Some twenty yards away were the dung-pits. The badger does not make a mess in its living quarters, but uses an outside toilet which it positions a short distance from its front door. Its cleanliness is further shown by its arrangement for other domestic waste. Down a slope was an area used to dump the waste from the interior of the home, like used bedding (a heap of grass and leaves) which had been carried out and thrown a discreet distance from the entrance. In winter the female might carry the bedding out to air and then return it for further use.

I knew the inside would consist of a labyrinth of tunnels and chambers, but I could not guess how large this particular sett would be. Perhaps there were other entrances and exits, but I did not have the time to search. I was happy that I had found her sett and made my way down the hillside to my waiting car.

From time to time I returned to her crossing-place but seldom saw her. I decided then to christen her 'Belinda' for reasons which now escape me, and then I saw her again. She was crossing the road in that familiar ambling gait and managed to scramble over the awkward fence. This time she appeared even heavier with cubs, and I knew that a sow could carry anything up to five young. Maybe Belinda would produce a large family.

My frequent excursions to this place revealed that she crossed the road around midnight, give or take twenty minutes either way. I knew that her route back to the sett would be the same each time, having been on a hunting expedition. Badgers enjoy their food, but are not particular what they eat – insects, beetles, worms, mice, wasps and bees are all fair game, and the thick coat of this animal makes it impervious to the anger of wasps or bees when under attack. Fruit are enjoyed too, and it's not unknown for a wandering badger to scent its way into an orchard to feast upon fallen apples.

Knowing of the animal's fondness for fruit, I did wonder if I could tempt Belinda from her sett with a few choice raisins or sultanas. Badgers love these fruit and I had heard tales of country folk making friends with them by using this bait. The badger is a one-man beast, however, and such a friendship can be somewhat tenuous.

Feeling there was little to lose and a lot to gain I began one of my night-duty patrols with a pocketful of raisins and later made my way to the edge of the sett before the usual time of Belinda's evening stroll. I placed a handful of raisins near the entrance and adjourned to a nearby hiding-place. It would be very foolish to shine my torch upon the mouth of the sett, so I relied on my night sight and was eventually rewarded by the grunting approach of the stout lady. She was grumbling and puffing as, heavy with cubs, she climbed the slope towards her sett. As she approached the entrance, she smelt the goodies and was clearly suspicious. I'm sure she'd never before been presented with foreign fruit but after a couple of exploratory sniffs she devoured them happily and vanished inside.

For a time this became a regular night excursion for me, both on and off duty. Each time I would drop a handful of raisins near the entrance and watch her enjoy them. Sometimes I would speak aloud from my hiding-place, talking to her as I had the day I helped her over the fence. The sound of my voice did not appear to alarm her and I began to wonder if she would respond to the raisins if I was closer to them. Maybe she already knew their presence was the work of humans. Maybe she knew I was there.

By now she was very heavy and I guessed birth was imminent. Spring was just around the corner as February moved along with its usual dose of rain and chill. Badger cubs are usually born in February and I knew that a happy event was expected very soon in this sett. I decided to test her tameness.

One night while on patrol I placed a handful of raisins outside the sett and squatted nearby within what I reckoned was the range of her scent. The night was dark, albeit not pitch black, and I could see the sett entrance quite clearly. The raisins were in a small heap in their usual place but nothing happened. Time dragged. My feet grew cold and I wondered if Sergeant Blaketon would be looking for me; maybe he'd find the parked car and wonder why it was deserted in such a remote place! I could always tell him I was seeking poachers . . .

Then she emerged. The distinctive grunting noise alerted me and suddenly her long snout appeared from the darkness below ground. She was quite visible due to the bright black-and-white pattern on her face. Without stopping she lumbered into the open air, sniffed at the raisins and began to eat. I spoke in a soft voice; she started, looked up briefly, but continued to eat. Undeterred, she gobbled up the tasty morsels with her piggy eyes fixed on me. I did not know whether she could see me, so I remained motionless, all the time talking soothingly to her. In my presence she consumed every morsel.

When she finished I dug into my pocket and produced more, tossing them before her. I thought she would take fright and run, but she didn't. She looked at me, then nibbled the extra helping. I threw more, closer to me this time and she came forward.

I had heard a lot about the ferocity of an angry badger and knew that one bite from those strong jaws could fracture my wrist or severely injure me, but I also knew of their trust in man. The badger is possibly unique among wild animals because it has no natural enemies in this country, its only foe being man. Man has tortured and destroyed badgers for centuries, sometimes under the name of sport and sometimes out of sheer ignorance of their value to the countryside. For example, badger-baiting was once a common sport. In this bit of fun a badger was tied to a post and had his jaw fractured; dogs were then turned upon him to tear him to pieces and in spite of his handicaps the mutilated animal would give the bloodthirsty spectators value for their dirty money. Today the threat comes from hunters armed with fearsome badger tongs, long steel tools which are thrust into the setts to drag the seized victim to the surface, where it is shot. Badger pelts have been used to make fur coats, their fur also making useful shaving-brushes and their heads have been fashioned into sporrans. In addition, many are killed simply for the fun of it, and some are slaughtered because it is feared they spread bovine tuberculosis among cattle.

In spite of everything a badger will still befriend a man.

But Belinda was safe from all this, at least for the time being. But was I safe from her? Did pregnancy make the sows dangerous? I talked softly, throwing more raisins to the ground and she took them all. She came closer, not as cautiously as I had anticipated. My heart was thumping as I tempted her to my hand. She moved slowly but clearly loving the raisins; she was very wary of me as I froze in my squatting position. I was literally inches from the pregnant sow.

Then I found I had run out of raisins. I scraped a dozen or so left in the corners of my pocket and placed them hopefully in the palm of my hand. I held them out for her, hoping the scent of my nervousness would not alarm her. It didn't.

Those narrow little eyes, close to the front of her snout, peered at me as she calmly nibbled the goodies from my hand. Then, quite abruptly, she turned and ambled off to seek more natural foods. I watched her go and lost her in the gloom, although I could hear her noisy progress through the undergrowth. Finally everything was silent.

It was an amazing experience and I will never forget those

precious seconds when she came so close to me, apparently without fear. I returned many more times to the sett during the following days but didn't see her. I knew the reason. She would be giving birth to her youngsters and looking after them. I wasn't sure whether the cubs remained in the sett for long periods of whether the parents took them out to learn the vital craft of survival. I had never seen the boar, although I must admit the difference in the sexes is not easy for humans to determine. The only real guide is that the adult boar's head is flatter and wider than that of his lady companion.

During the spring I paid several return visits during the midnight hours but didn't see Belinda. There was no sign of her on the road either and I began to wonder whether she had fallen foul of some badger hunter or been knocked down by a passing car. I searched the locality for signs of a carcase, but found none.

Then one balmy night in early summer I decided to walk up to her sett. It was very mild and light, a typical summer's night in June and I was not even wearing a tunic. I was dressed in shirtsleeves and police trousers, but I had my torch and, optimistically, my pocket was full of raisins. The sett still bore signs of being occupied and I felt sure she was there. I placed a handful of raisins outside the entrance and settled down for one of those long vigils. This time it was reasonably pleasant, as the night was so mild.

All about me were the night sounds of summer. Insects were busy among the trees, an owl hooted somewhere beyond my vision and there were countless unidentifiable sounds within the woodland. Little animals scurried about their business, perhaps investigating me, and I heard the twitter of birds disturbed by other creatures as they roosted above and around me. Among all this I sat still upon a convenient rock, watching the black mouth of the sett. Anticipation made the time pass quickly, and I must have missed at least one of my hourly points. I forgot the passage of time as I sat and listened to the night, and then the morning sun began to brighten the

sky around me. It was time to leave. It was just after three
o'clock.

Then there was movement. I froze.

Deep in the blackness of the miniature cavern I detected
movement. I couldn't be sure what it was, but something
definitely moved. I daren't budge, not now. My leg had
developed pins and needles, but I dare not shift it. I was
delighted when Belinda's familiar mask appeared, moving from
side to side as she sniffed the air, her sensitive snout unerringly
guiding her to my pile of raisins. She found them and grunted
in what I took to be a note of satisfaction, and then I saw her
family. Four miniatures of herself lurked in the background
and as she grunted at the food, they all emerged to join the
feast. They would be very handsome brocks, I knew, when
they grew up.

I watched in silence and remained utterly motionless, lest
I disturb this fascinating family breakfast. When they had
consumed the small meal they all looked about and sniffed
the air. I'm sure they scented me, but remained close to their
mother, who seemed to reassure them that this alien smell
was friendly. I talked softly, and the cubs all darted off, but
returned seconds later when I continued to speak in a low
voice. I held out a handful of raisins, which Belinda took from
my still hand, but the cubs did not venture so close to me.
They remained behind her, clustered in a cautious knot and
then as their mother continued to enjoy her early morning
snack they began to play and tumble with one another,
apparently oblivious of my presence.

Belinda finished her meal and I was gladdened to see her
join them in a hectic five minutes of boisterous play. Then
quite suddenly they all stopped and she ambled off down the
slope, with her playful brood romping behind.

I never saw them again.

Many weeks later I learned that Belinda was probably the
sow cub found by a local farm lad. That cub had been
orphaned by dogs during a raid on a local sett and the lad,
who lived in nearby Ploatby, had taken the cub home. There

he had reared it with affection but had left the district soon afterwards. The cub had been returned to the wild. Reports which reached me suggested that the badger, now fully grown, was sometimes seen in the locality and fed with tidbits by gamekeepers and farmers. If this was the same sow it would explain her lack of fear of me.

Later that year I found a badger's body near the roadside. I was sure it was one of Belinda's cubs because it was near their crossing-place. The badger had a fractured skull and was badly injured about the body, a casualty of a modern motor car accident.

Although I went to the sett from time to time I never saw Belinda or her family and I often wonder what happened to them. Badgers' families occupy their homes for centuries, and I did wonder if she had met some horrific fate at the hands of an unscrupulous human animal. I will never know.

In those days badgers were not protected by law, but in January 1974, the Badgers Act of 1973 became effective and protected this creature of whom Winston Churchill said, 'You are the most ancient of Britons.'

The badger has lived for centuries in North Yorkshire and this rural county welcomes his presence amongst us. It is very significant that the nation's first prosecution under that new law was undertaken within North Yorkshire, an indication of our local respect for Brock.

But I wonder if the law would have protected Belinda from her fate?

5

'He did not know that a keeper is only a poacher
turned outside in, and a poacher is a keeper
turned inside out.'

Charles Kingsley – 'The Water Babies'

For extremely personal reasons Claude Jeremiah Greengrass
took a late stroll in Brock Rigg Wood. This is an afforested
area on the hills above Aidensfield and, like much of the
district, it is owned by the Forestry Commission. Members
of the public are permitted to walk along its tree-lined roads
for the purpose of bird-watching or nature study, and the
procedure is to obtain the requisite pass from the local office.
This document must be produced upon demand to anyone
authorised to ask for sight of it.

So far as I know, Claude Jeremiah did not possess such a
document and indeed, that was not the kind of formality that
would unduly worry him. He rarely bothered with licences of
any kind. His woodland stroll in the small hours of a September
morning was destined to involve me because I was engaged
upon one of my periods of night-duty.

The trouble started when Claude Jeremiah found a set of
antlers lying on the ground of the forest. It was a magnificent
full set, abandoned due to the normal processes of nature, by
a male red deer. For this cunning little fellow the antlers
presented an opportunity to make a shilling or two by selling
them to a local antique shop. Mounted on a polished
mahogany base they would look beautiful above the door of
someone's house, so Claude Jeremiah promptly decided to

take them home. He would clean them and fix them to a suitable plaque, and sell them.

On the face of things it was a perfectly reasonable decision. The snag was that Claude Jeremiah Greengrass did not know the provisions of Section 2 of the Deer Act, 1963. This probably had little bearing on events because, if he had known, it would not have made the slightest difference to his actions. He would still have taken those antlers from the wood; he was that sort of villain. Acting in accordance with his instincts, therefore, he began to walk in triumph from the pine forest, proudly bearing aloft a particularly fine set of red deer antlers.

But even the best-laid plans go wrong: Claude Jeremiah had not bargained for the presence of Mr Archibald Flint. Mr Flint was a gamekeeper employed for the sole purpose of discouraging poachers and vandals. He was a dedicated keeper with some years' expertise and there were few men in the area who knew more about wildlife and the host of laws which protect nature from poachers and their ilk. Flint was a genuine expert, both in practice and in theory.

Having heard the twig-crackling approach of Claude Jeremiah Greengrass around one o'clock that morning Mr Flint sought refuge among the shadows on his hilltop kingdom. He was able to silently follow Claude Jeremiah about the woods and watch every move he made.

Because he was a stealthy man with many years of practice Mr Flint had followed the blissfully happy Claude Jeremiah for a considerable time before the latter had accidentally stumbled across the discarded antlers. It is interesting to speculate upon the thoughts ranging through Flint's skull as Claude Jeremiah's torch identified them as something special. And when Claude Jeremiah picked them from the ground Flint must have suffered chest pains. By 2.30 that morning Claude Jeremiah was leaving the woods with the antlers firmly in his possession. It was then that Archibald Flint pounced. He made threatening gestures with his twelve-bore shotgun and encouraged Claude Jeremiah to walk in front of it to a small gamekeeper's hut on the edge of the forest.

It was soon after this stage that I entered the story. Mr Flint telephoned our Divisional Office to announce his success and I was dispatched in the little Ford car to rendezvous with Flint and Greengrass in the isolated hut.

An oil-lamp was burning because someone had stolen the electric bulb, and I found Mr Flint sitting at one side of the rough wooden table with Claude Jeremiah sitting at the other. His brown, leathery face was wrinkled in disgust as the sombre gamekeeper maintained his vigil with the gun pointing directly at him across the table. The antlers in dispute rested on the table.

I entered breezily and said, 'Well, Mr Flint, what is it this time?'

Flint poured out the story of his careful surveillance of the prowling poacher and during this account Claude Jeremiah sat motionless and speechless. He had been to court enough times to know that any interruption was futile. It was far better to hear out the opposition because he'd then know the strengths and weaknesses of the other's story. He would get his opportunity to deliver a speech in due course.

I listened as the gamekeeper spoke in short, clipped phrases as if giving evidence in court, but I did not make any comment. I just gathered facts. I lifted the antlers, examined them and said, 'Well, Claude Jeremiah?'

'There's nothing wrong in helping myself to a set of antlers, Mr Rhea, is there? They were lying on the ground. Like a lump of wood. I didn't poach the deer they belonged to, did I? He knows I didn't. It was just the antlers.'

'He didn't kill the deer, did he?' I asked Flint.

'He did not,' said Flint emphatically. 'He took antlers. Antlers are part of a deer. It's in the Deer Act, Constable. It is an offence to take deer.'

'I did not take deer, Mr Rhea,' cried Claude Jeremiah, and I must admit I felt sorry for him. If I'd found his handsome set during one of my patrols I might have been tempted to keep them.

'Is it alleged that he took a deer?' I put to Flint.

'Deer and part of deer are the same; Section 9. By taking part of a deer he's committing an offence which is equal to taking a whole deer. Antlers are part of a deer, Constable.'

'Show me.'

The gamekeeper sighed and produced a small handbook from his interior pocket. He flipped it open at the relevant page. I peered at it in the flickering light and saw the vital words.

'He's right,' I said to Claude Jeremiah. 'It means court for you.'

'I'll be a witness,' volunteered Flint.

I knew of no power to arrest Claude Jeremiah for this offence, therefore I made a note of his personal particulars, which I knew by heart anyway. I cautioned him in the traditional way by telling him he was not obliged to say anything, but whatever he did say would be taken down in writing and may be given in evidence. I concluded by saying he would be reported for taking a deer at night, contrary to The Deer Act, 1963.

'I just took the antlers, that's all,' was his reply, which I noted.

I let him go but retained the antlers for evidence. I told Mr Flint that he would be informed of the court date in due course and that Claude Jeremiah would receive a summons. The formalities over, I gave Claude Jeremiah a lift back into Aidensfield and dropped him near his home. During that short trip he expressed his hatred of gamekeepers in general and Archibald Flint in particular, but refused to tell me why he'd been prowling around Brock Rigg forest during the night. After our chat I resumed my patrol.

In Eltering Police Office I entered the saga in my notebook and checked with Stone's *Justices Manual* on the veracity of Flint's claim. That reference book appeared to support his believe that antlers were classified as entire deer and I found no previously decided cases which might counter this. In short, it would be for our local court to determine this important issue.

Within a few days I had typed my account of the incident and had obtained a long written statement from Archibald Flint. He compiled his statement as a policeman would, and appeared overjoyed at actually catching this notorious local poacher red-handed. I've no doubt that Claude Jeremiah had been in those woods on many previous occasions without being caught, so perhaps this was justice of a kind. But we were not judging previous occurrences, and I submitted my report through Sergeant Blaketon, who agreed with everything Flint said and informed me he would recommend prosecution.

At first I did wonder if a written caution might have been appropriate rather than a hearing in court, but later agreed with Blaketon's decision. With a man like Flint pushing for a conviction it was best to let Eltering Magistrates' Court decide the issue. The matter would thus receive a public hearing.

In due course summonses were issued and the participants instructed to be at Eltering Magistrates' Court at 10.30 a.m. one Thursday morning. Alderman Fazakerly was Chairman and his accompanying magistrates were Mrs Pinkerton and Mr Smithers, with the efficient Mr Whimp as clerk of the court. The hearing opened with the usual applications for extensions of hours at local pubs and our case was first on the agenda.

'Claude Jeremiah Greengrass,' called the usher, and the untidy figure of my beat's most notorious criminal shuffled forward and stood before the assembled Bench.

'Is your name Claude Jeremiah Greengrass?' asked Mr Whimp.

'Aye, it is,' smiled Claude Jeremiah having answered this question in this court many times before.

'Listen carefully as I read out the charge. When I have finished you may plead either guilty or not guilty. Is that understood?'

Greengrass nodded.

'Claude Jeremiah Greengrass. You are charged that, on Friday, 27th September last, you took a deer during the night, that is between the expiration of the first hour after sunset and the commencement of the last hour before sunrise, contrary to section 2 of the Deer Act, 1963. How do you plead?'

'I didn't, sir. All I took was a pair of cast antlers, honest.'

'Am I right in thinking it is your intention to plead not guilty?'

'Yes, sir. I'm not guilty. I didn't take a deer, Your Worships, I found a set of antlers, old ones they were. That's all.'

'Thank you. You will get an opportunity to address the court. In the meantime you may sit down until it is your turn to give evidence. The offence with which you are charged is a summary offence and must be dealt with by this court.'

Mr Whimp sat down with a flourish typical of magistrates' clerks everywhere as Sergeant Blaketon rose to address their Worships. He was a fine figure of a man, standing in this rural centre of justice as he outlined the facts of the case. He summarised the evidence which would be given by Archibald Flint and called the gamekeeper to the witness-box. Flint gave a textbook account of the incident and concluded by producing Exhibit 'A', the antlers, duly labelled.

Next was an expert witness from the Forestry Commission, a Mr F.N.Z. Carruthers who told the court that the antlers were those of the red deer (*Cervus elaphus scoticus*), a species which frequented the plantation, although rare in other parts of England. It was plentiful in Scotland.

I was then called to give my evidence. I had to tell the court that, acting upon information received, I proceeded to Brock Rigg Plantation where I saw the accused and a set of antlers. I told the court of my brief interview, my cautioning of the defendant and his replies. I told of my seizure of the evidence, which I had labelled Exhibit 'A' and now produced.

When Mr Whimp asked Claude Jeremiah if he wanted to ask me any questions he leapt up and asked, 'Did I have a deer with me, Mr Rhea?'

'No, Your Worships,' I said. 'Just a set of antlers.'

'So I didn't take a deer,' and he sat down in triumph.

There being no further prosecution witnesses and no defence witnesses, next in the box was Claude Jeremiah Greengrass. He elected to give evidence from the witness-box and solemnly took the oath before beginning his account.

'I've always wanted a set of antlers, sir, to hang on my wall. I knew they'd put red deer in those woods, to see if they would breed. You don't get many red deer in England, sir, do you? Scotland, yes, but not England. Anyroad, I went up that night for a look around, just in case there was some lying discarded, you understand. The bucks discard their antlers, you see, knock 'em off on tree branches. Well, I found yon set, nice pair they are too. Just lying on the ground. So I picked 'em up, and got to the edge of the wood when Flint caught me. I didn't kill the deer to get them antlers, honest. They was just lying there.'

No one wished to put any questions to Claude Jeremiah Greengrass because the facts were not in dispute, and he was allowed to stand down. Alderman Fazakerly leaned from his lofty seat and whispered to Mr Whimp. I heard the loud whisper.

'I fail to see the point of this case,' he said. 'The fellow has obviously not killed or taken a deer, even if it was at night.'

'No, sir,' advised the patient Mr Whimp. 'That is not the allegation.'

'Isn't it? Then what is?'

'The case is based on the definition of a deer, sir.'

'Oh,' blinked Alderman Fazakerly. 'Is the prosecution trying to say that a set of antlers is a deer?'

'That would appear to be the interpretation, Your Worships,' smiled Mr Whimp. 'The relevant authority is in the Deer Act, section 9,' and he handed up a copy of Stone's *Justices Manual*, open at the correct page. I knew what it said, for I had read it some days ago. It stated that for the purposes of the Deer Act, '*a deer means deer of any species and includes the carcase of any deer or any part thereof.*'

'The antlers are not a carcase, are they?' simpered Mrs Pinkerton.

'No, but they're part of one,' grunted Mr Smithers. 'And they are part of a deer. The Act says that part of a deer is a deer.'

'It seems a bit hard on the fellow, doesn't it?' the Chairman whispered. 'It's not as if he's been poaching red deer, is it?'

'The Act says it is illegal to take deer at night,' Smithers spoke bluntly. 'He's admitted that, so he's guilty. Part of a deer is the same as a whole deer. The law says so.'

'Mrs Pinkerton?' asked the Chairman.

'The law is the law, so I must agree,' she simpered.

'Thank you,' the Chairman smiled. 'I also agree. He's guilty. What about a penalty?'

The advisory Mr Whimp came to the rescue. 'The offence carries a maximum fine of £20 for a first conviction,' he said smugly.

Fazakerly pursed his lips. 'I'd prefer an absolute discharge on this occasion. As you are aware, that is legally a penalty and a conviction, although it carries no fine or other sanction.'

They all agreed, so Alderman Fazakerly raised his head and addressed the assembled court, including Claude Jeremiah Greengrass.

'Claude Jeremiah Greengrass,' he cleared his throat in a judicial manner. 'The Deer Act was created to protect these beautiful creatures from poachers, and Parliament has seen fit to regard parts of a deer as equivalent to the complete animal. Because you have admitted taking antlers at night you are therefore guilty of the offence as charged.'

'Never!' cried the defendant.

'Is anything known against the accused?' Alderman Fazakerly asked Sergeant Blaketon.

Blaketon read out a list of his previous convictions, petty as they all were.

'Hm. Nothing serious, and no previous deer-poaching, eh? Well, Mr Greengrass, on this occasion we are prepared to grant you an absolute discharge. This means that, although you have been found guilty, there will be no penalty and no conditions as to your future conduct.'

'That's very kind of you sir, very kind indeed,' and the relief was clear in his voice.

Sergeant Blaketon jumped to his feet.

'Would Your Worships care to make an order for the disposal of Exhibit "A"?'

'Ah, of course. Well, as it was clearly found on Forestry Commission land, it must belong to them. The court therefore orders that the antlers be restored to the Forestry Commission. Perhaps Mr Carruthers will accept them?'

Carruthers smiled. 'In the event of a penalty other than a fine, Your Worships, I am authorised to donate them to the defendant, as a gift.'

'Then let it be done,' smiled Alderman Fazakerly.

And the weathered face of Claude Jeremiah Greengrass broke into a cheeky smile. Flint, on the other hand, turned a deep purple, and failed to appreciate this court's administration of rural justice.

Poachers are an integral part of village life. They are not all of Claude Jeremiah's calibre, although a rural beat like Aidensfield certainly possesses its share of grouse-grabbing villains. Most are local folks, men whose ancestors have been poachers over countless generations and for whom poaching is a natural pastime like walking or breathing. Coping with them is never difficult because the gamekeepers know them and know how to deal with them, albeit unofficially at times. For the gamekeeper and the local poacher the eternal contest is almost like a game – sometimes you win, sometimes you lose. In many cases a friendly rivalry exists, although it can be a serious contest at times.

Part of the reason for the cosy attitude is that the poaching laws are so mysterious to those who do not understand their requirements. They create offences which are not theft but which involve trespass. There are many offences within the scope of the poaching laws, and the illegality is created when poachers *trespass* in pursuit of game. The actual taking of game cannot be theft because the creatures are wild by nature, consequently it is trespass which forms the basis of the offences.

This makes it fun for the poacher. The sport can be compared with schoolboys sneaking into gardens to steal apples, although it must be said that there is big money in poaching and that pinching apples from gardens *is* theft!

It is the likelihood of big money that attracts carloads of highly skilled and ruthless poachers from the cities. These are the real villains, and they are a far cry from the village poacher who takes the occasional pheasant or salmon for his family lunch. These rogues journey into the rural regions of Yorkshire, there to give the estates a 'bashing', as they term it. They've even been known to use explosives to stun fish in rivers, in order to collect them in large quantities, while some of the cunning methods used to catch game-birds are fascinating. For example, raisins are sometimes soaked in brandy and this gets pheasants so drunk they cannot fly off. A drunk and disorderly pheasant is a curious sight.

My beat was attractive to poachers because it was the location of several large country estates. Some possessed the traditional lord of the manor and a large mansion for him to live in. These people were good to me and were good to the local residents, consequently none of us disliked people of quality. In fact, they were good for the district because they provided work for the communities and therefore helped preserve village life. Their extinction will be a tragedy for England.

For the poachers of industrial West Yorkshire, however, the presence of such happy hunting-grounds within an hour's drive of their back-to-back homes or high-rise flats was very tempting and challenging. There were reports of luscious pheasant, succulent partridges, juicy salmon and other culinary delights, all waiting to be taken by skilful and daring men, and quite free of charge too. All that was needed was a little time and patience. One of my regular and important duties was to liaise with gamekeepers and keep their lordships informed of trends and poaching intelligence. Like all country policemen I reckoned it would be nice to arrest an organised bunch of poachers.

An opportunity to do that arose one autumn evening. I was on night-duty and had elected to patrol the village on foot, for it was a Saturday. On that night especially, the local people liked to pop out to the pub for a noggin or two. I entered the Brewers' Arms at Aidensfield shortly before 10.30 to pay my customary uniformed visit. I knew the appearance of a uniformed bobby was appreciated by most landlords who wanted rid of hangers-on and who liked to go to bed at the same time as everyone else. I poked my head around the door to let everyone know I was about. The place was full; there was noise, laughter, happiness and music and there seemed to be no juvenile boozers or troublesome characters.

I waved across the sea of heads at the landlord, who saw me and waved back. Word would get about that the law was prowling and the drinkers would go peacefully to their homes. One or two locals made jokes about my presence and I was preparing to leave when the landlord hailed me.

He didn't shout for me; he just raised his hand and I recognised the signal. He wanted help or advice. This prearranged signal did not attract attention, so I went outside to wait. He followed and joined me soon afterwards, panting slightly.

'Glad I caught you,' he said. 'Did you notice those men in the corner?'

I shook my head. The place had been packed and, besides, not all the regular patrons were known to me.

'Strangers,' he said. 'I don't know them, but Sam overheard them talking.'

'Go on, George.' He was also called George, like the landlord of the Hopbind Inn at Elsinby. I wondered if all landlords were known as George.

'They were talking of giving his Lordship's river a bashing tonight,' he told me. 'Sam definitely heard them. Salmon, you know.'

'Thanks.' I valued this information. 'Has the river been done before?'

'Once or twice, down at Victoria's Bend.'

'Victoria's Bend?' I didn't know it.

'Half-way between here and Ploatby. It's a wide, sweeping bend in the river, and I'm told there's salmon in there, lots of them. It's named after Queen Victoria – she used to come and stay at the Hall, and liked to sit down there near the river in the summer. It's been called Victoria's Bend ever since.'

'I know it now.' I recognised it from his description. 'Right, thanks George. I'll inform the keeper.'

'He's in hospital, broken ankle,' George said.

I cursed under my breath. I'd have to cope myself, for I was the only policeman on night-duty, although Sergeant Bairstow was on patrol elsewhere in the Sub-Division. I peered at the two suspicious men through a side window so I'd know them again, then rang the sergeant from my own office. He was out and his wife did not know where he was, but she did inform me that he was expected back about one o'clock in the morning. He was obviously supervising several night-duty constables.

I decided to visit the location of the anticipated bashing in order to familiarise myself with the layout of the ground, river and trees. I walked along the rocky path which followed the line of the bubbling water and came to the long, sweeping curve in question. I knew this to be the haunt of succulent salmon and wondered about their habits and movements. I spent some minutes there, trying to work out the likely movements of the poachers.

In order to catch them I would have to wait in hiding until they proved the purpose of their visit by lowering lines or nets into the water. Those actions alone would be proof of their intent and I could give such evidence in court. But I had to see them do it. I found a convenient clump of bushes about fifteen yards from the river bank and concealed myself behind it. From here I had a clear view up river towards the direction from which the anticipated poachers would come. I looked at my watch. It was just after eleven o'clock.

I waited for about an hour and a half and began to wonder

if my time was being wasted. Maybe we'd panicked? Maybe it was a joke between the two men? I thought of all the other things I could usefully be doing, like drinking tea in friendly houses or shaking hands with yet more door-knobs in Ashfordly. Maybe the pub had done this to get me out of the way, so they could drink late? All manner of thoughts, nice and nasty, passed through my mind as I waited among the shrubbery and then I became aware of the approach of two men.

They walked very quietly, using the same path I had walked along. Even in the gloom I could see they carried rods, nets and gaffs, and wore waders. They were well equipped for their mission. As they neared me I could hear them whispering softly and soon they found a small promontory about fifty yards beyond me. They settled upon this, rigged up their rods, nets and gaffs and prepared for their vigil. I watched them all the time, making notes of the precise time and their actions. I waited. It would be nice to catch them red-handed with a salmon – that would be perfect proof. Should I wait for that? Or pounce now? I had enough proof to justify action.

Suddenly the water broke violently and there developed a fierce thrashing and lots of vile cursing; they'd got one, a big one, judging by the fight it was creating. The water turned white about their feet as they gradually hauled the catch towards the shore. I saw the glint of the cruel gaff as it embedded itself into the flesh of the fish. Still thrashing wildly the gleaming fish was lifted bodily from the water and cast deftly on to the bank where the men pounced upon it. It would be swiftly killed.

As they worked on their prize I crept from my hiding-place and was upon them before they realised I was there. I said all the proper things about being caught poaching, cautioned them officially and 'seized' their lines, rods, gaffs and nets, plus the salmon. That was my evidence. I had half expected them to make a run for it, but they didn't. They accepted their arrest most peacefully and I marched them back to the village and up the hill to my police house. They made no excuse and never attempted to escape from me. I was thankful, if surprised, at their meek submission.

I rang Sergeant Bairstow because he would have to officiate in the office as they were charged. He was now at home, it being half past one in the morning, and I passed on my glad tidings. He grumbled and cursed because I'd got him out of bed, but I chose to ignore his feelings as I prepared to drive my prisoners into his office. He would charge and bail them.

In the car the two poachers remained silent and I found it most surprising that these men were models of good behaviour. I'd heard of poachers attacking bailiffs, gamekeepers and policemen while in the act of making arrests, and I'd also heard of poachers running into the darkness never to be seen again. But these characters never spoke a word in anger, and never gave me a minute's trouble.

They provided their names and addresses. Both lived in York and seemed quite blasé about us keeping their expensive tackle. Charlie Bairstow bailed out each man in the sum of £25 to appear at Eltering Magistrates' Court in two weeks' time, to answer several poaching charges. They hadn't a licence to fish for salmon or trout, and were to be summoned for several fishery offences. All these were listed, and the police would act as agents for the Fishery Board because there were offences involving their activities on private land.

At the conclusion of the formalities the men apologised profusely for their actions and left the office. I remained behind to provide a quick account for Sergeant Bairstow and he listened intently.

'Nice work, Nicholas,' he smiled. 'You've made a couple of good arrests there. Night poaching, eh? The magistrates will love this one.'

'Thanks, Sergeant.'

'Now you'd better go and get the others.'

'Others?'

'Yes, others, Nicholas. There will be others, probably several of them.'

'There was only that couple, Sergeant.'

'That's right. They would be the advance party, sent deliberately to get caught. Think about it, Nicholas. Think about tonight's events. Those men enter a local pub where strangers are immediately recognised, and they begin talking about giving his Lordship's river a bashing. Why do that? Why tell the locals what they're up to? You are told and you lie in wait – they turn up laden to the eyeballs with fishing gear and you arrest them. A good job, well done. But it's all too easy, Nicholas. Did you notice how they left this office? They didn't ask for a lift anywhere, did they? I'm bloody sure their car isn't in Ashfordly, not when they were drinking in an Aidensfield pub. Someone would be waiting for them. Now they'll all go back to Victoria's Bend and give those salmon a real bashing. The money they'll make tonight will pay the fines of the two volunteers and everyone will be happy – except his Lordship.'

I considered his theory. It seemed feasible and I must admit that I had been surprised by the submissive attitude of the two poachers. I thought it all over right from the start, and reckoned Charlie Bairstow was right.

'I'll go back and arrest the others, Sergeant.'

'Not on your own, you won't. This needs more of us – the next lot won't be as gentlemanly as your first catch.'

'There's only you and I,' I said.

'Then I'll organise help,' he assured me. 'I can rustle up a constable from Eltering, and I believe the dog section is on patrol in Malton. They've been to a late-night dance – they can be here in half an hour.'

'Shall I go and keep observations?' I asked.

He shook his head.

'No, think it through, Nicholas. What is going through *their* minds right now?'

'They'll be waiting until the coast is clear,' I said.

'And is it clear? If you were a villain, doing what I believe they're doing, would you consider the coast to be clear?'

'No, not until the bobby has gone to bed.'

'Exactly. They'll be waiting for you to turn in.'

'I'm on nights,' I said.

'They won't know that. There's no reason why you shouldn't *pretend* to go to bed, is there?'

'Ah!' I got the gist of his thinking, then realised my pretended return for bed would arouse Mary and the children.

'Right,' he said. 'Go home. Park your motor-bike in the garage and go into the house. Go through all the motions of going to bed – lights on downstairs, office light on. Office light off, kitchen light on as if you're having a cup of coffee. Bathroom and bedroom lights. OK?'

'Yes, Sergeant.'

'Then when the house is in darkness creep out and make sure no lights are on. Meet me at 2.30 behind the Brewers' Arms, on foot. Wait there until I arrive with reinforcements.'

'Yes, Sergeant.'

'I'm sorry if it disturbs your family, but it's a worthwhile job.'

I left Ashfordly police office on my motor-cycle and chugged noisily home. I hoped my furtive activities would not cause too much upset among my family, but they were accustomed to the strange comings and goings of my motor-cycle. I placed the machine inside the garage and went through the routine of booking off duty and going to bed. Inside the house I switched on the kitchen light as I walked through to the office and switched on the kettle for a coffee. In the office I sat at my desk to write up my notebook as I would have done. Then I switched off the office light, adjourned to the kitchen and brewed myself a drink. I took it into the living-room, making sure all the lights were on, and I enjoyed the brief rest. Upstairs there was not a sound. I hadn't wakened them.

Having enjoyed the drink I pretended to climb the stairs to bed. Lights went off and on as I went about my fictitious movements, but there was not a murmur from the family. It made me realise how easy it is to burgle a house . . .

Once all this performance was over I crept out of the house, which I left in total darkness, and made my way on foot down to the village. It was about 2.20 and there was not a soul about. I crept into the pub car-park and was greeted by the rapid flash of a torch. Sergeant Bairstow had arrived.

'OK?' he asked.

'Fine,' I said. 'And not a murmur from the kids.'

'Good, let's go. Is there an approach for us that isn't direct from here?'

'We can go through Home Farm fields,' I told him.

'Lead on,' and I realised he had an army of policemen with him. Two men whose names I did not know were in the shadows, each with a police dog and there was another tall, senior police constable who I guessed was from Malton.

We marched through the darkness with me leading the way. We did not speak as I led them through a small copse and into the fields of Home Farm. We kept close to the hedges, which provided shelter, and after twenty minutes I halted them.

'The river is down there,' I said, pointing to the brow of a small hillock. 'Behind that hill the bank goes fairly steeply towards the river. The banks are lined with bushes and trees. The curve known as Victoria's Bend is down there – that's the favourite place for salmon.'

'I don't know what to expect,' said Bairstow. 'I don't know how many we'll find – if any! I imagine there'll be those we nicked earlier and their mates. Maybe two carloads. Seven or eight of 'em,' and he outlined a plan of action. We would use our torches or police whistles as signals.

'The dogs can cope,' said one of their handlers, when I expressed concern that the poachers might be armed.

'We'll use one dog at each side of them,' said Bairstow. 'And one of us at each side too. I'll stay with Nick – he knows the lie of the land.'

Two constables, one of whom was a dog-handler with his Alsatian straining at the leash, vanished to my right and were quickly lost in the shadows. They moved silently across the turf, climbed the fence and were soon moving through the woodland towards the river bank on my right. Bairstow, the other dog-handler and I crossed the fence to our left and clambered down the hillside. I felt we were making far too much noise, but Bairstow didn't call for silence.

Soon Sergeant Bairstow halted and pointed.

'There!' he whispered, and I followed the line of his outstretched arm.

Silhouetted against the silvery sheen of the moving water were several heads, all working at the river's edge. I could hear the roar of the rapids higher upstream, and realised this noise would conceal our movements. I counted five men. I guessed there would be more, the others perhaps posted as look-outs.

We were below the skyline and, as we neared the water's edge, the woodland thinned considerably. Finally we reached the riverside path. Bairstow waited for several long, agonising minutes and then flashed his torch twice, very quickly. The response came immediately – two flashes. The others were in a similar position, ready for action.

We moved forward, knowing our colleagues at the other side were doing likewise, closing in and making a sandwich of the poachers. Then up went a warning shout. It surprised us all. We'd been seen.

'Bailiffs!'

A man had been concealed behind a bush on the river bank and we almost tripped over him. Too late we realised he was there. He ran from us, shouting his warning as he rushed towards his pals.

Sergeant Bairstow did not flap. He simply stood his ground, pulled out his police whistle and blew it. It was the first time I'd heard a police whistle used on duty, and it galvanised us into action. The dogs were told to 'speak' and began to bark as Sergeant Bairstow called upon the poachers to stand still or be bitten in some very painful places. Four of them stood rock still, but one tried to escape by climbing over a fence into the fields beyond.

The look-out had vanished too, but a dog handler now called to them all, albeit addressing the man heading for the railings.

'Halt or the dog comes after you!' he bellowed. The running

man did not halt. He ran for all he was worth and I heard the handler tell his dog to deal with the escaper. He slipped the lead and with a glorious bound the agile dog leapt in pursuit of the frantic man. The other dog barked encouragement from the distance and it seemed as if this character was the only one foolish enough to attempt to outrun the dogs. Its handler followed with fitful strides as the bounding dog pursued the foolish poacher.

He could never hope to outdistance the dog, but someone must have given wings to the fellow's heels, for he did manage to clamber over the fence and was precariously balanced on top when the dog arrived. In the dim light we could see the drama. The man was balanced on top of the railings and was preparing to leap down into the field. At the precise moment he took off, the dog leapt up and seized his arm. With a cry of horror the man fell and we heard the tell-tale growlings and snarlings of a police dog which had cornered its prey.

'Leave!' cried the handler, and the dog sat back on its haunches, tongue lolling as it watched the sobbing, terrified youth. The others in the meantime, including the look-out man, had been gathered into a huddle and were guarded by the other dog. Its presence was enough to guarantee their co-operation.

The attempted escaper, who had fallen head first into a bunch of nettles, was gathered up and brought back.

We seized their gear for evidence, took them all to Ashfordly Police Station and bailed them out to appear before Eltering Magistrates' Court in due course. It was a skilful gang from Leeds, but the pair we'd caught earlier was not among them. None of this gang admitted knowing the other two, but I didn't believe them.

From our point of view it had been a good night's work, and I collapsed into bed at 6.30, tired but happy after the night's events. I told myself that when I woke around lunchtime I would ring his Lordship to acquaint him with our overnight success. He'd be pleased, I knew; maybe we'd each receive a complimentary salmon!

But his Lordship woke me at 8.30 by banging on the door of the house and demanding to see me. Mary had to arouse me, due to his insistence, and I staggered bleary-eyed downstairs to find him in the lounge, flustered and angry. Very angry indeed.

'Poachers!' he shouted. 'I had poachers last night, Rhea! Down at Ferris Bridge. They've given me a right bashing and here's you, lying in bed all day . . .'

I groaned.

6

'His motorcar was poetry and tragedy, love and heroism. The office
was his pirate ship, but the car his perilous excursion ashore.'

Sinclair Lewis – 'Babbitt'

In my early days in the Police Force it was considered by
those in authority that motor cars were not for ordinary
policemen, either at work or at play. That a constable could
or would ever own a car was something abhorrent and this
thinking was reflected in the fact that police houses had no
garages, police stations had no parking places and police
training centres issued 'Guidance to Students on Arrival'
without once mentioning a motor car. Perhaps Scotland Yard
did not subscribe to this image because old films about the
police invariably showed a long-snouted Wolseley roaring out
of the pearly gates of that famous Police Headquarters. Indeed,
many police forces later advertised Henry Ford's cars in
sombre black garb as they rushed up and down main roads
with 'Police' written all over them. In those days 'Police' was
synonymous with efficiency and quality, and I'm sure the police
forces who used Ford cars provided useful, albeit unconscious,
recommendation for Mr Ford's engineering skills. Another
peculiarity was that detective story writers rarely used motor
cars in their yarns to convey detectives around, even though
some of their detective inspectors did dress for dinner and
take sherry in country houses.

The reality of police thinking suggested that a constable
driving a car was akin to a gardener using his master's Rolls-
Royce, so the perambulations around our beats meant we

had to rely heavily upon our feet or else use very ancient pedal cycles. Cycles were unreliable because the lamps never worked and the tyres were always flat. Official cycles were large, upright monsters, painted black all over and sporting a chain guard. For years they provided the traditional mode of transport for the travelling constable, and still do in some areas. The constable went to work upon it, did his work upon it and travelled home upon it. Some forces actually paid an allowance to those who used their own pedal cycles for duty, and as this was based on the mileage covered on duty, little books were issued to the riders, in which the official mileage was recorded and checked carefully by the sergeant.

Eltering's official cycle was rusty and unfit for duty. The inspector requested a replacement; in fact, he was extremely daring because he applied for two county bicycles, basing his claim on the fact that the establishment of his officers had doubled since 1910 and new roads, coupled with expanding villages, had brought more people within range of our patrols. Much to his surprise his wish came true – the Police Committee at County Hall considered his application and allocated two new pedal cycles to Eltering Police Station. Sergeant Blaketon was appointed officer in charge of county cycles and promptly numbered them 1 and 2. He issued a mileage book to each machine. No. 1 cycle was to be used as the main machine, with No. 2 being used only in emergencies or when No. 1 was otherwise engaged. After each journey the mileage book must be completed, showing the date, times and places visited, with the name of the rider in charge at the time. He further instructed that after use the cycles had to be checked for cuts in the tyres, damage or loss of wind; the lights must be checked and the saddle cleaned for use. In this manner, therefore, the constables of Eltering became mechanised.

It was some time before I understood why Eltering managed to acquire two cycles. A few years later I learned that the Police Committee had been considering the issue of motor cars to selected town stations like Eltering. It transpired that the inspector had applied for two pedal cycles and had put up such a good argument for them that the Committee felt Eltering did not require a car. Ashfordly got a little car and so did Malton, while Eltering continued for years with pedal cycles.

A little Ford Anglia did arrive in due course, and indeed most rural stations eventually possessed one of these delightful vehicles. At the larger stations the Superintendent had a large Ford, usually a Consul, while the inspector made do with a Morris Oxford. No one else was allowed to use these sacred treasures and they were treated like pots of gold. The Superintendent's car was cleaned, oiled and maintained by a mechanically qualified constable, who also lit the fires, looked after stray dogs, cooked the meals for prisoners and did every other job around the station. He also spared a moment for the inspector's car, but studiously refrained from interfering with the pedal cycles. Another less talented officer cared for these machines.

It goes without saying that it was never easy travelling from place to place during routine duties. If our cycles lacked the speed necessary to reach emergencies while they were still emergencies we had to improvise and we did this by standing in the middle of the road in full uniform with hand raised. This was guaranteed to stop most vehicles and in this grand manner we begged or bullied lifts, or we took a bus.

Under no circumstances must we use either the inspector's or the Superintendent's car. Even though they were official vehicles, it was understood they were official only to those exalted ranks, and were most definitely not for the likes of working constables rushing off to deal with burglaries, rapes, sudden deaths or mayhem of other kinds. They were used to convey the higher ranks to their dinners and other important social functions.

There were occasions, however, when ambitious constables let their crime-detecting ardour get the better of them to such an extent that they made use of the Superintendent's car. The horror of such an action was too fearful to contemplate, but this happened to me on one occasion.

I was working 'office nights' at Divisional Headquarters during a shortage of men, and the time would be around two o'clock in the morning. The telephone rang, a rare event in that station at any time, but particularly so at this early hour. I answered it. A very anxious gentleman was calling from a kiosk in the market-place and his message was to the effect that his car had just been stolen and was, at this very moment, being driven out of town at the hands of an unscrupulous villain. The gentleman provided the registration number and a brief description of his vehicle, so I asked him to make his way to the office where a colleague would look after him. Meanwhile I would give chase. There was not a moment to lose.

I rang Control Room and provided them with a description, saying the stolen vehicle was heading towards York. Control Room promised assistance in the shape of a modern, highly sophisticated police patrol-car. I could hardly set off in pursuit on my motor cycle – by the time I'd got myself dressed in my plethora of gear, the car would be miles away. I decided to use the Superintendent's car, for it was parked in the station garage. I made this decision in the full realisation that my career might come to a sudden end, but villains are there to be caught. I might just catch this one. If I did nothing about it my career could come to a similarly swift end.

The gleaming car awaited. Its keys dangled from a hook in the Charge Office. Feeling almost as if I was taking this car without lawful consent I took the keys and raced around to the garage. Within seconds I was on the road and enjoying the chase. There is little doubt that these official cars were beautifully maintained and tuned. The policemen who looked after them nursed a deep pride in their work, and all vehicles were in a superb condition. There was not a scratch on this car and its paintwork gleamed. Its engine purred like a contented cat and I found myself humming with sheer enjoyment as I sped through the sleeping town in pursuit of the stolen car. This was the life!

I switched on the radio, gave my call-sign to Control Room as I booked on the air, and smiled at the consternation of those listeners-in who would think that the Superintendent was not only out on patrol, but hotly pursuing a stolen car. Such is the effect of a personalised call-sign like Mike One Zero Papa. I listened to the commentary on the radio – a York constable was heading towards me, hoping to head off the vehicle, and it was a fair bet that one of us would halt the flight of HAT 101. That number was etched into my memory.

I sped along the fine surface of the main road with the wind whistling about the car as I drove to its limit. I touched 100 m.p.h. and the car remained as steady as a rock. I had been mobile for some ten minutes when I heard Control Room announce to all involved in the hunt for HAT 101 that a village petrol-pump owner had heard a noise and had seen the car-driver helping himself to a tankful of fuel. I knew the village. It was off the main road, so I turned off its long straight carriageway and bore along the peaceful dark lanes. I urged the willing vehicle into the bends and along the straights at speeds which would have terrified me under normal circumstances. There was a maze of lanes here, but I knew I wasn't far from the village in question. The car could be in any of these lanes.

Quite suddenly I came up behind the stolen car. It seemed the thief had not realised he was being chased because he was pottering along at a fairly sedate 45 m.p.h. I was now faced with the problem of stopping him. This was not easy, especially on such narrow lanes, and it was before the days of blue revolving lights and flashing police signs. I had to rely on my headlight dip switch, horn and my voice. There was no loud hailer fitted to this car – some of the more splendid patrol-cars possessed loud hailers from which booming voices, amplified many times, could halt a thief in seconds and arouse half the town in the process. But I had none of this sophisticated equipment so I shouted out of the window, blared my horn and flashed my lights. It had some effect.

The driver thought I wanted to overtake him, so he pulled

into the side of the lane to allow me through. At that stage, it seems, he realised it was a black car with no markings but containing a chap in uniform bent on stopping him. Quite understandably, he accelerated. I did likewise. Suddenly we were roaring alarmingly along the narrow lanes with lights flashing and horns blaring. Tall, thick hedges rushed at us on the corners, and hills yawned before our noses. Houses tore past and cattle shook their heads in bewilderment. How long we careered like this I do not know, but it seemed like hours. Then very unexpectedly he turned sharp left, which meant I had to brake urgently. Tyres screamed as I attempted his sudden change of direction and I found he had careered through an open farm-gate and was currently sinking into a foul-smelling pond. I stopped at the edge as he clambered across the roof of the car, now up to its axles in slime, and I said, 'Come on, you're under arrest.'

'Oh, bloody hell!' he said in evident resignation and he came quietly as arrested persons tended to do in those halcyon days. I conveyed him to the police station, where a sergeant now waited. The formalities of searching him, questioning him and eventually charging him were completed and the perplexed owner was taken out to retrieve his car from the pond. We drove the Superintendent's car on that trip too, and used a tow-rope to haul the abandoned vehicle from its soggy parking-place.

By six that morning the excitement was over. The man had been charged and would appear at court that morning. Meanwhile he would remain in the cells as a guest. The loser had got his car back, the farmer into whose pond the stolen car had dropped would have a tale to tell at market and I would be roused from my sleep by nine o'clock, only three hours later, in order to attend court and give my evidence. In those days policemen weren't supposed to need sleep.

I attended court and the case was rapidly dealt with, the thief pleading guilty to the offence of taking and driving away a car without the consent of the owner. He also pleaded guilty to careless driving, and using the car without insurance. I gave evidence in the formal manner drummed into us at training school and he got away with a total fine of £65, and had his licence endorsed.

I was then ordered into the inner sanctum, wherein dwelt the Superintendent. I expected praise for my part in effecting the swift arrest of the car-thief, but instead found myself facing a very red-faced and irate Superintendent who waved an official log-book at me. It belonged to his car.

'This!' he simmered. 'This book – last night you drove over 100 miles in my official car – my car. Two trips, each of fifty . . .'

'Yes, sir,' I said.

'But this is the *Superintendent's* car!' he bellowed. 'It is not to be used for routine patrolling, not under any circumstances and certainly not by a constable.'

'I was chasing a stolen car, sir,' I began to explain. 'I had no other means of catching the thief,' and went into a long-winded and fairly exaggerated account of my escapade.

He fumed and panted as I continued, but my reasons were totally invalid. I almost felt he was going to charge me with taking and driving his car without consent! He told me again that Superintendents' official cars were not to be used for routine police work, they were for supervisory duties. In short, I got the bulling of my life and retracted from the office with my pride wounded. There was no doubt in my mind that if I had not used the Superintendent's car that thief would have escaped. I was convinced my actions were justified.

Higher authority didn't think so. My actions that night led to a Divisional Order which stated quite categorically that the Superintendent's official car must never be used for routine police patrol duties. It was a supervisory officer's vehicle for use by supervisory officers on supervisory duties.

Like all such orders, however, there was an escape clause. This allowed the car to be used for emergencies, but this permission was qualified by saying it could be done only by the personal consent of the Superintendent.

The inevitable happened. I was on night-duty some weeks

later in the same police station when an almost identical event occurred. A householder heard noises in the street and looked out of his bedroom window in time to see his Morris Minor vanishing from sight. He immediately rang the police station and I answered the telephone; the result was a repeat performance of the previous escapade, except that I rang the Superintendent at home to get his personal permission to use his car.

Three o'clock in the morning is never a good time to arouse anyone from sleep, let alone one's superior officer, but he was very good about it. He said I could use his precious car to chase the thief. Actually, he had no alternative – to have refused would have created all manner of problems if I had had to explain to an even higher ranking officer how I had been refused permission for operational reasons. So the chase began.

This crafty character selected a winding route which twisted through many villages. I knew it well, even though it was pitch black and even if I was perhaps a little more tired than I should be. But I knew the roads this thief was using, and like the previous case I guessed he would not realise he was being followed by a keen young constable.

I pressed the accelerator and the finely tuned car responded. It took me into those bends and along those lanes with a whirr of tyres and a flash of speeding hedges, villages and lanes. I was enjoying myself; this was great. It was better than watching Edgar Lustgarten's films or re-enacting a Scotland Yard chase in a Jaguar or something equally splendid. I was thrilling myself as I hurtled along those lanes in the Superintendent's lovely vehicle.

Everything went well until I ran off the road. I still cannot remember where the road went, but I do recall sitting in the car and leaning forward at an alarming angle. The front wheels were in a ditch and the rear ones were spinning uselessly in mid-air. I switched off the engine, disengaged the gears and clambered out, dropping like a pilot from an aircraft as I landed on the grass verge beneath. The car smelled very hot and there were enough sods of grass lying about to carpet a cricket pitch.

I was totally alone. The place was deserted and I had not arrested this thief. Luckily, the car radio still worked, so I called for assistance.

I had a very long and painful report to submit when I returned, and the Superintendent said he had no wish to see me.

I understand he was very upset about it.

Because policemen rarely owned vehicles they experienced great pleasure when sitting in the passenger seat of a shining black police patrol-car. Riding in one of these gleaming machines was the next best thing to owning one, and the truth was that official motor cars remained a luxury in many forces even into the second half of the twentieth century. Supervisory officers did use them, but not constables on routine patrols.

It will be appreciated therefore that the opportunity to actually *drive* a powerful police-car was considered one of the greatest possible honours. This honour was occasionally bestowed upon selected personnel who formed a specialised unit known as the Road Traffic Division.

Men selected for this duty were undoubtedly the *crème de la crème* of any police force. Not only had they proved themselves good practical police officers in the traditional style, but they had also shown themselves highly skilled in driving, even managing to retain their smartness in spite of the shiny seats of their trousers and the paunchy bellies which resulted from too many hours in the driving-seat. These were the swashbuckling heroes, men with hair styles reminiscent of RAF officers during the war, always well groomed and eye-catching. These were ladies' men, an élitist group with a penchant for obtaining cups of coffee in highway cafés and an ability to control a speeding car in all conditions. They were to the police service what fighter pilots were to the Royal Air Force.

They created legends in their own time. There were tales of skilled patrol-car drivers waltzing their cars beautifully on ice, tales of high-speed drives across the moors to rescue suicidal men hanging by ropes from beams of ancient inns, and daring chases to capture stolen vehicles or meet superintendents at rendezvous points. Whatever they did became a talking-point over coffee from our night-duty flasks; it was all thrilling stuff.

For the young policeman whose mode of conveyance was his feet this was a lifestyle to dream about. To become a patrol-car driver was the ambition of many and the lot of a few. As if in answer to our dreams it was deemed by higher authority that all young constables should undergo a short attachment to Road Traffic Division.

This was to familiarise us with the miracles performed by this group of specialists, so that we knew their abilities and capabilities. Thus in the course of our duties we could call upon their expertise, and it was hoped we would make greater use of these fine fellows in moments of stress or dire emergency. The cars used by these giants were different from ordinary police vehicles – they had radios for one thing, and their speedometers had been rigorously checked over a measured mile in order that speeders could be safely prosecuted in court. These cars had signs right across the front which said POLICE and which could be switched on at night. Their commodious boots were full of paraphernalia to deal with traffic accidents, like a broom for sweeping up broken glass and a shovel to put it on, a tape measure, cones for warning oncoming drivers, a first aid box, balls of string, lifting gear and a host of other useful things. Unlike modern police cars they did not have blue flashing lights, noisy horns and sneaky computers like VASCAR to trap speeders.

There is no doubt that these shining black cars held a certain enchantment and offered a romantic interlude in the average bobby's career. An attachment to Road Traffic Division, however short, must be considered a step towards this Valhalla. It so happened that my fortnight's attachment coincided with a period of night-duty, which meant I was allocated a night patrol in a warm police car. The arrangement was that I patrol my patch as usual, albeit in the company of a seasoned patrol driver, and our joint manoeuvres would satisfy his patrol requirements in addition to providing supervision of my beat during those nights. It seemed a reasonable compromise and I looked forward very much indeed to my introduction to Road Traffic Division's marvels and mysteries.

On the first evening I presented myself at Ashfordly Police Station, where it had been arranged that my driver for the shift would collect me at 10.20. I was armed with a flask of coffee, tin of sandwiches and my trusty torch. At the appointed time my heavenly chariot arrived. It was a shining black Ford Consul known as Mike One Five, pronounced Mike One Fifer in phonetic jargon, and alternatively referred to as M15. The car's unfortunate call-sign led to it being known as Mystery One Five or the Secret Service car and its driver was PC Rupert Langley.

He was a thirty-year-old married man with a lovely wife and two equally lovely children. Rupert and his family had transferred to the North Riding Constabulary from Kent because his wife loved horses and wide open spaces. Malton, with its racing-stables and accessibility to the moors and dales, seemed a perfect posting although her love was for hunting and hacking rather than racing. None the less, it was an ideal place for the Langley family to grow up.

Rupert was at least six feet two inches tall with a slim, athletic build topped by a mop of wavy black hair. The women he met at work and at play fell instantly in love with his dark, thoughtful eyes and it was said that many deliberately drove their cars carelessly or parked illegally in the hope he would take down their particulars. In spite of his sun-tanned magnetism he never strayed from his family home and was always faithful to his wife.

Few disliked Rupert, and I was delighted he was to show me the work of Road Traffic Division. He was highly articulate and very amusing, two talents that were quickly in evidence as he introduced himself and showed me around his car. It was clearly an object of pride for him as he explained how to operate the radio and how to use the various call-signs favoured by Road Traffic Division. He explained all about the speedometer, so accurate and tested regularly for evidential purposes, the specialist tools and equipment in the boot and finally the PA. I did not know much about the latter device, but studiously observed him as he operated a switch on the dashboard.

'That switches on the PA,' he said, as if I knew all about it.

'Does it?' I wondered whether to show my ignorance but he recognised my uncertainty.

'Public address system,' he clarified the point. 'About half our fleet is fitted with the public address system. It's a loud-hailer device, really, worked off the battery. I just speak into the handset of the official radio,' he picked up the handset, 'and switch it on. Then I can talk to crowds of people outside all at once, or get cars to move aside or stop. Warn folks about lost drugs or bad road conditions. That sort of thing. It's marvellous. You can tell a whole street about a gas leak in no time.'

To demonstrate it he switched on and said into the handset, 'Good evening friends.' Outside the car his words boomed and echoed about the police station and I felt sure they would be heard as far away as the market-place. I wondered what the towns people would think as those words filled the night air, and guessed a drunk or two might suddenly become sober.

Having seen the magic of the car I climbed in. I was now officially an 'observer' and as such would be responsible for noticing offenders and incidents during this shift. I would also have to provide supporting evidence for any court case secured by Rupert.

Not knowing what excitements lay in store we set off smoothly, the beautifully tuned car transporting us in sheer luxury. We accelerated out of the police station yard and made for the tiny town centre. The official radio burbled quietly from the dashboard. It was my job to show Rupert around Ashfordly and district and I felt he was worthy of being shown some of our secret places, where tea and buns could be obtained at all hours. It was his task to educate me about the skills of his specialist department and our mutual task was to police the area tonight.

Rupert talked freely and I found him easy and entertaining to listen to. As a southerner, he had found the North Riding people to be somewhat blunt at first, but had since grown to like and respect them for their toughness and straight speaking. He had grown fond of the North Riding countryside too, and talked of making it his permanent home. He liked his work, he was happy with his car and appreciated the opportunities provided for him. In short, he was happy; a rare and contented man.

Our first tour of duty was spent getting to know each other, and attempting to understand each other's mode of working. Nothing of any great significance arose but our second shift was to prove much more interesting. We stopped one or two motorists to advise them about faulty lights, and I toured my vulnerable properties to check for signs of illegal entry. In this way we successfully combined our roles, and my beat remained peaceful.

Towards midnight we found ourselves in Brantsford market-place and Rupert decided to park for a few minutes to observe the passing scene. This is always a useful exercise, although Brantsford dies at 10.30. That is the time the pubs close and, as that event had passed quietly, our vigil was distinctly lacking in action and pace. To be truthful, that was the situation until a stray dog appeared.

It was a cur dog, a type very common among the moorland farmers of this region. They are small, hardy animals, predominantly black with patches of white fur, and this one emerged from a side street to sniff the cool night air. It cocked its leg against a lamp-post and wandered into the main street. It was quite alone.

I noticed Rupert lift the handset of his radio, but I did not link that action in any way with the dog. Next he pressed the PA switch. This meant the public address system was alive.

That which followed was quite surprising. Rupert lifted the handset to his mouth and began to produce the most realistic sounds of a dogfight I've ever heard this side of Percy Edwards. The amplified battle cries reverberated across the town and it was as if all the hounds in hell were fighting in Brantsford High Street. The innocent cause of this commotion stood in the middle of the road, highlighted by a street-lamp with its hair standing on end, its tail as erect as a flagpole and its teeth bared in a realistic grimace as it sought its hidden foe. Rupert continued to growl and snarl until several doors opened and many lights came on; people came to see what was happening and one pub was cast open to discharge a late-night party into the street. Everyone wanted to observe the fight but all they found was a very puzzled cur dog alone in the middle of the street.

Then Rupert stopped.

It was amazing how busy the small town had become and we now had something and somebody to watch. From the excited voices of the pub crowd it seemed they were members of a 21st birthday party which was being held for the landlord's daughter. The entire gathering from the pub was now in the street, all clutching glasses of drink and seeking nearby nooks and crannies for the dogfight. Up and down the street windows had opened both upstairs and downstairs, and curious folk leaned out, asking questions of one another and expressing their concern about uncontrolled dogs. The party-goers provided a backcloth of coarse humour for the roused slumberers, and among all this speculation and commotion the bewildered dog wandered about, now totally unconcerned about the flap it had caused.

Rupert sat with a big smile on his face and I laughed quietly at his side. It was almost like watching a live stage performance, with no idea what was to follow.

'You've certainly livened up this place!' I chuckled. 'It's quite busy now.'

'It works wonders when things are quiet,' he said, taking out his pipe and lighting it. 'I find it fascinating to watch people as they hunt the dogfight. When they go in I'll do it again, briefly. They'll all rush out again – they'll talk about it for ages afterwards.'

And he did. Ten minutes later the cur had vanished and the drinkers had returned to their party. The windows had been closed, the doors had been locked and the town restored to its normal state of tranquillity. Rupert's second impression resulted in the ghastly amplified sound of dogs fighting to the death, two killers snarling their vengeance upon each other, howling and barking in the darkness.

From our vantage-point we enjoyed a repeat performance as more lights came on, more doors opened and the party-goers rushed out once again, laughing and shrieking as they nervously sought the Hound of the Baskervilles. By now my sides were aching with suppressed laughter but Rupert simply sat there, nursing his pipe as he observed the bewildered people trying to solve the mystery. I wondered what kind of rumours would be rife in the little town tomorrow, and tried to visualise what Sergeant Blaketon would do when the tales reached his ears. He'd probably arrange a purge upon stray dogs.

'Let's take a walk,' Rupert said quite suddenly, stuffing his pipe into the car's ashtray. We left the warmth and security of the car, walked into view of the people and patrolled the High Street much to the relief of the residents. Several asked if we'd heard the dogfight, and Rupert denied it. He explained that we'd just arrived, although he did mention a cur dog which was now trotting peacefully home along Junction Terrace. The final scene in this drama was an invitation to join the birthday festivities. We did this and enjoyed them tremendously. I could see that Rupert's talent was already paying dividends.

During the nights which followed I was to learn more of his unique and fascinating talent. In similar moments of inactivity I would ask if he could mimic particular sounds and would challenge him with requests to copy things like squeaking gates or a roll of thunder. Invariably he could oblige. Sometimes his art was undertaken in the privacy of the car without coming to the notice of the general public, but by far the most interesting sessions were those broadcast through the public address system of his patrol-car.

I have seen women blush delightfully at a loud and sincere wolf-whistle coming from somewhere beyond their ken. I have seen those silly people about to jay-walk or drive their cars out of parking areas without looking, pull up sharply in the face of Rupert's stern warnings. I've known him bid 'good morning' to his friends in this way and 'goodnight' to home-going drunks. I've seen him remind his wife, whom he noticed out shopping, to bring home his favourite cheese or some meat for the cat. I've also watched him mischievously make totally unidentifiable sounds – one example is a simple clicking noise, the sort one does with one's mouth to encourage a horse to trot. When done through an amplifier in the street the noise can be very baffling and it's good fun to watch the genuine bewilderment on the faces of those who cannot identify it. Other small intriguing noises included clicking his fingernails into the mike, drumming his fingers on the side of the microphone, scraping a matchbox's sandpaper with a thumbnail or simply yawning loudly.

But it was his ability to imitate specific sounds which I found most interesting. He could produce an excellent cuckoo and I'm sure he was the cause of many rural folk writing to their newspaper to boast of hearing the season's first cuckoo. I have often wondered how many early cuckoos were Rupert idling his time in a layby. The blackbird's alarm call and the honk of a pheasant were nicely done too, and I'm sure he created despondency among the wildlife on my beat. I could imagine the local birds and beasts hearing these alarm calls and accepting them as genuine before scurrying to safety.

It is difficult to highlight the most memorable of his imitations, but two remain etched in my memory. The first occurred in the very early hours of one morning when we had been diverted to the seaside town of Strensford upon a rather urgent enquiry. It was almost an hour's journey from our beat, but as Rupert was the only patrol-car driver on duty that night, it meant we had to undertake the task. We left Aidensfield at eleven to arrive about midnight and deal with the inquiry. It was no more than a traffic inquiry from a southern police force, but it demanded the knowledge of an expert Road Traffic officer because it involved the misuse of a Goods Vehicle Carrier's Licence. I didn't understand the urgency but went along and learned something of this branch of traffic law. We concluded at 1.30 and decided to have our meal-break at Strensford.

We could have gone to the police station, but it was a lovely summer morning with a clear, bright sky, so we decided to enjoy our sandwiches and flasks on the clifftop. There we could enjoy the superb views out to sea and watch the coasters sailing by. Rupert knew the town sufficiently well to select a quiet parking place overlooking the harbour.

He was a fascinating companion. He boasted a fund of interesting stories and seemed to know a little about everything. Fortunately, he was not a boastful type and it was during this conversation that he reminded me of the part played by the little man who sat in the little office at the end of Strensford's ancient swing bridge.

From our vantage-point, we could see the bridge. It was of Victorian vintage and spanned the middle harbour, the only link between the east and west sides of the town. Being old-fashioned it was operated by the man who sat in the tiny round hut at one end. When a ship came into the harbour and wished to proceed into the upper reaches to berth it had to make its presence known to the bridge man. He would then open the bridge to allow it through. Passages of this kind were done only at high tide and, as high tide varied from day to day, the town was frequently brought to a standstill as a slow-moving ship sailed upstream between the open halves of the bridge. There was nothing anyone could do about it, and the bridge became a popular tourist sight.

'I'll show you something,' he said when we had finished our meal. He started the engine and drove down to the harbourside, where he parked in the shadows of the fish-sheds with the lights off. 'See the little hut on the bridge?'

'Yes,' I said, for I knew it well.

'The bridge man will be in there now. It's manned for two hours either side of high tide. I can see his light on.'

He flicked the switch of his PA and proceeded to give a first-class imitation of a ship's hooter. He gave three blasts, each very slowly and each reverberating above the sleeping roofs of the town. To my ears it was a perfect reproduction of a ship's hooter and I felt sure the population of Strensford would never know it was a fake.

'That was good,' I said sincerely.

'Watch the little hut,' he smiled, getting out his faithful pipe.

After a few minutes a little man rushed out, peered into the darkness of the lower harbour and then uncoupled some links at the centre of the bridge. He remained on the half nearest our side of the water and I watched the massive bridge begin to open. He had set the mechanism in motion before emerging and, very slowly, the two halves split at the centre, each swinging open and moving the entire structure to the sides of the river. When it was fully open the halves halted and I could see the figure of the little man standing expectantly on the edge of his half. He was peering towards the sea.

Rupert started the car engine and drove out of the fish-sheds. When he was on the road he switched on his headlights and cruised towards the bridge, where a closed gate prevented sleepy drivers leaping off the edge and into the water.

'Evening, Harry,' he got out and shouted at the fellow, who still gazed out to sea.

'Morning, Mr Langley. You haven't seen a ship down there, have you?'

'Not where we've been,' smiled Rupert, strolling to the gate and leaning on it.

'I could swear a hooter went, honest.'

'Hooter?'

'Aye, a ship's hooter, three blasts. The signal to open the bridge. Didn't you hear it?'

Rupert shook his head solemnly. 'Not me, Harry.'

'It must be my age,' said Harry walking towards us. He remained with us for about three minutes, during which time no ship materialised from the darkness.

'I'm going barmy,' he said and re-entered his little hut to set in motion the machinery to close the bridge. He repeatedly uttered sighs and said he couldn't understand it; he could have sworn he'd heard the signal to open up. Rupert never made the bridge-man any wiser and we each received a cup of tea from him. We whiled away an hour in his company, listening to tales of his seafaring days. Like all old men he loved to reminisce.

And so it went on, each night producing another sound from the strangely constructed throat and lips of PC Rupert Langley. He imitated the crowing cockerel of dawn and I'm sure many a worker has rushed off early because of it. He did a useful motor-cycle scrambling sound and wasn't bad with a car's horn. Howling dogs and braying donkeys were easy and on one occasion, he excited an entire coachload of day-trippers.

This happened in Eltering during a night-patrol. The party had enjoyed a full and merry day at the seaside, having concluded their outing with a visit to a late-night club. They had left the club around two in the morning and their coach stopped at an all-night café in Eltering for toilets, tea and coffee. Their choice was a transport café, very pleasantly clean and a point of attraction for night-duty policemen.

The truth is that we fancied a cup of tea about 3.30 that morning and decided to visit that same café. We arrived in the car-park just as the trippers' bus began to disgorge its load. Before we had time to climb from our vehicle the entire contents of the coach had formed a long queue in the narrow doorway. It stretched halfway across the car-park, and the solitary fellow on duty would take ages to cope with this lot.

We remained in the car, watching the queue with sorrow. The more we thought about our lost cups of tea the more thirsty we became.

Then I saw Rupert's eyes twinkling. Out came his pipe, which he lit among clouds of pungent fumes and, as I guessed, he picked up the handset. What was he up to now?

With the handset close to his mouth he began to produce a sound like a distant wind. It whistled slightly, then gradually intensified and changed its note. Now it was just like a jet aircraft. As Rupert increased the volume of the noise I realised that the tail-enders of the tea queue were all peering up at the sky, seeking the elusive and noisy aircraft.

The note grew louder. Then he changed its pitch. Suddenly he produced another sound as if the engine was spluttering and backfiring. It sounded as if an aeroplane was coughing alarmingly, and he followed with a high-pitched whistling, for all the world like a crashing and doomed aircraft. The bewildered queue was buzzing with excitement and anticipation, with all eyes raised to the dark mysterious heavens as the unknown aircraft entered its final seconds.

Then the crash. How he produced this I do not know, but he crouched over the handset with his hands cupped about his mouth as he produced the most realistic and horrendous sounds of an aircraft in its final agony. He followed this masterpiece with the muffled roar of its inevitable crash, accompanied with more distant rumblings and explosions. Then there was a long period of extreme silence. The queue members were stunned and bewildered.

'Let's go,' he announced.

Lights blazing and two-tone horn blaring he spun the wheels of the police car as he emerged from the car-park, wheels and tyres shrieking as he vanished along the road. A matter of yards away he turned suddenly right. I had no idea what he was up to, but once off the main road he manoeuvred the car through the back lanes of a housing estate and minutes later re-appeared at the café. He doused his lights and waited a short distance away.

All the waiting queue members were scrambling aboard their bus, with the driver urging them to hurry. Then the bus raced off the way we had just travelled, everyone anxiously seeking the scene of the plane-crash. When it had gone, we pulled into the car-park for the second time, parked and emerged triumphant from our seats. We were enjoying a lovely cup of tea by the time the bus returned. Everyone was in a state of high excitement, and we said it was a false alarm. We couldn't explain the noises they'd heard.

It was a foregone conclusion that one night something would go wrong. A talent of that kind used in these circumstances must inevitably bring trouble of some kind, and I think Rupert knew this. His twinkling sense of humour and love of people and their reactions kept his talent within reasonable limits and it is fair to say that no harm was ever done. He knew when to stop and many victims of his jokes never knew they had been hoaxed. Many of his impressions resulted in little more than talking-points or unexplained mysteries.

It was said that the inspector and the sergeants knew about his activities, but he always took care to practise his deception when no supervisory ranks were around. Very occasionally he would direct something specifically towards them. He could imitate footsteps, for example, and I've seen him sit in his car in the shadows and imitate a woman's high heels clip-clopping along a footpath. And I've seen the smile of expectancy on Sergeant Bairstow's face as he waited for the vision of loveliness to appear. Then Rupert would materialise instead. I've known him imitate a galloping horse at night with the same result. It was all good, harmless fun.

But in the early hours of one spring morning things went wrong. I was with him at the time and can smile now, although it provided a few hair-raising moments.

It was a lovely morning in late April and we had almost completed a full night's tour of duty, being scheduled to come off patrol at six o'clock. It was about a quarter to five and the sun was striving to make the coming day warm and beautiful.

The dew of night covered the choice grass about us and the birds were waking the countryside, all competing for the crown of champion of the morning chorus.

We had concluded a long, careful patrol of the district and had a few minutes to spare before returning to Ashfordly, where I would book off duty. Rupert brought the car to rest on a small hillock at the side of a rural lane, a vantage-point regularly used by sightseers during fine weekends. It provided a fine view of Ryedale and was perfect for a picnic. Behind us were the open moorlands, stretching loftily into North Yorkshire, but before us, on the bottom side of the road, was a pasture full of very contented cows. As we parked they peered balefully at us, as cows tend to do, and one or two took a step nearer out of sheer curiosity. This is a feature of cows – they do like to know what's going on, but within a few minutes they had accepted as harmless the big black shiny creature with bright eyes. They returned their attention to the succulent grass.

There must have been fifty all told. They were all chewing their cud and munching very noisily without a care in the world. Their only worry would be milking-time in a couple of hours or so, followed by a gentle meander back to this field. It was a life of sheer pleasantry, and these cows looked very satisfied with their lives.

'I can do a lovely randy bull noise,' announced Rupert, taking out his pipe.

I laughed. 'Randy bull noise?'

'A bellow, I think it's termed. It has quite a dramatic effect on cows, you know, particularly in the spring.'

'Has it?' I wasn't convinced.

'That's when a young cow's fancy lightly turns to thoughts of randy bulls,' he said.

I chuckled at his description. 'What happens?'

'I'll show you.'

With no more ado he laid his pipe to one side, switched on the PA and cupped the handset in his hands. He bent to his task and there emerged from the loudspeaker on our front bumper the most awful bellowing noise. I watched the cows. Without exception they pricked their ears and looked in our direction. As one they stared at the big black bull who was calling to them so lovingly.

'See! I've got their attention!' he smiled, returning to his task.

He repeated the love-sick bellowing and the amplified noise echoed about the landscape. The cows loved it. They began to walk towards us. The entire herd was moving.

He repeated the exercise, his eyes closed tightly with concentration as he fought to produce exactly the right sound. By now, the herd was in full gallop, responding to his music . . .

'Hey!' I nudged him. 'They're coming for us . . .'

'Just curiosity,' he replied. 'Cows are like that,' and he didn't look up from his work as he began another love-call. This final one galvanised the eager cows into a frenzy of activity, and the entire herd was now in full flight and heading for our car.

At the approaching thunder of hooves he looked up.

'God!' he cried, and in an instant started the engine. He rammed it into first gear and we roared from our vantage-point as the leading cow crashed through the fragile hawthorn hedge in a passion of lust. She was followed by all the others and as we roared along the road the entire herd galloped after us.

My final memory that night is our speeding car tearing along a rural lane, hotly pursued by fifty love-sick maidens, all with their tails in the air.

Thus ended my first lesson with the Road Traffic Division.

7

'Keep the home fires burning while your hearts are yearning.'
Lena Guilbert Ford – 'Keep the Home Fires Burning'

In their early days some police forces combined law enforcement with fire-fighting and indeed many pioneer police officers were equally skilled in both roles. As the police became more professional and their area of responsibility more specific their fire-fighting duties were cast aside. Today the Fire Brigades and the Police Service work side by side at many incidents and indeed continue to share buildings in some places. The modern policeman does not possess a fund of stories connected with fire-fighting, although I do like this old yarn.

In the days when police did fight fires a large blaze broke out in a well-known store in York, and the police were called to the scene. Unfortunately, their horses were all engaged upon a ceremonial occasion and none was available to haul the fire fighting appliance to the fire. Undeterred, the chief rushed into the street and halted the first vehicle he saw, a large cart drawn by two equally large horses. He commandeered these for the job.

After skilfully harnessing them to the fire-tender the fire-fighters climbed aboard and whipped the surprised horses into a gallop. Unaccustomed as they were in this task the gallant animals responded magnificently and were soon galloping through the quaint streets, *en route* to the blazing building.

The machine careered across the River Ouse bridge and

there was the fire. The driver tried to bring his team to a halt,
but they were having none of that! They continued past the
seat of the fire and, in spite of yells, shouts, whips and other
methods, they refused to stop. The horses eventually ran
themselves to a standstill some three miles on the road to
Tadcaster. From that date spare horses were available in case
of emergencies.

When I joined the Force those days had long passed and
the Fire Brigade was a modernised unit noted for its
extraordinary speed, coupled with sheer efficiency and ability.
Even though we were two quite distinct organisations,
however, the police initial training course contained
instructions on how the police should co-operate with the
Fire Brigade.

If my memory has not faded, a complete lesson was devoted
to the police duties and responsibilities at fires. This was
considered necessary because the work of a police officer
inevitably brings him to the scene of most fires and it was,
and still is, essential that a patrolling bobby knows what to do
when faced with an emergency of this kind.

We were taught that, when patrolling our beats, we had to
familiarise ourselves with the locations of all turncocks,
principal fire hydrants and their water-supplies. For the latter
we often relied on rivers, canals, reservoirs, tanks and the
like. We had to know the local procedures for calling out the
Fire Brigade and were exhorted to discover the whereabouts
of essential equipment like blankets, ropes, sheets, sand,
tarpaulins, sacks, ladders, buckets and a host of other useful
things.

Another aspect of our local knowledge was that we were
expected to know who was likely to be in a particular building
at any one time, or who to contact out of normal office-hours.

It was always useful to know if a building had a resident
caretaker and which buildings were deserted at night,
weekends, holidays or other times. The intricacies of
emergency fire fighting apparatus had to be understood and
it was prudent to visit buildings with a view to learning the

location and *modus operandi* of those items.

All this was drummed into us at training school in a one-hour lesson and we were then compelled to learn, parrot-fashion, our responsibilities at the scene of a fire. These were resolutely hammered into our brains, just as children learn their arithmetic tables and alphabet. The result was that we never forgot them. I remember our responsibilities, for they conveniently provided ten answers, which made them a very handy examination question.

They were:

(a) Ascertain whether the fire service has been called; if so, by whom. If not, do so IMMEDIATELY;

(b) save human life;

(c) save animal life;

(d) save and protect property;

(e) prevent stealing;

(f) assist the Fire Brigade;

(g) divert traffic where necessary;

(h) keep a record of important matters;

(i) if the building is unattended, inform the owners or keyholders;

(j) in large outbreaks, ensure police reinforcements are available.

Once those points were firmly implanted in our brains it was deemed acceptable to turn us loose to hunt for fires. In reality, there was a lot more to the practical application of our duties, but those ten points did remain implanted in the brains of police officers who assisted at fires. It was rather like checking off a shopping-list.

In addition to those pertinent points there was the responsibility of knowing what to do at the scene if we were the first to arrive. For example, we had to attempt to cut off the fire's supply of air, we had to search buildings for casualties and beware of weakened walls or floors. In the event of chimney fires we were advised to help the householder remove the fire from the grate and shift any inflammable material from the vicinity of the fireplace. Rugs, furniture, curtains and so forth had to be taken away from the heat and one suggested method of stifling the blaze was to shove wet sacks up the chimney. I learned that finding wet sacks was never easy.

We must always be aware of the risk of inhaling smoke or lethal fumes and were told to crawl about burning buildings on our hands and knees to avoid those problems. This is the advice given:

> 'Remember, heat rises and with it, smoke. When in smoke, CRAWL and keep your nose and mouth near the floor. You will get air, you will see and you will not trip up.'

I felt it was sound advice and it did provide a memorable mental picture of a fire-fighting constable. We were taught that the best way to remove an unconscious person from a smoke-filled room is to drag him along the floor. This could be done by tying the casualty's hands about one's neck and crawling with him between one's legs. The advice continued, 'Proceed downstairs backwards, supporting the patient's head and shoulders.' It was all good stirring stuff.

To escape from upstairs windows we had to lower ourselves until hanging by the fingertips on the window-ledge, then kick backwards and drop with bended knees. We had to beware of arson, and therefore preserve what we could at the scene, like cans of paraffin, matches, electrical devices and so forth. We were reminded of the various legal rules appertaining to fires. For example, at that time it was an automatic offence for anyone in a town to allow a chimney to catch fire, and it was equally illegal for anyone to knowingly make a false alarm call.

Like firemen, the police had certain powers to enter premises in which a fire had broken out or was suspected, when entry was necessary for the purpose of extinguishing fire, and this could be done without the consent of unhelpful, obstructive or absent owners or occupiers. If necessary, we could break in. Furthermore, the senior police officer present could close any street or regulate traffic whenever necessary or desirable for fire-fighting purposes, and in the absence of a police officer, those powers were given to the senior fire officer.

Armed with this kind of close knowledge about my powers, duties and responsibilities I sallied forth into the world beyond training school and felt rather more confident than some of my colleagues, so far as fire-fighting was concerned. This was because, as a member of the Royal Air Force during my National Service, I had compulsorily attended a two-week fire-fighting course near Blackpool. There we were lectured about the various types of fires, about methods of putting them out, about how to shout 'Water On' and 'Water Off' at the right time, how to hold a hose as the power of water was pumped through, and how to climb ladders correctly.

In a rural area like Aidensfield, however, all this knowledge and training could be wasted. The likelihood of a fire was remote, or so I thought.

As it happened, they seemed to break out all over the place. I doubt if there were more than usual in other places, but a village policeman knows everything that happens, and whereas most fires do not reach the ken of the public because they are minor ones, they are made known to the local police officer, even if they are nothing more than chip-pans bursting into conflagrations.

One of my first problems with a fire occurred at the Moorcock Inn, some miles beyond my village. It lies on a lonely road which spans the spacious heights of the North Yorkshire moors. It is a fine old coaching inn of considerable interest, and one of its noted and much publicised claims to fame was its peat-fire.

Peat provides a most useful fuel in moorland homes. It burns very slowly and steadily, and throws out a considerable heat. It is dug from the moors after which the square turves are neatly piled into stacks to allow the wind to pass through and dry them. These are known locally as 'rickles' or even 'rooks', and can be seen dotted across the windswept heights.

When the peat is dry it makes a beautiful fire. It is enhanced by an interesting smell which is a permanent feature of peat-burning homes and which can sometimes be recognised at a distance when tramping across the moors. Many a sensitive nose has identified peat-smoke rising from isolated chimney-stacks.

The Moorcock Inn, being very isolated and therefore liable to be cut off for weeks in the winter, solved its heating problems by burning peat. Outside the cosy inn numerous heaps of peat were stacked, while inside the bar was a traditional peat-fire, complete with traditional peat-smell. That fire has burned through some of the worst winters on record, and even though local coal supplies have failed to reach the inn the establishment remained warm and cosy, a true bastion of delight against the storms outside. Just as it had sheltered marooned coaching-parties in bygone days, so it now offered the same hospitality to lone motorists or even modern coach-parties.

It was a modern coach-party which created something of a storm *within* that peaceful place. At the time the inn was not cut off by snow, although it was a bleak winter's night when the party arrived. The coach was full of young men, about forty in number, and within seconds that peaceful rural haven was transformed into a maelstrom of arms, legs, tongues and shaking heads, accompanied by loud voices and hearty laughter. Clearly, members of the party were enjoying themselves and very soon the strong Yorkshire beer did much to further that happy state.

In their mellow mood it was not long before the cheerful bunch discovered the history of the peat-fire burning so gracefully and pungently in the grate beside them. Legend said that the fire had never stopped burning for 125 years; it had burned continually during that time in spite of hot and cold days, fuel shortages, sick landlords, tired and lazy staff and spells of isolation during the long winters.

As interest mounted in this piece of history it transpired that the boisterous party was a rugby football team and its supporters. A reputation of the kind enjoyed by this fire presented a challenge to these men – if that fire had burned for a century and a quarter it seemed to be their earth-bound duty to extinguish it. A rapid conference was held and, within minutes, six volunteers stepped forward to put out that ancient moorland blaze. The method proposed was to do so in the manner expected of a beer-swilling rugby football team.

The six stood proudly before the smouldering chunks of peat and in spite of angry representations from the unhappy landlord they opened their trousers, took out their hoses and promptly began the task of extinguishing the fire. Their team mates gave them valuable support during this performance and shouted encouragement from the ranks, while a second team stood by to continue, should the first effort end in failure.

I arrived not by choice but by coincidence. By then the deed had been done and the merry coach had left for a famous West Riding of Yorkshire town, noted for its own strong beer and rugby team. Unaware of these very recent events I walked into a bar seething with furious locals and reeking of something which was definitely not peat-fumes. When I expressed my distaste at the aroma the landlord told his sorry tale and led me to the fireplace. Its contents looked dead. The old stone hearth contained little pools of liquid and the lumps of half-burned peat showed no signs of life. I knew I was witnessing the end of an historic era.

One hundred and twenty-five years of history had been snuffed out within seconds. It was not surprising that the regulars were very, very angry and complained bitterly to me. I turned to the landlord and asked,

'Is this an official complaint?'

'Is it summat you can deal with?' he asked.

'Not really,' I said, racking my brains to determine whether it was a criminal offence to urinate upon a peat-fire. I wondered if the actions qualified as malicious damage to a fire but knew of no such provision, although there was a possibility that their actions could be construed as 'conduct likely to cause a breach of the peace'. This is an offence which can occur only in a public place, so that raised the question of whether a bar was a public place . . .

'There must be summat I can do about it,' he said, ruffling his hair. 'They've ruined my main feature – folks come miles to see that fire. It's the longest burning fire in the country, and they've put it out! That's criminal! It must be. There must be summat you can do!'

'I think it's a civil matter,' I pronounced. 'You should see your solicitor – he might be able to claim damages or compensation for you.'

'That's no good,' he snorted. 'It'll take ages to fix that, and besides, there's no guarantee I'd win, is there?'

'In that case, it hasn't been put out, has it?' I stated firmly.

'It has, there's not a sign of life. See for yourself.'

'It's still burning,' I said to him, equally firmly and hoping he would get my message. 'They didn't succeed did they? In spite of their watery efforts, your peat-fire is still burning.'

One of the regulars, an old farmer with skin like leather and a curved walking-stick in his hand, said, 'Nay, it's nut oot, Harry. It's bonning yit, Ah can see it. It just needs a spot o' help . . .'

'You could tell the local papers,' I suggested. 'Imagine the publicity – a team of West Riding rugger players trying to put out a North Riding peat-fire that's burned for a century and a quarter – and failing. You've got all these witnesses who'll swear to that failure, hasn't he, lads? You wouldn't let Lancastrians put it out, would you?'

The others, including the landlord, remained silent, not apparently understanding the import of my statement. I tried again.

'The fire didn't go out, did it?' I spelled out the situation. 'Those silly bloody rugger players did not succeed, did they? We couldn't let 'em beat this pub, could we? You're all witnesses – you can all say they failed, can't you?'

And then they all laughed.

'By lad, thoo's reet,' said one of them, and the gnarled old fellow with the stick stooped to peer into the smelly grate.

'It's bonning yit!' he said smugly. 'Nay, Harry, them daft buggers didn't kill it.'

As Harry went back to his bar feeling happier, if a little puzzled, we collected a few pieces of paper, some dry kindling sticks from the shed behind the pub, and we gave a burst of assistance to the struggling peat. The underparts had not been dampened and, very soon, the peat ignited and returned to its old smouldering ways.

I did wonder whether the challenge would be accepted by lots more passing teams, and suggested that Harry placed a second fire in an outbuilding, especially for them to pee on. He said he'd consider it.

A local paper got hold of the tale and published a lovely piece about the resilience of the fire and it gained some valuable publicity for the inn. Even today that pub boasts of its longest-living peat-fire, about which legend says that not even a noted rugby team and several gallons of strong Yorkshire beer could extinguish it.

The next fire I had to cope with occurred in the early hours of one morning while I was on duty at Eltering. It had been a very peaceful night with no occurrences and by three o'clock I was beginning to feel rather bored and tired.

Then I smelled smoke.

As I stood beside the telephone kiosk outside Eltering Post Office I could smell smoke. It was drifting from somewhere behind the main street, apparently from a clutch of buildings although the darkness made it impossible to see its source. I wandered up and down the street, sniffing the night air while trying to trace its origin.

Then I heard a voice behind me.

'What's going on, Rhea? You're like a bloody greyhound, sniffing like that.'

Sergeant Blaketon had emerged from one of the alleys in time to see my perambulations with nose aloft.

'I can smell smoke, Sergeant. It's not far away.'

'It'll be a bonfire,' he said. 'Somebody will have lit a bonfire and it'll be smouldering. They do that, you know.'

'It's not that sort of smell,' I insisted. It wasn't a bonfire smell. Bonfires have their own distinctive smell and this was different. It is difficult to describe a smell, but I knew this was definitely not a bonfire. I continued to parade up and down the street, sniffing and looking for signs of smoke. He joined me, and together we promenaded, noses in the air, sniffing loudly. It must have been a strange sight.

'Bonfire,' he said eventually. 'I can smell it now. Bonfire, Rhea.'

'No, Sergeant,' I argued. 'It's not a bonfire!' and then I saw the faintest wisp of grey smoke drifting past the illuminated windows of the telephone kiosk. 'There!' I pointed. 'It's floating past the kiosk.'

'Bonfire,' he affirmed.

I decided to explore. I was very unhappy about this, for it was most certainly a strange smell, not the scent of burning garden rubbish. By peering into the night sky against the reflection of the town's few remaining lights I hoped to catch sight of more drifting smoke. And I did. I saw a considerable plume rising from an area tucked in the middle of a cluster of ancient buildings, just behind the main street.

'There!' I pointed out the grey pall to Sergeant Blaketon.

I galloped towards it. That part of Eltering is a maze of narrow passages and tiny alleys where dozens of small houses are literally clustered on top of one another. Their age and construction means they are tinder dry, their old wooden roofs and beamed ceilings being perfect fuel for a major blaze. And, I knew, there were no gardens in that part of town. This was no bonfire.

Blaketon followed my urgent dash and I could hear him panting through the dark passages. We didn't know where we were going, for each passage had others leading from it, and in those narrow confines I could not see the smoke against the night sky. I was guided by my sense of smell and the smell was intensifying. Now I heard the crackling of flames.

Round the very next bend I found it. It was a narrow cottage tucked into the corner of an alley, and it was half-timbered. Through its ancient mullioned window I could see the glow of a fierce blaze. The entire room was burning brightly, and the upper storey window was missing, casting a thickening blanket of smoke across the nearby roofs. Sergeant Blaketon arrived seconds later and we stood for a moment, awestruck at the sight of this tiny cottage, as its interior glowed a fierce and menacing red.

'Fire Brigade!' he gasped. 'Police – ring for them too, Malton.'

I galloped back to the kiosk and dialled three nines for the Fire Brigade before panting out my story. I was out of breath and had difficulty gasping out the address, but soon convinced the recipient of the urgency of my call. I told the police at Malton and asked for assistance; rapid help was assured.

I ran back to the scene and found Sergeant Blaketon, his face glistening with perspiration in the red glow, knocking on doors and attempting to rouse the sleeping occupants of adjoining premises. He was running up and down, thumping doors and shouting, 'Fire, fire . . .'

I did likewise.

In the light provided by the blaze I could see more of the burning cottage. It was tucked into a corner of a small, cobbled square deep in the heart of old Eltering. All around were lots of similar buildings, all with tiny windows, old doors and low ceilings, ancient and tinder dry. If this fire spread . . . It reminded me of the Great Fire of London . . . the potential inferno didn't bear thinking about.

'It's a warehouse,' Sergeant Blaketon yelled above the roar of flames. 'Full of toys and games. Nobody inside, thank God . . .'

Although we knocked on neighbouring doors nobody responded. Not one person answered. The Fire Brigade arrived very quickly and soon had their thick hoses snaking through the passages. Men in dark uniforms and shining helmets arrived and the place became a hive of organised activity. Firemen with breathing apparatus and powerful lights battered their way into the blazing building to search for casualties as I continued to knock on doors.

As we worked a senior Fire Officer halted us. 'You'll have to evacuate these houses,' he ordered. 'If this blaze gets away from us the whole lot'll go up. People an' all. I hope we can contain it but . . .' and his voice tailed away.

We tried again. I counted the cottages in question. There were only six. I had been to every one several times, and so had Oscar Blaketon. We were beginning to think they were all empty, perhaps kept as holiday cottages, and then I heard the swish of curtains being drawn open. I looked up and a man's face appeared at a bedroom window. He glowed orange in the bright light.

'Out!' I shouted above the noise and saw the horror on his face as he stared at the blazing inferno only yards away. 'Out – anybody else in there?'

The face vanished and I hammered on more doors. By now there was a tremendous amount of noise at the scene – firemen were working and shouting, water was hissing, fire crackling, timbers falling, slates crashing and Sergeant Blaketon hammering on doors with his truncheon. How anyone could sleep through this din I do not know. If it took our combined efforts to rouse the orange-faced individual, there could be more people in bed, so I concentrated on the house which had produced the face.

As I hammered, a frightened feminine face appeared, wearing long blonde hair. 'Out!' I cried at the top of my voice, cupping my mouth with my hands. 'Hurry up, for God's sake . . .'

She vanished, but still no one emerged.

Anxious firemen were rattling doors, banging dustbins and generally creating as much noise as possible. At last it had some effect. More curtains opened, more glowing faces appeared and more people began to move about inside those threatened houses.

'Take 'em away, out into the main street, for safety,' Sergeant Blaketon ordered. 'Get their names, ask how many folks were inside. Everyone must be accounted for.'

The senior Fire Officer was dutifully organising his men and other nearby residents who had arrived to watch, as I moved away from the immediate vicinity. I stood aside, and my little group of bewildered people began to grow as the startled sleepers emerged from their six tiny houses. All wore casual clothes – sweaters and light trousers – and as they assembled in a huddle near me, I asked, 'Anyone left inside?'

No one spoke. They were all too shocked.

I called to Sergeant Blaketon. 'Sergeant,' I cried. 'Can we check inside every cottage, one by one? I think they're all here now.'

A fireman answered. 'Aye,' he said and promptly vanished inside the nearest. As he did this a couple emerged from another and soon I had six shivering couples standing around me. We waited as the fireman bobbed in and out of the houses and eventually declared every one empty.

Meanwhile three fire appliances had parked in the street and their long, snaking hoses were pumping gallons of water into the blazing building. The firemen were doing a good job, their chief mission being to prevent the spread of flames. I felt they were gaining the upper hand.

'Come on,' I said to my group. 'I've got to check you all.'

Like sheep the six men and six girls followed me along the dark alley until we arrived in the main street, aglow with lights and throbbing with action as the three appliances worked their way into the coming dawn. From the safety of the street I could see the dull red glow that now brightened the sky, and the flicker of red at the distant end of the passage.

People were standing around in nightclothes, and in the midst of all the activity and interest I drew my little notebook from my pocket, moved the survivors into a shop doorway and prepared to count them.

'Well,' I tried to be cheerful, 'you're all safe. I'll need your names, please, for accounting purposes. We'll have to make a detailed inspection of every affected house and premises, to check for missing persons. It's routine.'

No one spoke.

I wondered if they were all in a state of deep shock.

'Come along,' I coaxed them. 'Names. How about you?'

I addressed a young man with a mop of untidy black hair. He looked at the others and his facial expression told me that something was not quite as it should be. I then looked at his companions. Six pretty girls. Six young men. Six young men with six pretty girls, all shy.

Who owned the cottages? I did not know because Eltering was not part of my own regular beat and these night visits provided only a cursory knowledge of the town.

I slowly looked them up and down.

'Local folks?' I asked.

The one I had addressed shook his head. 'No,' he said. 'We're on holiday.'

'A conference, actually,' chipped in a second youngster, a man.

And a girl giggled.

'Look,' I said, my notebook open in the palm of my hand, 'I've got to take your names because I've got to check the safety of everyone. That's all.'

I was recalling the ten points I'd learned at training school, one of which was to keep a record of important matters. I reckoned this was important.

The first man gave me his name. I noted it, and asked for his address. 'This address, you mean?'

'Isn't this your home address?' I put to him.

'Do we have to? Give our home addresses?' he asked.

I was beginning to understand.

'Look,' I said firmly. 'All I'm concerned about is the safety of the people in those cottages. Why you are here does not concern me. If something is bothering you,' and I looked from one to the other, 'then say so. I'm discreet enough not to let anything slip, if that's bothering you. If I know your problem I can cope with it. If I don't know it . . .' I left the phrase unfinished.

'OK,' the spokesman said. 'I'm staying at No. 3.'

'What's the alley's name?' I asked.

'Cross Alley,' he said. 'Houses 2 to 7 are rented as holiday accommodation. No. 1 is that store, a toy-shop store. They're all owned by the same man, the shopkeeper. We've rented the cottages for a holiday. There's no more of us – just the twelve.'

'So there's no problem. Now, names, please.'

Full appreciation of their dilemma now dawned on me. Not one of these men was married to the girl with whom he had been discovered. One could now understand their reluctance to leave the cottages in spite of the threat by fire, and I've no doubt they all hoped it would be extinguished before it led to the discovery of their love-nests. But things don't work out quite like that.

I took down their names, with two of the girls crying softly into their boyfriends' arms, and eventually Sergeant Blaketon appeared and asked, 'All safe?'

'All accounted for, Sergeant,' I said with confidence.

'Smashing. They've got the fire under control. The cottage will be a wreck, a total loss I'd say, and the contents. Looks like an electrical fault. You folks will be all back soon. They've stopped it spreading. Panic's over.'

An hour later I was sitting in No. 3 with the young man to whom I had first spoken and his girlfriend. Three firemen were with me, all enjoying cups of tea and biscuits. Sergeant Blaketon and another police sergeant from Malton were in another cottage, and in every house a little party was being held. Outside a pair of vigilant firemen continued to play their hoses into the gutted cottage and kept the smouldering heap of burnt-out toys from breaking into a new blaze.

By six o'clock that morning it was all over. The firemen had gone and I was alone with my young couple.

'Thanks for the tea.' I prepared to leave too. 'Sorry you've been disturbed.'

'It won't get into the papers, will it?' asked the girl, called Susan.

'The fire? I reckon it will. It'll be in all the local papers.'

'Oh God!' she cried. 'I hope my husband doesn't find out.'

'He won't, Sue.' The man curled his arm about her. 'I'm in the same boat – my Anne thinks I'm at a conference.'

'Your names won't be released.' I was the only person with their names. 'If the Press do ring tomorrow your names won't be released by us. If they call here don't tell them who you are and don't allow them to take your pictures. Just say you are all safe and intend to continue your holidays.'

'I'll tell the others. Thanks.'

'Don't mention it, but,' I smiled, 'off the record, who are you?'

'Office workers,' he said, smiling ruefully. 'Income tax officials, actually. The chap with this block of cottages owns a shop, as I said. We know him. He let us all book in – we're six mates from one office – and we said to our wives that we were going off to a conference. These are six girls from the office – they said the same to their folks. Delicate, you see.'

'Very delicate,' I agreed.

I felt like asking if any of them worked on my income tax returns, but my question might have been misinterpreted. I remained silent and wished them a happy conference, or perhaps I should have said congress.

But I still wonder if any of those youngsters deal with my income tax returns.

A strange provision relating to fires was drummed into us at training school, where we were told that it was illegal to allow one's chimney to catch fire. Anyone whose chimney did catch fire was therefore to be reported and summoned to appear before the local magistrates' court. If they were found guilty the fine would be a maximum of ten shillings (50p). The statute which created this offence was the Town Police Clauses Act of 1847 which was, and still is, in force in some urban areas. One major problem was learning which urban areas were affected; furthermore, it did not apply to rural districts. This meant that rural chimneys could happily catch fire and belch forth smoke without offending against this law, although the Public Health Act of 1936 did create something called a 'smoke nuisance'. This could be dealt with by a local authority.

Smoke nuisances of the latter kind were not of great concern to the patrolling policeman, although reported chimney fires did mean a visit to the house in question for the purpose of reporting the unfortunate individual whose chimney had let him down. More often that not the case never reached court, as the offender would receive an official written caution from the Chief Constable. This was infinitely better than facing a court.

It must be said that few policemen sought chimney fires; official notification was left to the Fire Brigade, some of whose officers seemed to enjoy reporting these minor disasters to us so that the necessary legal procedures could be implemented.

In the rural areas, however, it did not really matter to the policeman whether or not a chimney caught fire. It was not illegal on my beat and my time at Aidensfield did not involve me in any such crisis. Certainly, there were chimney fires and much surplus smoke was cast high into the heavens, but summonses were never issued.

Another factor was that country folk were rather particular about keeping their chimneys clean. They employed some ingenious methods to maintain them in a clean condition, and a good old rural recipe was to burn potato peelings in the fireplace with a dash of salt. This was to prevent an accumulation of soot in the chimney. Many rural men swept their own chimneys, having purchased the necessary equipment, and there were others who reckoned such expenditure was unnecessary.

Instead, they adopted natural methods, one of which was to obtain a thick bunch of holly and lash it tightly together so that a kind of rough broom head was formed. Ideally it should be wider than the chimney. It was then tied to a long rope and in order to use this device, two people were needed. One carried the holly to the top of the chimney and perched this on the rim. The rope thus dangled down inside and the second man seized the end. He then pulled it down inside the chimney and his mate pulled it up again. This was a very effective brushing device but there is nothing to indicate how the man at the bottom kept himself clean. It was reckoned to be a good system for those rurals who burned only wood, because wood-burning residue rested in all kinds of places within the chimney breast. The springiness of the holly was sure to remove it.

Another system was to obtain a large piece of holly and ensure it was dry. It was then lit so that it burned fiercely and cast via the fireplace up into the chimney. If things worked out correctly the rising draught would carry the blazing object right up the chimney and out at the top, thus dislodging the soot along its roaring route. If the holly lodged along its route, the chimney might catch fire, but this served the same purpose, if a little dramatically.

One of the finest methods was to carry a live hen to the top of the chimney and drop it down. Its urgent flappings during the descent removed all the surplus soot, which promptly fell into the hearth and often spilled into the room. If one was not careful, the hen, very relieved at reaching base, ran about in sheer happiness and left a trail of soot as it squawked and flapped in blessed joy. I have no recipe for cleaning sooty hens.

If rural folks had recipes for cleaning chimneys, they also had recipes for putting out chimney fires. The simplest was to shut all doors and windows, and stop up the bottom of the chimney with a piece of sacking saturated in water. In addition some would throw salt on to the fire with sulphur if available. This was considered a good substance to throw into the grate if the chimney was blazing because it exhausted the fire's supply of oxygen. This seemed a favourite method because the fire starved itself to death.

I have seen chimney fires roaring like jet aircraft, and at times the chimney stack has grown practically red hot with smoke and flames belching out. Such fires are fed from below by powerful draughts which produce the roaring noise. Surprisingly, little or no damage is done, but one problem in the countryside is that many cottages were built in such a way that timber sometimes entered the chimney breast. The ends of the beams were exposed in the chimney and many farms have wooden beams beneath their fireplaces. Lots of old chimneys have ledges and shelves inside, the outcome of rough building techniques, and if burning soot accumulates in those areas the result can be danger to the house. Hens or burning holly were useless if these areas got alight; the only answer was lots of water.

A chimney fire of this kind occurred in a small terraced house at Aidensfield as I was patrolling the village. I was first upon the scene. The cottage belonged to a retired postman called Horace Hart, a widower who kept his home immaculate. It seemed he'd forgotten to arrange the annual sweeping of his chimney, and when I arrived it was well alight, belching forth magnificent clouds of dense black smoke in spite of the wet sack Horace had stuffed aloft.

He had called the Fire Brigade from a neighbour's house and I decided to await its arrival. There was nothing anyone could do in the meantime. Ashfordly Fire Brigade comprised a happy band of part-timers who had to leave their daytime jobs or their firesides and rush to the Fire Station, praying earnestly that their Fire Appliance would start.

As this was late one evening with men about their homes I felt reasonably confident that the Brigade would make it. As a crowd gathered to observe events, Horace's chimney was puffing out huge clouds in fine style. It was a classic chimney fire.

Among the neighbours who gathered to watch was the man in the adjoining cottage. His interest was not difficult to understand, for he emerged spluttering and coughing his anger that such a thing could happen, especially as the two houses were linked. This was Lieutenant-Colonel (retired) Jasper Q. Clarke, who lived there with his sister and who pompously strutted about the village organising the lives of others and complaining incessantly about the noise from children, aircraft, tractors, radio sets, ice-cream vans, cars, motor-cycles and seagulls. Some bicycle bells also annoyed him.

Fortunately for him no one had complained about the noises made by Lieutenant-Colonel (retired) Clarke, but his anti-social activities did excite comment among the locals. He was a smart little man with a bristling grey moustache and grey hair cut in a military style. He wore hacking jackets and cavalry twill trousers, brogue shoes and occasionally a monocle. So perfectly did he play his part that sometimes I wondered if he was a confidence trickster pretending to be a retired army officer, but his credentials seemed genuine.

His presence among the observers led to comments about black deposits falling upon his garden and house and the dangers thus presented to his property by the inferno in the chimney right next to his. He kept darting into his own house to check it wasn't ablaze, and it seemed his sister was away for the evening. He had reason to worry, however, because these cottage fireplaces were back to back, with their chimneys rising parallel with one another. They emerged in one chimney stack, albeit with separate chimney-pots.

With the anxious little man pacing up and down, the village awaited the arrival of Ashfordly Fire Brigade. When it arrived twenty minutes later the chimney was still belching black clouds and Horace continued to dampen the sack which filled the base of his stack. Clearly, the internal timbers or sooty deposits on the ledges inside were still burning, and this was dangerous. Unfortunately for Horace it seemed that Thirsk Races had been held that evening, and every member of the Fire Brigade save one had taken the opportunity to watch a local horse. It had won, and they had gone out celebrating; they had not yet returned. The Fire Brigade therefore arrived in the person of one man, and he was driving the appliance.

He knew it was a chimney fire before embarking upon this trip, and was prepared to tackle the blaze alone, an idea that held some hope. In my capacity as local constable, however, I offered my help, casually mentioning my RAF Fire Fighting Course and the instruction received at Police Training School.

The fireman, a butcher from Ashfordly, said he appreciated my offer of assistance. He would have to operate the machinery of the fire appliance and asked if I could manage the hose. Proudly, I said I knew how to hold a nozzle and knew all about shouting 'Water On' and 'Water Off'.

Thus the fire-fighting team was prepared. After inspecting the seat of the fire the fireman announced that something inside the chimney was ablaze. This confirmed our diagnosis. It might be sooty accumulations or it might be some exposed timbers, either of which needed water to extinguish it. Horace was therefore advised to remove all his furniture from the room in question, because the resultant mess would be pretty ghastly. Aided by the onlookers we had the room clear within five or ten minutes, and removed the sack from the chimney. This created some extra smoke and served only to feed the fire.

Because I was operating the hose I had to climb the ladder of the fire appliance with the hose, and direct the jet down the chimney. Through a series of switches on the fire appliance a ladder crept skywards until it came to rest very close to the belching chimney. My duty was simple – I had to climb the ladder in the manner taught me at the RAF Fire Fighting Course and direct the nozzle down Horace's chimney until the fire was extinguished. It was a simple task.

I began my journey. The ladder shook and trembled as I climbed in the approved style, clutching the hose in the recommended manner. Finally I reached the chimney stack. Thick smoke was pouring out and my eyes began to smart. There was barely room to breathe among the swirling clouds as they moved about me, sometimes totally enveloping me and sometimes letting me bathe in the glow of the many lights below. In spite of the heat from the chimney and in spite of the effects of the smoke and in spite of the darkness and danger, I managed to seize the nozzle in the correct hold and direct it into the chimney-pot. My eyes were aflame by this time, smarting and running with tears, I was coughing violently, my hands were burning and I turned my head to avoid the thick, rising mass of muck and soot.

But the all-important nozzle was in position. I was ready.

Half closing my eyes against the swirling, stinking cloud I reached out and by touch confirmed that the nozzle was firmly inside the chimney-pot. I shouted, 'Water On.'

There would be a short wait as the water rose to the occasion, and through smarting eyes, I looked down upon the little crowd below. Lieutenant-Colonel (retired) Clarke had rushed indoors yet again to check his house and all eyes were upon me. Lights and torches beamed their rays in my direction, and from my vantage-point I could see the powerful jet of water thrusting its way along the hose. I watched mesmerised as the flat empty hose thickened rapidly and grew round as the water approached the nozzle. It straightened out the bends and jerked the hose into life, forcing it to kick against the strain. At that precise moment the wind changed direction and I was totally smothered in a moving mass of smoke. The hose was bucking in my grasp.

When this happens the force is tremendous and threatens to jolt the nozzle from your grasp. It must be held firm at all costs, otherwise it can leap from your grasp and cause severe injuries to anyone nearby. Blinded by the smoke and heat I hung on for all I was worth. The nozzle moved within the chimney-pot – I felt it slide under the pressure, but the smoke concealed it. I clung to it as it writhed and bucked in my tight grip, and listened as the powerful jet gushed down the chimney. Once it was pouring out of the nozzle I settled down to hold it tightly in position, my eyes smarting and my lips dry with the dirt and heat.

Then there was a tremendous commotion below.

Lieutenant-Colonel (retired) Jasper Q. Clarke ran out of his house, smothered from head to toe in a thick black horrible mess. His eyes were the only white spots about him as they peered beseechingly from the mask fate had donated him.

I had put the hose down the wrong chimney.

8

'And many a burglar I've restored
To his friends and his relations.'
Sir William Schwenck Gilbert – 'Trial by Jury'

Sir William Schwenck Gilbert (1836-1911) achieved operatic success when he worked with Sir Arthur Seymour Sullivan (1842-1900), but it was the former who coined the oft-repeated phrase about what happens when 'the enterprising burglar's not aburgling'. Not many other writers feature the burglar in their works – they favour murderers and confidence tricksters, highwaymen or kidnappers and in fact the burglar is frequently portrayed as a simple fellow clad in a striped sweater bearing a sack with the word 'swag' across the front. In spite of the burglar's lack of appeal as a creature of drama, his deeds are dark and sinister because he breaks into the castle of man and the plain fact is that burglars are not universally loved by their public.

None the less, the burglar was greatly loved by lawyers. He made money for them because the nature of the crime lent itself to many hours of legal wrangling, discussion, fee-earning and decision-making in High Courts. He also provided legal authors with a good deal of fascinating copy, while the constable in his infancy must learn and understand the intricacies of this crime.

For hundreds of years burglary could be perpetrated only at night, and this fact alone gave it a certain stature. Today things have changed, and burglary may be committed at any time of the day or night.

When I joined the police service, therefore, burglary was a night-time crime and had to be prevented at all costs. If a burglary was committed on one's beat it was considered akin to allowing a murder to happen or a rape to occur, consequently every police officer did everything in his power to prevent burglaries.

There is a certain fascination in the history of the crime. Ancient legal writers tell how houses, churches and even the walls of cities and their gates were legally protected from being breached by villains who wished to steal. Chester and York are examples of such cities. The earliest known name for the crime was *burgh-breche* and its Latin name around AD 1200 was *burgaria*. Today we would not regard breaking into cities through their walls as burglary, but it was once part of this old crime. By the Middle Ages, however, it had come to be applied only to dwelling-houses, although for a time churches were encompassed within its provisions because they were regarded as the dwelling-house of God.

Such thinking pervaded through the development of criminal law and led to all manner of beautifully argued High Court decisions. Such discussion became facetiously known as legal fiction, and included arguments such as whether a tent could be a dwelling-house or whether movable structures like caravans and houseboats, or even flats, were dwelling-houses. A building could be considered a dwelling-house even if no one lived in it at the time, but the main point of the crime, when I joined the Police Force, was that it could only occur between the hours of 9 p.m. and 6 a.m., the period between those times being regarded as 'night'.

Because burglary was regarded so seriously, night-duty constables paid great attention to the likelihood of burglars being abroad on their beats, and a thorough knowledge of the ingredients of the crime was drummed into us. We had to recognise a burglar when we saw one, not because of his striped sweater and bag of swag, but because of his ability to commit acts which were within the wording of the legal definition of burglary. The legal definition was completely changed by the

Theft Act 1968 but I can still recall the old one which created such gorgeous decisions in court.

It was provided by Section 25 of the Larceny Act 1916 and read as follows:

'Every person who in the night
(i)   breaks and enters the dwelling-house of another with intent to commit any felony therein;
or
(ii) breaks out of the dwelling-house of another having
      (a) entered the said dwelling-house with intent to commit any felony therein;
      (b) committed any felony in the said dwelling-house shall be guilty of felony called burglary and on conviction thereof liable to imprisonment of life.'

That definition was instilled into us at training school so we would never forget it, and it was an interesting crime to study. There was a very helpful mnemonic which helped us to learn its provisions. It was: IN BED.

We learned the provision of the crime by writing those initial letters in this manner:

I   -   Intent.
        Intent to commit any felony therein.
N   -   Night.
        Must be committed at night, i.e., between 9 p.m. and 6 a.m.
B   -   Breaking.
        There must be a breaking, either constructive or actual. Mere entry without a breaking does not constitute burglary.
E   -   Entry.
        The house has to be entered by inserting either some part of the body like a hand or an instrument like a hook on a stick.
D   -   Dwelling-house.

It had to be a dwelling-house of another, not a shop,
factory, school, church or other building. These are all
catered for in other sections of the Larceny Act 1916.
Houses broken into during the daytime are separate
offences.

That, then, was burglary as learned by young constables until
1968 and as we patrolled our beats during those long night-
hours we were always alert for the possibility of houses being
burgled or were seeking incidents which would exercise the
practical side of our instruction.

For example, did 'breaking' include climbing down a
chimney, or was the lifting of a cellar-flap within that meaning?
In one case the burglar got stuck in a chimney because it was
of inadequate proportions and he had to be pulled clear.
Certainly entry via a chimney was 'entry' for burglaries, but
could it, in all honesty, be regarded as a 'break in'?

If a person smashed a window in order to climb in, that is
actual breaking, but the legal fiction of criminal law was
stretched to its limit by calling some entries *constructive
breaking*. For example, if our enterprising burglar tricked his
way into a house or bullied his way in and thus got someone
else to open the doors and break the continuity of the building,
that was known as constructive breaking. We were told that
this properly fell within the maxim '*qui facit per alium facit per
se*', which was probably very important. But suppose the
criminal climbed through a window that had not been glazed,
or simply opened a door which was not locked? And suppose
he broke into a cupboard?

These, and many more imponderables, exercised our minds
at training school and provided marvellous ammunition for
examination questions. Having studied all aspects of the crime
and learned the value of all the words in the definition we
were presented with baffling questions – we were asked about
evil-doers who broke into houses with an intent to rest their
weary limbs and not commit felonious deeds therein. Were
they burglars? Should we consider some other form of

nocturnal illegality? One enterprising felon said he'd entered a house at night to see the ghosts which were said to haunt it, while another said he'd entered to attack a horse. The latter raised the question of whether a stable is a dwelling-house. It might be, if it is *attached* to a dwelling-house . . . but the fellow did not intend to kill the horse, but merely to stop it winning a race. Is that felony? And suppose a boy broke into a house to wind up all the clocks?

Thus our mental gymnastics continued in the shape of examination questions and finally, having studied past centuries of case law, we were cast out to apprehend real burglars. In truth they were very few. If such offences did occur they were usually recorded as 'housebreaking' because it is not easy to prove beyond all doubt that the crime had been committed during the night. Apart from making the police station statistics less alarming by revealing a spate of illegal nocturnal enterings at the houses of others it was far easier to prove that a housebreaker had paid a visit. For example, if a householder woke up at 6.05 a.m. to find his house had been broken into during the night, how could he prove it had occurred before 6 a.m.? Not a chance! It might have happened at 6.02 a.m., so it was recorded as housebreaking, an infinitely less serious breach of the law. By this method, the police prevented many burglaries.

On my rural beat at Aidensfield I could ponder upon Gilbert and Sullivan's burglars and cut-throats, gurgling brooks and merry village chimes, but I did wonder if such evil-doers ever paid visits to my beat. The first indication that they did visit me came one lonely summer evening.

I was patrolling in Eltering, performing one of my periodic night-shifts in the small market town, and made my midnight point outside the post office. It was known to the telephone operators who occupied the first floor that policemen stood outside that kiosk at approximately midnight. Sometimes, if a friendly operator was on duty, we would be invited in for a cup of tea, always taking care to dodge the sergeant.

On such an evening, therefore, I was studiously loitering

beside the silent kiosk when the upper-floor window opened and a man's head appeared, framed in the light.

'Officer,' he said, not recognising me as a local policeman. 'There's burglars, I think.'

'Burglars!' Horror made little mice with chilly feet run up and down my spine. 'Where?'

'Either in the Youth Hostel or at the Youth Club,' he said. 'I'm not sure which.'

My mind rattled off the definition. A Youth Hostel could be a dwelling-house, but a youth club? Could that be classified as a store? School? Warehouse? Or even a dwelling-house if someone lived on the premises?

'Why can't you be sure?' I asked from below.

'They've a party line,' he said. 'They've knocked the telephone off the hook and I can hear them – they're talking and I've heard money rattling.'

'And you don't know which place it is?'

'No,' he said, and at that moment Sergeant Bairstow appeared adventitiously from the shadows.

'Trouble, Nicholas?' he asked.

'Burglars, Sergeant,' and I gave a brief account of my puzzling conversation with the telephone operator, who still dangled from the upper window, waiting for instant action from us.

'We can't ring them to find out, can we?' He rubbed his chin.

'No, Sergeant,' I agreed with this diagnosis.

'So it's either the Youth Club or the Youth Hostel,' he said, still rubbing his chin. 'And they're still inside eh? This will be great, Nicholas, if we catch 'em red-handed. Right, we'll investigate,' and he turned his eyes heavenward. The operator had, in the meantime, vanished inside, but returned to announce, 'They're still there, and they're smashing something open. I can hear them.

'Thanks, we're off to attend to it. Don't alarm them.'

Twenty yards farther along the road Sergeant Bairstow halted and it is prudent to recall that this was long before the days when policemen had radio sets and motor cars. Our assets were two feet each, and our problem was that the two buildings in question were at least a mile from each other.

'We'll check the Youth Club first, together. It's the most likely to be done,' he advised.

The decision made, we hurried along the narrow streets to the building which housed the Youth Club. It had once been a school and was perched on a patch of land adjoining the river which twisted through Eltering. It was a tall building of Victorian bricks and boasted a lot of attics, staircases, roof windows and hidden corners. It was surrounded on three sides by a high brick wall, inside which was an area once used as a playground. Now it was marked with lines for a multitude of ball-games. The fourth side abutted the river, from which entrance on foot was impossible.

If the burglars were in here how had they entered?

The door into the yard was locked, so I had to climb over the wall. As it was over ten feet high I had to get a 'leg up' from Sergeant Bairstow, but in no time I was perched on top and faced a long drop into the yard beneath. I lowered myself gently and dropped the final feet, striking the concrete well below street level. I was now alone in the enclosed area and moved gently across the yard, seeking indications of felonious persons. I tried the two doors which led into the buildings – there was not a sign of a break-in. The place was in darkness and was secure. I shone my torch on all the windows – all were locked and not one was broken.

Somehow Charlie Bairstow had clambered to the top of the wall and sat astride it, shining his torch on to all the roof windows, the roof lights and other likely places of entry. Nothing. It seemed this place was secure.

'I'll check the river side,' I said. This meant inching my way along the side of the premises, through a narrow alley full of old bottles, leaves and tins, until I found myself peering over a high wall above the river. And there, moored to the wall, was a small rowing-boat. It was empty and parked on a patch of thick black mud.

My heart began to thump. They *were* here, inside, right now. If we could surround the building we'd get them!

I shone my torch along the wall and found a likely place of entry – a window set high in the riverside wall. I could just see it if I stood precariously on the wall, hanging on to a tree and leaning out across the exposed mud. But that window was not broken, nor was it open. I could even see the catch – it was locked. Maybe they'd got inside and closed the window to conceal their presence?

I ran back to Sergeant Bairstow and whispered to him.

'There's a rowing-boat down there,' I said. 'It's tucked into the bank, just below a window, but the window is locked.'

'I'm coming down,' and he lowered himself gingerly into the yard. After I had showed him the stationary vessel we both checked every inch of that building and found not a solitary indication of felonious entry. Wherever possible we shone our lights through ground-floor windows, but never saw any indication of villainy.

'That boat's got nothing to do with it,' he announced. 'I'm sure of that. It'll be a club boat, a privately-owned one even. Nothing to worry about.'

'Let's get the keyholder out,' I suggested, wondering how we were going to climb out of the yard. The wall was far too high.

'Ring the office from the kiosk up the street,' he said. 'Tell them to get the keyholder out and come here as fast as possible. Meanwhile, we'll check the Youth Hostel. I'm convinced the burglars aren't here.'

In spite of the boat I had to agree. We managed to climb out of the yard by teetering along the riverside wall and into the back garden of a neighbouring house. From there we tiptoed into the street via the garden path. Before leaving, we made a final check, but came away satisfied that not a solitary window or door had been burgled. That Youth Club was as safe as Fort Knox.

'It's a queer job,' he said for no apparent reason as we turned for a final look at the deserted building. I felt it was offering us a challenge; was the felon inside, laughing at us? If he was he must have gone through the roof.

'Come along,' Charlie Bairstow said. 'Youth Hostel next. I wonder if that telephone operator was imagining things?'

In a very isolated position, the Youth Hostel was known to have cash on the premises, in addition to food and drink. It presented a very likely target, so we hurried about our business. It stood near the castle, about a mile out of town and this meant a long, panting hike through the streets. With Sergeant Bairstow puffing and panting, we both climbed through narrow alleys to the long, low-roofed building. It had once been a row of miners' homes, and had long since been converted into a Youth Hostel of considerable charm.

It was in total darkness. Like the Youth Club it was difficult for two of us to surround it, so we each went a different way, each creeping around the peaceful spot. We examined doors, windows and other points of possible entry. I found nothing insecure, and met Sergeant Bairstow heading towards me.

'Nothing, Sergeant. It looks secure.'

'So does my half,' he said. 'Test mine, and I'll do yours.'

And so both of us concluded a complete tour of the Youth Hostel without finding any insecurities. There was no trace of felonious entry. Our next task, to be completely certain, was to rouse the warden.

She was a fierce lady of indeterminate age and sex, but, considering we knocked her from her slumbers about one o'clock in the morning, she was surprisingly affable. When she had learned of our business we were invited inside; there we searched the office and examined the entire building, including the safe. And the telephone was still on its stand. This place hadn't been burgled. So it must be the Youth Club.

We declined her cup of tea saying our inquiry had taken a turn for the urgent, and hurried back into town. My legs were aching after the variety of exercises they had recently endured, and Sergeant Bairstow was panting like 'a broken winded gallower', as we say in North Yorkshire. Before long we were back at the dark and brooding Youth Club. The keyholder hadn't arrived yet.

'I'll check again,' so I ventured down the neighbouring garden path and along the wall which bordered the river. And I noticed the boat had vanished!

'Sarge!' I called, ignoring the need for caution. 'Sarge, here!'

He came panting to the wall top and I worried momentarily for his safety as I pointed to the vacant space.

'That boat's gone,' I said stupidly.

'We've missed 'em.' He sounded very sad. 'You know, Nicholas, I've never caught a breaker red-handed in my whole career. And I could have tonight, eh? And they were there all the bloody time . . . How did they get in? It must have been a duplicate key job.'

As we discussed that and other possibilities I heard the sound of a large key in the lock of the gate which led into the yard, and I went with lighted torch to greet the keyholder. Sergeant Bairstow followed. A small, meek man wearing a sweater and old slacks entered and blinked as our lights picked out his pale face.

'I'm Sergeant Bairstow,' said Charlie.

'Mr Woolley,' he said. 'Youth Leader. They said it might be burglars.'

'We think so,' and the sergeant outlined the story. Nervously Mr Woolley approached one of the doors and inserted his key. It opened with a slight squeak and he stood back to let us in. I entered, followed by a tired Sergeant Bairstow, while Mr Woolley came a shaky third, putting on the lights. He led us to the office – sure enough, the telephone had been knocked from its stand and was still dangling at the end of its wire. The desk drawer had been forced and all the cash taken, together with other valuables like drink, cigarettes and sweets. It had been a thorough raid.

Mr Woolley sank to the floor and sighed heavily, while Bairstow cried, 'God! We'll cop it for this . . . We could have had them. I could have caught them . . .'

I was curious to know how they'd got in, and began a tour

of the brightly lit place, seeking the point of entry. And I found it. I found a staircase which led from the centre of the club and twisted high towards other floors, four flights in all. Each landing had a tiny window and one of those had been broken; entry had been via this point, and I realised it was impossible to see it from ground level. It opened across a hollow in the roof and was totally invisible from below.

I wondered how they'd reached that point from the boat, for there was no drain-pipe at that side of the building. They must have been human flies.

The outcome of our *faux pas* was that the CID were called in. They came to fingerprint the place, including the telephone, which was eventually replaced on its stand. A check by Mr Woolley showed that some £32 had been stolen, in addition to food and drinks worth about £9. I told the detective sergeant about the boat and he smiled, saying,

'Crafty sods, eh? Coming in boat? Can you describe it, Nick?'

'Just a small rowing-boat,' I said. I hadn't noticed its colour or anything else about it, except that it was small, perhaps a two-seater. I did remember seeing a small quantity of water in its bottom and told him that.

'We'll run a check on all boats,' he promised.

And so we adjourned. We searched the town for signs of burglars wandering about, and I checked all the riverside boats to see if I recognised the one they'd used. I didn't. Finally I went to bed, tired and upset that we'd missed the villains. When I came on duty the following night I found a note from the detective sergeant. It simply said, 'Check the Youth Club again – we're still interested in that boat.'

I wondered if this indicated information that they might return? CID intelligence must have unearthed some reliable gen. I might catch them red-handed this time! Accordingly, I journeyed to Eltering and made it my business to check the Youth Club once more, very, very thoroughly. I tiptoed through the neighbour's garden as before and once again crept along the riverside wall.

My heart leapt!

It was there. Lying low in the water was the boat in exactly the same position as last night, and my heart was beating so violently that I felt it would disturb the burglars. I then realised that if the burglars were expected, the CID would have arranged a reception party. They were probably inside too, waiting . . .

I shone my torch on the boat. It was a battered old craft, now that I began to examine it more carefully. And that damp patch in the middle . . . it was mud! Just like the surrounding mud of the river bed, now exposed. It had a massive hole in the bottom. It was derelict. It could never float in a million years, and couldn't have sailed anywhere this century!

And high tide was coming in . . .

Even this far inland the river was tidal, and with a sinking heart I realised what had happened. In the time we'd been at the Youth Hostel, the water had risen a few inches, sufficient to cover the wrecked boat.

So they hadn't burgled by boat.

They must have simply climbed over the wall, shinned up a drain-pipe and broken in through that lofty hidden window. And it wasn't a dwelling-house either, so it couldn't be classed as burglary.

We wrote it down as office-breaking, but the typist misspelt it as officer-creaking. Maybe it wasn't a mistake?

In very erudite terms the detective sergeant told me to be more careful with my observations in the future and Sergeant Bairstow was instructed to keep a tight eye on local towns and villages at night. I knew the senior ranks weren't very happy about our detection rate and did not want a repeat of the Youth Club fiasco. Sergeant Bairstow considered it his duty to teach the constables under his wing something of crime prevention techniques. He taught me how to walk in the shadows, to check suspicious vehicles, to note the movements of suspicious people and to record a host of other minutiae, any one of which could be instrumental in detecting a crime.

Charlie Bairstow became very burglar-conscious and persuaded the Crime Prevention Department to play its part. Together we advised shopkeepers and householders about leaving windows ajar, especially those on the ground floor, and we reminded them not to leave newspapers protruding from letterboxes, or allow full milk bottles to remain on the doorsteps for days. We described them all as invitations to burglars.

One of Sergeant Bairstow's pet themes was 'keys hanging on string'. If he had a favourite 'don't' this was it. He would preach the gospel at schools and Women's Institutes, for it was a very common practice by householders to leave the door key hanging on a piece of string behind the letterbox. How easy it is for the burgling gentleman to locate and use; Sergeant Bairstow failed to understand why intelligent people left their keys for burglars in this fashion. Lots did it, and lots got burgled. It was his antagonism to this practice that caused us a slight problem one night.

I was walking down Partridge Hill in Eltering, intent on checking an office-block at the bottom, when I espied Sergeant Bairstow waiting for me. He stood beneath a lamp standard and smiled warmly as I approached.

'All correct, Sergeant,' I assured him.

'You've not checked those offices yet?'

'They're next on my list, Sergeant.'

'Then tell me what you see wrong, Nicholas.'

I checked the door at the entrance and it was locked. All the ground-floor windows were also locked. The place seemed impregnable. Then I recalled his current obsession about keys on string and glanced at the front door. The letterbox was standing open; in fact, it was non-existent and in its place was a large, oblong hole through which letters were pushed. It was high in the door in a vertical position, like a large figure 'I' in the centre panel. And behind I could see a piece of string. I smiled.

'This, Sergeant?'

'Well done, lad. Good observation, you know. Yes, now that

is a foolish example, isn't it? We just lift out the string . . .' and he hooked his forefinger behind it and hauled about three feet out. A Yale key dangled from the end. Smiling at the success of this practical tutorial, he said, 'and we fit it into the lock.'

Sure enough it worked. The key was clearly shared by all the users of the premises, for the door swung open. We went inside to check that burglars had not done likewise. The interior boasted half a dozen locked doors, and upstairs was a similar arrangement. These doors led into small offices rented from the owner of the building, and every office was secure. None the less, he had a valid point. A breaker-in could lurk inside, securely hidden from the outside world, as he carried out a furtive raid on one of the offices.

When we had been right round the internal route we returned to the front door. He paused and said, 'We'll remove it, for safety,' and with no more ado Sergeant Bairstow untied the string from its hook above the letterbox and said, 'We'll fix it to the bottom.'

A large screw protruded at the bottom end of the letterbox gap, and he carefully tied the string to it, saying, 'This'll prevent it being noticed so easily.' He left he key dangling inside the door, but its lifeline was now safely concealed from the outside world. We left and I slammed the door. The office block was now secure.

I was about three strides away when I realised, with horror, what we'd done.

'Sergeant,' I called, halting abruptly.

'Yes?'

'They can't get in now, can they?'

'They can, they know where the key is. The burglars don't.'

'But they can't reach it. It's hanging *below* the letterbox, and it's impossible to put a hand through that small gap to get hold of the string.'

He stood in silence for a few moments, and then said, 'Oh, bloody hell!'

We examined the door. Sure enough, the gap was there

but it was far too small to accommodate anyone's fist, let alone a policeman's. No one could reach that office key. I visualised lots of irate office workers tomorrow morning, all hammering on their door or ringing the Superintendent to complain about interfering policemen. Try as we might we could not reach that string.

'Oh, bloody hell!' he said again. 'What can we do?'

'We need a bit of wire,' I suggested. 'A stiff bit to hook it out.'

'I know where we can find some.'

He led off at a fast trot and we were soon tramping around the backyard of an electrical contractor's premises where scrap of all kinds abounded. His torch eventually located a length of thick wire about eighteen inches long. It was pliable enough to bend, yet strong enough to remain in any selected shape.

Marching triumphantly through the town with this up his sleeve he and I returned to the door. I now wondered if we were committing the crime of 'possessing housebreaking implements by night'. The wording of the offence did qualify it by adding 'without lawful excuse', and I wondered if ours was a lawful excuse? It was too late to worry about our actions, because Sergeant Bairstow was already at the door, asking me to stand guard in case anyone came. I had to whistle if someone approached.

From my vantage-point I saw him shape the piece of wire into a long straight piece with a large angled hook at the bottom and a type of handle at the top. Carefully he inserted his improvised key retrieval device into the narrow letterbox. He missed. He cursed. He must have missed several times and he cursed several times before he asked me if I could help, as my fingers were probably more nimble than his. I did. I inserted the hooked wire and played around with it inside the door, groping for the elusive length of string. I must admit it took a lot of finding and I missed it several times. Then I felt it. The key moved and rattled lightly against the timbers of the door and I gently lifted my piece of wire. And out it came. Sergeant Bairstow was delighted. He proudly opened the door and we restored the key to its former place.

He wasn't happy about the key so visibly hanging behind the open letterbox, but felt there was little he could do that night. He'd speak to the office workers at a later date.

'Some folks deserve to be burgled,' he said as he strode away.

I began to wonder if I would ever deal with a genuine burglary, but it was my old adversary, Claude Jeremiah Greengrass, who remedied that defect. Quite suddenly he found himself charged with burglary but the circumstances were bizarre, to say the least. They could only happen to Claude Jeremiah Greengrass.

Once upon a time, as the best stories begin, there lived in the hamlet of Briggsby a highly desirable young lady whose husband was supposedly sailing around the world on a Merchant ship. He had never been seen in the village, and to relieve her extensive boredom the young lady sought solace in other men. Many paid visits at late hours and spent a considerable amount of their free time comforting her and seeing that her taps did not drip.

She lived in a picturesque cottage just off the main street. It was in a quiet cul-de-sac, a veritable dream house rented from the local estate and cared for by a succession of male visitors. The lady in question, called Cynthia, was a pretty creature in her late twenties. Rather petite and slender in stature she had pleasing dark eyes, a mop of dark hair and a skin which attracted the sunshine so that it always bore enviable honey tans. Her generously proportioned figure was equally interesting and she had a passion for tennis and other games where short shorts were worn. These activities allowed her to display those lovely brown limbs and magnificent brassiéred outline.

That Cynthia was highly attractive was never in doubt, and even the ladies of Briggsby realised this; the men, on the other hand, did not worry too much about the absent husband and indeed, were very happy that he never turned up. Many took to walking their dogs past her house at night, and some would pop down there to change a wheel on their cars because it was a traffic-free lane. Others would ask to borrow her ladder, and some would allow her to use their lawnmowers. Cynthia had a lot of friends among the men.

She gained even more admiration when it was learned she went to bed without the encumbrance of a nightdress. Furthermore, it was understood on good authority that she did deep-breathing exercises and chest-expanding motions in front of uncurtained windows. As this was a very quiet rural lane ending in a cul-de-sac it might be thought that no one would notice such activities. The truth was that the track was almost permanently full of men and dogs, cars and cycles with punctures, wheelbarrows with broken bearings or men merely passing that way because it was the shortest route to somewhere or other.

Word of Cynthia's overt charms eventually reached the ears of Claude Jeremiah Greengrass. Claude, being a somewhat devious and cunning fellow, did not resort to the blatant ruses of the villagers, but decided, after a few beers, to explore the situation for himself in his own inimitable manner.

He selected one Friday night in August, a balmy evening replete with the scent of roses and honeysuckle. It was the night of the full moon and he had been to Ashfordly for a drink or two, having travelled there on his trusty cycle. He was meandering his weary way home, around midnight, when he chanced to pass the road end which led to Briggsby. Cynthia's hamlet. Her accessibility had frequently tantalised him and he had often considered the things he'd like to do to her and with her. Now he had an opportunity to put his dreams into action and turned his front wheel firmly towards Briggsby's main street. Very soon he was cycling down the street on well-inflated tyres, and without tell-tale impediments like lights and conscience.

Unbeknown to Claude Jeremiah the object of his passion was lying in bed awaiting the arrival of an adventurous lover. She had done her chest-expanding exercises and gone through her deep-breathing routine, to the enjoyment of a nearby field, and now lay in bed, naked, to await her visitor. The man, it seems, had assured her of a most unusual evening, with excitements galore, promising a variety of skills he'd learned in the Middle East when serving with the Marines. Cynthia lay in bed, anxious and eager, and in her moments of blissful dreaming almost lapsed into a fitful sleep. It is fair to say that her romantic expectations had clouded her powers of observation, because it was at that moment that Claude Jeremiah Greengrass arrived outside her house.

The audience had dissipated and he was alone, and he stood for a few moments, outside her privet hedge, to contemplate the situation. He knew of the ladder others had borrowed, and rapidly made a sortie to the side of the cottage. He found it beneath an open shelter and bore it triumphantly to the peaceful garden. Acting very silently and with extreme care, he placed it against her window-sill.

The window was open, he noted, as were the curtains. He had anticipated this, having done a little homework. Inside, he guessed, lay the deliciously naked Cynthia; the beer in his belly and the moon in the sky had given him a drive unknown for years, and at this stage all caution was thrown to the winds. He stepped into her garden, moving wraithlike across the lawn until he was at the foot of the ladder. His poacher's skill took him this far without a sound. Then, in an unexpected spasm of urgency, he removed all his clothes, with the exception of his socks. For reasons best known to himself he retained his socks. It might have been to stop splinters getting into his feet, but no one really knew the reason for this action.

Fully aroused by this time and perfectly capable of carrying out the rapist's act which he intended Claude Jeremiah climbed the ladder, hoping for instant action. Standing firm and upright on the ladder he reached the window-sill, spotted the catch on the window and released it to raise the bottom half of the already open sash window. It slid gently open with the faintest sound. He thought lasciviously of the lovely woman lying just inside.

At this stage of the expedition he could see her lovely shape beneath the thin sheet, inviting and welcoming. He sat astride the window ledge to manoeuvre himself into the room. Her bed was close to the window, and he sat there, gazing at the tantalising creature so close to him. One leg was dangling outside the house, the other inside; he was literally half inside and half outside the house.

It was at this stage that events staggered him almost to the point of impotence. By the light of the moon two bare white and sensuous arms reached from the bed as the naked shape of Cynthia cast aside the sheet, seized him in a particular place with a squeal of sheer enjoyment and literally dragged him on to her bed. Never one to waste an opportunity, Claude Jeremiah enjoyed himself as only a wildly encouraged man can under such uninhibited circumstances, and after a frantic breathless thirty minutes with never a word spoken he flopped at her side, exhausted but deliriously happy. No one would ever believe this, no one.

Not yet satisfied and wishing to attempt something even more exciting she reached out with a sexy hand and switched on the light.

And she screamed. She screamed and screamed and screamed.

It was the wrong man.

Her unexpected and violent reaction to his presence galvanised the naked Claude Jeremiah into the speedy escape action for which he was noted in poaching circles, and he vanished down the ladder in his socks. As he clambered to safety, she rang the police, crying 'Rape, rape, rape.'

By sheer chance I happened to be in Ashfordly as the 999 call came through, and with Sergeant Blaketon at my side I drove urgently to Briggsby. There we interviewed the greatly distressed young lady and promptly mounted a search for the rapist in black socks. We found his clothes at the bottom of the ladder and immediately I knew who it was.

'I know who these belong to, Sergeant,' I announced proudly.

'Then you must arrest him,' he said. 'Burglary.'

'Burglary?' I cried.

'Yes, PC Rhea, burglary.'

'What about the rape accusation?'

'We must interview the lady at length, in the presence of a policewoman,' was all he said.

While he waited for the policewoman to be roused and called to the scene I went in search of Claude Jeremiah. I knew he was either faced with a two-mile walk across the fields in his stocking feet or a very chilly cycle-ride. I searched for his cycle and failed to find it. He'd be riding home, bareback! I jumped into the trusty little Ford and simply drove along the most obvious route to Claude Jeremiah's home.

I found him about a mile from Briggsby, bathed in perspiration and as naked as the day he was born, except for his socks.

He halted as I pulled up beside him.

'Evening, Mr Rhea,' he said affably. 'Nice night.'

'Lovely,' I agreed. 'Where have you been?'

'Visiting a lady friend,' he said. 'Then she got stroppy and kicked me out.'

'Where?'

Standing on the verge in his socks and beginning to shiver in the cool breeze, he told me his story. I allowed him to ride home with me in close attendance, so that he could put on some clothes. We'd need his discarded articles for evidence of his presence, should he decide to dispute that.

'She invited me in, Mr Rhea,' he insisted as I later drove him to the police station at Ashfordly for further questioning. 'I'll tell you what I did.'

And he repeated the story that I have told. As we waited for Sergeant Blaketon and the policewoman I brewed a cup of tea and we sat down to enjoy it. Claude told me quite candidly of his adventure that night and was clearly shaken when I informed him we may consider charging him with rape, and would certainly charge him with burglary.

'I'll admit I *intended* to rape the nympho,' he said, 'but there was no need, Mr Rhea. She grabbed me and the next thing she was doing everything to encourage me. She went wild, honest. It was great, smashing. I've never been done like that in years. It was when she put the light on that she made the fuss.'

Sergeant Blaketon returned with the policewoman and when Claude Jeremiah explained his part in the incident Oscar Blaketon looked utterly baffled. We locked Claude Jeremiah in a cell as we discussed the case. He had the woman's side of the tale.

She had been expecting a lover. She admitted that. Cynthia had been promised an exotic evening full of Oriental mystery so when the ladder and the naked man appeared at her window she thought it was her Knight in Shining Candour. Unable to contain her ardour she had seized him expertly and had clearly admitted she'd dragged him into bed, actively encouraging what followed. Her story tallied exactly with Claude Jeremiah's.

'It's hardly rape, Sergeant.' I recalled the definition of the crime. Rape was defined as 'unlawful sexual intercourse of a woman against her will by force, fear or fraud'. Certainly Claude's activities had not been against her will, nor had there been any force, fear or fraud of the kind required by law to fulfil the definition. He had not fraudulently gone about his business.

'There is a definite burglary, PC Rhea. We can get him for that. He *intended* rape when he entered the room. That qualifies as burglary.'

Together we examined the essential points of the crime in an attempt to determine which offence fitted the latest exploit of Claude Jeremiah Greengrass. To be guilty of burglary his actions that night would have to include all the points of the definition. I remembered the mnemonic – IN BED.

I – Intent. I knew there must be an intent to commit a felony – any felony. Rape was a felony. That intention must have been in his mind at the time of breaking and entering her house. This could be a tricky point to prove. Claude Jeremiah certainly had had that objective in his mind *before* entering; in fact, it had been in his mind right until he'd got his leg over the window-sill. I visualised interesting legal battles over this point.

N – Night. Yes, this fitted the definition. It had occurred around midnight.

B – Breaking. There must be a breaking-in. I knew that the mere lifting of a window already open and not fastened in any way could not be construed as 'breaking'. But he had opened a catch on this one; he admitted that. He had further opened an already open window. Was this sufficient to constitute a 'break'? The court must decide.

E – Entry. This had certainly occurred. I felt the court would have to think carefully about this aspect. Entry by part of the body was sufficient and I wondered precisely what she had seen silhouetted that night. Which part of his excited body had been first to enter her house? This was very important because the intent to rape must be present in the accused's mind at the precise moment of entry into the dwelling-house. The court's discussion on this aspect could be interesting.

D – Dwelling-House of Another. That point was satisfied.

'Well, PC Rhea, it's your case. Do we charge him with burglary or not?'

'We might consider "Entering a house in the night with intent to commit a felony",' I suggested by way of negotiation.

'No good,' he said. 'It's a question of intent. A question of precisely when he had in his mind the intention of rape. If he broke in, or merely entered without breaking in, with such an intent in his mind at that precise instant, we've got him for something. Burglary maybe, some other lesser offence perhaps.'

'Let's charge him and let the court decide,' I suggested, thinking of Eltering Magistrates in all their splendour.

That was our only hope. We could not dismiss the offender because the public could allege complicity, negligence or inefficiency on our part, so we had to proceed, even though proof of any precise crime was difficult to produce. It all depended upon the verbal admission of Claude Jeremiah Greengrass, who was astute enough to talk his way out of anything.

Due to its serious nature burglary was not triable at the local magistrates' court, for it was an indictable offence and must be tried before a jury; it could, however, be dealt with at Quarter Sessions.

Before Claude Jeremiah appeared at Quarter Sessions or the Assizes the magistrates would have to consider all the evidence in what were known as Committal Proceedings. These were designed to determine whether or not there was sufficient evidence to justify a trial at High Court, so our local magistrates would have to listen to both sides of the drama. Having listened they would then decide whether or not Claude Jeremiah Greengrass should stand trial.

With due solemnity the magistrates assembled on a date shortly after the alleged crime, the bench comprising Alderman Fazakerly, Mrs Pinkerton and Mr Smithers, with the precise Mr Whimp as Clerk of the Court. Claude Jeremiah faced this impressive array of personages as Mr Whimp fussed over the pile of papers in front of him.

Because this was a committal hearing Claude Jeremiah was not given leave to plead because the purpose of this exercise was not to establish innocence or guilt. It was merely to satisfy the examining magistrates (Fazakerly, Pinkerton and Smithers) that there was enough evidence against the accused to justify a trial.

Sergeant Blaketon, being the prosecutor on this occasion, made a short speech which outlined the facts. Witnesses were then called, Cynthia being the first. As she was examined in the witness-box her statement was taken down on a typewriter. It was a long, laborious process known as 'taking depositions', but it had to be done. Having made her statement, Claude Jeremiah could cross-examine her. Being the man that he was he did not bother with solicitors or counsel, knowing sufficient about the law to conduct his own defence. He knew he was not a burglar.

'Cynthia,' he began, knowing his Christian name technique would impress their Worships. 'The Court has heard how you were lying naked in bed, waiting for your lover. I appeared at the window. Did you or did you not take hold of me and pull me into your bed?'

'Yes, but I thought . . .'

'Did you recognise me?'

'Well, I thought . . .'

'What did you see exactly?'

'Just an outline, on the window-sill . . .'

'Before that?'

'The ladder. The noise roused me, I was dozing. Then you, somebody, climbing up. Standing on the window-sill or ladder maybe, to lift the window. Just an outline, like a dark shadow.'

'But outside?'

'Yes, outside.'

He turned to face their fascinated Worships. 'At that stage, Your Worships, I must admit I had the intention of raping Cynthia. But that intention vanished as I entered the building.'

'Go on,' invited Alderman Fazakerly, leaning forward and drooling slightly.

'Cynthia,' said Claude Jeremiah eloquently. 'Did any part of my body enter your house as I stood on the top rung of that ladder?'

The court, and Cynthia, burst into a fit of filthy laughter, for one's idea of a sock-clad, rampant rapist, all rarin' to go, standing naked atop a ladder with perhaps a portion of his anatomy protruding into the dwelling-house of another, was too much to bear.

'No,' she said eventually.

'Thank you. The point is, Your Worships, that I did not enter that house while my intention was to commit rape. What happened next, Cynthia?'

'I closed my eyes.'

'Ah!' said Alderman Fazakerly, relieving the tension of the court. 'Why did you close your eyes, my dear?'

'I thought it was my friend – a lover – I wanted to pretend

I was asleep, he likes that, you see . . .'

'So you didn't see what the accused did next?'

Claude Jeremiah filled in the next stage of the story. 'I unlatched the window at the sides where it was locked, lifted it and sat on the window ledge. I put one foot inside and one arm inside. Half of me was inside, and half outside. My head was inside, I think . . .'

'Then what?'

'Cynthia,' said Greengrass beaming like a barrister in full flow. 'That's when you saw me.'

She nodded.

'What did you do?'

'I thought it was Arthur. It looked just like him, the outline, you know . . .'

More giggles.

'So I just grabbed him and pulled him on to my bed. It was just under the window.'

'And you encouraged me, actively, to have intercourse with you?' smiled Claude Jeremiah, almost delirious at the memory of that night.

'Well, yes, but I thought . . .'

'So, Your Worships, all thoughts of rape left me when she hauled me into bed. This was no rape of an unwilling woman, no felonious entry into the house, although it nearly was. You cannot prosecute a man for his thoughts or desires, only for his illegal misdeeds. I submit, Your Worships, on behalf of myself, that there is no case to answer. I ask that I be discharged.'

It was a most impressive speech and I wondered where he had learned to speak like this.

Cynthia signed her deposition, following which Claude Jeremiah gave his own evidence. He was closely examined by the prosecution and signed his deposition, which totally refuted any allegation of burglary or rape. The magistrates signed all the depositions, then adjourned to make their decision.

The court devolved into a muffled chatter, interspaced with

moments of rude laugher until the door at the rear of the bench opened and the majestic line-up returned, unsmiling.

Claude Jeremiah stood to attention as they took their seats and courteously remained standing as they settled upon their chairs.

'Claude Jeremiah Greengrass,' said Alderman Fazakerly. 'There is considerable doubt as to the precise timing of events that night. The crime of burglary, so adequately explained by Sergeant Blaketon, does not seem to have been fulfilled. We find there is insufficient evidence to justify a committal for trial on indictment on a charge of burglary. As no other charges have been levelled against you, we dismiss this case.'

'I'll get him one day!' I heard Blaketon growl, but I must be honest when I say I doubted this very much indeed.

9

'Tell him his pranks have been too broad to bear with.'
William Shakespeare – 'Hamlet'

The solitary policeman who patrols the streets and lanes at night regularly finds himself with the time and the opportunity to contemplate. He finds himself thinking about the meaning of life and there are many sage sayings which adequately illustrate his mental attitude during those long, silent hours. The poets have endeavoured to capture the character of night and have produced fine phrases like 'ships that pass in the night' or 'the shades of night which fell so fast'. Policemen, on the other hand, are much more practical and tend to consider 'nights that are lang and mirk' or 'long, long wintry nights' or the 'longest night in all the year'. If policemen do lean towards poetry they consider themselves 'sentries of the shadowy night' or even 'sons of the sable night'.

It may be possible to fill a book with such quotations but police officers are not keen on ratiocinative quotations, unless they are created by themselves. Although night-duty does give time for the constable to produce words of wisdom, this seldom happens. Instead, the quiet times breed mischief.

One passable form of activity is to play jokes upon one's colleagues. One advantage of this is that it is possible to use the whole district as a playground, but a distinct disadvantage is that one becomes so involved and excited that one forgets that the public sometimes suffer from a lack of sleep and peer out of their windows. Another important factor is that sergeants, inspectors and even superintendents have a nasty habit of creeping up on the frolicking policemen and this leads to all kinds of disciplinary trouble.

In general, though, the pranks are harmless. One very popular prank was to creep around the police officers' bicycles, which were parked all night outside the station, and remove their saddles. These were concealed, and the morning witnessed several poor bobbies, tired after their night-patrols, cycling home in curious positions, not daring to sit on the dangerously protruding seat-pillars. By the next night the seats had returned. Another trick was to remove one pedal, so that the constable had to cycle home by using only one leg. Alternative caps would be switched on the hat rack, so that it was a most difficult job to find one's own headpiece. All good, harmless fun.

In addition to these internal pranks many tricks were played in the streets. It was the misfortune of most new constables to be the victim of such pranks, but at a small station like Aidensfield or Ashfordly it was very unlikely that I would become a victim, because our night-duty stints were often solitary affairs. None the less, the possibility always remained, particularly when patrolling the streets of nearby Eltering or Strensford. When working in a strange area one had always to be alert to such possibilities and I bore this in mind when working at those stations.

I remember one poor young constable, newly arrived from the City of London. At the tender age of twenty he had only a few months' service in that Force and had transferred to the north to be near his fiancée. He was given the task of patrolling a beat in Eltering, and had the misfortune to encounter Ben and Ron, the two traffic terrors. Over one of our mid-shift breakfasts they casually mentioned that it was the duty of the town night-shift man to arouse the local keeper of the dog's home. They told that constable that the keeper liked to be up at five o'clock in the morning in order to exercise and feed all the inmates. Because he was notoriously bad at getting out of bed he had left a standing request for the night-duty policemen to rouse him at five. The police had agreed because his father was a magistrate in York.

That is what they told the poor young constable. It was, of course, a load of rubbish. Even worse was their recommended method of rousing him. These merry-making constables coolly told the youngster that the only way to rouse the sleepy keeper was to kick and hammer loudly on his door for a full five minutes. They carefully told him which door to use.

And so the diligent youngster had gone about this duty. The result was that the entire town was roused by the continued and irate barking of dozens of stray dogs, an action which did arouse the puzzled keeper.

Another prank was perpetrated by a sergeant who dressed as a roadsweeper and cleaned the streets in the early hours of the morning. He performed his dramatic role whenever a new constable was patrolling, and it was a comparatively simple operation. He borrowed a barrow and broom from the Highways Depot and, dressed like a tramp, swept the town at 3 a.m. or thereabouts. He did this to test the reaction of the constable concerned. But what does a constable do when he sees a roadsweeper at work so early?

Sergeants, I suppose, are just as guilty as their men for playing tricks on one another or upon their subordinates, although it must be said that many of these were done with valid reasons. For example, many night-shifts tolerate one constable who cannot remain awake, especially when on office-duty. Tricks were played on him in an attempt to keep him awake.

One of the funniest of this kind involved my pal Dave at Brantsford, who nodded off in the middle of a long report about an alleged case of careless driving. I had been on night-patrol with Sergeant Bairstow and he decided to call on Brantsford Police Office on a routine visit. Dave was on duty. The lights were on and we made no pretence about being silent. It would be around five o'clock in the morning.

Inside we found Dave. He was sitting at the typewriter, with his elbow on the desk and his head resting on his upright hand, fast asleep. More amazing, there was a cup of cold tea dangling from his upright hand, the handle hooked upon one of his fingers. The cup was about half full and somehow, his hand supported both a cup and his head. The unfinished report was in the typewriter.

'Look at that!' grinned Sergeant Bairstow. 'It's bloody amazing – he's out like a light.'

'Shall I wake him?' I asked

'Not yet,' he grinned. And Sergeant Bairstow crept into the office and climbed on to a chair. He carefully opened the face of the wall clock and moved the pointers forward from 5 to 7.30. Then he beckoned me to stand where I was. He joined me.

For a moment he watched the snoozing Dave and his amazing cup of tea, then shouted, 'Morning, PC Watts.'

Dave jerked into instant life. His tousled head shook into wakefulness as he struggled to open his eyes and the cup now jolted so much that he poured its contents all over the blotting-pad.

'Sorry,' he apologised. 'You surprised me.'

'Is that important?' asked Bairstow, indicating the unfinished report.

'I'm going on holiday, Sergeant, when I finish at six, and wanted it done by then.'

'Six?' a puzzled expression appeared on Bairstow's face and I realised he was no mean actor.

'Nights,' Dave replied in all innocence. 'I'm on nights – I finish at six, Sarge, and we're going straight off in the car. We've a ferry to catch at Hull . . .'

'I thought you were on early turn,' said Sergeant Bairstow, frowning and looking at his watch.

This action caused Dave to turn and look at the clock behind him, and he leapt from the chair. 'Half past seven!' he cried. 'Bloody hell, I should be driving through York now . . .'

'York?'

'Yes, on the way to Hull . . . I was supposed to be on the road by half six . . . bloody hell . . .'

And he began ripping out his unfinished report, rushing

round the office, tidying up and generally generating something of a whirlwind as we stood and watched. He mopped up his spilt tea and I could see he was terribly agitated.

I wondered what the sergeant would do next. He did nothing.

'Sorry, Sarge,' cried Dave, almost running out of the office with his hat on the back of his head and his jacket open.

'Thanks, Sarge, I mean . . .'

And Charlie Bairstow allowed him to leave. The last I saw of Dave that morning was his flying figure as he tore from the police station to rouse his family. Only then would he realise what had really happened.

The truth was that Sergeant Bairstow had used this method to give him an hour off duty before going on holiday. It was also a reminder that one should not fall asleep on duty, and I knew Dave would always remember this lesson.

'Come along, Nicholas, it will be six o'clock by the time we return.

A lot of pranks were undertaken to relieve the crushing boredom, but others were perpetrated to teach less friendly policemen a lesson. It must be said that every police station, large or small, has its own rotten egg. He could be too keen on prosecuting the public, too hard on kids, or simply a misfit among his fellow officers. Such policemen are unpopular, even among policemen.

There are many kinds of unpopular cops – it might be a youngster from an upper-class background who thinks himself superior to his colleagues, it might be a brain-box who has passed all his exams and is good at academic subjects, but hopeless at practical policing, or it might be a keen officer who books every possible defaulter for the most trivial offences. Whatever their faults, disliked officers can be treated with considerable contempt by their colleagues.

Such a fellow arrived at Eltering a few months after I was posted to Aidensfield. He was a tall, Nordic-looking character with high cheekbones and wavy blond hair. He considered himself God's answer to Romeo and, worse still, he came from the south. This accident of birth immediately segregated him from the Yorkshiremen about him. It must be said, however, that his southern nativity alone did not cause any real rift because Yorkshiremen are kind enough to such unfortunates to attempt a programme of conversion. During this intensive course the incomer would be taught the ways of Yorkshire folk and would begin to understand their wiles. If such incomers were wise they would accept the lessons or respect the advice given. If they were stupid they would attempt to outwit the Yorkshiremen.

This particular constable, whose name was Sean O'Malley and who looked nothing like an Irishman, was none the less christened 'Paddy' on the day he arrived. His first action was to promptly let everyone know he resented this name because he wasn't Irish. 'Sean' was acceptable, he said, nothing more, nothing less. So Sean it was to his face, and Snooty or Paddy behind his back.

His attitude soon upset the local constables and indeed the populace. The local police were upset because he scathingly compared the tiny market town of Eltering with the busy metropolis of London, and he upset the residents by coldly reporting them for all manner of curious offences like tethering mules on the highway, shaking mats before 8 a.m., having shop-blinds less than eight feet above the footpath, fixing flower-pots on window-ledges without securing them, repairing cars in the street and many similar wrongs. He seemed to revel in unearthing the most unrealistic laws to enforce.

This made him less than popular with the sergeants, who disliked having to submit his reports for consideration by their superiors. It alienated him from his superiors because they had to make decisions whether or not to prosecute these startling illegalities. He once set about proving that a local tramp was an incorrigible rogue by using the full weight of the Vagrancy Act 1824, and even tried to prosecute a fairground fortune-teller for being a fraudulent medium. He had a passion for inspecting old motor vehicles in the hope he would find horrific crimes created by flapping mudguards, ineffective warning instruments, mobile cranes with wheels too large, agricultural tractors used for purposes not connected with agriculture, rakish cars bearing dangerous mascots, trailers without the requisite number of attendants, solo motor-cycles towing trailers and a multitude of parking positions which he believed were causing unnecessary obstructions.

The snag was that all the farmers ran old bangers. These unclean vehicles would carry corn, corpses, sheep, pigs and hens, vegetable produce and sometimes even people. It was not prudent to ask whether these were 'social, domestic and pleasure' purposes, nor was it deemed wise to ask if the car was taxed only for private use. Sean's activities meant that every trip into town was a financial hazard because of a possible court appearance, so people did not venture into Eltering if he was likely to be on duty. As a result the economic future of Eltering, especially on market day, was threatened.

The result was that Snooty Paddy believed he had cleaned up the town. Gone was the huge number of horrendous offences which had threatened the security of the town before his arrival. Now there was a market-place peopled by law-abiding citizens and a handful of cars with no faults. All the faulty ones stayed at home, or else went to Harrowby market.

The sergeants spoke to this man in an effort to encourage him to take a more realistic view of life, and a more reasonable approach to the public. But their efforts failed. Sean knew his law and it was his duty to enforce that law. There would be no discrimination, no favouritism, no slacking, no question of preferential treatment. If an offence was committed, that offence would be reported by him for summons.

His activities around the undersides of cars, lorries and buses caused him to be known as Gravel Knees, a derisory nickname which he failed to discover.

The problem facing his supervisory officers was how to

cure him of his disease. Doing one's job correctly in the police service is never easy, for there is always that element of society who feel they have been badly treated or have suffered some injustice. Men like Gravel Knees believe they are treating everyone alike and that their actions do not lead to injustice. In truth, they are a menace to society. To rigidly enforce every rule, law and order down to its full stops and commas, is stupidity at its very worst and persecution at its best.

I am reminded of the old saying, 'Rules are made for the obedience of fools and the guidance of wise men', and most police officers feel this is a good guide to sensible law enforcement. Gravel Knees was a fool and discussions about him were held in high places, even in very high places. We learned he had left the Metropolitan Police due to antagonism from senior officers. Down there, it seems, he had enforced the Metropolitan Police Act with such fervour that he undid years of good crime detection work by other officers. Men, like detectives, rely on the public for freely given crime-busting information and spend years building up relationships. Good informants were getting booked by Gravel Knees for various social evils like getting drunk or quitting their cars without switching off the engine, and thereafter they refused to co-operate in the fight against serious crime.

If Gravel Knees was rigid in his attitude towards the law, he was equally rigid in the application of his duty. If the sergeant told him to patrol the town and personally try every door-knob he would do exactly that without any question. An order was an order. He did not question authority of any kind, being firmly in the belief that those who issued orders had Guidance From Above, and that there were many sound reasons for the orders in question. The man was almost an automaton.

His peculiar attitude to life set us talking one night. I was on duty, patrolling my beat in the little Ford Anglia, and halted at Eltering for my morning break at 2 a.m. Gravel Knees was assigned to Eltering town that same night. At our mid-shift meal-break was Vesuvius from Malton, the two Road Traffic lads, Ben and Ron, Sergeant Bairstow, Gravel Knees and myself. It made a cosy gathering, all of us sitting in the tiny office with mugs of tea and sandwiches. We chattered like pals of many years' standing, such is the camaraderie of the police service.

During our discussion the question of blind obedience arose and Ron skilfully manoeuvred the subject to the testing of door-knobs.

'I maintain that not every door-knob should be checked,' he pontificated. 'I mean, there are places that no one in his right mind is going to enter unlawfully, so why check them?'

'I disagree,' said Sergeant Bairstow. I now knew him well enough to spot a very cheeky gleam in his eye. 'Every door should be checked. If our orders say we must check every door, then that's what must be done. Orders are not compiled without good reason, Ron. They're often the product of past experiences.'

'The point I'm making,' returned Ron, 'is that common sense must be used in the interpretation of orders. I mean . . . Let's see . . .' and he thought for a few moments. 'Suppose you haven't checked something like the monumental mason's backyard – it's full of half completed tombstones and slabs bearing inscriptions. Who's going to pinch anything from there, I ask you? So why worry about checking it for security?'

'Go on, what's your point?' I wondered if he and Charlie Bairstow had pre-arranged this little chat. It had the hallmarks of a lead-in to something else.

'OK. My point is this. I am patrolling my beat and I am very aware that I have not checked that gate. The yard might be open. It is a few minutes to knocking-off time. If I go and check that yard I will be half an hour late into the office, and this can cause concern to the office staff and to my senior officers. They may think I've been attacked or something. So I omit to check the yard and return to the office on time. I think I've made the right decision, and I base that on the grounds that a check of such an establishment is not justified in those circumstances.'

'I disagree,' came in Gravel Knees. 'If you did that under the circumstances you describe you would be disobeying a lawful order. There is no excuse for that, no excuse at all.'

'Balls!' said Ron, scornfully.

The conversation continued in this vein until it was time to leave, and I commenced the second half of my tour of duty, thinking over Ron's discussion with Sergeant Bairstow. It had been a strange conversation, I decided, and I wondered why they had chosen to talk about tombstones and graveyards. I got the answer the following night.

We were all in the same police station at the same time. Some had come in early for their meal-break and the argument was still raging. Gravel Knees was at the centre of it, receiving what we call a 'lug-hole bashing' from the others. I must say he held his ground well, and all his arguments appeared to be backed by a close study of the rules. In that sense he was unshakeable.

Having eaten, Vesuvius left early to continue his patrol and within five minutes Sergeant Bairstow also left. Ron and Ben remained with me and Sean O'Malley, alias Gravel Knees. The tempo of the discussion subsided.

Ron and Ben kept it alive, but only just, saying how terrible it would be if every motoring law was strictly enforced. England would become a police state, Ron reckoned, but O'Malley could not see this. He maintained that rules were for a purpose and they must be enforced if that purpose was to be achieved for the good of society.

Precisely at the end of his forty-five minutes' meal-break, Gravel Knees left the office. I was now alone with Ben and Ron.

'I hope you won't grow into that kind of copper, Nick,' said Ron. 'Rules, rules, rules . . . people like him are incapable of using their initiative.'

'He'll grow out of it,' I said, not being able to think of anything more apt at the time.

'He won't,' Ben swore. 'Blokes like him are with us for ever.'

'He's in for a shock tonight,' said Ron, smiling at me.

'Shock?' I puzzled.

'They've set him up for a little test,' said Ron. 'It'll either make him or break him. Tonight he will decide whether every rule needs to be rigidly enforced, or he will decide that, on occasions, rules can be relaxed or ignored, depending upon prevailing circumstances.'

'How?' I asked, full of interest.

This is what occurred.

The prime movers in this escapade were Sergeant Bairstow and Vesuvius, and it seems that the basic idea had come from Vesuvius. One of the lock-up properties on O'Malley's beat that night was the mortuary, and Vesuvius knew that it contained a corpse. This was not unusual, because that mortuary often had overnight guests and one of the keys was retained at the police station. The building was sometimes checked by the officer on night-patrol and on several occasions new or inexperienced constables had terrified themselves by shining their torches on to handsome bodies laid out for further attention.

Vesuvius considered that O'Malley should be put to the test and he selected the mortuary and its current occupant for the job. Sergeant Bairstow had agreed to this course of action.

Knowing how rigidly O'Malley worked they reckoned he would leave his meal-break at 2.30 a.m., patrol the town centre for some forty-five minutes and then head for the mortuary, which was behind a small chapel. His estimated time of arrival was 3.20 a.m. on a cool autumn morning.

Such was Vesuvius' dedication to the task in hand that he entered the mortuary at 2.30 and sat in the clinically cold place for three-quarters of an hour with his right hand immersed in a bucket of icy water. This had the effect of reducing the temperature of that hand almost to freezing point, but he endured this discomfort for the sake of Eltering town.

He positioned himself behind the inner door, and left the outer door unlocked. The theory was that O'Malley would check it at 3.20 a.m. or thereabouts, find it insecure and walk in. If he obeyed the dictates of his conscience he would enter the mortuary to make a thorough check. Vesuvius was relying on that.

Inside, therefore, Vesuvius waited behind one of the inner swing-doors, and on the stone slab immediately inside was the corpse of an old gentleman, emaciated and naked. Sergeant Bairstow was crouched at the far side of the corpse, and a close observer would have noticed a broom in his hand. The head of the broom was beneath the shoulders of the dear departed as he lay upon the slab. His frail old head dangled over the end with its eyes uppermost.

Vesuvius waited with his right hand in the bucket of icy water as the long minutes ticked by. In the dim light which filtered into the place from the town outside the stark white corpse could be seen but nothing else. The place was as still as death; there was not a sound.

'Any sign of him?' asked Sergeant Bairstow in a hoarse whisper.

'Nothing,' replied Vesuvius.

3.20 came and went. And then there were sounds outside. A heavy, measured tread could be heard upon the flagged path, and Vesuvius whispered, 'He's here, Sarge!'

Only now did he remove his hand from the water and dry it on a towel he had borrowed, tossing it into the corner behind the door. The outer door rattled as someone tested the knob. The door opened and they heard the faintest of squeaks as it admitted the visitor. Vesuvius smiled to himself. Bairstow whispered, 'Ready?'

Then the inner door creaked as the handle turned slowly. The knob rattled very faintly as it opened inwards, to the left. Behind the other inner door, the one on the right, there waited Vesuvius of the Icy Hand.

A torch was clicked on. The sombre place was filled with light as the figure stepped forward and, at that precise moment,

Vesuvius reached from the shadows with his horrible hand to seize the hand of the visitor and draw him into the mortuary. As that icy cold and damp hand seized the other, the corpse groaned, or so it seemed, and slowly began to sit upright, its pale thin body indistinct in the gloom away from the shaking torch.

From the terrorised visitor there came the most awful shriek of horror as he turned and ran from the premises. His throat was struggling to make coherent sounds as he galloped outside. Vesuvius smiled a victory smile.

'We've done it, Sarge.'

'At least the lad came in, eh? Lots wouldn't. That body was heavy. I thought he was going to slip off the brush-head.'

'My hand's bloody cold!' Vesuvius stuffed his chilled hand deep into his pocket for warmth.

Congratulating themselves the two conspirators left the mortuary and locked the door. But as they walked away the figure of PC Sean O'Malley was walking boldly towards them.

'Good morning, Sergeant,' he said very pleasantly. 'I was just coming to check the mortuary.'

'Just coming?' smiled Bairstow. 'You've not been?'

'No, I got delayed.'

'You did?'

'Yes, Sergeant, a minor delay, but a delay none the less.'

It was too dark for O'Malley to see the swift glance that passed between his colleagues.

'Anything serious, Sean?' Bairstow used his Christian name quite affably.

'A car without lights, Sergeant.'

'Really, where?'

'Just around the corner. The minister of the chapel, in fact. Well, to be honest, his wife. Mrs Sheila Newby. A nice lady.'

'You've booked her, at this time of the morning?'

'I'm afraid so, Sergeant. It seems her sister-in-law was very ill, so she and her husband, the Reverend Newby, drove over to Bradford to be with her. They remained until the early hours and drove back, returning home a few minutes ago. I chanced to be in the street and noticed that the rear light on the offside was not working. I decided to interview the driver and make a report. As it happened, the car turned in nearby, to the Manse. I interviewed the driver, who is also the owner of the car, that is Mrs Newby, wife of the minister of this chapel. I have reported her for not showing obligatory lights during the hours of darkness.'

'You haven't, Sean!'

'Rules are rules, Sergeant.'

'So what are you doing now?'

'I have inspected the documents relating to the car and they are all in order. I am now resuming normal patrol, Sergeant, and was on my way to check the mortuary for security.'

'You've not been in?'

'No, but the Reverend Newby has.'

'Has he?' chorused the plotters. 'When?'

'Just now. He flew past me, I'm afraid, on his way home, and wouldn't stop to talk. Perhaps he was very upset at his wife being reported . . .'

'How did *he* come to check the mortuary, Sean?' Bairstow's tone hardened.

'When I was interviewing his wife he suddenly remembered that he had left it open for a body to be taken in, a sudden death of a tramp. He is a key-holder, on behalf of the chapel, you see. He thought he would rush around just to check while he was on his feet. As I said, Sergeant, he's been but did not stop to talk to me. One cannot always be popular, can one, if one does one's duty? The poor man. Fancy having a wife who doesn't care enough about her vehicle to see that the lights are correct and in working order.'

'The mortuary is locked now,' said Sergeant Bairstow softly.

'I'll just check it to be sure, Sergeant. I believe in doing things myself, just to be on the safe side. Shall I see you again?'

'Not tonight,' said Sergeant Bairstow. 'Tomorrow perhaps, eh, Vesuvius?'

'Yes, Sergeant,' smiled Vesuvius, who didn't really like ministers of religion either.

10

'Oh woman! Lovely woman! Nature made thee to temper man.'
Thomas Otway – 'Venice Preserved'

It was Ogden Nash in his declining years who said he preferred to forget both pairs of glasses and to pass his time saluting strange women and grandfather clocks. The performance of night-duty is somewhat similar because the creatures one sees in the fading light may be precious friends of the opposite sex for whom a whistle might be appropriate, or they might be ogres in the form of sergeants, inspectors or even superintendents from whom constables prefer to conceal themselves.

During that overwhelming tiredness which descends at the dead of night other shapes can be seen, horrid, ghostly outlines which are the figments of sheer exhaustion coupled with an overworked imagination and bad eyesight. It is these mis-shapen things that, I am sure, gave rise to the tales of medieval monsters, dragons, evil spirits and devils. In a normal state of health and vision these can be seen to be trees, rocky outcrops, lamp-posts, pillar-boxes and even reflections.

Apart from seeing visions, there is little doubt that the night-hours have a randy effect upon the male person, and policemen are no exception. The ratio of ordinary males to police males is such that there are many more ordinary males who feel randy at night and who seek to satisfy their lusts in strange places. This is not to say policemen don't satisfy their lusts – it is merely to point out that any night will witness fewer lusty policemen than lusty males of other kinds. The satisfaction of lust can become illegal, but more often than not it is merely embarrassing, sometimes to the participants and sometimes to the beholders.

Patrolling constables often stumble across couples who are actively engaged in a demonstration of mutual affection. This is one of the unforeseen concessions of working night-duty, for if one cannot enjoy those pleasures oneself because of one's devotion to duty, there seems no reason to deny the same pleasures to the people under one's care.

Love therefore continues unabated at night. It happens in bed, in doorways, in cars, in alleys and shop doorways, in cinemas, in seaside shelters, hotel bedrooms, Italian gardens and even on the top of ornamental rockeries and beside fishponds.

If it happens out of doors it is fairly certain the policeman will find it and be suitably embarrassed. It is possible that if it happens in bed the policeman will be involved. If that sentence can be interpreted in more ways than one, what it really means is that love in bed can cause what we term 'a breach of the peace', if the man and woman are not married to each other. These rows or disturbances are known as 'domestics'; love really has little to do with such traumatic events, although sex has a lot to do with it, and it is not uncommon for a man to leap into bed with a woman who is not his wife, then for the husband to return and make a disturbing discovery. It happens all the time and trouble brews; the police are called and another domestic problem is wrapped up with a summons and lots of local publicity.

Ingenious and skilful lovers find places where they cannot be caught and where prying eyes cannot see them. In truth there is no such place but lovers are blind to this simple fact. Off they go in their passion-wagon to carry out their nefarious activities in conditions of total secrecy, while in truth the whole world knows about it. Little men with binoculars and dirty raincoats know about them, children know about them, poachers and gamekeepers know about them, other lovers know about them and you can bet your last penny that the local policeman knows about them. Unlike the rest he keeps this information to himself because it might become useful ammunition at a later date. Exactly how useful will never be known in advance, but the natural condition of a constable tells him that secrecy is by far the best policy if he catches a local celebrity in furtive turmoil with 'another woman'. Such information is carefully noted for future reference.

Incidents of this kind so often involve people you would never believe would get into such interesting situations. Policemen learn never to be amazed at anything, but there are times when we are truly surprised.

One of my surprises involved Miss Prudence Proctor. For some months I did not know she existed, but gradually the name cropped up on male lips from time to time, and I began to grow curious about the personality who bore that name. By dint of careful, if oblique questioning, I learned that she lived in Elsinby, occupying a small cottage which nestled behind some trees. It was therefore out of sight from the road through the village, and the approach was along a short, muddy lane. The lovely yellow stone cottage with its red pantile roof squatted among the trees and there was a patch of pleasing rose-garden and lawns before it.

I learned, through more diligent inquiries, that the back of the house excited a good deal more interest than the front, particularly among the male population. This was due to its balcony. It seems that the balcony had been constructed by a previous owner and it led from the french windows of the main bedroom, now excitingly occupied by Miss Prudence Proctor. She lived alone, I discovered, and for many weeks I never set eyes on the lady.

Eventually I noticed her walking proudly down the village street *en route* to the post office. At the time I did not know that this was *the* Prudence Proctor of whom I had heard so much, because she was a very smart middle-aged woman walking erect and confidently towards me. She would be about forty years old, I estimated, with dark hair bound about her head and lashed into a tight bun. Her face was pink and pleasant, and she had a lovely smile. She nodded 'good morning' to me as I patrolled along my way. She wore a sober grey two-piece costume, white blouse with a red bow at the throat and a pair of black court shoes. She carried a black handbag and did not wear a hat.

From her appearance I judged she was either a top businessman's secretary or a schoolteacher, or maybe someone in the professions like a doctor, dentist or barrister. I was to learn subsequently that she had no known occupation and appeared to live on private means, although she did occasional work with the BBC on audience surveys and similar statistical experiments. She was not married and, I understand, never had been. She lived alone in that delightful cottage and kept two ginger cats. She was quiet, law-abiding, attractive and articulate, the sort of woman any man would be pleased to know, on both a professional and personal level.

At our first meeting she stopped me to ask advice. She had a nephew, she said, who was shortly leaving school and he had expressed an interest in the police service as a career. He wanted to join as a cadet and hoped to become a full-time member of the regular force.

After outlining the necessary qualifications I offered to obtain some leaflets and brochures for the lady and asked her name. Then it was that I learned she was the famous Miss Prudence Proctor of Acorn Cottage, Elsinby.

Her physical appearance made me unsure whether I was talking to the person whose antics set the village men aflame with passion from time to time. But if local information and gossip was accurate, then this indeed was the lady. After noting her name and address and promising faithfully I would secure the necessary information, I bade her 'good morning' and off she went, walking proudly about her business.

I found it very, very difficult to accept that this was the woman whose name was always on the male lips of Elsinby. There must be some mistake; they must be wrong. This was a straight, serious, even dowdy woman and I began to wonder if the men were involving me in some weird and obtuse type of Yorkshire joke.

A week later I received the necessary literature from our Recruiting Department and decided to call at Acorn Cottage to deliver it. I undertook this duty during an evening patrol and it would be around seven o'clock when I called. Prudence answered my knock dressed in a long, close-fitting woollen dress. Over a cup of tea she told me that she had knitted it herself. She provided me with biscuits and I answered all her questions about a policeman's life. In all, I spent about an hour in her company and found her very intelligent and interesting.

I saw no more of her for several weeks. Because of what I had heard I must confess I did not seek her out, nor did I venture to call upon her to find out how her nephew had progressed with his application. The next time she crossed my line of duty was one night in early August. The air was balmy and mild with the scent of honeysuckle and roses, and all about Elsinby the cornfields were a glow of yellow. The summer fruit was ripening – blackberries, apples, pears, plums and wild berries abounded, and the late summer was ideal. It was a lovely time to live in a rural community.

I was on night-duty and had decided to drive the little Ford around my own patch to check some of the pubs. Day-trippers and visitors were in the district and some tended to abuse the hospitality of the landlords by staying late. This created antagonism among the local drinkers because it was their privilege to drink after hours, being friends of the licensees. Such privileges must not be abused.

For this reason I liked to pop into my local pubs just before closing-time to eject everyone, and the appearance of the uniform was generally sufficient to do the trick. At 11.10, therefore, I popped into the Hopbind Inn at Elsinby, which was heaving with warm bodies and thick with heavy smoke.

'Time, gentlemen, please,' called George when he espied me, and the usual deathly hush descended. Gradually everyone drank up and left, one by one, the visitors being the first to remove themselves, and the local folks hanging back as they always did. During the exodus, one of them sidled up to me and whispered, 'Full moon tonight, Mr Rhea.'

This was Isaac Samuals, a local poacher.

'Is it?' I asked, wondering why this should be of interest to me.

'Aye, midnight or thereabouts. Full moon.' He could see I was not comprehending the hidden significance of this occurrence. 'You know!' he said, pointing vaguely to a locality behind the pub, somewhere out in the woods.

I scratched my head. 'Sorry, Zaccy,' I had to admit defeat. 'I'm not with you.'

'Full moon,' he repeated in a stage whisper. 'You'll be there, eh?'

I must have looked decidedly stupid because he led me outside and said, 'Acorn Cottage – we're all going up there, now.'

'Why?' I asked in total innocence.

'Thoo knows,' he said, his old head nodding in its own secret language. 'Full moon . . .' and he nudged my arm, grinning all the while through his assorted black teeth.

'Can I come?' I had to ask, wondering if their full-moon sojourn was legal.

'Aye, course you can. We all are.'

'Show me.' I was interested and still did not link this with Prudence.

He led me stealthily out of the back door of the Hopbind Inn and along a stony lane with a row of cottages and a school at one side. We turned left at a junction in the lane and I found myself tramping across leaf mould and grass as he took me, by the light of the moon, through a woodland glade.

The path was clearly defined by the passage of many feet and we climbed through picturesque wooded areas in almost total silence. As a poacher he could negotiate woodland more silently than a ghost, and I was equally accustomed to being silent, although I couldn't compete with him in these surroundings. We made our way steeply into the wood until we veered left and returned towards the village, albeit at a higher level.

Within five minutes we were in a wooded glade, deep among the trees, and I was surprised to find about twenty men there, all totally silent. Some turned and smiled as I made my way into the arena. I now realised we were directly behind the home of Miss Prudence Proctor. It was now that I saw the famous balcony, showing clearly in the night due to its coat of brilliant white paint. The cottage was in darkness.

'What's going on?' I whispered to Isaac.

'Thoo'll see,' was all he said, nudging me and laughing softly. 'Thoo'll see, Mr Rhea.'

It was clear that no further enlightenment was to be given, so I waited for about twenty minutes, wondering if Sergeant Blaketon was looking for me. I daren't leave now, for I was sure all was going to be revealed. Several more gentlemen arrived to make a considerable audience in the wood, every one of them standing silently behind Acorn Cottage.

Then things began to happen. The french windows of the bedroom were opened on to the balcony and I could just distinguish two long, smooth arms pushing them open. The bedroom inside was in darkness, and then lights came on. These were not the normal household lights, but were in brilliant and exotic colours – red, green, purple and many others, all combining to give a low, vibrant hue to the room. Pulsating music then began to sound from that room; it was a tune I did not recognise, but it had a hint of gypsy magic as it came from the record-player, amplified so that we could hear it clearly. Finally, Prudence appeared.

Silhouetted against the colourful background and sensuously bathed in alternating colours, was a tall woman in swirling drapes of some lightweight fabric, silk, maybe, or satin or even something more flimsy. To the stirring intensity of that music she began to dance on the balcony. Her hair, long and dark, swirled as she moved and her eyes flashed in the changing light.

The long-playing record provided a selection of vibrant

music which grew faster and faster and more furious as we watched. The lights changed all the time, sometimes very low and dim, exchanging suddenly to bright and piercing rays as they focused on the entrancing woman who danced before our eyes. Faster and faster went the music, faster and faster went Miss Prudence Proctor until the thin veils began to disappear. With the skill of a professional strip-tease artiste, she began to remove her veils, one by one, gracefully and sensually, all the time maintaining perfect time to the changing mood of the music.

I looked at the men. They were transfixed. Their eyes were glued on the unbelievable scene before them, and I smiled. They'd have to pay pounds for this sort of entertainment in the city, yet here she was, free and totally uninhibited, providing an exotic evening for her audience in a Yorkshire wood. As the music intensified so did she. As the first record finished the second dropped into place to continue the rhythm as more veils were discarded. It was clear that every one was going to be removed tonight.

And they were. One by one she removed her seven gossamer veils in movements that spoke of total devotion to her art. She was aided by a lovely body against a backcloth of moving light and throbbing music. In that sylvan setting her rustic audience made not a sound. There were no whistles, applause or shouts – nothing. It was as if they knew that any sound from them would stop the show, perhaps for ever. It would be like waking up before the end of a wonderful dream.

But the display did end. The final veil was discarded in a smooth and beautiful movement to reveal the mature splendour of this strange and compelling woman. At that point the music stopped and the lights went out. She vanished as suddenly as she had appeared.

Silently the awestruck men returned home through the wood, not speaking and not making a sound. They would tell their wives they'd been talking late at the pub, and no one would be any wiser.

'Does she know you lads watch her?' I asked Isaac when we neared the village.

'Nay, lad,' he laughed. 'She's no idea.'

Personally I doubted this, but did not press the matter.

'How did you know she'd do that?' I asked him.

'It's full moon,' he answered. 'She does it at every full moon.'

He made that statement as if it explained everything. Perhaps it did.

If frustrated ladies wish to prance around naked at full moon in the privacy of their own homes it is barely a police problem. On the other hand, there are many ladies who are not frustrated and who relieve their pent-up emotions by lovemaking in all sorts of unlikely places. While this is likewise not a police problem *per se* it is true that many a night-duty constable has helped cars out of rivers and bogs in which they have inexplicably found themselves while their occupants were busy with other things. Similarly, many a policeman has stumbled across couples busy in public places like car-parks, pub forecourts and even in the street. I was once told of a naked pair hard at it in the back seat of their Ford Consul in full view of the incoming customers at a local pub. They seemed totally unabashed by the interesting display they were providing and, although none of the drinkers complained, the landlord did ring me about it. He didn't want the reputation of his pub tarnished by powerful rumours of open-air orgies.

I proceeded to the scene, as we say in official jargon, and sure enough the story was accurate. A naked man and woman were very actively making love in the car, apparently oblivious to the fact that their performance was in a very open and public car-park. Acting in the best interests of the general public, I tapped on the window. After the passage of a moment or two it was wound down by a man looking very flushed about the face and perspiring somewhat from his recent exertions.

'What's up, mate?' he asked, wiping his brow.

'You realise where you are?' I put to him, wondering how to open this conversation.

'Aye,' he said.

'Well, you're causing embarrassment,' I continued. 'The folks in the pub are embarrassed.'

'Not them!' He wiped his brow again. 'They'll be lapping it up. Look, it's not illegal, is it?'

'It depends where you do it and who you do it with.'

'She's the missus.'

'Whose missus?' I asked the obvious question.

'Mine,' he said flatly. 'She's my missus.'

'Well, can't you go home?'

'Home?' he growled, peering up at me. 'I have no home. We live with her parents, the bloody in-laws. Her mother's an interfering old cuss and we haven't a minute to ourselves. Paper-thin walls, an' all. No privacy even in bed. We can't relax, there's no fun. So we go out and do it in the car.'

'But not on a pub forecourt?'

'Couldn't wait,' he said. 'Look, mate, I'm sorry if I caused upset, honest. I thought the windows were steamed up.'

'They are,' I agreed, 'but the light from the pub shines right in, and although you couldn't be seen in detail, there's no mistaking what was happening.'

'There's no peace, luv,' he said to his wife. 'Come on, let's go.'

'There's a disused aerodrome a mile up the road,' I advised him. 'First turn left.'

'Is there?'

'Let's go there,' said a sweet voice from the depths of the car, and they did. I checked that his number was correct and tallied with his name. The woman really was his wife. I felt a twinge of sorrow for people who live in conditions so appalling that they must carry out this most private of acts in a public place. Privacy is a valuable commodity.

There are many furtive lovers who perform in public places which they believe to be private, and they do so because they do not wish to be caught by their respective husbands/wives/

boyfriends/girlfriends/lovers. In truth, illicit romance of this kind is usually discovered and a tryst of this sort captured our imagination late one Friday night.

We are fortunate in North Yorkshire to have lots of open countryside and spacious moorland areas which are ideal for those who wish to 'get away from it all', even for an hour or two. Many of the moorland heights and green valleys have become rendezvous points for lovers of all ages and both sexes, and if one travels around at night, like policemen do, one sees cars, vans, tents and uncovered people dotted about like daisies on a lawn. The period of peak activity is around eleven o'clock in the evening which broadly coincides with pub closing-times. Some of the very hardy and determined remain there until one or even two o'clock. On a winter's night this demands devotion of an extraordinary kind.

Such a couple were John Withy and Sheila Grove. John was about thirty-three years old, married with two children, and a painter and decorator by trade. He was a busy man who successfully ran his own business and, although he worked long hours, he did have a certain amount of freedom of movement. This was usefully employed among the many desirable ladies he met in the course of his work, lots of whom wanted their fronts decorating. As a consequence John had many romances, most of which were short-lived in the extreme, even as short as half-an-hour, but once in a while he would find someone with whom he fell deeply in love.

Such a woman was Mrs Sheila Grove. She was a delightfully vague sort of girl whose husband was a commercial traveller. He was away from home for lengthy periods and Sheila grew somewhat lonesome. John had been contracted to paint the Grove household and, as a consequence, Sheila invited him in for a cup of tea. From that stage the romance blossomed. Sheila, however, was a crafty lover and, upon realising what the neighbours might think, took great pains to conceal her new-found friendship. She let the kettle steam up the kitchen windows or met John away from the family home.

Romances of this kind never escape the notice of

neighbours. Neighbours see all, hear all and say everything; what they don't see they invent, and what they can't invent isn't worth thinking about. Word therefore got around to everyone except John's wife that he was very busy decorating Mrs Grove's panels and architraves. John, meanwhile, had informed his wife that he was working late on an important and rushed job, which to a certain extent was true.

Much of his overtime and rushing was spent in his little van high on the North Yorkshire moors on the edge of Aidensfield beat. His favourite pitch was a lofty spot on a moorland ridge beneath some pine-trees. A small knot of pines grew from this exposed ridge and they were bent due to the prevailing winds never dying away, but this slender row of timber provided some sort of shelter for his little van, marked 'Withy – Decorator'. It would proceed to that lovely place once or twice a week, and inside its cosy interior John and Sheila would commence their stripping and pasting.

During my routine patrols I passed the van several times but did not disturb the happy couple. It was a very lonely area and they caused no harm to anyone. I did not investigate because I knew who it was and what they were doing, and it was no part of a policeman's duty to interfere with moral misbehaviour of a personal kind. I did wonder, however, when and how their little game would be discovered. Invariably, such liaisons are discovered and I felt sure John and Sheila were no exception.

It was very appropriate that their meeting-place was known as Lovers Leap, for legend said that, years ago towards the turn of the century, a young couple leapt to their deaths from this point. This was due to some parental opposition to their romance.

Sometimes on my day off I would walk here with Mary and the children, for the vantage-point provides a wonderful view of the surrounding countryside. It is breathtakingly beautiful. From the small plateau beneath the stooping firs the ground falls steeply away across a heathery and bracken-covered hillside. That hillside is covered with young silverbirch trees, knotted briars and acres of tightly growing bracken as it slopes steeply into a ravine many feet below.

The ravine contains a moorland stream of purest water which bubbles happily over granite as it makes its way, full of minerals, to the sea. Beyond is the wild, colourful expanse of the North Yorkshire moors with Fylingdales Early Warning Station in the background and, beyond that, the romance of the wild North Sea.

At night the view is equally grand because the valleys and hillsides are dotted with tiny lights, shining like glow-worms, and the dark block of moorland suggests intrigue, danger, mystery and of course, romance, just like the inside of Withy's decorating van.

It was to this location, therefore, that John Withy and his van, with Sheila at his side, proceeded one night, intent upon a spot of dressing down and undercoating. I was on duty at the time, patrolling in the little Ford Anglia, and had no occasion to visit Lovers Leap that night – not initially, that is. From what I learned later it seems that the happy pair, excited and keen, had reached the site of their future passion. In the cosiness of the decorating van, with its load of paint, wallpaper, ladders and associated tins and bottles of fluid, they had commenced their evening ritual.

Kisses and cuddles developed into slaps and tickles, and in no time at all their clothing was thrown off as they settled down to the real business of the evening. The two warm and naked bodies writhed and pumped in sheer ecstasy, although they were rather hampered because they had to manipulate themselves into all kinds of positions on the front seats. Unfortunately, the rear of the van was laden with tomorrow's wallpapers, paint and brushes, cleaning fluid, and there was no room for humans in love. This did not deter John and Sheila – in fact, it spurred them to make a decent job on a poor location, and soon the little van was bouncing rhythmically to the movements of the blissful pair.

Their frantic and ecstatic writhings performed a small act which was destined to lead to their eternal embarrassment.

Their movements knocked the handbrake of the little van and it released its grip on the vehicle. Slowly but surely the handbrake abandoned its post under the undulating movements of the couple, and the vehicle began to move, very slowly at first.

In their climaxing moments the couple did not notice this gentle movement and before long the van was running down the slope. Very slowly it moved from its parking-place while every delirious action of the pair inside gave the van more momentum. Soon it was travelling quite fast and before John and Sheila realised what was happening the van was careering out of control down the steep, bracken-covered slope of Lovers Leap.

It was too late to stop it. Panic-stricken, John leapt from the object of his passion and managed to open his door, shouting for his lover to jump. Both jumped out. There was nothing else they could do. They rolled over and over in the thick bracken, Sheila screaming with fear, pain and shock as the bouncing van careered along its downward route, rattling and crashing through the thick undergrowth and demolishing a host of tiny silver birches. It could go no farther than the gully.

As expected there was an almighty crash as the van and its contents dropped like a stone into the ravine and burst into flames. Petrol, paint and the paraphernalia of decorating, all combined to create a time-bomb within the van. An enormous explosion followed as the entire thing blew up. Fires broke out along the hillside as the dry bracken began to burn, and soon the intense flames of the blazing van roared into the heavens, illuminating the night sky for miles around.

The couple whose hot passion had literally set the countryside alight stood naked on the hillside, clutching one another and bleeding from numerous scratches and cuts. Sheila was crying softly into John's arms as he simply stood there, spotlighted in the dancing flames and not daring to believe this had really happened.

The noise and brilliance of the display attracted the

attention of many eyes, and in no time the police station and fire brigade offices were notified. Emergency fire tenders roared to the scene, and I was contacted at a telephone kiosk only minutes later. The constable at the desk at Malton gabbled something about an aircraft crash and immediately I was roaring to the location. There was no difficulty tracing the scene, for once I gained the elevation of the hills I was guided easily by the flames and smoke. I was first to arrive and I parked among those bending pines, wondering what had caused this turmoil. The entire hillside was ablaze, crackling and roaring in the eternal wind.

And there, shining in the light of the fire, I saw two naked figures struggling up the hillside towards me. The man was clutching a weeping woman as they struggled, bleeding and battered, towards my car. And they wore not a stitch of clothing between them. There were all kinds of jokes I could have made at that point, but while it was undoubtedly the place for a joke it was certainly not the time. I called to them and suggested they get into the police car. Inside there was my cape and an overcoat, and I advised them to use those while I decided what to do about the blazing moor.

I ventured part of the way down the hillside and got as far as a small area of burning bracken, which happily had been contained by a patch of sphagnum moss. From there, I could see the van deep in the gully, still burning fiercely and emitting sparks and fumes in its death throes. It was beyond any help. As I climbed back up the steep incline, the fire brigade arrived and I was able to inform the leading fireman of the situation.

My chief concern was that the whole moor would catch fire, a regular event on these hills, but it seemed the fortunate location of the sphagnum moss had largely eliminated that likelihood. Members of the brigade ventured down the slope and finally began to spray the burning wreck with foam, smothering the blaze and quenching the flames. Others tackled small pockets of fire among the vegetation, and the moor was given a liberal soaking of water. This soaking continued, using water from the gully, just in case the fire did penetrate the upper layer of moorland topsoil. But within a couple of hours the fire was out and the brigade left the scene. It hadn't been as bad as we had feared.

Back at my car, I found Sheila shivering in my cape and John wrapped in my overcoat. She had dried her eyes but was in a state of shock as he sat dumbfounded with his arm about her.

'So what happened?' I asked.

He told me his story.

'You've got some explaining to do,' I added when he had finished.

'What can I tell the wife?' he pleaded. 'What shall I do?'

'I'm not going to put ideas into your head, John,' I said. 'But first you need clothing.'

'My husband has some old clothes,' Sheila offered. 'I can tell him I threw them out.'

'How can I explain to my wife?' John pleaded. 'What will she think if I turn up in different clothes?'

'I'm sure you'll think of something.' I returned to the driving-seat and started the engine. 'Well, who's first?'

'My house,' Sheila said.

'What about the hospital for a check-up?' I suggested.

'Not likely, there's enough explaining to do,' John said. 'We're all right, apart from cuts and bruises.'

'Take us to my house,' Sheila repeated. 'Your overalls are still there, aren't they, John?'

'So they are,' he smiled. 'Yes, do that. I'll manage somehow.'

I took them to Sheila's home and went inside with them, each as naked as a babe. They were not shy in my presence and when both were dressed, Sheila in a sweater and slacks and John in his overalls, I had a coffee with them.

I left feeling it had been an interesting night. Days later I could not confirm a rumour that John's van had been stolen while he was on the job, although the rumour circulated the village for weeks. I have no idea how John explained to his wife about his missing clothes, but I can confirm they were not reported lost or stolen.

* * *

If love and its side effects cause problems to people beyond the police service they also create problems within. Policemen are like other lusty male humans who, from time to time, succumb to the charms of lovely ladies who are not their wives or sweethearts. Many have risked their careers for a few moments of tender illicit love.

It is refreshing, therefore, to discover a policeman who loves his wife so much that he risks his career to spend blissful moments in her company.

Such a man was constable Simon Simpkins, a tall, slender, twenty-two-year-old with a penchant for quizzing scooter-riders and an intense dislike of children who sucked ice-lollies. His arrival at Eltering coincided with the arrival of Inspector Bert Minskip at the nearby Sub-Divisional Headquarters. Both these arrivals coincided with my posting to Aidensfield and we met from time to time.

Inspector Minskip, it had been rumoured, was with us only temporarily, having been sent from one of the busy urban areas of the country where the pace and quality of life had been too much for his sensitive nature. Headquarters had considered it wise to post him briefly to a rural patch where life was pleasant and straightforward, where the people were human and where he could exercise a different sort of policemanship. His posting was a kind of official holiday, a period of adjustment and unwinding for him, a spell without pressures and lacking the problems of an inspector in a busy urban station.

The snag was that Inspector Minskip found the solitude and lack of sordid criminal happenings rather boring and he occupied his time in the close supervision of his men. This was disconcerting for rural bobbies, who traditionally enjoyed a great sense of freedom. The outcome was that instead of relaxing and enjoying his three months with us Inspector Minskip became very neurotic about the affairs of the station, the timings, personal lives and duties of those officers under his command. He was perhaps unfortunate that PC Simpkins, newly married and fascinated with his new life, was one of the officers beneath his care.

I met PC Simpkins once or twice and found him a very pleasant young fellow, if a little immature at times. Sometimes we shared night-shifts; from time to time when I was patrolling from Aidensfield he would be on duty in the southern area of our Division and we would meet at Eltering Police Station for a chat over our supper. He was keen to learn the job and was particularly anxious to understand the intricacies of traffic legislation as he had ambitions to become a Road Traffic patrol-car driver.

It was this ambition which appeared to upset Inspector Minskip. He believed that all good policemen patrolled on foot or on cycles, and that traffic men were not really police officers, but merely glorified forms of taxi-drivers. He therefore allocated to young Simpkins many tours of cycle duty, hoping to impress the lad that a constable aboard a pedal cycle can hear and see many things of value to a patrolling policeman.

One night in late summer I was patrolling around Eltering town when I saw young Simpkins on a pedal cycle. It would be around one o'clock in the morning and I stopped to speak to him.

'Morning, Simon,' I said, stepping out of the little Ford. 'Are you lost? You're a bit off your patch, aren't you?'

He smiled dreamily. 'Yes, I am, but I know you'll keep it to yourself. I'm going to have a quick visit to my wife. She gets lonely when I'm on nights.'

'Ah!' I understood the situation very well.

'I thought I'd manage an hour with her. I reckon this bike'll get me there and back without being missed.'

'Isn't Inspector Minskip around?' I asked.

'No, he saw me at 11 and said he was going home to bed. There's no sergeants on duty either.'

'Best of British!' I wished him and off he went, looking gladsome and elated.

He pedalled into the darkness with the official red light wavering slightly as he tried to coax extra speed from the cumbersome machine. I watched him turn a corner to pedal his way to his love-nest. He would have to report at Eltering at six o'clock to book off duty, so that gave him plenty of time to achieve his purpose, and he would have to risk the consequences of missing one or two points.

It was with considerable surprise that I found Inspector Minskip waiting for me at my four o'clock point at Whemmelby Kiosk. Like young Simon I thought he'd gone to bed. Clearly that had been a tale to lull the men into a false sense of security, and he had taken the decision to drive into the wilds to check that I wasn't sleeping on the job. I wondered about Simon . . .

Inspector Minskip asked if everything was correct and I used suitable noises to assure him that I had the entire Sub-Division under my firm control and that no villains were abroad.

'Have you seen young Simpkins?' he asked after the formal business was over.

'No, sir,' I said firmly.

'I've searched all likely places for him,' said the inspector. 'I'll bet the young bugger's sneaked off home to see his missus. He can't keep off her . . . he'll wear himself out. You know what these newly-weds are.'

And off he went.

It was clear to me that he'd suspected the love-sick constable of sneaking home during duty-time and had hatched this little plot to catch him. That meant trouble for young Simon and I wondered what Minskip would do next.

Unfortunately, I had to return to my own area and was not able to witness the end of this story, although the finale did reach me in a roundabout way, as stories are prone to do in police circles.

It seems that a highly satisfied Constable Simpkins left his love-nest on the official cycle to wind his contented way back to Eltering Police Station. There he would report off duty and go home again, lucky chap. The cycle was going well, the morning was fine and dry; he was completely happy and very much in love with his beautiful wife. In spite of his euphoric state he was very alert and I am given to understand that it was with considerable surprise that he noticed the bulky figure of Inspector Minskip standing beneath a street-lamp. He was positioned near a roundabout on the approaches to the town.

Constable Simpkins knew the game was up, but he had almost a quarter of a mile to consider his next action and dream up his excuses. There was no other road which could be used as an escape route. Minskip had obviously observed his approach, for he had stepped from beneath the street-light and now stood in the middle of the road, awaiting the cornered youngster. As he cycled those final, nerve-racking yards, Simpkins could see his career evaporating. There'd be no motor patrol, he would be disciplined and kicked out of the service with a black mark for ever against his name. All this crossed his mind as he cycled closer to the waiting inspector.

How much of the story which follows is the untarnished truth and how much is the result of subsequent retelling by fascinated *raconteurs* will never be known, but an account of the finale to this drama circulated our Sub-Division like this:

It seems that the waiting inspector called upon PC Simpkins and his bicycle to stop and explain their presence at this place. Simpkins, however, had totally ignored that order and had cycled a few yards past the inspector, where he had dismounted and leaned the cycle against a street-light. Without a word to the puzzled inspector, PC Simpkins had swiftly climbed up the lamp-post to sit astride the crossbar at the top. There he had clung to the lamp standard rather as a monkey would do. And there he sat, never speaking a word to the bewildered inspector below.

We were assured that Inspector Minskip had stamped, ranted and raved at the base of the lamp-post, shouting orders for the constable to descend and threatening all kinds of dire circumstances when he did. The outcome was that PC Simpkins simply remained where he was. He had said not one word and had merely gazed heavenwards into a sky brightening with the light of a new day. As Minskip had circled the base, sometimes threatening, sometimes pleading, PC Simpkins had never moved one inch, nor had he spoken one word. It had been as if he were never there.

We are given to understand that this performance lasted some twenty minutes after which Inspector Minskip announced he was going back to the office to report the matter to the Superintendent by telephone. He would arrange for a sharp disciplinary lesson for young Simpkins.

Inspector Minskip had then walked away, huffing and puffing his indignation and anger, and had undertaken the long walk back to the police office on foot. Having been such a keen advocate of foot patrols he could scarcely have used a car.

Once the inspector was out of sight, PC Simpkins had descended and rapidly boarded his trusty cycle. He raced back to the office, beating the panting inspector by a good fifteen minutes. He had sufficient time to ring the duty inspector at Malton to express his concern about the mental attitude of Inspector Minskip.

'What's up, Simpkins?' the duty inspector had asked, noting the hint of positive alarm in Simpkins' voice.

'Well, sir, it's difficult, but Mr Minskip has just accused me of sitting up a lamp-post two miles off my beat. He didn't seem able to understand what I was trying to tell him, you see, and I was very worried, so I came straight here and rang you. I thought the Superintendent ought to know about it . . .'

And so, after a lengthy conversation with PC Simpkins, the inspector at Malton had telephoned the Superintendent at Divisional Headquarters. The matter had been sufficiently important to drag the great man from his bed, and he listened carefully to the constable's unlikely story.

There had been recent concern about the mental condition of Inspector Minskip; the constable's story sounded so unusual, so outlandish . . . The following day, lengthy interviews were arranged with him and he vowed he had never been off his beat and had certainly never shinned up a lamp-post.

The outcome of all this was that poor old Inspector Minskip was advised, in a manner he could not refuse, to attend the Police Convalescent Home for three months' complete rest. We understand he found it beneficial.

HEARTBEAT

CONSTABLE ACROSS THE MOORS
AND OTHER TALES OF A YORKSHIRE VILLAGE BOBBY

NOW AN ITV SERIES

Nicholas Rhea

Of the millions who have enjoyed ITV's popular series HEARTBEAT, none will forget characters such as Claude Jeremiah Greengrass, Sergeant Blaketon and PC 'Vesuvius' Ventress. And they will be familiar with the village of Aidensfield, at the heart of Constable Nick Rowan's North Yorkshire beat. Set in 1960s Aidensfield, this omnibus collection of stories, which together with Nicholas Rhea's other tales of a village policeman originally inspired the HEARTBEAT TV series, tells of all these characters and many more: of Claude Jeremiah's dog Alfred and his unfortunate incident with the budgerigar, of young PC Nick's first merry New Year's Eve in Aidensfield, and of the funeral of the ancient tramp, Irresponsible John. Humorous, touching and imbued with a deep affection for the Yorkshire countryside and its people, this heartwarming collection is a treat no HEARTBEAT fan will want to miss.

'Witty, warm-hearted and full of lovable rogues'
Northern Echo

Heartbeat is a Yorkshire Television series derived from the Constable Books by Nicholas Rhea

FICTION / TV TIE-IN 0 7472 4125 2

HEARTBEAT

CONSTABLE AMONG THE HEATHER
AND OTHER TALES OF A YORKSHIRE VILLAGE BOBBY

NOW AN ITV SERIES

Nicholas Rhea

In the quiet North Yorkshire village of Aidensfield
a policeman's lot is often a very happy one. So
found PC Nicholas Rhea whose colourful and
warm-hearted stories of his countryside beat in the
1960s are the inspiration behind ITV's enormously
popular drama HEARTBEAT, starring Nick Berry.
From skulduggery at the Aidensfield village whist
drive to Sergeant Blaketon's trials with a stranded
Humber Snipe, from Gold Top Gareth, the
kleptomaniac milkman, to Roy the devoted
sheepdog who stays with his master to the very end,
even in a hospital ward, PC Nick Rhea paints a
delightful, poignant and amusing picture of a police
constable's life in some of England's most beautiful
countryside thirty years ago.

'As with the Herriot series, the best humour comes
from the author's close understanding and
affectionate portrayals of the character of Yorkshire
country folk' *Northern Echo*

Heartbeat is a Yorkshire Television series derived
from the Constable Books by Nicholas Rhea

FICTION / TV TIE-IN 0 7472 4012 4

A selection of bestsellers from Headline